D1760348

The Grazier's Wife

A former English teacher, Barbara Hannay is a city-bred girl with a yen for country life. Many of her forty-plus books are set in rural and outback Australia and have been enjoyed by readers around the world. She has won the RITA, awarded by Romance Writers of America, and has twice won the Romantic Book of the Year award in Australia. In her own version of life imitating art, Barbara and her husband currently live on a misty hillside in beautiful Far North Queensland where they keep heritage pigs and chickens and an untidy but productive garden.

barbarahannay.com

Zoe's Muster
Home Before Sundown
Moonlight Plains
The Secret Years
The Country Wedding

BARBARA HANNAY

The Grazier's Wife

PENGUIN BOOKS

PENGUIN BOOKS

UK | USA | Canada | Ireland | Australia
India | New Zealand | South Africa | China

Penguin Books is part of the Penguin Random House group of companies
whose addresses can be found at global.penguinrandomhouse.com.

Penguin
Random House
Australia

First published by Penguin Random House Australia Pty Ltd, 2016
This edition published by Penguin Random House Australia Pty Ltd, 2017

10 9 8 7 6 5 4 3 2 1

Text copyright © Barbara Hannay, 2016

The moral right of the author has been asserted.

Cover design by Alex Ross © Penguin Random House Australia Pty Ltd
Text design by Samantha Jayaweera © Penguin Random House Australia Pty Ltd
Cover photographs – Farmhouse: Darren Schiller Photography, Woman: PeopleImages,
Horses: Janelle Lugge/Shutterstock
Typeset in Sabon by Samantha Jayaweera, Penguin Random House Australia Pty Ltd
Colour separation by Splitting Image Colour Studio, Clayton, Victoria
Printed and bound in Australia by Griffin Press, an accredited ISO AS/NZS 14001
Environmental Management Systems printer.

National Library of Australia
Cataloguing-in-Publication data:

Hannay, Barbara, author.
The grazier's wife / Barbara Hannay.
9780143785255 (paperback)
Subjects: Farmers' spouses--Australia--Fiction.
Families--Australia--Fiction.
Farm life--Australia--Fiction.

610.73430994

penguin.com.au

For Linsey and Julie

PROLOGUE

Ruthven Downs, Far North Queensland, 1970

Her husband was asleep at last.

Stella Drummond stood in the bedroom doorway, watching the steady rise and fall of Magnus's chest. He was sprawled on his back, fully clothed in stained moleskins, a checked flannel shirt and navy blue socks. She had managed to remove his elastic-sided boots when he'd collapsed on the bed, but she knew he was past caring about pyjamas.

His jaw was bristly white with at least two days' growth, his thick, grey-flecked hair a dishevelled cockscomb against the pillow, and his mouth hung open to reveal the gap where he'd lost a molar.

This was how Magnus always slept when he'd been drinking. Soon he would be snoring.

Stella was all too familiar with the pattern. After a day of uncommunicative moodiness, her husband would spend the evening drowning his sorrows in whisky. The drinking would be accompanied by roaring outbursts of rage and crises of logic that were often directed towards her, and she had no choice but to endure the tirades until at last he was overcome by blessed sleep. Then she could breathe a sigh of relief. The ordeal was over.

This evening, however, Stella felt no sweet ripple of relief. She was shaking with a harrowing fear.

This latest rage had been by far Magnus's worst. Tonight there had been consequences. Magnus hadn't merely given voice to his anger. He'd taken pen to paper and had written instructions for his lawyer, horrifying instructions that had broken Stella's heart. And filled her with guilt.

Now, a snore erupted from the sleeping figure, a snore so loud she feared the noise would wake him. Swiping at her wretched tears, she turned out the light and swiftly left the room. Timber floorboards creaked as she made her way down the darkened passage to the study, where a standard lamp cast a pool of yellow light over Magnus's desk and the dreaded white envelope.

Addressed in Magnus's thick, dark scrawl to Kenneth Woods, his lawyer, the envelope was sealed, but Stella already knew its contents. Magnus had made sure of that. He'd read his legal directive to her in his pompous, booming voice, taking sneering delight when he saw how badly it shocked her.

Naturally, he'd ignored her tearful pleas. 'Don't you bloody dare cry over spilt milk. You only have yourself to blame. You should have thought about the consequences before you snuck away with your fancy man.'

At least he hadn't been physically violent. Despite his increasingly drunken rages, Magnus had never raised a hand to Stella and she was grateful for that. She was grateful, too, that both their children were far away in Brisbane – Deb in her last year of art college and Hugh halfway through his university degree. She would have hated them to hear their father swearing at her as he had this evening, yelling and waving his fist as he hurled terrible accusations in her face. Accusations that were, sadly, true.

For Stella, however, the vile descriptions that still echoed in her head could never sully the beauty of the precious time she'd stolen to be with Tom Kearney. She could never regret going to Cairns to meet him. Those few, too brief, blissful days would be forever enshrined in her memory, bright and unsullied.

Deep within her, she nursed a reassuring certainty that her memories of Tom would sustain her through whatever grim trials life, or her husband, chose to throw at her. Her only regret was that all these years later, Magnus had finally, mysteriously, found out about Tom.

Predictably, Magnus had overreacted and jumped to wild, irrational conclusions, with the result that he'd insisted on making these drastic changes to his will. Now he planned to drive to Burralea tomorrow to deliver his instructions to their lawyer.

This was to be her punishment, but the changes he'd ordered were totally unreasonable. Crazy. Fuelled by jealousy and based on wrong assumptions.

Unfortunately, Stella knew that her husband wouldn't listen to reason, especially not from her, and although Kenneth Woods was an old family friend as well as their lawyer, she doubted that even he would be able to change Magnus's mind. Her husband's pig-headedness knew no bounds.

With a heavy sigh, Stella picked up the envelope, handling it cautiously between her thumb and forefinger, as if it were a bomb. She slipped it into the pocket of her apron, then made her way through the house to the verandah outside.

The night sky was filled with clouds, without a glimmer from moon or stars. Stella leaned forward, resting her forearms on the verandah railing, and looked out into a blackness so complete she felt smothered by it.

Down by the creek the mournful cry of a curlew drifted into the night in a soul-searing wail of despair.

I know how you feel, she told it silently and, despite the warm spring evening, she was swamped by a wave of hopelessness.

She shook the feeling aside. There was danger in indulging in maudlin thoughts and she turned her mind instead to memories of her arrival here at Ruthven Downs as a bride, remembering how she'd loved the homestead at first sight. She'd entered this marriage determined to be a good wife and mother and, for the most part, she'd succeeded. It had only been in recent years that Magnus's drinking had spoiled the delicate harmony she'd worked so hard to maintain.

Until now she'd managed to keep her marriage and her family on an even keel, and tonight she had to remain strong. Her son's future and the future of the Drummond family's vast cattle property now depended on her. She had to keep a cool head and think this problem through.

Even the bleakest situations could be turned around. There was always a solution, and she was grateful for the crucial lesson she'd learned many years ago. Too late.

She must never, *never* give up hope.

1

It had been a long day in the stockyards. As Seth Drummond drove his ute back down the winding, dusty track to the homestead, his thoughts were focused on creature comforts. A hot shower, a fried steak with onions, and a beer. Not necessarily in that order.

Rounding the last bend, he dipped his Akubra against the setting sun and saw the familiar spread of the home paddocks and the horse yards, their timber fences weathered to silvery grey. Beyond the low, sprawling, iron-roofed homestead with its deep verandahs and hanging baskets of ferns, a huge old poinciana tree shaded the house from the western sun.

At the perimeter of the paddocks, a meandering line of paperbarks marked the course of the creek, and as the setting sun's rays lengthened, the distant hills became folds of rumpled velvet beneath an arching sky that deepened from pale blue to mauve.

Seth had lived here all his life, but he never tired of this view, especially at the end of the day when the landscape was dappled with shadows and light.

Today, however, a strange car was parked near the homestead's front steps. The small, bright purple sedan looked out of place in this dusty rural setting.

Visitors.

On the passenger's seat at Seth's side, the blue cattle dog pricked up his ears and stiffened.

'Yeah, know how you feel, Ralph.' Seth gave the dog's neck a sympathetic scratch. 'I'm beat. Not in the mood for visitors.'

He edged the ute forward and as he did so, a figure rose from a squatter's chair on the verandah. A girl in slim blue jeans and a white T-shirt. She had a mane of thick, pale tawny hair, dead straight to her shoulders.

Recognising her, Seth let out a low whistle.

Joanna Dixon, the English backpacker, had scored a job as camp cook on last year's muster. She'd cooked a mean curry in the camp oven and she'd coped well on the job, giving as good as she got when the ringers labelled her the Pommy jillaroo and teased her about her toffy English accent.

Pretty in a slim, tomboyish way, with surprisingly cool, blue eyes, Joanna had flirted with Seth rather blatantly. But his job had been to lead the mustering team, not to be sidetracked by the chance of a roll in the swag with the hired help.

He had no idea what Joanna was doing back here now, but his recollections were suddenly cut off. Joanna was bending down to lift something from a basket on the verandah.

A small bundle. *A baby.*

Seth cast a quick glance around the homestead and lawns, but there was no sign of another woman. Joanna was holding the baby against her shoulder now, patting it with a practised air.

Fine hairs lifted on the back of Seth's neck. He went cold all over. *No, surely not.*

After the muster last year, Joanna had moved away from the district to pick bananas at a farm near Tully. Seth hadn't expected to see her again, and he'd been surprised when she'd turned up at the

Mareeba Rodeo a couple of weeks later, all smiles and long legs in skinny white jeans. She'd greeted him like a long-lost friend and had mingled easily with his circle of friends.

They'd enjoyed a few laughs, a few drinks. Later that night, primed with rum and Cokes, Joanna had knocked on his motel door. He hadn't turned her away that time.

Yanking a sharp rein on his galloping thoughts, Seth parked the ute next to her car. He drew several deep breaths and took his time killing the motor. There had to be a sensible explanation for this, an explanation that did not involve him.

Determined to show no sign of panic, he got out of the vehicle slowly. 'Stay here,' he told Ralph as the dog slipped out behind him. Obedient as ever, the blue heeler sat in the red dust by the ute's front wheel, his eyes and ears alert.

The girl on the verandah settled the baby in her arms. Seth removed his Akubra and ran a hand through his hair. After an afternoon in the stockyards, he was dusty and grimy: he'd been branding, ear-tagging and vaccinating a new mob of weaners, fresh from the Mareeba sales. He left his hat on the bonnet as he strolled towards the three low steps that led to the verandah.

'Hi, Joanna.'

'Hello, Seth.'

'Long time no see.'

'Yes.' She looked nervous, which was *not* a good sign. The girl Seth remembered had been brash and overconfident.

'How long have you been waiting here?' he asked.

'Oh.' She gave a shy shrug. 'An hour or so.'

'That's quite a wait. Sorry there was no one to meet you. I'm afraid I'm the only one home at the moment.' He forced a smile but it only reached half-mast. 'I thought you'd be back in England by now.'

'I'll be flying home quite soon.'

Relief swept through Seth. He'd been stupidly worrying about nothing. This wasn't what he'd feared. Joanna was leaving, going back to England.

'That's why I needed to see you.' Joanna dropped her gaze to the baby in her arms, then looked at Seth again. He could see now that her eyes were too big and too wide, displaying an emotion very close to fear.

Alarmed, Seth swallowed. His mind was racing again, trying to recall important details from that night over a year ago. Hadn't Joanna said she was on the pill?

He found himself staring at the baby, searching for clues, but it just looked cute and tiny like any other baby. Its hair was downy and golden as a duckling, and it had pink cheeks and round blue eyes. It was wearing a grey and red striped jumpsuit and he couldn't even tell if it was a boy or a girl.

He swallowed again. 'How can I help you, Joanna?'

Her mouth twisted, and she looked apologetic. *So* not a good sign. 'I've come to introduce you to Charlie.'

Whack.

'A – a boy?'

'Yes.'

Seth couldn't think. He was too busy panicking. 'Is – is he yours?' A stupid question, no doubt, but it was the best he could manage.

'Yes.' Joanna gave her lower lip a quick nervous chew. 'And he's yours too, Seth.'

Slam. It was like being thrown from a horse and finding himself on the ground, winded. Seth struggled to breathe. 'I don't understand.'

'I'm sorry.'

Joanna truly looked sorry. Unfortunately for Seth, this only compounded the situation. She'd always been so cool and self-assured, and now, as he saw tears glittering in her eyes, an incredible impossibility seemed scarily believable and – *damn it* – feasible.

'Didn't you . . . Weren't you on the pill?'

'Yes, but I'd started the pill mid-cycle and things hadn't settled down. Obviously, I should have been been more careful. I should have warned you, but I never dreamed . . . It was an accident, of course.'

Again she looked down at the baby lying in her arms. She touched his soft hair. 'I nearly didn't go through with it. I was so close to having an abortion. I had it all booked and everything. But I – I knew he was yours.'

She looked up at Seth with a sad smile. 'At the last minute I knew I had to keep him, Seth. I realised I had this little person inside me and I knew that one day he could inherit all this.' She gave a nod towards the wide, bronzed stretch of the Ruthven Downs paddocks.

Seth could only stare at her. He had no words. He was numb, dumbstruck. Trying to take in the horrifying news.

'Charlie's three months old. You can have a DNA test, if you like, but I swear you're the only guy I slept with around then.' Lifting her chin, she eyed him steadily. 'You're his father, Seth. Your name is on his birth certificate. He's Charles Drummond.'

Seth still couldn't think straight, but he forced his legs to move, to mount the steps. 'You'd better come inside.'

'Right, thanks.' With surprising speed, Joanna scooped up a bulging zipper bag and the basket, which Seth now realised was actually one of those capsules for putting babies into cars.

It was a lot to juggle when she had the baby as well. He wasn't keen to help her. It would be like admitting to a truth he didn't want to accept, but the good manners ingrained in him from birth were too strong. He held out his hand. 'I'll take those.'

'Thank you.'

The homestead door wasn't locked. Propping it ajar with one elbow, Seth nodded for Joanna to precede him into the central hallway. 'Lounge room's on the right,' he said, knowing she'd never been in the house before. When she'd been on Ruthven Downs previously, she'd only ever slept in the ringers' quarters or in a swag under the stars.

Now he followed her into the lounge room, still furnished with the same old-fashioned chintz and silky-oak sofas and armchairs that had been in the house since his grandparents' day. The long room was divided by a timber archway and at the far end was the dining area, dominated by a rather grand, mirror-backed sideboard where a collection of photos depicted the history of Seth's family. The Drummonds of Ruthven Downs.

Seth's great-grandfather Hamish Drummond was there in faded sepia, looking serious and heroic in his World War I army uniform. In another frame, Seth's grandparents stood together on their wedding day, his grandfather Magnus looking ever so slightly smug. Then his father, Hugh, as a baby in a long, white christening robe. His parents, rugged up in thick coats and scarves, on their honeymoon in the Blue Mountains. Seth was there too, aged around ten. He and his sister were both on horseback. There were even photos of his aunt and cousin.

Now, as Seth set the baby capsule and bag in a corner next to a faded gold and cream oriental rug, he felt as if the four generations of family photographs were somehow watching him. Reproaching him for fathering a bastard.

'Take a seat, Joanna.'

'Thank you.' She seemed as edgy as he was and she sat with a very straight back.

'Would you like a drink? Water? A cuppa?'

'I'm fine, thanks. I have a water bottle. I can't stay long.'

Seth frowned. He supposed he should be relieved that this was only a brief call. She was going back to England, so at least she wasn't planning to move in with him.

But there were so many questions. He was too tense to sit. 'How come this has taken so long?' He tried not to glare at her, but he had no hope of smiling. 'You've known about – about *him* for a year. Why suddenly decide to turn up now out of the blue?'

The baby gave a little mewing cry and she settled him against her shoulder and began to pat his back again. She drew a deep breath. 'Look, I know I haven't handled this well. For ages I tried to carry on as if the pregnancy wasn't really happening.'

After only the briefest pause, she hurried on with her story. 'I had a job on a property just outside of Broome, doing a little cooking and helping the kids with School of the Air. I often thought about getting in touch with you, coming to see you, but I – I was worried. I was worried about your family's reaction.'

Giving a sheepish half-smile, she quickly dropped her gaze. 'Then I saw on Facebook that your parents were away on holiday in Spain . . .'

A nasty chill streaked down Seth's spine. Joanna was spying on his family? He felt instantly defensive about his parents, who were away on their first overseas holiday, a long-overdue luxury that they both deserved so much.

'You mentioned that you'll be leaving for England soon.'

'Yes.'

'And you're taking Charlie.'

'No, Seth.'

Seth had been standing, but now, blindsided, his knees caved and he sank swiftly into the armchair opposite her. The truth was suddenly, painfully obvious. Joanna was dumping the kid on him. That was why she'd come. Now, while the baby's grandparents were safely out of the country. She didn't have the guts to face them as well.

'I'm getting married, you see,' she said matter-of-factly. With her chin high and sounding more like the calm and 'together' girl that

Seth remembered, Joanna added, 'It's been planned for ages. My fiancé is Nigel Fox-Richards.'

After an expectant pause during which Seth made no response, she continued less certainly, 'We didn't have a formal engagement, but it was all settled before I left England. Nigel's family has an estate in Northumberland. They're – they're quite well off.'

'How jolly,' Seth responded bitterly.

She had the grace to blush.

'So how does that work?' Distaste lent a hard edge to his voice, but he was too angry to care. 'Were you allowed your little adventure in the colonies before you settled down to married life in the castle?'

'Well, I suppose it was more or less like that. Nigel had this list of adventures, you see – trekking the Himalayas, sailing to the West Indies, hugging polar bears or whatever. He wanted to tick them off before he got too busy with the estate and our life together, so we agreed on eighteen months apart. Now Nigel's father's health is failing and it's time to take on all sorts of responsibilities.'

Bizarrely, Seth could already picture Joanna fitting into that scene. She certainly had the posh accent and he could imagine her in skin-tight cream jodhpurs and knee-high boots, a riding crop tucked under one arm, a string of pearls around her tanned throat.

'How does Nigel feel about Charlie?'

'He doesn't know about Charlie.' Her mouth tightened and her eyes were suddenly hard and determined. 'He's not going to know about him. He can't. He mustn't. That's the thing, you see.'

'No, I don't see.' Seth was on his feet again now, too angry to sit. 'You'd better explain. Preferably in words of one syllable, so everything's perfectly clear.'

Joanna sat even straighter, shoulders squared. 'I can't take Charlie back to England, Seth. There's no way that Nigel's family would accept him.'

So, at last, the truth. Joanna was going to marry her Lord Fauntleroy, and she needed to keep her Aussie bastard hidden.

Seth's anger spilled. 'For fuck's sake, Joanna, how the hell can you be so bloody casual about this?' Dramatically, he threw his arms wide. 'Oops, I've had a baby, and here he is, and now I'm off home to England.' He shot her his fiercest glare. 'Is that the best you can bloody do?'

He should have known she would give as good as she got.

'Don't forget, Seth,' she said coolly, 'you were as keen as I was at the time. And you were also pretty *bloody* casual about our relationship. When I left, I got a kiss on the cheek and a pat on the bum. Goodbye and happy memories of my trip Down Under.'

'Well, yeah,' Seth said defensively. 'But if I'd known this had happened, I would have –' He hesitated, unsure of his ground. 'I suppose I knew you would have done your best to help me, to look after me and Charlie. I never really doubted that. The problem was –'

Now it was Joanna's turn to hesitate.

'You didn't want my help,' Seth supplied. 'It would have complicated your life. I might have tried to ruin your plans.'

'Yes.' For a moment she almost looked penitent, but then she said calmly, 'Now it's your call, Seth. You asked me to make everything clear. And I'm asking you now – do you want Charlie, or not?'

No. Hell, no.

I can't possibly . . .

It was way too sudden. Most guys had nine months to get used to this sort of news . . .

For the first time, Seth looked properly at the striped bundle in Joanna's arms. The baby was curled up like a koala – his golden head lying against her shoulder and one small, dimpled hand resting on her breast. He had fat cheeks and neat little ears. His eyelashes were blond and his eyelids heavy, drooping sleepily.

This was Seth's son. His flesh and blood.

His son. If Joanna was telling the truth – and Seth suspected she was – this tiny scrap of humanity carried Drummond genes. He was Charlie Drummond. He was going to grow into a toddler, a schoolboy, a teenager.

A man.

I knew that one day he could inherit all this.

Emotion clawed at Seth's throat. Anger again, certainly. He was furious with Joanna for her secrecy, for treating him like a last resort. He felt fear, too, as he contemplated the responsibility suddenly landed on him. His lifestyle, his freedom – hell, his whole life as he knew it – would be totally stuffed.

And then, very much to his surprise, Seth felt another emotion emerging, something deep and primal and unexpected: a fierce welling up of protectiveness.

But hell.

'Are you expecting us – *me* – to take care of Charlie?'

Joanna nodded. 'That would be the ideal situation.'

'What if I told you that I couldn't?'

She drew a deep breath. 'I know this must be a terrible shock, Seth, and I apologise for landing it on you like this, but the only alternative I can think of is to hand him over to the state for adoption.'

Adoption? A ward of the state?

Seth was surprised by the vehemence of his reaction.

Heaven knew he didn't want a baby. He had a cattle station to run and while he knew a fair bit about caring for newborn calves, he knew absolutely zilch about looking after a human baby. More importantly, he thoroughly enjoyed being a bachelor.

Joanna's bombshell was as shocking and unwelcome as a grim health diagnosis for a person who'd always been fit and well. And yet . . . Seth knew that life could deal hefty punches from time to time. If he was honest, he'd had a pretty free run so far. He'd grown up in a beautiful part of the country, had enjoyed the fun of boarding school, representative rugby union, university. The life of a cattleman, the life that he'd always wanted, had been handed to him on a plate.

Joanna was right. When they'd had their careless, casual fling, he'd been a very willing partner. Now, he had little choice but to cop this blow. An unpleasant reality had to be faced and, to his own somewhat stupefied amazement, he was already coming to terms with this new and weighty responsibility. *Charlie*.

But there were still questions to be asked.

In a desperate bid to get his head straight, Seth marched to the French doors that looked out across the dusk-shadowed landscape. He saw the fiery glow on the rim of the distant hills. The evening star was already showing and he watched the flight of a trio of ibises, their long necks straining as they winged their way homewards.

He turned. 'Are you sure you've thought this through? Can you really give up your baby? He looks well cared for. I'd say you've been a good mother. How are you going to feel down the track, Joanna? Have you thought about that?'

'Of course.'

'Say he settles in here, becomes part of this family. How do I know you won't turn up in a few years' time to tell me you've changed your mind?'

'That won't happen, Seth.'

He might have rejected this assertion if he hadn't seen the silver glitter of tears in Joanna's eyes. Her mask had slipped and the pain and stoic resolution in her face told their own story. She had made a difficult choice and now she was determined to go through with it. All the way.

'Well,' Seth said quietly, as he eyed the bulging zippered bag, which presumably contained all the necessary equipment for the baby's care. 'I suppose you'd better show me what's involved in feeding him.'

She smiled shakily as he returned from the French doors. 'Here,' she said. 'You should at least hold him.'

Seth drew a sharp breath, then held out his arms, stiffly bent at the elbows.

'You can relax a bit. You just need to support his head,' Joanna said. 'His neck's not very strong yet.'

The little guy was now in Seth's arms. So small and warm. He felt his throat tighten.

'Is the name okay?' Joanna's eyes were too bright. 'I thought about asking you first, but I was too scared. I wanted to tell you about him, you know, face to face.'

Seth shrugged. 'Charlie, Charles, Chas – anything, as long as he's not called Chuck.'

For the first time, they both smiled. In his arms, the baby wriggled. 'Hey, Charlie.' Seth's voice was choked.

Charlie looked up at him, frowning like an old man with all the worries of the world, but staring solemnly, straight into Seth's eyes.

'G'day, little mate,' Seth said, and he was rewarded with a heart-breaking, toothless grin.

2

It was another perfect night in northern Spain. Jackie Drummond was practically floating with happiness as she strolled through the narrow cobblestone streets of Parte Vieja, the old quarter of San Sebastián. The autumn air was cold and clear, and Jackie, wrapped snugly in a newly purchased red and purple pashmina, could see patches of star-splashed sky between the spires and rooftops.

She loved the centuries-old feel of the place, the ancient stone churches, the solid arched doorways and the fountains adorned with baby angels. She loved, too, the warmly lit bars that rubbed shoulders with all this history, and hummed with a happy mix of tourists and locals.

In the bars people were drinking *sidra* and dining on the tantalising canapés called *pintxos*. Anchovy and olive, foie gras and caramelised onions, jamon and goat's cheese, crab and salmon. Meanwhile, mere streets away, the Atlantic Ocean hurled and thumped its might against the rocky foreshore, tossing white spray breathtakingly high.

For Jackie, everything about this city was exotic and exciting, so very different from rural North Queensland where she'd spent her whole life. Each new sight and sound and taste was fascinating. It was such a surprise. She'd never dreamed that travel could be so much fun.

For so long she'd resisted Hugh's suggestions about going over-seas. They had a time share in Noosa and she'd loved those annual holidays. She'd loved knowing exactly what to expect when she arrived. Why bother travelling to foreign countries when there were glamorous beaches and outstanding restaurants in their own state?

But here she was, finally in Europe with her husband and their friends, having the time of her life. Everything was working out just as Hugh had assured her it would. She'd been foolish to worry.

Unfortunately, worrying was second nature to Jackie. Even though she'd been married to her grazier husband for thirty-nine years, and they had two wonderful children anyone might be proud of, her humble past threw rather a long shadow.

She'd been Jackie Greeves before she was married to Hugh, and she'd lived with her mum in a run-down worker's cottage on the outskirts of Atherton. Her father, a timber-getter, had been killed in a logging accident when Jackie was four. After that, Jackie's mother kept a roof over their heads by washing and ironing and cleaning houses.

Her mum used to say that she didn't mind the work. Cleaning houses was good honest toil, she said, and she got to see how other people lived. And although a few rich kids at school made unkind comments, Jackie hadn't been an unhappy child.

It was only when she reached her pre-teens that she became conscious of the difference between her life and those of her friends. This was especially clear in the Christmas holidays, when her school friends' families towed powerboats to Lake Tinaroo and camped on its banks and waterskied. Others took off for even grander holidays down south at the Gold and Sunshine Coasts.

One year a classmate had invited Jackie to join her family camping at the lake. Jackie had gleefully accepted and she'd had a fabulous time, but she'd felt guilty about abandoning her tired, struggling mum, who never got to have a holiday. In the years that followed, as a sort of penance perhaps, she'd spent the weeks over Christmas working alongside her mum hoping to lessen her load.

It hadn't been easy, trying to convince her mother that she enjoyed helping with the mopping and vacuuming, but the reward had been that they could finish early and spend precious afternoons at home watching videos together.

Jackie and her mum shared a weakness for romantic movies and for butterscotch twirl ice-cream, and those afternoons were the hugest treat. They helped to ease the pain, too, when the other kids came back from their holidays with glowing suntans and exciting stories about skiing or surfing or going to Dream World.

As soon as she was old enough, Jackie had left school and got a job in the local supermarket. It had seemed sensible. She knew she could never afford to go away to university.

By contrast, her husband Hugh had grown up on the vast acres of his family's cattle property, Ruthven Downs, and he'd travelled away to one of the state's best boarding schools and then to university in Brisbane. Before he met Jackie, he'd spent a year backpacking around Europe and South America.

For Jackie, marrying Hugh had been a bit unreal, like one of the romantic movies she'd so adored watching with her mum. As his wife, she'd applied herself earnestly to helping him maintain Ruthven Downs as one of the most thriving and successful properties in the district. She had adapted quickly to life on the land and didn't mind the hard work and long days.

When Hugh had first suggested an overseas holiday, Jackie was anxious, especially when he mentioned the two other couples that they might travel with. She wasn't at all sure she would fit in.

She was quite at home mixing with cattle people, whose conversations revolved around family, the weather and the condition of stock or pastures. She was a stalwart of the local CWA, where she'd always felt very welcome and comfortable. But the proposed travelling companions were old school friends of Hugh's. Jackie was a little in awe of them and her old insecurities lingered.

Ian Kinsella was an architect based in Cairns and his wife, Shelley, had her own business, an elegant gift shop that sold exquisite soaps and hand creams and scented drawer-liners. They had a spectacular house in Edge Hill, surrounded by trees and looking out to beautiful views of the Coral Sea.

The other couple, Brad Woods and his wife Kate, were both lawyers in the Woods family firm in Burralea, a pretty town in the heart of the Atherton Tablelands. Brad was a third-generation Burralea lawyer. His father had been friends with Hugh's father, Magnus Drummond, so their connection went back to boyhood.

While Jackie had met these people on several occasions over the years, and no one in the group had ever made her feel inferior, she'd never felt completely relaxed around them. And of course she always tried too hard.

The first time she and Hugh had invited them to lunch at Ruthven Downs, she'd fretted over the menu and the table settings, the flowers, and even the guest towels in the bathroom. In the end everyone had been incredibly friendly, though, and that afternoon and other occasions since then had gone without a hitch.

And now, to her intense relief, the trip was working out beautifully, too. The three couples were sharing a three-bedroom apartment in San Sebastián and they'd fallen with surprising ease into a workable division of roles.

Kate Woods set out each morning while it was still dark – it got light at eight-thirty at this time of the year – and returned with fresh baguettes and delicacies from the bakery. Ian fancied himself as a

cook and on several mornings had produced scrumptious break-
fasts – either scrambled eggs with local herbs, or an enormous
Spanish omelette loaded with peppers and jamon.

Jackie's husband Hugh had chatted up the people at the info
centre and garnered tips about the best sights and day trips available. Brad found the best delis with gourmet Spanish cheeses and
meats, while Shelley hunted down the fashion shops and purveyors
of gorgeous leather handbags.

Jackie, the self-confessed novice traveller in the group, was
happy to be guided by the others and to make herself useful in the
kitchen, making the toast, unstacking the dishwasher, wiping down
benches.

At some point she'd been christened the 'Toast Master' and she
was secretly pleased. The nickname was a sort of validation for her.
She belonged.

It helped that the Basque territory in Spain was new to all of the
group, so they'd had fun making discoveries together. So far, they'd
tramped through several museums and art galleries, and had visited
the aquarium at one end of La Concha Bay and the funicular at the
other end.

They'd hunted down a restaurant hidden in the distant hills,
where they'd enjoyed a sumptuous lunch. And they'd visited farms
in the lush nearby countryside to see firsthand how sheep's cheese
was made, and how jamon ibérico was created from pigs fed on
acorns.

Now, this evening. They'd chosen to go back to a favourite restaurant opposite the Basilica of Santa María del Coro. As Jackie
filed in with their group, the place was alive with voices and laughter. Delicious aromas filled the air and people bustled about.
from the kitchen.

At first, it looked as if they wasn't a spot free, but they quickly
established a flirtatious rapport with one of the waitresses. Jackie

suspected he slipped her a very generous tip – and she managed to find room for them.

Happily, they squeezed onto wooden forms on either side of a narrow table and mulled over the menu. Slow-cooked beef cheek or something lighter? The goat's cheese and walnut salad?

Selections were made and wine was ordered. A ruby red carafe of *rioja* promptly materialised, accompanied by a basket of sliced baguette. From where Jackie was sitting, she could see through an open doorway to the basilica outside. It had beautiful, ornately carved doors and, on the wide stone steps in front, several groups of young Spaniards sat, enjoying the evening, sharing a joke, and tossing back their glossy dark heads as they laughed.

Momentarily distracted by their shining-eyed, youthful vitality, Jackie thought of her own children. Seth at home on Ruthven Downs, caring for the property, mending fences, checking the condition of the cattle, the paddocks, the dams, and ordering in stock feed if necessary. Their daughter Flora was in a very different scene. It still stunned Jackie that her daughter's years of hard work and endless practice had paid off and she was now a musician, a professional violinist in Melbourne.

She hoped her children were as happy as these carefree young people appeared to be.

Abruptly, she was dragged out of her musings by Brad, who was telling the group a story, recounting how he and Kate had first met when they were on a walking trail.

'It was on the Thorsborne Track on Hinchinbrook Island,' Brad was saying. 'And I came across Kate balanced precariously on a pebble-sized rock in the middle of a creek, trying to refill her water bottle.'

'And of course I saw Brad and immediately –'

'Fell in love,' supplied Shelley glibly.

'Fell in the water,' Kate corrected with a smiling eye-roll.

Brad's habitual grin was wider than ever. 'So then it was a case of a wet T-shirt with no competition.'

This brought a bellow of laughter from Ian and Hugh and a dig in the ribs from his wife's elbow.

'I must say,' remarked Shelley as the laughter died down, 'that's much more interesting than the way Ian and I met. We were at a party and a mutual friend introduced us.'

'Boring, boring, boring,' said Ian with a shrug.

Shelley laughed. 'And I turned you down three times before I took pity and agreed to go out with you.'

Her husband smiled. 'You were playing hard to get.'

'Clearly,' said Brad.

Jackie was intrigued. 'What made you change your mind?'

'Oh.' Shelley tucked an elegant wing of silver hair behind one ear. 'Ian sent me flowers with a note attached.'

At this point, Hugh joined in. 'And it was the message in the note rather than the flowers that did the trick?'

Now Shelley's smile was coy. 'Exactly.'

Jackie was dying to know more and she could sense that the others were as curious as she was about what Ian's message had said. But the waitress reappeared, her arms laden with their meals.

People began to eat. No one pushed Shelley to expand on her story and the subject was on the brink of being dropped completely when Brad, with a succulent piece of braised beef cheek poised on his fork, directed a grin towards Hugh and Jackie.

'What about you guys?' he said. 'I don't think you've ever told us how you met.'

Jackie gulped. She glanced at Hugh, who was sitting opposite her and smiling at her over his glass of *rioja*.

He sent her a wink, then he told them, 'Jackie was cutting my hair.'

Jackie knew it was silly to feel nervous. Being a hairdresser was nothing to be ashamed of, but she'd never talked about her past in this company. Now, as Kate's and Shelley's eyes widened with surprise, she felt her face go red.

'Really?' said Kate.

Shelley asked the obvious: 'Were you a hairdresser, Jackie?'

'Yep,' she said, almost defiantly.

'Our eyes met in the salon mirror,' said Hugh.

'And the rest is history.' Melodramatically, Kate pressed a hand over her heart. 'Oh, I can just picture it.' She managed not to sound patronising, for which Jackie was grateful.

'It was a very romantic moment,' Hugh agreed, speaking with the simple sincerity that Jackie had always loved.

And the truth was that she'd always thought their meeting *was* incredibly romantic. She would never forget the day the tall and handsome Hugh Drummond strolled into the salon where she worked in Atherton's Main Street.

Every detail was clear in her memory. Hugh had sat down in the chair and she'd arranged a cape around his shoulders. Their eyes had met in the mirror and he'd given her a warm, interested smile that made his lovely dark eyes glow.

Jackie had smiled back at him . . . and their smiles had gone on for far longer than they should have. In a movie there would have been sappy music playing. Eventually, Jackie had blushed and become flustered, but she'd managed to cut Hugh's hair without making a hash of it.

'It's no wonder you always look so good, Jackie,' Kate said. 'Hairdressers have such a talent for making the most of their appearance. A real flair.'

Jackie sent her a grateful smile and she decided then and there that it was time to stop worrying.

After dinner, they wended their way through the narrow streets filled with people, past bars that spilled yellow light onto the stone.

Near the edge of the bay they stopped at an ice-cream shop.

Part of the fun was lingering again over choices. Jackie opted for a dollop of tangy raspberry combined with the smoothness of hazelnut and cream.

She shared the ice-cream with Hugh, linking her arm through his and offering him bites as they took a path across a park between trees strung with lights. Everywhere she looked, locals were promenading, enjoying the autumn evening just as she was. A middle-aged woman pushed an old man in a wheelchair. A stylish young couple were out with a pram. A young girl in a red tracksuit jogged past them with three dogs on leads.

In the distance, someone was playing a guitar, sending cool, sensual notes rippling into the night. Jackie thought it was quite possible that she'd never felt happier.

'I'm having the best time.' She rubbed her cheek against Hugh's shoulder.

'It's worked out well, hasn't it?'

'So much better than I thought. And we still have Paris and London ahead of us. Two more weeks.'

Hugh laughed and, in a moment of uncharacteristic spontaneity, he burst into song. 'We've only just begun . . .'

An elderly couple walking past, arm in arm, smiled.

Jackie grinned back at them. She finished the ice-cream and found a tissue to wipe her hands. Their friends were a few metres behind them, lingering to read an inscription on a statue.

As they waited at a pedestrian crossing for the lights to change, Jackie asked, 'Do you find yourself thinking much about home?'

'Hardly at all.' Hugh dropped a kiss on the top of her head. 'I know the place is in good hands.'

She smiled. 'Yes, Seth was dead keen to have the run of the property, to prove how capable he is.'

'He's more than ready to take over.'

And then you could retire, Jackie thought. *We would have more time to travel.* It was an idea she could get used to.

They were crammed into the lift, which was climbing creakily to the apartment, when Jackie's mobile phone pinged with a text message. Unearthing the phone from her bag in the tiny space was next to impossible. She waited until they were back in the apartment and had flopped onto the lounge room sofas, as was their habit at the end of the day.

'Who's for a nightcap?' asked Ian.

'No more alcohol for me,' said Kate. 'I'm putting the kettle on.'

Jackie put her hand up for camomile tea. Ian began to pour whisky, while Kate headed for the kitchen. Jackie dug her phone and tortoiseshell-framed reading glasses out of her bag and then brought up the text message. It was from Rhonda Close, one of her CWA friends.

> *I saw Seth and the baby today. Wow!*
> *What a lovely surprise. Congrats, Grandma! xx*

Jackie blinked and reread the message, but it made no more sense the second time than it had the first. Rhonda must have got her wires crossed. Seth didn't have a baby.

Sorry, she wrote back. *I think you must have the wrong pers—*

Jackie stopped typing. Rhonda had to be mistaken, but to be on the safe side she would double-check the story with Seth first. If Seth had been seen out with a baby, he would have been minding it for a friend. There was bound to be an explanation.

It wasn't as if her son was in a relationship. There was no steady girlfriend, at least there hadn't been anyone serious in the last year.

Jackie checked the world clock on her phone. It was seven in the morning at home. With luck she would catch Seth before he headed out to work.

Across the room, she caught Hugh's eye. She rose and waved her phone at him. 'I'm going to ring Seth.'

Hugh looked surprised, but then he nodded. 'Give him my best.'

She went through to their bedroom, which looked out onto a central courtyard above which clotheslines were strung between windows. Earlier that day she'd done a little hand-washing, and her tights and knickers were still hanging alongside two of Hugh's shirts.

She unpegged the shirts and put them on hangers, then stowed the underwear in a drawer in the wardrobe. She closed the window, drew the curtains, and sat on the bed. Pulling off her boots and wriggling her stockinged feet, she thought again about Rhonda Close's message.

Rhonda was a bit prone to jumping to conclusions. She must have been mixed up.

The phone rang and rang.

'Hello,' Seth said at last, a little breathlessly.

'Seth, darling.'

'Mum?'

'Yes, how are you?'

'Fine, thanks. How's Spain? Are you still enjoying yourself?'

'Yes, it's absolutely wonderful here. The weather's perfect and I love San Sebastián.' Jackie would have expanded on all the things she loved about Spain, but she heard a sound in the background. A cry, a bleat, that might possibly have come from a baby. 'Seth, I got the strangest text message from Rhonda Close.'

'Oh?'

'She's congratulating me on becoming a grandmother. She said she saw you in town with –'

Abruptly, the noise in the background grew louder. It was a wail.

Most definitely a baby's cry.

'Can you hang on a sec?' asked Seth.

'Of course,' Jackie choked out, and she sat in stunned silence with the phone pressed to her ear.

What on earth was going on? Had a woman moved into the homestead with her baby? A friend in need?

She tried to think of anyone in Seth's circle of friends who'd been pregnant or had a baby recently. When she drew a blank, her mind started throwing up other possibilities that she just as quickly dismissed.

She mustn't panic. She just had to be patient. Everything would make sense in a moment.

'Hello?' said Seth's voice after what seemed like an eternity. 'Are you still there?'

'Yes.' Jackie forced false brightness into her voice. 'Is – is everything all right, Seth?'

'Yes. I mean, well, something's come up. But I've got it all under control. I didn't want to bother you. There's nothing really for you to worry about.'

'But there is a baby?'

'Yeah. I'm afraid it's true, Mum. You're a grandma.'

3

Hugh poked his head around the door. 'I thought you might have fallen asleep. Your camomile tea's getting cold.' He was smiling as he held out a mug, but the smile quickly vanished. 'Jackie, what's wrong?'

She was still dazed and shaken as she told him about Seth and the baby and the English backpacker, who'd already gone back to England. She hadn't cried until now, but Hugh's shocked expression sent her reaching for the travel pack of tissues on the bedside table.

Hugh put the mug down, then sat with his arm around her shoulders. When she had wiped her eyes and taken a sip of tea, he asked quietly, 'Is Seth sure the baby's his?'

'That's the first question I asked him.' Jackie dabbed at her eyes again. 'I asked him several times, actually. He got fed up with me. He said what does it matter? His name's on the birth certificate and there's no one else putting his hand up to be the baby's father.'

Hugh let out his breath in a low whistle.

'Don't worry,' Jackie added stoutly. 'As soon as we're home, I'll get a DNA test done. I know they can do it from a strand of hair.'

Hugh frowned rather sternly at this, but he didn't argue. 'How old is the baby?' he asked.

'Three months.'

He gave a helpless kind of shrug. 'Well, I suppose the timing's right. The muster was a little over a year ago.'

'This liaison,' Jackie said, using her fingers to make air quotes around the word, 'didn't happen during the muster. Seth and this girl met up a bit later at the Mareeba Rodeo, after she left us.'

'Oh, I see.'

'I must say I'm relieved about that,' she added. 'There's so much bad press about foreign backpackers and rural workers being pressured into sex on the farms where they're working.'

'For God's sake, Jackie. Seth would never –'

'I know, I know,' she said quickly. 'Just the same, there'll be tongues wagging.'

Hugh shrugged again, back to his unruffled self. 'I remember the cook,' he said. 'What's her name again?'

'Joanna.'

'Joanna, that's right. Joanna Dixon. She was a pretty good camp cook. Got on well with the stockmen.'

'Clearly she got on very well with Seth.'

Hugh didn't smile. He gave a thoughtful nod and then a small sigh. 'And now we have a grandson.'

'Yes, and his mother's high-tailed it back to England to take up a new life without him.'

'That's a turn-up for the books.'

Jackie wondered if her husband was thinking, as she was, about the way this should have happened. First a wedding, where a lovely daughter-in-law was welcomed into the family. Later, the happy couple sharing their exciting news. And then months of delightful anticipation while Jackie knitted bootees and made a patchwork quilt for the baby's cot.

'What kind of girl leaves her baby behind?' Hugh asked. 'In

this day and age when there's no stigma attached to being a single mother?'

'A girl who's going to marry a very wealthy Englishman,' Jackie told him. 'A girl who doesn't want her mistakes in Australia ruining her chances.'

Hugh's gaze was serious now as he stared at the carpet with a thoughtful frown. 'Is that what Joanna told Seth?'

'Yes, she's got a fiancé back in England. Can you believe it? The poor baby. How could she be so heartless?'

'I wonder what are the chances of her changing her mind.'

'Seth doesn't seem to think she will.'

'Well, she's already sprung one huge surprise. I hope to God that she doesn't deceive him again.'

'I know. That's what worries me, too.'

Together, they sat in gloomy silence as the reality of the new family situation sank in. It wasn't pleasant to know that the mother of their grandson could be so cool-headed and selfish.

'I suppose we should be happy. At least the baby's perfectly healthy,' Jackie said after a bit. 'But it's all so –'

She was about to say that it was all so sad, but she stopped herself. Seth hadn't sounded sad. He'd sounded amazingly calm. Calm and smiling. She was sure she'd heard a smile in his voice, which, under the circumstances, was quite remarkable.

'How the hell will Seth manage?' said Hugh. 'He'll have to hire a nurse. Has he done that already?'

Jackie shook her head. 'You'll never believe this. He's hired a couple of stockmen to look after the cattle and *he's* looking after the baby.'

'Seth?' Hugh's jaw dropped. For the first time in a long time, he looked in danger of losing his cool. 'You mean he's changing nappies and getting up for feeds in the middle of the night and walking the floor – everything?'

'Apparently.'

Jackie had to press her fingers to her lips to stop herself from crying. This was so very, very different from the way she'd expected her son's life to turn out. Seth was almost thirty, in the prime of his life, a popular and eligible young man.

Hugh looked stern. 'He won't be able to keep that up forever.'

'I know. Seth said it's just for the first few weeks. He said everything to do with the property is under control and he wants to get to know the baby. He wants to *bond*.' She smiled shakily.

Hugh slipped an arm around her shoulders again. 'We should be proud of our boy. He's facing up to his responsibility like a man.'

'I guess.' Jackie's voice squeaked, and this time she couldn't hold the rush of tears. Hugh's arms tightened around her, hugging her close to his chest, and she cried hard.

She wasn't completely sure why she was crying. In her early marriage, she'd known the deep disappointment of several miscarriages, so a part of her welcomed any baby with joy. But she was certainly disappointed that this baby was going to shape Seth's future, when it should have been the other way around.

'I'm not desperately sad,' she said, when Hugh released her and handed her another tissue,

'I know. But you've had a shock.'

'His name – the baby's name – is Charlie.'

'Charlie,' Hugh repeated quietly. 'Charlie Drummond.'

She thought she could almost hear a note of pride in his voice.

Her mobile phone pinged again. Cautiously, she picked the phone up and put on her reading glasses. 'Seth's sent us a photo.'

She tapped the screen and together they stared at the tiny picture. It was a selfie of Seth in a grey T-shirt, with two days' growth of beard, his thick, dark hair tousled as if he hadn't combed it in days. But he was grinning as he held a baby in the crook of his arm. The baby was incredibly cute, with a splash of golden hair and huge blue eyes.

'Oh, he's gorgeous, Hugh.'

'Yeah, he's certainly a cutie.'

The photo had been taken in the kitchen. Jackie could see an empty baby bottle with a teat and a tin of formula on the stone-topped bench behind Seth. She could also see, through the back doorway, a glimpse of gum trees and sun-lit paddocks.

Without warning she was hit by a rush of homesickness.

'I think he looks like his mother,' said Hugh.

'Well, she is blonde, isn't she?'

'Sort of, but then so are you.' With a fond smile, her husband ruffled her hair.

Jackie's natural colour tended towards mousy and she'd been lightening it for many, many years, since her hairdressing days. She might have commented on this, but she was distracted by a new, alarming thought.

'Hugh, should we go home?' The question burst from her.

'Break our holiday?'

'Yes.'

Dismay washed over her husband's face. 'I – I don't think that's necessary.'

'I just thought Seth might need us.'

'Does he look like he needs us?'

Jackie had to admit there was no sign of strain in Seth's smile. 'He didn't tell us about Charlie's arrival, so I don't suppose he expects us to come rushing back.'

'I think he'd be upset if we did.'

'Yes, probably.'

'He's doing the right thing. We should let him get on with it,' Hugh said proudly.

'But eventually –'

'Eventually, we'll work something out. Once we're home, we'll tackle this as a family.' He sent her a questioning glance. 'Does

Flora know about the baby?'

'I'm not sure. I'll send a message back to Seth to tell him we think Charlie's wonderful, and I'll ask him if he's been in touch with Flora.'

When this was done, she nodded towards the lounge room. 'Should we tell the others?'

'There's certainly no need to tell them tonight, not when they're all unwinding before bed.'

Jackie accepted this with a shrug. She wasn't looking forward to sharing this news. Becoming a grandparent was an important rung on the ladder of life, but she had hoped it would be a joyful occasion, not one wreathed in question marks and foisted on her out of the blue. She remembered how relaxed and incredibly happy she'd been a mere half hour ago, before she read Rhonda's message. Now she doubted she would sleep at all.

4

Hi Seth,

What amazing news! I can't believe I'm an aunty. I adore the photos. Charlie is sooo cute. But I'm still trying to wrap my head around the fact that he's yours! Even harder to credit is that you're going to look after a baby all by yourself! Wow, that's sensational. Truly heroic, big bro. I wish I could help – not that I know anything about babies.

Do you know about wind? Veda, a friend who plays cello, had a baby last year and his colic became the bane of her life. She has all sorts of theories about burping babies, but I suppose Mum will be able to set you straight with that when she gets home. Oh, and did you know it's good to play Mozart to babies? It's supposed to boost their brainpower.

On the music front here: we have a new conductor who's come over from Europe on a secondment. Enrico Pauli. He's a young hot

shot and we're so privileged to work with him, but he's really hard
to follow. At the first rehearsal I couldn't get the hang of his beat.
Even James, the concert master, was having trouble.

We had another rehearsal yesterday and that was better. And
Enrico's energy is rubbing off. He's got the musicians enthused.
Even the older, stodgier members of the orchestra are lifting their act.
Usually they're checking their watches and muttering about going
over time, but there wasn't a murmur from them last night.

I'm going to have so much fun shopping for Charlie.

Love,

Aunty Flora

To: Jackie Drummond
From: Flora Drummond
Subject: Huh??

Hi Mum, thanks for passing on that pic of Charlie. What a cutie he is.
It must be killing you that you're not home to cuddle him (it's killing
me!), but I'm so pleased to hear that you're having a great holiday.
You guys really deserve it.

I gotta say, though, just between you and me, I can't understand
how that girl could have just dumped her baby on Seth like that
without any warning. After going to all the trouble of carrying him for
nine months and giving birth, how on earth could she abandon her
own son? It's very strange.

I guess that baby doesn't know how lucky he is to have a dad
like Seth.

Keep on having fun.

Lots of love,

Flora xx

To: Flora Drummond
From: Seth Drummond
Subject: Re: Go Daddy!

Hi Floss,

You ask if I know about wind. I now know more than I'd like to,
I'm afraid. I've read just about every site there is on the internet,
trying to work out the best ways to burp this windy little son of mine.
I've walked with him over my shoulder, gently stroking his back. I've
sat him on my lap with a hand supporting his stomach. I've paced
the floor, I've jogged, I would have stood on my head and wiggled
my ears if I thought it might help.

Sorry, that's probably too much information. Just believe me,
the sweetest sound you could ever hear is not a violin played in the
moonlight, but a baby's burp and then silence.

I read that female ears are pitched somehow to super-react to
a baby's cry, but it only took me a week to tune in to his wavelength.
BC (before Charlie), you could have dropped a forty-four gallon oil
drum off a ute outside my bedroom window and I wouldn't have
stirred. Now I wake at two in the morning and leap out of bed,
adrenaline pumping, at the merest squawk.

Hey, thanks for the Mozart tip. I tried playing 'Eine Kleine'
to Charlie to soothe him, but I'm afraid he didn't seem to like it.
Must take after me, he prefers *Sunrise over Sea* by John Butler Trio –
I don't know what that will do for his brainpower. I've also
downloaded a white noise app to see if that will help with getting
him to sleep.

Becoming a parent is both amazing and frightening. But he's
a good kid, really. You can tell he doesn't really want to cry. We'll
get there.

All the best with the orchestra. Remember in *Ghostbusters* when
Bill Murray told Sigourney Weaver that she was the best cello player

in her row? I'm sure you're the best second violin :)

    Love,

    Seth

To: Jackie Drummond
From: Flora Drummond
Subject: Welcome home

Hi Mum,

    Thanks for your email. So lovely to know you're back in Oz and on the home front again, ready to back up Seth on this amazing parental adventure. Now I might get to hear more deets about Charlie. Seth has been in touch, but it seems like he's too busy to write very often.

    I'm getting pretty busy too, actually. Rehearsals are hotting up for the opera season. Glamorous as that sounds, the reality is that every night I'll play a hundred times more notes than Oliver and I'll be paid half as much. (Who's Oliver, you might ask? He's a singer, a tenor that I've started seeing. A couple of sopranos in the chorus are dead jealous, tee hee.) And of course I'll be down in the pit and not up on the stage in the limelight, so I won't get nearly as much love from the audience either.

    Don't get me wrong, I'm not feeling sorry for myself, just pointing out the way things are in the music world. But I shouldn't complain. At least I have a full-time job with the orchestra. The singers are only on short-term contracts and have to have day jobs as well. Oliver works in a bank.

    Would love to hear how things are with you guys. How's Dad? Who's pacing the floor with Charlie now?

    F x

To: Flora Drummond
From: Jackie Drummond
Subject: Re: Welcome home

Thanks for the welcome, Flora. It's so lovely to be home, especially now that we're over the jetlag.

We're totally in love with the new little member of our household. Charlie reminds me so much of Seth as a baby, even though he's much fairer. I'm going to help with babysitting, of course, and I'm quite excited about that (now that I'm over the shock of instant grandmotherhood). I wish we could have been here to help Seth from the start, but your father thinks it was a good thing that Seth and Charlie had a few weeks on their own to sort themselves out. Seth's certainly bonded with the little fellow.

Would you believe Seth's also talking about building his own separate cottage? I don't suppose I should be so surprised. Your brother's always had a mature, independent streak, hasn't he? But building his own place will be so much extra work for him when he's already juggling the cattle work and the baby.

I will take your father's advice, however, and 'butt out'.

Your friend Oliver sounds very interesting. I hope you continue to enjoy his company. It would be lovely for you to have a boyfriend who shares your passion for music. Any chance of a photo?

Love,

Mum xx

To: Flora Drummond
From: Seth Drummond
Subject: Catch up

Hi Floss,

Happy New Year! Sorry for my silence these past couple of months, but the building project is well under way. It's just a very simple kit home, but that's fine for Charlie and me. Can't believe he's almost seven months already.

I've needed a fair bit of Mum's help with minding the little bloke. Unfortunately, you can't really use a power drill or a nail gun with a baby slung on your back. They don't make dust masks or earmuffs small enough.

I've been putting in long hours though, and I reckon I should have this place finished in another week or so. Then maybe Charlie and I can get into some kind of routine.

I've also done a little more experimenting with music, hoping to find something Charlie really likes and that helps him to sleep. 'This Lullaby' by Queens of the Stone Age and 'Fear of Sleep' by The Strokes were kinda successful, but his very favourite is Pearl Jam's 'Better Man'. I don't suppose anyone's done a study on the effect of Pearl Jam on a baby's brainpower, but clearly, the little guy has taste!

Enjoy Melbourne. I grin every time I think of my little sis sipping a latte, or hanging out in some trendy rooftop wine bar. After all those years of practising scales – scraping horsehair over catgut – you've earned a chance at the good life.

Seth x

To: Flora Drummond
From: Christy Hargreaves
Subject: Your brother

Hi Flora,

I hope all's going well in Melbourne. We miss you! But it seems your brother's making up for your absence. Several young mums saw him with his baby at the doctor's the other day and now practically every female in Mareeba is gushing and gossiping about him like he's one of the Hemsworth brothers. Honestly!

They thought Seth was incredibly cute, the way he was so proud of Charlie's weight gain, and asking the girls questions about the best cream for rubbing on a baby's bum etc.

Word on the street: Charlie's mother has gone back to England to marry another guy. I suppose you'd know all about that, but don't worry, Seth will have no trouble at all in finding someone to take her place.

Cheers for now and enjoy the big smoke,

Christy

5

It was still dark when Alice Miller woke and her first thought was that she was back in Brisbane at her grandmother's house in Ashgrove. Something about that scenario wasn't quite right though. She was too aware of the silence. There was no hum of morning traffic penetrating from the street outside. In the distance a rooster was crowing.

Of course. How could she have forgotten?

A wave of desolation rolled over Alice and she shivered, remembering yet again that her grandmother was dead and she was completely alone in the world.

Surely twenty-seven was too young to be the only family member left, but that was how it was for Alice.

Her parents and her baby sister had died tragically in a car accident when she was ten. Seven years later she'd lost her beloved grandfather. And now, after another decade, her grandmother – who for all these years had been her guardian, her provider and her best friend – was gone too. Her aunt and uncle who lived in Thailand were hardly ever in touch, so they barely counted.

Alice lay very still with her eyes squeezed shut, determined not to cry again, but she couldn't stop her mind from replaying the events that had marked the finality of it all. The funeral service had been held at the brick church on Waterworks Road that her gran had attended every Sunday. It had been followed by a gathering back at the house, which was mainly for the diminished circle of her grandmother's friends: people from the bowls club, and her gran's nearest and dearest from church – Peg Glasgow, Dulcie Forrest, Michael and Jean Brown.

At least Alice was familiar with what her grandmother's circle expected – cups of tea, glasses of sherry, plates of pikelets with jam and cream, fruit cake – and their messages of condolence had been sincere.

'You were always so good to your gran.'

'Elsie was lucky to have you to look after her.'

'She was so proud of you, Alice.'

But the group hadn't hidden their dismay when Alice told them she was putting tenants into her grandmother's house, the only home she could really remember, and moving away.

So very far away, to a place her grandmother had talked about frequently . . .

Enough.

Alice opened her eyes.

Already, dawn was making its presence felt. A pale grey light glimmered at the window and she could see the outline of her bed, covered by the bright rose-and-aqua Indian throw that she'd bought at a market in Cairns. In the room's corner, a silvery shimmer gleamed from the oval mirror on the wardrobe door.

This was her new home in Burralea, a tiny village on the Atherton Tablelands in Far North Queensland. Her new life had begun last month when she'd signed the lease for a quaint little shop with a sizeable space at the back – complete with a scarred and battered but quite usable workbench – and a small, one-bedroom flat overhead.

Slipping from the bed, Alice could feel the hope bubbling afresh in spite of her lingering sadness. She pulled her dressing-gown on to ward off the early-morning highlands chill, and went to the window and leaned out, taking in the main street.

The solicitor's office was fancy and modern with plate-glass windows and sliding doors, but mostly, the shops in Burralea were old like hers. Both the chemist and the hairdresser had brass plaques over their doors proudly showing the date they were built in the 1920s.

In keeping with the town's tourist image, the older shops had been carefully gentrified. Now, restored and repainted, the street also boasted large garden pots on the footpaths and lampposts with hanging baskets overflowing with bright petunias and daisies and dainty blue lobelia.

The overt quaintness and nostalgia of the town appealed to Alice. In fact, she loved it. While her friends embraced streamlined architecture and the wonders of flat packs from Ikea, Alice was a girl with one foot in the past.

So yes, this place suited her. From her first-floor vantage, she could see clear to the end of the street, where a white mist lingered along the creek, trailing like a soft cloud through the thick trunks of the remnant rainforest that lined the creek's banks.

Taking a deep breath of the fresh mountain air, she caught a hint of wood smoke from the chimney of the pink house on the corner. She heard the rooster crowing again, followed by the high-pitched call of a scrub hen, and then the softer notes of a rainforest pigeon. Soon there were other birds whistling, twittering and warbling, adding their songs to the dawn chorus.

Alice felt her spirits lift. After such a short time in Burralea, her move to the far north still seemed like a huge and rather wonderful adventure.

It had begun with the long and arduous three-day drive up the Bruce Highway with her little ute piled high with all her worldly possessions, including her grandfather's precious woodworking tools. Having initially found this place over the internet, she'd arrived at Burralea and made the exciting final inspection, pleased to discover that the reality exceeded her expectations.

She had signed the lease agreement, moved into the new flat and then had come the best part of all. The day after her arrival, she'd scoured the second-hand shops on the Tablelands for bits and pieces of furniture, both for her own use, and to restore and sell.

This was to be her new business. She'd already hung up her shingle, a simple wooden sign that said *Alice Miller, Furniture Restorer,* along with her phone number. Two days ago, she'd made a circuit of the shops in Innisfail, Babinda, Cairns and Mareeba. It had been quite a long day trip, half of it spent travelling, but Alice was happy with the loot she'd collected. Now she was the proud owner of a Baltic pine chest of drawers, a mahogany wardrobe, a kitchen dresser, a milking stool and several old mirrors. The chest of drawers was for her own use. The rest she was in the process of restoring for future sale.

She was feeling quite optimistic. With enough money to tide her over for the time being, she had planned to settle into this new life quietly. But already she'd sold one of the refurbished mirrors to Tammy, the hairdresser down the road, and there'd been telephone enquiries from people looking for unusual gifts, and walk-ins that had brought her paying customers.

Just yesterday, a woman from a cattle property on the other side of Mareeba had brought in the detached top section of a lovely old sideboard, carefully wrapped in a sheet and stowed in the back of her ute. She wanted the sideboard's mirror done up in time for her husband's birthday party.

'The sideboard's very old,' the woman, whose name was Jackie Drummond, had said. 'It's been in my husband's family for generations and the mirror's become spotty over the years.' Then she'd pointed to the office across the road. 'I know Brad Woods, the solicitor. He told me about you.'

The solicitor had wandered over to Alice's shop last week and poked his head through the doorway to the workshop, offering a cheery smile and a welcome to the neighbourhood. After chatting for a bit and showing a healthy curiosity in the work she was doing on the mahogany wardrobe, Brad Woods had invited her to join him and his wife and several locals at the pub that Friday evening for an easy meal.

Alice had accepted the invitation and the evening had been very pleasant, a firsthand experience of country-town friendliness. Another tick in the box for Burralea.

'Brad told me you can fix old mirrors,' Jackie had said. 'I think he said you re-silver them. Is that the right term?'

'Yes, that's right.' Alice stifled the nervousness that squirmed, momentarily, in the pit of her stomach. She'd re-silvered several old mirrors in Brisbane. It had been a tricky task to master, but she'd followed the detailed instructions her grandfather had written in his 'Blue Book', and they'd all turned out just fine. She was only nervous now because this was her first important job in a brand-new business.

Carefully, she studied the lovely old bevelled mirror. 'There's one small scratch in this corner down here. I can try to hand-polish it, but I can't guarantee I'll be able to get rid of it.'

'Oh, that's okay,' said Jackie with a breezy wave of her hand. 'It's mainly the spots I want to clean up.'

Alice nodded. 'Re-silvering is perfect for clearing up age spots. Your mirror will look as good as new.'

Jackie had been delighted and had made a joke about clearing her own age spots. They'd agreed on a price and now Alice had planned to start the job today, right after her breakfast.

Sunlight streamed through the French doors that looked from Alice's workroom onto the rather wild garden and the dank rainforest beyond the back fence. The day was windy, though, and she kept the doors closed. A branch of a lilly pilly tree scratched at the glass as she gently laid the top piece of Jackie Drummond's sideboard on her workbench.

Pulling her long curly hair away from her face, she twisted it into a careless knot. Anticipation hummed inside her as she ran her fingertips over the smooth silky-oak frame. Alice loved furniture liked this, the glowing amber-toned timber, the carved panels beneath the mirror and the decorative posts on either side of it. She loved the craftsmanship and the elegance, but also the history and the romance of knowing that others had loved it before her.

Her reflection in the speckled mirror stared back at her and she saw her pale oval, too-serious face, her auburn hair still trying to curl despite being pulled back. She wondered how many others had looked into this silver rectangle. Part of her enjoyment of working with old things came from imagining those faces from the past.

She pictured a 1920s bride on her wedding day, smoothing a simple, brow-hugging veil over her sleek bobbed hair. A young soldier proudly adjusting his chinstrap and the angle of his slouch hat.

She saw a fair-haired mother in an elegant 1940s gown, holding up a rosy, round-cheeked baby, the two of them laughing at their reflections.

Lovers. Their glances meeting in the mirror. Covert smiles.

Okay. Enough.

Alice shook her head to clear it, and focused on the job at hand. Her first task was to remove the backing that held the mirror in place.

Thin sheets of silky-oak veneer had been secured over the back using tiny tacks. Black smears showed on the timber where many of the tacks had corroded. Alice set to work carefully, using a pair of long-nosed pliers to gently prise the tacks from their holes and then, with a thin chisel, she lifted the veneer.

She went about the task methodically, unhurriedly, just as her grandfather might have done many years before her.

So many hours of her childhood had been spent in the garage at the bottom of their garden. Sometimes her grandfather had let her help him with sanding and polishing, and she'd taken such pride in her work. He'd praised her to the skies and her love of the trade had been born.

When all the tacks were free, Alice lifted the timber veneer and set it to lean safely against the far wall. Returning to the mirror, she discovered a layer of padding stowed behind it.

Actually, it wasn't mere padding, she realised on closer inspection. It was a thick manila envelope addressed in shaky handwriting.

For the Drummond Family.

Frowning, Alice picked the envelope up, gave it a light dusting with a dry rag and turned it over. On the back was the sender's address, in the same shaky script: *Stella Drummond, Ruthven Downs, November 1970.*

A chill skittered down Alice's spine. Something about this discovery unsettled her, even though she knew it shouldn't. This wasn't the first time she'd found a surprise inside old furniture.

Once before, when she was working for a restorer in Brisbane, she'd found a wedding ring that had been wedged in the back of a drawer thirty years earlier. Returning it to the owner had been a joyful occasion. Another time, she'd come across a copy of a Brisbane newspaper from 1915, which had also been placed behind a mirror in a sideboard, presumably as kind of time capsule for subsequent owners.

Alice had shown it to the sideboard's owners and they'd been delighted, and had agreed it should be returned to its hiding place. When Alice had reassembled the newly silvered mirror, she'd added a *Courier Mail* from the current day.

Those finds had been fun, but this felt different. This almost certainly was different. This envelope had the appearance of a private family document. There were definitely papers inside.

Testing the flap with a fingertip, Alice discovered that it wasn't sealed. Gingerly, a little guiltily, she lifted it. There was another envelope inside and folded pages that might have been a letter.

She knew this was none of her business and she resolved not to remove anything, but when she tilted the packet ever so slightly, she could read the thick, spiky handwriting on the second envelope.

Instructions pertaining to the will of Magnus H Drummond.

Alice gasped. *Holy shit.* What was this? She was sure Jackie Drummond knew nothing about it and suddenly her curiosity was replaced by concern. Instructions pertaining to a will sounded scarily serious, something that she shouldn't hang on to any longer than necessary.

She thought briefly about speaking to Brad Woods, the solicitor and Drummond family friend across the road, but she just as quickly dismissed the idea as inappropriate. This was a private matter. She'd taken note of Jackie Drummond's phone number yesterday, so the sensible thing to do was to call her.

Jackie answered quickly. 'Oh, hi, Alice. How's the mirror?'

'It's fine,' Alice assured her. 'No problems. But I've found something rather interesting stowed behind it.'

'Really?'

'Yes, there's an envelope addressed to your family.'

'Goodness. How mysterious.'

Jackie sounded amused and Alice didn't want to alarm her. Rather than telling her about the will she said simply, 'I have to collect something from Mareeba, and this afternoon's as good a time as any. I could drop it off at your place.'

'Well, that's very kind. Are you sure it's not too far out of your way?'

Alice wasn't totally sure of the location of Ruthven Downs, but Mareeba was only half an hour away and she had Maps on her phone. Besides, she wasn't especially busy just yet, and she would feel happier when this envelope and its contents were where they belonged. With the Drummonds.

6

Alice had probably driven more kilometres in the month since she'd left Brisbane than she had in all the years before that. Driving in the country was a very different matter from the rush and impatience of city traffic, however.

Today was sunny, the sky a perfect blue with soft white clouds, and farmlands spread on either side of the road like giant patchwork quilts. Paddocks of green pasture dotted with black and white dairy cows were interspersed by earthy blocks scattered with the remains of harvested cornstalks, or fields of legumes topped by lacy white flowers. In other paddocks, plantings of young macadamia trees were protected from the wind by borders of she-oaks.

Every so often a farmhouse appeared, framed by a garden and shade trees and lawns as smooth as bowling greens. Looming beside or behind the houses, large, open, corrugated-iron barns were filled with hay bales, and machinery sheds sported expensive harvesters and tractors.

As she drove further north, the smaller crops gave way to coffee and avocado plantations. Fields of sugar cane stood tall, their fluffy mauve spearheads waving in a light breeze. A sign for a roadside stall announced red pawpaws for sale.

Around Mareeba the country became drier, the pockets of lush rainforest replaced by straggly bush. Alice called in at the second-hand furniture store, then pressed on along the Mulligan Highway. A road sign pointed north to Lakeland and Cooktown, legend-ary towns of the far north, frontier country that had always held a mysterious glamour for her.

It was exciting to know that although she would only cover a small section of this road today, if she kept going, she would end up at Cape York, the very northern tip of Australia.

Here the landscape was dotted with skinny gums and giant anthills as well as lovely green lagoons, and pale grassy paddocks where white and grey beef cattle grazed. In the distance a blue ridge of mountains loomed.

The road dipped down over a pretty creek lined with weeping paperbarks, and it was on the other side of the next rise that Alice saw the impressive, solid-timber fence and gates, and a sign painted in black and white reading *Ruthven Downs*.

Jackie had warned Alice that the chain on the gate wasn't locked. Curiosity mounting, she turned off the bitumen, closed the gate carefully behind her, and continued along a well-graded dirt road.

She began to feel a little nervous. Apart from yesterday's meet-ing, she knew nothing about the Drummonds, but she'd instinctively liked Jackie. A slim blonde, probably in her late fifties, she'd been simply dressed in well-cut jeans and a white collared shirt tucked neatly into place with a brown leather belt. Her jewellery – gold ear-rings and a chunky gold chain – had looked expensive, befitting a successful grazier's wife, but there was nothing snooty about her.

To Alice, Jackie had seemed very down-to-earth and friendly.

She was still thinking about this and reassuring herself that she was doing the right thing when her ute rattled over a cattle grid and the track emerged into open country again. Now she drove between

paddocks where beef cattle grazed, then past stockyards with weathered timber fences. Beyond these lay the long, low homestead.

Alice's stomach tightened and she glanced again at the envelope
lying on the passenger's seat beside her. For the Drummonds' sake,
she hoped that the papers inside were nothing more than interesting
facets of family history that had been hidden away for safekeeping.
But now that the handover was imminent, she couldn't help worrying.

Had it been her imagination, or was there something sinister
about that thick, black handwriting with instructions pertaining to
the will of Magnus H Drummond?

Why on earth had it been hidden?

Pulling up in front of the homestead, Alice did her best to shake
off the sense of foreboding. A glance in the rear-vision mirror showed
her the extra freckles she'd gained since moving to the north. She
tucked a stray strand of hair behind an ear and forced a smile. The
smile looked nervous and she tried again. That was better.

Okay. Deep breath. Stay cool.

Collecting the envelope, she climbed out of the car. There
were only three short steps to the verandah. A dog barked as she
approached, and she saw a blue cattle dog rising from his shady spot
on the verandah beneath a hanging basket of ferns.

She supposed she should have known there'd be a dog on a property like this. She hovered on the bottom step, not sure if she should
continue.

But the dog didn't look too ferocious, so she bravely continued
and in a matter of moments, she was knocking at the open front
door and looking down the homestead's central hallway where a
row of Akubra hats hung on the wall.

The dog barked again and almost immediately Alice heard footsteps. Not the light steps of a woman, but a heavy-booted stride.
Her heart sank and she prayed that Jackie was close behind.

'Easy, Ralph,' called a male voice, and then a figure appeared, backlit by the afternoon sunlight streaming through windows at the far end of the hallway. Alice could only see his silhouette – broad-shouldered, narrow-hipped, the suggestion of low-slung jeans.

It was only as he got closer that she realised he was young, around her age. And shirtless. Make that shirtless *and* impressive. A silly pulse started in her throat and she tried not to stare at the sudden appearance of bulky brown shoulders, of veins snaking over muscled arms, a broad bare chest, a scattering of hair arrowing downwards.

'Hey, there.' He gave his chest a self-conscious scratch. 'I was – ah – was expecting one of the ringers.'

With that he turned and snagged a shirt from the row of hooks on the wall in the hallway. The shirt was soft cotton, a faded blue, the same colour as his eyes, and he pulled it on and did up the buttons.

Alice supposed she should be grateful, but it was like a striptease in reverse. As each inch of that intriguing chest disappeared, she had the devil's own job to keep herself from staring.

But it was time to remember exactly why she was here.

'I was hoping to see Jackie,' she said, keeping the envelope flat against her side. 'I spoke to her this morning. I phoned her.'

'Ah.' Amusement shimmered in his smile. 'So you must be the furniture restorer?'

'Yes.' Alice was used to guys smirking when they heard about her job. Defiantly lifting her chin, she said, 'I'm Alice Miller.'

To his credit, this guy didn't smirk. 'Hi, Alice. Seth Drummond.' He offered her his hand and his grasp was firm. 'My mother mentioned that you might call in.'

So, this was Jackie's son. His shoulders were now straining the shirt's seams, but Alice carefully directed her gaze away from him and down the hall. 'Is Jackie in?'

'No, I'm afraid something came up. Some drama with the CWA

cake stall and she had to race off. But she said you might be dropping off a packet or something?'

'Yes.' Alice would have preferred to speak to Jackie, but she supposed it was okay to hand these documents over to her son.

She held out the envelope.

'Thanks.' Seth looked down at the envelope, frowning, then turned it over and read Stella Drummond's name on the back. His frown deepened. 'Where'd you say you found this?'

'It was hidden behind the sideboard mirror.'

'Hidden?'

'Well, I'm only guessing, but it was jammed between the mirror and a sheet of timber veneer.'

Seth pulled a face. 'Weird.' He gave the envelope a thoughtful tap. She noticed that his hands were strong and tanned and slightly rough-looking, no doubt from working with cattle and mending fences, or whatever it was that cattlemen did.

'Thanks for bringing this out here,' he said. 'I'll make sure Mum gets it.'

Her task was complete. She gave a little nod and took a step back.

Seth Drummond let his smiling gaze linger on her a shade longer than was necessary. She knew he was checking her out, but it was a bit silly of her to be glad she'd worn her favourite paisley print smock teamed with dark green jeans.

'Great to meet you, Alice,' he said. 'Might see you around some time.'

She was tempted to respond with a smile, but she was afraid it would be too coy. There was something different about Seth from the city guys she'd known, an air of practicality about him that seemed somehow more intensely masculine. And, to Alice's annoyance, he made her feel flustered, like an awkward teenager.

Ignoring the fluttery sensation, she said simply, 'I'll give Jackie a call when the mirror's ready.'

'Sure. Thanks.'

She turned quickly and marched with businesslike briskness across the verandah, down the steps and back to her car. She didn't look at Seth Drummond again as she climbed in, started the motor and put the ute in reverse.

Out of the corner of her eye, she was aware that he remained standing, one big shoulder propped against the door jamb, watching her as she backed away. She felt stupidly self-conscious, but fortunately she didn't back into the ornamental birdbath that stood right on the edge of the lawn. As she turned the steering wheel and shifted into drive again, she put her foot down a little too hard. Fine gravel sprayed from beneath her tyres as she took off.

What an idiot she was. Her face was flaming.

Metres down the track, she realised she was still going too fast when she hit the first cattle grid. The ute didn't just rattle over the grid this time. There was a loud crunch and a jarring sensation under her wheels.

Guiltily, and a hell of a lot more cautiously, Alice edged her vehicle forward. All seemed fine at first, but then it happened again. Another jarring, scraping sound. Oh, God, what had she done?

She pulled off the track and got out. Almost immediately she saw the flat back tyre.

Shit. She was so angry with herself. How could she have been so stupid? So flustered by a guy? It wasn't as if she'd lived under a rock and had never encountered the male of the species. In fact, she'd become rather jaded about men after her most recent dating experiences and she'd vowed to be cool-headed from now on. And she knew damned well that she was supposed to slow down over cattle grids.

Now, the eucalyptus smell of gum trees and a faint whiff of cow manure reminded Alice that not only did she have a flat tyre, she was also many kilometres from the nearest service station. She let out a heavy sigh and felt the afternoon sun, bright and hot on her neck and arms. She was a pale-skinned redhead and she hadn't brought a hat.

She didn't risk a glance back to the homestead. With luck, Seth Drummond hadn't witnessed this debacle. She didn't want his help. She didn't need it. She knew what to do, or at least she knew in theory how to change a tyre, though the last time this had happened she'd been on a busy Brisbane road in peak-hour traffic. Her gran had been a passenger and they'd called the RACQ.

She would be embarrassed to call the RACQ now, especially when part of her reason for moving north had been to prove to herself and to the world that she was independent and strong.

Okay.

These trials were supposed to be character-building.

With deliberate calm, Alice selected a wrench from the toolbox in the back of the ute. It was awkward trying to free the spare wheel that was bolted to the back of the cabin, but she persisted.

Luckily, the bolts weren't too tight, and once the spare was free, she set it with the jack, the wrench and a screwdriver on the grass. Step one was complete.

She was crouching beside the deflated tyre, levering the screwdriver behind the rim of the hub cap, when she heard footsteps on the track. Then Seth's voice.

'That's bad luck.'

Alice grimaced, and she was tense as she turned to him. 'I'm afraid it's more like bad management. I hit the cattle grid too hard.'

Seth gave an easy shrug as he strolled towards her. In no time he was crouching beside her, examining the tyre. 'This tread looks pretty worn. There's a good chance it was about to go anyway.'

Which still amounted to bad management as far as Alice was concerned. She should have checked the condition of her tyres after the long journey north.

'I can change it in no time,' Seth offered.

Alice flushed. 'That's a kind offer, but it's okay, thanks. I know what to do.'

'Yeah, I'm sure you do.' His smile was friendly rather than patronising. 'But you might find those wheel nuts hard to loosen. Garages often put them on with a rattle gun and it takes sheer brute force to shift them.'

'Oh.' Alice didn't fancy the embarrassment of rejecting Seth's help and then having to knock on his door and ask for it five minutes later. 'Well, all right.' She tried to sound gracious, despite the dent in her pride. 'Thank you. That – that would be helpful.'

'There's only one hitch.' As Seth took the screwdriver and freed the hub cap with impressive ease, he shot Alice a quick, almost apologetic glance. 'I need a favour from you in return.'

She went very still, suddenly uncertain and uncomfortably aware that she was alone in the bush with a towering man who was virtually a stranger.

'I've left my son asleep up at the house,' Seth said.

His son? Her mind had been travelling down a completely different track. It took a moment to regroup, to realise that Seth wasn't putting the hard word on her.

Instead, he had a son, which meant he was probably also married, and, to her annoyance, this brought a flurry of stupid disappointment. And confusion.

She could have sworn that just a few minutes ago, this guy's manner had been borderline flirtatious.

That lingering smile . . .

Might see you around some time.

'Charlie's sixteen months. He's due to wake up any minute,' Seth said. 'Would you mind nipping up to the house and keeping an eye on him?'

'I . . . ' Alice knew nothing about children. Not a thing. For her own very good reasons, she avoided them. But really, in this situation, what choice did she have? 'I – I guess.'

Seth grinned. 'That'd be great. There's no one else home, so just go right in. Charlie's in a room down the hall. Second doorway on the left.'

With that, he picked up the wheel wrench and began to attack the first bolt. Alice gulped, and felt helplessly manipulated as she turned and hurried back up the track to the house.

The front door was still open and she stepped inside, walking on tiptoe. The house was lovely and old, with large rooms that opened onto deep shaded verandahs. It had a quiet charm about it that spoke of another era. It was the kind of place she adored.

Under other circumstances she would have taken her time, lingering over details – the deep, six-paned, casement windows, the leadlight panels in the front door, the soaring ceilings, the carved timber fretwork above the internal doorways.

Today, however, she stuck to her mission and continued resolutely onwards, past the big lounge room on the right and the bedroom on the left. Seth had said the baby was in the second room on the left and Alice expected to find a nursery, but when she reached this doorway she realised it was an office.

A large, vintage, silky-oak desk with a green leather top stood squarely in the centre of the room. On it were a very modern laptop and printer and a basket overflowing with opened mail.

The baby was in a portable cot in the corner. Alice wondered if Seth and his wife had another house on the property. Perhaps the baby's mother was at work in town, but those details became irrelevant as Alice stood in the doorway.

From here she could see him, a small figure, still asleep and lying on his back, dressed in a pair of denim overalls and a long-sleeved navy and white striped T-shirt.

A lightning-quick flash of fear zapped through her.

She couldn't help it. She knew it was irrational, but it was an instinctive reaction, a phobia really, that she'd carried from childhood and had never been able to shake off.

She was calmer about getting close to a giant spider than to a human baby, but she forced herself to be sensible now. She took a step into the room, just to make sure that Seth's little son was still breathing.

His chest was moving softly and Alice let out her own breath that she'd been holding. Charlie was cute, a toddler, a proper little boy. Charlie Drummond.

Unlike his father who had thick dark hair that curled at the ends, Charlie's hair was straight and glowing golden in the sunlight that streamed through the window. His skin was clear and looked incredibly soft and baby-smooth. His cheeks were flushed with sleep, his eyelashes long and fair. One chubby little foot was bare and the other was covered by a black and yellow striped sock. The discarded sock lay in a rolled-up ball in a corner of the cot.

He was cuteness personified.

And for Alice, that was a problem.

All babies were cute. Cute and vulnerable and helpless. Just as her baby sister, Daisy, had been as she'd lain in hospital after the car accident that had killed their parents.

Alice had been eight when Daisy was born. Such a thrill it had been to have a tiny sister and Alice had always felt protective of her, like a second mother. All these years later, she was still plagued by the terrifying memory of her little sister wreathed in bandages, with IV and monitor tubes everywhere. Every day for a week her grandmother had taken her to sit in the scary hospital room. Watching Daisy. Watching Daisy's pale sleeping face and her one, tiny, unbandaged hand.

Even though Daisy had been drugged and asleep, Gran had read her stories in her lovely gentle voice. Beatrix Potter and AA Milne.

The stories were too old for Daisy really, but Alice had listened while she stared at her sister's delicate fairy fingers, at their pearly miniature nails. She hadn't been allowed to touch, so she'd sat very still, willing those fingers to move.

And she'd watched the only part of Daisy that did move – her stomach – going slowly up and down, up and down, up and down. But after a week, the movement had stopped and the monitors had begun to beep madly. Nurses had come running.

'Daisy, Daisy!'

'Call for Dr Knowles!'

'Ring Pharmacy!'

At the age of ten, Alice had been well aware of the change in the nurses. She'd seen the way their usual calm confidence gave way to distress and alarm. She'd seen the raw anxiety in their eyes, had been able to hear it in their voices.

Alice had known they were on the edge of panic as they shooed her and her gran from the room and firmly shut the door. Alice had never been allowed back in. She never saw Daisy again, only a tiny white coffin covered in flowers.

Now, she pressed a hand against her thumping heart and took a step back from the cot. She would wait in the lounge room. If Charlie woke he would no doubt cry out and she would hear him.

As she backed away, she distracted herself by taking a curious glance around at the Drummonds' office. One wall was filled with shelves holding thick ledgers and serious-looking tomes that seemed to be mainly about cattle management. There were also photos of men on horseback, their faces shaded by wide-brimmed Akubras, and pictures of enormous bulls with prize ribbons around their necks.

On the desk sat a silver-framed photo of Jackie with a pleasant-looking man who was probably her husband. The shot looked like a holiday snap. A sunny blue sea with sailing boats sparkled in the background. It had been taken somewhere in Europe perhaps. The couple had their arms around each other and looked incredibly happy.

And the envelope that Alice had handed over to Seth for safe-keeping now lay next to the computer, one corner resting on the keyboard, as if Seth had dropped it there ever so casually. Alice wondered if Magnus H Drummond had sat at this very desk to write his instructions for his lawyer.

Thinking about that, she felt an inexplicable, uneasy shiver.

She looked again to the cot in the corner. And froze.

Charlie's eyes were open. His eyes were light blue like his father's and he was lying there, staring at Alice. Then, as he continued to stare, he frowned at her and his bottom lip trembled.

Oh, no. Was he going to cry?

She didn't know what to do. Should she speak to him? Go to him and pick him up?

It must be terrible to be a baby and have to lie there helpless, waiting for a stranger to pick you up.

Charlie, however, was far from helpless. With the ease of a monkey, he rolled over to his knees and a moment later he was standing, clutching the sides of the cot. But he was still staring at Alice with those huge blue eyes. And she was sure that he didn't trust her. She didn't blame him.

'Hello, Charlie.' She tried not to sound nervous. Babies were probably like animals and could tell if you were nervous. 'Have – have you had a nice sleep?'

The little guy continued to stare at her in silence, while keeping a death grip on the edge of the cot.

Alice tried again. 'Your daddy's fixing my car,' she said.

This time his face crumpled and he let out a wail. 'Daddy!' he bellowed, showing two small white teeth in his lower gum. 'Dadda! Daddeee!'

Oh, help. Clearly the mention of his father had been a major mistake.

Alice didn't have a clue what to do now, but she had no choice but to try to soothe him. Hurrying forward, she picked him up. He was heavier than she'd expected, and strong. He twisted and squirmed.

'Hey,' she said in her most soothing tone as he tried to hurl himself out of her arms. 'It's okay. I'll take you to your father.'

'Daddy!' he cried again, and this time his sturdy little body trembled with a shuddering sob.

Alice tried to jiggle him up and down, as she'd seen other people do with babies. To her relief it seemed to work. Charlie stopped crying and stared at her, but his eyes were still glistening, and his long lashes were wet with tears. It was an unnerving sight.

'You're okay,' she said. 'I'm not going to hurt you.'

It didn't work. Charlie wriggled and squirmed again.

'Down!' he demanded.

Alice wondered if he could walk.

'Down!' he screamed, kicking fiercely into her. She set him down carefully.

Charlie could walk, all right. He took off at a great pace, running out of the room with one foot in a sock and the other bare, wailing as he went. 'Daddy! Daddy!'

Alice hurried after him, terrified he would slip as he tottered precariously over the polished timber floorboards. She could picture him with a bruised forehead, a split lip.

'Charlie,' she called as she caught up. 'It's okay. Please don't cry.' She couldn't bear this. She was almost in tears herself. 'I'll take you to Daddy.'

She had no idea if the baby understood, but he must have realised that his father wasn't anywhere close by, and he allowed her to scoop him up once again. His soft, tear-stained cheek bumped damply against hers and his little hands clutched at the fabric of her smock. He smelled of shampoo – baby shampoo, she guessed – and her heart might have melted if she hadn't been so nervous.

She hurried outside. From the verandah she could see her white ute on the side of the track and a figure crouching beside it.

'See?' she said, pointing. '*There's* your daddy.'

Charlie's lip protruded and he frowned again, obviously not sure if he should believe her, so she took off at once, across the verandah, down the steps, taking a shortcut over the grassy lawn. The sooner she delivered Seth's son to his father the better.

Luckily, Seth had worked quickly and by the time they reached him he was tightening the bolts on the new wheel.

He rose from his task and grinned at Alice and Charlie. 'Were you making all that racket?' he accused his son, and he gave the little boy a playful poke in the stomach.

'Dadda!' Charlie was all smiles now and holding out his arms.

'Are you behaving yourself for Alice?'

'Dadda,' he wailed, once again trying to hurl himself earthwards.

'Hang on a sec, little mate.' Seth was sterner now. 'Be a good kid for Alice for just a bit longer and let me finish fixing her car.'

'Why don't you take him now?' Alice said. 'I can finish the wheel.'

This brought a puzzled smile from Seth. Clearly, he thought she was crazy to suggest swapping the task of holding a baby for tightening wheel nuts.

He had a point, of course. Her avoidance of small people *was* crazy and, as often as possible, she hid that side of herself from the rest of the world. If she was brutally honest, she'd moved away from Brisbane in a bid to escape babies.

With all her friends either getting married, or on the verge of settling into long-term relationships, babies had started to arrive in her social circle. Currently, at least three of her girlfriends were pregnant and Alice hadn't wanted to hang around for the births. While she was in awe of her friends, who approached motherhood with no apparent trepidation, she'd felt compelled to flee from those happy family scenes.

From the safety of Far North Queensland, she planned to morph into a kind of modern-day fairy godmother. One who sent her friends' children lovely gifts from afar.

Right now, however, she could hardly dump Charlie. In response to Seth's questioning gaze, she gave a carefully nonchalant shrug and left him to finish with the wheel nuts while she wandered, with his son still in her arms, over to the barbwire fence at the edge of a paddock.

'Cows,' she told the tiny boy, pointing to a herd of grazing silvery beasts.

Charlie grinned. 'Moo!'

'That's right. Good boy.'

But even as she said this, an unwanted memory stirred, smoke from a witch's cauldron, and she heard her mother's voice, light and loving, echoing down the years . . .

What does the cow say, Daisy?

Moooooo.

Good girl.

A shiver ran through Alice. She gave a fierce shake of her head, trying to dismiss the memory, but she couldn't hold back the emotions that accompanied it.

'Okay, that's done.' Seth was grinning as he approached them.

Alice blinked hard, hoping to hell that no tears showed.

He frowned at her. 'Are you okay?'

'Sure.' She dredged up a smile. 'Thanks so much for doing that. It probably would have taken me hours.'

'No problem.'

She held Charlie out, keen to hand him over. Seth looked down at his hands and gave them a swift wipe on the back of his jeans.

'Thanks,' he said as the little fellow leaped gleefully into his arms, but he shot Alice another thoughtful, searching look.

He'd probably never met a woman who was so eager to hand back his super-cute son.

Alice's arms felt strangely empty and she folded them over her chest. 'I guess I'd better get going then.'

Seth nodded.

'Bye, Charlie.' Alice reached out, almost but not quite touching the baby's bare toe with her fingertip, and she tried not to notice the charming picture the two of them made, the dark-haired, big-shouldered man holding the sweet, golden-topped cherub. But she did notice that Seth was still frowning.

The look in his eyes might have been puzzlement. Or disappointment. Which didn't really make sense. Why should he give a toss about her motherly instincts?

She wondered again about Charlie's mother. Was she at the CWA with Jackie? Working in town?

Alice chose not to ask. Her work here was done.

Hastily, she stowed the tools and the damaged tyre in the back of the ute. 'Well, thank you again,' she told Seth. 'I'll ring Jackie when the mirror's ready.'

'Yeah, sure. The spare looks okay, but don't forget to get your old tyre replaced.

'I won't.'

He raised a hand as she slipped behind the wheel.

Charlie waved too. 'Bye, bye,' he called, all smiles now that he was with his dad.

'Bye, Charlie.'

She drove off without looking back, annoyed with herself for wasting even so much as a moment on fancying a man who was a father and, more importantly, in a relationship.

She'd made that mistake once before, only that time she and the lowlife had been on five dates before she'd discovered he had a wife and two kids.

Now, as Alice rounded a bend, a cold, lonely cloud settled over her, a sense that she was forever doomed to watch other people's happy lives from the outside.

Damn. She was supposed to have escaped all that.

———————

Jackie didn't open the envelope until after dinner, when she took a mug of hot chocolate through to the office. She hadn't told Hugh about Alice Miller's discovery. It might have been a bit awkward, possibly leading to difficult questions about why she was in a hurry to have the mirror rejuvenated. She hadn't yet told him about the party she'd planned.

She'd decided it should be a surprise. If Hugh knew about her plans, he'd say there was no need for a fuss and want to call the whole thing off. But he deserved a proper celebration. Jackie knew their family and friends would turn up, and it would be good for her successful but overly modest husband to have to sit and listen while people said nice things about him.

Even without the party arrangements, they'd both had a busy day. Hugh and Seth had been up at the crack of dawn, heading off to mend fences on the western boundary, while Jackie minded young Charlie. This afternoon, Jackie had found herself dashing into Mareeba at the last minute to fill in on the CWA cake stall.

By the time she'd got home, there'd been dinner to cook and she hadn't felt inclined to raise the subject of the hidden envelope over crumbed cutlets and a nice glass of red.

Now, as she entered the office, all she wanted was a little quiet time to herself. The only sounds in the house were the soft hum from the dishwasher in the kitchen and the murmur of British voices drifting from the lounge room where Hugh was watching one of his favourite crime shows.

She saw her grandson's portable cot in the corner of the office and smiled.

Charlie would be asleep now, she thought, sending a fond glance through the window to the faint glow from Seth's cottage down by the creek. She still marvelled that Seth had insisted on building a separate dwelling for himself and Charlie. It was only a simple, easy-to-build kit home, but it served Seth's purposes well, and Jackie was immensely proud of the way her son had shouldered the unexpected responsibilities of fatherhood.

Seth had a talent for cattle management as well, though, so the family had come to a satisfactory arrangement where Jackie usually minded Charlie for three days a week, and he went to day care in town for two days. Depending on the season and the work required, they shared Charlie on the weekends, but Seth always cared for the boy in the evenings. For over a year now, he'd hardly ever gone out at night, and he'd managed his son's feeding, bathing and bedtime routine with surprising ease.

As for Charlie, he was such a cheerful, healthy, easy-natured little chap that Jackie and Hugh had been smitten from the moment they'd set eyes on him, and the problems Jackie had fretted over simply hadn't arisen.

Now, as she settled at the desk, she looked forward to checking her emails to see if there were any more responses to the party invitations she'd sent out yesterday evening. She'd spent ages at her laptop, designing the layout for the invitation, selecting just the right photo of Hugh, and fussing over the wording, the perfect font and colour scheme. She'd even found a *Top Secret* overlay and she was very happy with the result.

When she'd made a quick check this morning, three acceptances had already arrived in her inbox. Two of them were from the Woods and the Kinsellas, which was no surprise, but she ticked their names off on her list.

Jackie had a weakness for lists. Already she'd compiled a host of them for this party. One list for invitees, another for household tasks such as cleaning windows and shampooing carpets, another for the catering requirements, and yet another for menu options.

For the next few weeks, her focus would be the party and tonight, she really didn't want to have to deal with this envelope. A quick check of her emails was all she wanted, followed by a sneak peek at Facebook.

She didn't post much about herself on Facebook, but she loved the glimpse it gave her into other people's lives – showing who among her friends was on holiday, or who had welcomed a new grandchild, started a new hobby, or lost a beloved pet.

But the envelope, sitting where Seth had left it next to her laptop, was rather hard to ignore.

To the Drummond Family.

Jackie eyed it with a measure of mistrust. The once-white paper was smeared with a cobweb and it was dirty around the edges after years of being crammed behind the mirror.

Why had it been hidden?

Secreted?

It was all rather intriguing.

She turned the envelope over and gave a start when she saw Stella Drummond's name and address on the back. This was Hugh's mother.

Stella had been widowed before Jackie and Hugh were married. They'd have been happy for her to stay on at Ruthven Downs, but she'd chosen to move into a cottage in Atherton, which was less than an hour away and where she'd lived very happily for many years.

Stella had died only a few years ago. Before that, Jackie had visited her regularly, taking her casseroles or fruit cakes. Having lost her own mother many years earlier, she'd been pleased that she and her mother-in-law were quite close, especially as Hugh's sister, Deborah, always seemed to be terribly busy.

Deborah and her son, Xavier, lived further away, in the rainforest near Cape Tribulation. Deborah was an artist and she was always going to workshops or giving workshops, or helping to organise art exhibitions, so it had fallen to Jackie to take Stella to appointments with her GP, or down to Cairns to see specialists.

Deborah had been happy to let Jackie do this, even though she seemed to resent the close bond that developed between Jackie and her mother. But then, Jackie's relationship with Hugh's sister had always been strained. To begin with, Deborah, who proudly wore her prematurely grey hair long to her waist, had stated openly, almost tauntingly, that she refused to set foot in a hairdresser's.

Jackie hadn't minded about that, but she'd been upset when she'd overheard Deborah referring to her as 'Hugh's blonde, size-eight trophy wife'.

There'd been other niggles with Deborah that Jackie had learned to live with, but now, she had to wonder if her bond with her mother-in-law hadn't been as close as she'd presumed either. It was a shock to realise that Stella had hidden papers behind the mirror.

Why had she never mentioned this? It wasn't as if she'd suffered from dementia. Her body had become increasingly frail, but to the very end, her mind had remained as sharp as a tack.

Rather nervously, Jackie lifted the unsealed flap on the envelope. Inside, there was another envelope and a wad of closely written pages. She set the smaller envelope on the desk, frowning at the bold black handwriting.

Instructions pertaining to the will of Magnus H Drummond.

Oh, dear God. Jackie's heart gave a terrible thump. What on earth was this? Why would Hugh's father write instructions for his will?

Or rather, why would Stella hide his instructions?

She wondered if the accompanying pages would explain.

Carefully, and with a sickening sense of foreboding, she unfolded the thin pages and saw that they were covered in Stella's handwriting. With a shiver, she quickly folded the pages again.

She really should show this to Hugh. Stella and Magnus were his parents, after all, and he'd been the main beneficiary of his father's will. Whether these documents were important or not, Hugh should be the first person to read them.

Jackie dithered, however, trying to decide whether she should disturb Hugh tonight. He was completely relaxed and enjoying his show. Should she risk ruining his chances of sleep?

A beat later, she reasoned that any news these papers contained couldn't be urgent, not after all this time. Of course it could wait till morning.

With this dilemma resolved, Jackie was about to slip everything back into the envelope when she was gripped by an impulsive, fierce curiosity.

She wouldn't touch Magnus's envelope, but perhaps she could take a peek at Stella's letter. She certainly wouldn't read all of it, that was Hugh's prerogative, but a quick glance at the first paragraph would reassure her that it was nothing too serious.

This thought had barely formed before Jackie's hands, almost of their own desperate volition, opened the pages and smoothed the creases. She thought briefly of Pandora opening that fateful box, and she was as tense as a spy on a window ledge as she skimmed Stella's opening lines.

I have done a terrible thing, but before you condemn me, please let me explain how these sorry circumstances arose. I shall try to be brief and to the point, but I need to start at the beginning . . .

7

It started in Singapore towards the end of 1941 . . .

'Sister Murray?'

Stella was painting a young Australian soldier's back with iodine when she heard her name called. Turning from her task, she saw Freddy Cornick, a tall, willowy brunette who volunteered at the hospital two days a week. Freddy was an American, married to a British businessman. They had made their home here in Singapore, and while Freddy wasn't much older than the newly arrived Australian nurses, she acted rather like a mother hen around them.

Stella smiled as she approached. 'Hello, Freddy.'

'Hi there.' Freddy came closer and peered with interest at Stella's handiwork. 'I see you're busy.'

'Too right,' chimed in Stella's patient, a cheeky young private from Tasmania called Jimmy Downs. 'Sister Murray is saving my life.'

'I'm almost finished,' Stella told him.

Jimmy had been admitted with a severe case of prickly heat, brought on by Singapore's steaming humidity. Stella had been treating him for several days now, washing his rather skinny back and then either rubbing the inflamed skin with antiseptic cream or paint-ing it with iodine.

He was forced to lie on his stomach for this procedure, and now he had to twist around awkwardly to address Stella and Freddy. 'You can't leave yet. Sorry, Mrs Cornick, but Sister Murray and I need a little privacy.'

'You don't say,' Freddy remarked dryly.

'I'm going to ask her to marry me.'

Stella laughed to cover her surprise. Her nursing experience in Queensland had mainly focused on women and babies. She was still learning the ropes when it came to dealing with flirtatious Aussie soldiers.

'My dear boy,' Freddy told Jimmy lightly, 'half the men in this hospital want to marry Stella. I'm afraid you'll have to stand in line.'

Stella rolled her eyes at this blatant exaggeration, but it had the desired effect of subduing the young man while she finished attend-ing to his back.

'Now stay flat on your stomach for at least fifteen minutes,' she told him as she gathered up the bottle of iodine and the kidney basin with used swabs. 'Is there anything else you need?'

'Your undying love?'

'See you later, Private Downs.' Stella sent him a smile as she left.

Outside on the verandah, Stella's attention was momentar-ily captured by the stunning view. The hospital overlooked one of Singapore's wide avenues, busy with motor cars and trishaws and bordered by trim green verges and rows of clean white government office buildings. Beyond this Stella could see the cranes on the busy docks and the glittering sea where brown-sailed junks and hard-worked freighters were bathed in the glare of tropical sunshine.

She had been in Singapore for three weeks now and she still found this view captivating, but she turned quickly to Freddy. 'You wanted to speak to me?'

'Yes, honey, I came to offer an invitation. Guy and I are throw-ing a dance party at Raffles on Saturday week. It's a regimental do, or at least that's Guy's excuse. He's buddies with the entertainment officer, but as far as I'm concerned it's just a wonderful opportunity for a fabulous party.'

Freddy offered Stella her most winsome smile. 'And I really want you to come.'

Before Stella could respond, Freddy quickly added, 'I've checked your roster and I know you're free. *And* you won't be on your own. I've already invited Peg and Vera and Jean. They've all said yes.'

Stella hadn't yet looked at the following week's roster, and she wondered if Freddy had sweet-talked a superior into accommodat-ing her plans. She couldn't help smiling at the woman's forwardness, but everyone liked Freddy and she got away with all sorts of things that others wouldn't attempt. She was also one of those amazing women who managed to carry an air of glamour, even when rolling bandages or emptying bedpans.

For all these reasons and more, Freddy's invitation was excit-ing. Raffles Hotel, so perfectly positioned with a view out to the sea, was the ultimate in luxury hotels, the jewel in the crown of opulent, exotic Singapore. Stella had been there once, briefly, for afternoon tea, but never in the evening for a proper party.

'Please don't tell me you've already had a better offer,' Freddy added quickly. 'I know you young, pretty nurses are deluged with invitations.'

Surprisingly, this was true. Stella had been quite amazed by the busy social life in Singapore. When she'd signed up to join the Australian Army Nursing Service, she'd expected to be transported into the thick of the conflict in the Middle East or Europe. Her mother had been in tears.

'Don't worry,' Stella had tried to reassure her as they hugged for the last time on the homestead verandah. 'I'll come home from this war and marry a grazier and have six strapping sons.'

They'd laughed at this and wept a bit more. Then Stella's father, the manager of the cattle property where they lived, had driven her into Hughenden in his battered old truck. From there she'd begun the long journey south to Brisbane for further training at the Redbank Military Hospital.

On boarding a troop ship some weeks later, Stella and the other nurses had been surprised to learn that the vessel wasn't heading for Europe as they'd all expected, but was bound for Singapore.

Stella had been abysmally ignorant about Asia and she'd had no idea what to expect. Arriving at the docks, she'd been hit by a potent mix of smells from the damp, earthy tropical vegetation and from the piles of dried fish and sweet spices waiting to be unloaded from junks.

She'd soon learned that Singapore was not only a very busy and significant port, but was also considered an impregnable garrison, completely safe from invasion. By some incredible stroke of luck, Stella and her fellow nurses had arrived in a fascinating haven. Despite the dreadful war raging in other parts of the world, the mix of Chinese, Indians, Malays and Brits who made up Singapore were enjoying 'life as usual'.

Actually, the level of luxury that the British in Singapore enjoyed was quite an eye-opener. Their social life was extremely active and everyone, including their military, was having a 'jolly good time'. Young nurses were in great demand and there'd been a string of invitations to attend golf or tennis parties, swimming afternoons, cocktail parties and any number of dances.

'How lucky are we to have ended up here?' Stella's friends were almost hugging themselves with delight.

Yes, the Japanese were making waves, but they were a long way to the north, and Singapore was safe, would always be safe. Apparently *everyone*, even Churchill, was definite on this point.

Singapore was an unassailable fortress.

Reassured, Stella found the place wonderfully exciting, even if she did feel guilty about having so much fun in the middle of a terrible war.

And now, an invitation from the Cornicks, to Raffles Hotel, no less.

'Thank you so much, Freddy,' she said. 'I'd love to come.' But she was already wondering if she would have either the time or the spare funds from her meagre allowance to shop for a new outfit. A party at Raffles demanded something rather special. And expensive.

'Oh, and one more thing,' Freddy called as Stella was about to hurry off to the next ward. 'I know you're busy, but if you can spare the time to come up to the house, I'll find you a beautiful little something to wear.'

'Oh, no, I –'

Freddy held up her hand. 'Relax, Stella. I've tons of gowns I'll never wear again.' With narrowed eyes, Freddy tilted her head and looked Stella up and down. 'I'd say we're pretty much the same size, but if anything needs to be altered to suit you, I'd be very happy to organise that.'

Stella was too surprised to think of an appropriate response.

'There's no need to look so shocked.' Freddy grinned and gave an airy wave of her hand. 'Ah Lan's a genius with a sewing machine. Dressmaking miracles happen here all the time.'

'But that's too kind. I couldn't –'

Again the other woman stopped her. 'Honestly, honey, the army pays you peanuts and I love playing fairy godmother. Indulge me. It'll give me a buzz.' She cocked her head to one side again, appraising Stella. 'You're so fair and I'm so dark, anything we choose will look completely new on you. And I think I have just the thing.'

In their nurses' quarters that evening, the girls who'd been invited had a quiet confab.

'It's ridiculously generous of Freddy,' said Peg. 'I suppose we're being brought in to make up the numbers.'

Vera gave a shrug. 'I don't mind. It's all terribly exciting and I plan to have a jolly good time.'

'Of course. That's what Freddy wants,' added Jean. 'And in return, all we have to do is dance at Raffles with handsome English officers. I'm not complaining.' Closing her eyes, she gave a dreamy grin. 'I reckon it could be a night we'll remember for the rest of our lives.'

Stella knew she was silly to feel guilty.

And Freddy was as good as her word. By the following Saturday morning, the girls had visited the Cornicks' big, old-fashioned bungalow, set back behind a swathe of palm trees and green banana plants. The selection of outfits had been made, the alterations completed, and the lovely gowns delivered to their quarters by one of the Cornicks' Chinese boys.

Vera was to wear a softly clinging gown in pale blue georgette. For Peg there was a lovely dark green, floor-length dress decorated with sequined leaves, and Jean was to wear a very becoming pink and grey gown. For Stella, Freddy had insisted on a dramatically simple affair with a sleeveless black velvet bodice and a white satin full skirt.

On the night of the party, the girls felt like princesses as they climbed into one of Singapore's many yellow Ford taxis.

From the moment Stella arrived at Raffles Hotel on that hot December night, *everything* felt different. It was almost as if the rambling, ornate *grande dame* of hotels had cast a spell.

Excitement gave her goosebumps as their taxi pulled up on the circular driveway, where bright lights spilled from the palatial interior.

Stepping out of the taxi, she felt the sleek, silk-lined bodice of Freddy's elegant gown lying cool against her skin and the full skirt swishing and rustling about her ankles. The other girls were as keyed up as she was, and too awed to speak as they proceeded through the doorway into the white marble entrance hall.

Here, elegance and grandeur abounded. The central atrium, bordered by Corinthian columns and enormous flower arrangements, soared three storeys high.

Vera's eyes were almost out on sticks as she looked about her. 'Pinch me. I'm sure I must be dreaming.'

'I know, it's so grand and beautiful,' said Stella. 'It's hard to believe we're supposed to be at war.'

'Oh, don't even think about the war tonight,' Jean scolded. 'We don't want to spoil this by feeling guilty.'

Stella knew this was sensible advice. She took a huge breath and let it out slowly, reminding herself to calm down. This was simply a bit of fun, but she couldn't shake off the skin-tingling sense that it would be no ordinary night.

A Chinese waiter, dressed in a starched white uniform, offered them drinks from the enormous tray he carried. The girls helped themselves to pink Singapore slings and the boy pointed the way to the Palm Court Wing where the Cornicks' party was already under way.

Even before the girls reached the huge salon, they could hear a band playing one of the latest American hit tunes. Saxophones, trumpets and clarinets . . .

You made me love you . . .

Then Freddy, looking splendid in a slinky black and silver gown, came hurrying towards them with her arms outstretched. 'Oh, there you are, lovelies. Don't y'all look beautiful. Come on and join the crowd.'

In full mother-hen mode Freddy ushered them into the throng, and it was all rather dazzling. The musicians were playing on a dais decorated with potted palms, women in gowns of every pretty hue were dancing with military men in full regalia. The dancers spilled onto wide balconies that opened off the main room, and beyond this were floodlit lawns and gardens dotted with bright bougainvillea and majestic, fan-like traveller's palms.

'Dinner will be served out there,' Freddy told the girls, waving an elegantly manicured hand towards the long tables set on the lawn and covered with white linen. 'Now, I see you already have drinks, so come and meet people.'

Freddy didn't elaborate on exactly which people she planned to introduce the girls to, but it was soon clear that she had certain young officers in mind.

Strangely, whenever Stella looked back on that night later, she could never really remember meeting other men besides Tom. There'd been a lot of smiling and chatter as introductions were made and she knew she must have spoken to and danced with other men.

She could remember the stifling heat of that night, despite the fans circling overhead. It had been so hot and humid that the band played only slow tunes. Dancing any faster made people too sweaty.

Somewhere in the general buzz and fun, Stella heard the name Tom Kearney, but that had meant very little until she looked up into the face of a tall, smiling English soldier.

Many times afterwards, she'd pondered the mystery and magic of attraction. What had drawn her so forcibly to Tom? There were so many good-looking officers at the party that night and they'd all looked their dashing best in their beautifully cut, dark blue dress uniforms. Some of them had been impossibly handsome, like matinee idols. And yet she'd fallen fast and hard for a lanky fellow with mid-brown hair and a longish, suntanned face.

Within moments of meeting Tom, she was entranced by the sparkle in his silvery grey eyes, by the way his skin creased deeply at their corners when he smiled, making them narrow to twinkling, intriguing slits.

Stella had met many British soldiers since she'd arrived here and often, when they heard she was Australian, they wanted to call her 'cobber', or to crack jokes about Aussies having to walk upside down on the bottom of the globe. To her delight, there was none of this from Tom.

He didn't seem compelled to talk about Test cricket or kangaroos or boomerangs either. He seemed genuinely interested in *her*, made her feel as if his smile was only for her, as if she was the only woman in that crowded Palm Court.

It was quite spectacular really. From the moment they stepped onto the dance floor and Tom took Stella's hand in his, with his other hand at the small of her back, she was exquisitely aware of his touch. Just like that – *zap* – the slightest brush of his body against hers was electrifying. She'd never felt so switched on and *alive*!

Even for the keenest of couples, however, it was too hot to stay on the dance floor for very long. Cool drinks were soon needed. Stella and Tom took their long glasses, clinking with ice cubes, to the edge of the balcony and set them on the stone balustrade.

From here they looked out across the gardens to the smooth, moonlit sea. Leaning against the cool stone, they talked, and Stella discovered that conversation with Tom was every bit as enjoyable as dancing.

She found herself telling him about growing up on the cattle station at Hughenden and how she'd been interested in nursing from a very young age. She even told him about the manual of bush nursing she'd found at the homestead and how she'd used it to teach herself to treat sick animals on the property.

In turn, she learned that Tom was an engineer who'd grown up in Richmond on the Thames and that he'd been working in Malaya for several years before the war, which no doubt explained his suntan. He'd joined the army as soon as war was declared and had gone back to England for training.

'Do you still have family in London?' Stella asked, thinking somewhat fearfully of the Blitz.

'Not at the moment. My sister's married and lives in Wessex, but her husband's away in the navy, so my parents are living with her.'

'You must be pleased about that. The damage in London has been terrible.'

Tom nodded. 'I spent years at university learning how to build bridges, and now the world's gone mad trying to blow up as many bridges or buildings as possible.'

'Or blow up people,' Stella added quietly.

'Yes, that too.'

They were silent for a bit then, looking out across the gardens while the scent of frangipani and jasmine hung in the still night air and dancing couples drifted and swayed behind them. The band was playing 'Moon Love', a haunting tune that seemed to roll over them in waves.

Stella wondered if Tom was thinking about the war. She almost asked him this, before she remembered her promise to Vera that she would try to forget about the war for one night.

She fanned her face with her hand. 'It's very humid, isn't it? I thought there might be a breeze out here.'

'You need a *punkha wala*.'

'What's that?'

'One of those fellows with a fan. Your own personal servant whose sole job is to keep you cool.' Tom grinned as he said this.

Stella smiled, too, and the sad, dreamy music swelled dramatically. 'That music's beautiful,' she said. 'But it's sad, too.' For some reason she couldn't explain, the music made her think of lovers being parted.

'It's adapted from Tchaikovsky,' Tom said. 'I believe he was very depressed when he wrote it.'

'Really? Are you a musician as well as an engineer?'

'No, but my mother's a pianist and she lived in hope that either my sister or I would inherit her talent. She was always dragging us off to concerts.'

'Did you enjoy them?'

'I did, actually.' Another smile, and a sparkling flash in his eyes. 'But they didn't turn me into a musician.'

Stella thought how different Tom's life had been from hers. Surely, there couldn't be two places more different than an outback Australian cattle station and a home near the Thames in London. And yet here she and Tom were now, both many miles from their homes and brought together by war.

'How do you feel about being posted here?' she asked.

Tom lifted an eyebrow. 'About being here in Singapore? At a party like this, instead of blowing up bridges or being shot at?'

'Yes.' Although, when he put it like that, her question did sound rather silly.

He took a moment to answer. 'It's like being a toy soldier.' There was a hint of bitterness in his voice and he was no longer smiling.

'It's unreal,' Stella suggested.

'Yes. We're in a weird kind of limbo – not working at the things we were trained to do, but not fighting either.'

'That's exactly how I feel.' It was a relief to have found a kindred spirit. 'I mean, we do have patients at the hospital, of course, but the work's pretty easy compared with what nurses are facing in other posts.'

She finished her drink and set the glass down. 'I know the authorities here have prepared for the worst – just in case. They're storing food and blood for transfusions and such, but they're still telling us that the war can't reach us here. And even some of the soldiers are joking about it, saying the Japs are too short-sighted to shoot straight.'

Tom's eyes were serious now. For a long moment he seemed quite sombre as he looked at Stella, but then he took her hand in his. 'For your sake, I hope they're right.' And his face creased into one of his heart-lifting smiles.

8

It was the wrong place and the wrong time, but falling in love is rarely convenient and meeting Tom changed me forever.

When dinner was served, Stella and Tom sat together. It made perfect sense to them. Stella's friends were busily flirting and laughing with a group of young officers at the other end of the table. Only Freddy appeared to notice them and she seemed beside herself with delight, beaming at Stella whenever she caught her eye.

It was all rather magical, dining out on the lawn under the stars.

'The only time I've eaten outdoors like this was when we had campfires down on the creek bank,' she told Tom.

'That sounds like fun. What did you eat?'

'Oh, sometimes stew in a camp oven, or fried sausages, or perhaps fish if Dad was lucky enough to catch some.'

'And you would have looked up at the stars and seen the Southern Cross?'

'Yes.' She smiled at the memory of the glittering night skies in outback Queensland. 'What about you? Have you enjoyed many outdoor meals?'

'Only in Malaya, really. And even then, not all that often.'

A beautiful orchid had been set at each place and the meal was three courses with fish, followed by steak and then mango pudding and ice-cream, and, of course, it was utterly delicious. Between the courses a speech was delivered by the regimental commanding officer, a white-haired man with an impressive moustache and a uniform covered in braid and an astonishing display of medals.

After dinner, Tom danced with Stella again. By now the other men had got the message that they should keep their distance. For this night, at least, Stella was his.

But despite the lovely attention Tom paid to her, he didn't try to kiss her on that first night. There was no stealing away to a dark corner of the garden. He was a perfect gentleman. She was both pleased and disappointed, which didn't really make sense.

He did, however, ask her if she was free the next day.

Stella didn't hesitate. 'I'll be on night duty, so I don't have to be in the ward till eight tomorrow evening.'

'That's wonderful. What say we meet up in the morning, then? I can show you parts of Singapore you haven't seen yet.'

Her insides were leaping with excitement, and when she thanked him she was surprised that she managed to sound so composed.

Stella's friends, however, weren't so sure about this invitation. Going in groups to a party was one thing. Dancing all night with the same fellow, then seeing him again the very next morning was another matter entirely. In the taxi on the way home they put their case quite bluntly.

'We're in the middle of a war, Stella. There's no point in getting serious about an English soldier.'

'I'm not *serious* about him. I've only just met him.'

Peg rolled her eyes. 'Oh, sweetheart, pull the other one. We saw you making sheep's eyes at him.'

Sheep's eyes? How embarrassing. Had she really been so obvious?

'Not that I blame you, really,' Peg added kindly. 'Tom's quite a heartthrob. But that's the problem.'

'Where does he plan to take you?' Jean sounded like an overly concerned aunt.

'I'm not sure,' Stella admitted.

'Probably to Robinson's,' suggested Peg. Robinson's was an extremely popular restaurant in Raffles Place. 'Or maybe to the Sea View Hotel.' This venue was a couple of miles out of town on the East Coast Road, a popular meeting place for Sunday-morning drinks.

'Tom said he'd like to show me places I probably haven't seen,' Stella told them.

Vera was studying her with shrewdly narrowed eyes. 'Avoiding the crowds.'

'No, he's lived in Malaya and he knows all sorts of things about the Far East.'

'Hmm. I'd say you've got it bad, love.'

'I haven't. I told you he's just – just a nice fellow.' Even to Stella's ears this wasn't very convincing.

Vera shook her head. 'Just be careful, won't you?'

'Of course I'll be careful.'

But she was so keyed up she barely slept that night.

As she'd expected, when she met Tom next morning, he didn't take her to Robinson's or to the Sea View.

'I thought you might like to see Chinatown,' he said. 'We can walk from here if it's not too hot for you.'

Stella, basking in the warmth of his smile, was open to any

suggestion. 'I'm happy to walk. I come from Queensland, so I'm used to the heat.' She didn't add that Singapore, almost sitting on the equator, produced a drenching humidity beyond anything she'd experienced at home.

Tom took her arm. 'Perhaps I should buy you a parasol.'

But she was wearing a fairly wide-brimmed hat and there were shady trees for at least some of the way, and sometimes a shop's awning offered respite from the tropical sun. Catching sight of their reflections in a shop window, Stella thought they looked rather perfect together – the tall, straight-backed Englishman in his khaki battle dress and the fair-haired girl in her best cornflower blue linen and white sandals.

Of course, having Tom's company made the excursion special, but Stella was fascinated as they left the space and orderliness of the government and business sections, with traffic policemen on every corner, and discovered that Chinatown, mere blocks away, was a completely different world.

Here, instead of grand colonial buildings, golf clubs, green parks and gardens, the streets were narrow and crowded, the buildings tall and flimsy, with brightly coloured washing strung on poles from the windows.

The shops were tiny, little more than holes in the wall, but they displayed an impressive array of foodstuffs both inside and out. Tom pointed out lacquered ducks, and shark fins that were apparently used for making delicious soup. In narrow doorways cane baskets were piled with ginger-root and dried mushrooms, and bottles of pickled cabbage.

There were hawkers, too, carrying bamboo poles on their bony shoulders with heavy containers of food dangling from each end. A family sat on the side of the road, eating from tiny bowls with chopsticks.

'The food here is amazing,' Tom said. 'Have you ever tried a

Chinese steamed dumpling?'

'No. Are they safe to eat?'

He laughed. 'Perfectly safe.'

Around the next corner, he stopped at a stall where a little man squatted beside a wood-fired burner. To Stella's surprise, Tom spoke to the man in rapid Chinese and she was promptly handed a pair of wooden chopsticks and a small blue and white bowl with two fat, savoury-smelling dumplings.

'Let me pour a little soy sauce for you.' Tom tipped dark salty liquid from a tiny white jug.

'It smells really good,' Stella admitted. 'But I've no idea how to use chopsticks.'

'You hold them like so.' Tom demonstrated. 'Hold the upper stick like a pencil.'

She tried to copy him.

'That's right. Now, you move the top chopstick up and down and keep the lower stick steady between your middle finger and the base of your thumb.'

He waggled his upper chopstick and Stella tried her best to do the same, but the sticks slipped out of place.

'You show me how to eat one,' she said, and was instantly mesmerised as Tom deftly lifted a dumpling from his bowl to his mouth.

She watched his lips close over the soft pastry and was hit by a ridiculous burst of heat that had nothing to do with the tropical climate.

'Your turn,' he said with a smile.

But when she tried to follow his example, her dumpling kept slipping from the chopsticks back into the bowl.

'Here, let me.' Setting his bowl aside, Tom took Stella's chopsticks and expertly lifted a dumpling to her lips. He smiled his endearing, crinkly smile. 'Open wide.'

Stella knew she was blushing. Her heart had picked up pace too.

It was unbelievably intimate to have Tom feed her, his gaze focused on her mouth, and she was ever so flustered. Luckily, she managed to eat the dumpling without coughing or choking.

And it *was* delicious.

'Thank you,' she said. 'That's –'

The dark heat in Tom's eyes sent the rest of her remark scattering to the four winds. All she could think about was how attractive he was, and the message in his eyes suggested that he felt the same way about her. She sensed that if they hadn't been in a bustling street in Chinatown, he would have taken her into his arms and kissed her there and then.

Instead, their gazes locked and time seemed to stand still while a fresh tide of heat rose into Stella's cheeks. Tom's eyes were shimmering as he and Stella smiled at each other.

It was Stella who looked away first. She took her chopsticks from his hand, speared them inelegantly into the other dumpling in her bowl and proceeded to eat it.

Tom chuckled. 'That's very bad manners, you know.' But he didn't look as if he minded in the least, and after they'd thanked the bowing and grinning Chinaman, Tom casually dropped an arm around Stella's shoulders. 'Would you like to see the Indian quarter? It's not far from here.'

Of course she said yes.

Again within a few streets, the atmosphere changed, this time to a gentler, almost indolent pace. Handsome Indian men in shirt tails or women in vivid saris strolled hand in hand with their beautifully dressed children. Others lolled in doorways, lips stained red from chewing betel nut.

And now the smells were of chillies and curry and tropical fruit – mangoes, pawpaws, star apples and lychees. Tom bought Stella a bag of lychees to take back to the nurses' quarters.

'This is almost like having a whirlwind tour of Asia,' she said as they walked on past brilliantly coloured market stalls. 'What about the Malays? Where do they live?'

'They tend to be gathered on the outskirts. On the edge of the rubber or coconut plantations, or in fishing villages.'

'There's an amazing mix of cultures here, but you Brits are certainly the power base. And you have most of the wealth.'

'That's true,' Tom agreed, and added more soberly, 'for better or for worse.'

They were making their way back along Orchard Road when they passed a news-stand broadcasting the headlines in the *Malaya Tribune*:

27 JAPANESE TRANSPORTS SIGHTED OFF CAMBODIA POINT

Tom stopped, frowning at the sign.

'Where's Cambodia Point?' Stella asked.

'At the southern tip of Indo-China.'

'So the Japs are getting closer?'

'Yes, quite close.'

'Do you think they're headed for Malaya?'

Tom gave a slight nod. 'This certainly puts them within striking distance.'

He was clearly concerned and went into the shop to buy a newspaper. Stella watched his frown deepen as he emerged, his focus entirely on the front page.

'It says the ships are steaming west,' he told her.

'Towards Malaya?'

'Yes, either Malaya or Southern Siam. There's also an official announcement telling people not to travel. They're urging anyone on holiday to come home.' Tom's face was grave, his mouth tight, turning down at the ends. 'Maybe now they'll listen to us.'

'Us?'

'The engineers. The military minds have been blocking our

suggestions.' He let out a heavy sigh as he folded the newspaper. 'I was posted back here to work with Brigadier Simson, the chief engineer, primarily because I know the region and its people so well. We had instructions from the War Office to add to the fixed defences in this area.'

He gave a slow, almost weary shake of his head. 'The brigadier and I travelled all over Malaya. We saw so much that needed to be done, but every defence project we've suggested has been turned down by the military leaders here in Singapore.'

'That's crazy. Why?'

His shoulders lifted in an unhappy shrug. 'General Percival has deemed it unnecessary. Claims it wouldn't be good for morale.'

'For heaven's sake!' For the first time since she'd arrived in Singapore, Stella was gripped by a sense of foreboding. Had everyone, including the British general, been fooling themselves about the region's safety?

'Look, I'm sorry.' Tom tapped the folded newspaper before tucking into his belt. 'This latest news isn't good. I'm afraid I'll have to cut our outing short. I should get back to the barracks.'

'Yes, of course.' Stella was fighting a mix of disappointment and concern, but she managed to smile as she held out her hand. 'Thank you for a lovely morning.'

Tom smiled. 'We don't have to say goodbye just yet. I'll walk you back to your quarters.'

He took her hand, linking his fingers through hers. They walked on and Stella wondered if this would be the end of their acquaintance. If the war reached Malaya, Tom was likely to be posted to the mainland. The hospitals would get busier. Everything would be frantic. There was a chance she might never see him again.

His hand tightened around hers. 'You're worrying, aren't you?'

'No.'

'Liar.' His eyes flashed and he gave her hand a squeeze. 'Don't worry. I'm confident you'll be safe here.'

'I was thinking about you, actually. You might have to go away.'

They had reached the shade of a poinciana tree. Its canopy was like an enormous green umbrella dotted with red flowers and it hung out over a high white wall to cover the footpath. The ground beneath was soft with a layer of tiny fallen leaves.

Tom stopped and drew Stella deeper into the shade, lifted his hands to her shoulders and held her in front of him.

His grey eyes were serious and yet they shone with a light that set her heart hammering. 'And I'm thinking about you, Stella. We've known each other less than twenty-four hours, but already you've become incredibly important to me.'

There was a ragged edge to Tom's smile. 'Whatever happens, I absolutely *have* to see you again. Whether it's tomorrow, next week, or at the end of this bloody war, I'll find you. I need to see you again.'

Stella nodded fiercely, biting back tears. 'Yes. I want that too.'

Ever so softly, Tom traced the curve of her cheek with the backs of his fingers. 'I think you're the loveliest girl I've ever met.'

Stupidly, she wanted to howl, but then Tom drew her closer into the shadows, gathered her close, and kissed her.

So thrilling, that first touch of his lips. The sweetest sip, a gentle invitation.

It set Stella trembling.

Her lips parted, needing more. Her hat slipped sideways and tumbled to the ground and the bag of lychees followed, landing in the bed of leaves with a soft plop. She lifted her arms, anchoring her hands behind Tom's neck as her body swayed against his. And now he wrapped his arms even more tightly around her as he kissed her again.

Stella had been kissed by men before, but she'd never been overcome by the rush of emotion that filled her now. The streets of Singapore, the heat and the smells of the tropics faded. Her entire focus was swept up in Tom's kiss. It was like catching a wave, the two of them carried together, riding its crest, rushing towards an unknown destiny.

They were both rather quiet when, at last, they walked on. Their kiss had been a sobering thing. An exciting, untimely revelation.

At the gate to the nurses' quarters they said goodbye.

'I'll be in touch as soon as I can,' Tom said. 'In the meantime, please take care.'

'All right. Thanks. And – good luck with everything.'

He flipped her one of his cheering grins. 'You too.'

When Stella reported for duty on the ward that night, she was glad to have the distraction of work. After saying goodbye to Tom, the rest of the day had dragged. Her friends were either working or asleep, or at a swimming party, and she'd wandered about in a daze, doing a little hand-washing, trying to write a letter to her family.

But she'd been too distracted to concentrate properly and she'd made so many mistakes that she'd had to restart the letter three times. In the end she'd given up and had tried to sleep, with little luck. Tom was the problem, of course.

Now, on the ward, however, Stella drew on the discipline she'd acquired during her training. Here there were beds to be made, patients to bath, temperatures to be taken and charts to be filled. Medication had to be handed out. It was time to stop mooning.

At just after four o'clock in the morning, the hospital was quiet as Stella tiptoed through the darkened wards. She checked that the patients were sleeping comfortably, rearranged a pillow, offered a glass of water to sip, made sure the fans were still doing their job of stirring the hot, torpid air.

In the vain hope of finding a breeze, she moved to a window. From here she could see the lights of the city spread out like a map. A step sounded behind her and she turned to see Peg, who was also on night duty.

'Hot, isn't it?' Peg said softly.

'Yes, I was hoping for a breeze.'

Peg pushed the window wider, and they caught the scent of wild ginger and the sound of frogs peeping in a pocket of the jungle that fringed the city. 'No chance of a breeze.' Peg turned to Stella. 'So how was your outing with Tom?'

'Lovely. We went to Chinatown. Tom speaks Chinese and he tried to teach me how to use chopsticks.'

'A handy skill.'

'I was hopeless.'

Stella watched the silhouette of a freighter moving in the harbour and remembered the Japanese transports steaming towards Malaya. 'Did you see today's headlines?' she asked Peg. 'Twenty-seven Jap ships are heading for Malaya.'

'Really? Gosh. What did your Tom think about that?'

'I think he's pretty worried, actually. He suggested that the military bigwigs here are a bit too complacent.'

'Well, they certainly haven't ordered a blackout.'

'No. Not even a brownout.'

As she said this, Stella heard the droning of plane engines. The night sky was dark and cloudy, so she couldn't make out the shape of the planes, but suddenly there was a flash of fire and the loud *crump* of an explosion.

She almost cried out in fear.

'What was that?' asked Peg, but almost immediately there was another blast.

Peg pulled back from the window. 'It can't be a raid, surely?'

'I don't know,' Stella said helplessly. There'd been no sirens, but even as she said this, she heard the drone of yet another plane and another horrifying *crump*. The floor beneath them seemed to shake and there was a sound of breaking glass.

'Sister!' a terrified voice called from a bed behind them. 'What is it? What's happening?'

For the rest of her shift, Stella was busy calming worried patients and attending to their needs. Throughout this time, she wasn't really sure what had happened. It was only at the shift changeover that the news arrived. Seventeen Japanese planes had dropped bombs on Singapore.

By the end of the day, the news was worse. The Japanese had landed at Kota Bharu in Malaya and, astonishingly, they'd also bombed an American naval base in Hawaii called Pearl Harbor.

This terrible war now involved America and was escalating and spreading at a scary pace. Stella was a little ashamed of her first thought, that she would probably never see Tom again.

9

Jackie looked up from her reading, aware of the sudden silence. Hugh had turned off the television and, for a moment, there was no sound at all. Not a whisper within the house or throughout the dark bush that stretched all around them. Then she heard Hugh's footsteps as he went through to the kitchen. The swish of the tap as he rinsed the mug. The slight clink as he set it on the drainer.

Any moment now, he would arrive at the office doorway.

Jackie dropped her gaze quickly to Stella's pages. After reading just a few crowded paragraphs, she'd become completely absorbed in her mother-in-law's story. So far, she had no idea how wartime Singapore was connected to Magnus's instructions to his lawyer. The full story was probably huge.

One thing was certain. It was too late at night to start sharing this with Hugh now. They'd never get to sleep. As Hugh's step sounded in the hall, she shoved the letter and the two envelopes into a drawer in the desk.

She was snapping the drawer shut as he appeared at the doorway.

'Still working?' Hugh smiled at her. 'What is it? CWA?'

Unfortunately for Jackie, she was a terrible liar. 'No. I'm just – um – fiddling. You know, Facebook.'

'Ah.' Tall, lean, and tanned after a lifetime of hard work in the outdoors, Hugh relaxed his shoulder against the door jamb. 'So what's the latest gossip?'

'Oh –' Jackie grabbed at straws. 'The Eriksons are on holiday in the US, visiting their son in Los Angeles. And the Greens have a new grandchild. A little girl called Cora.'

Hugh's smile hinted at puzzlement. 'I'm sure you told me that two days ago.'

'Did I? Sorry.' Jackie's mind raced. It was just as well she'd never taken up spying as a career. She wouldn't have lasted two minutes. But she really couldn't tell Hugh about the envelopes. Not now. That was, most definitely, a task for daylight.

'Are you sure you're okay?' Hugh asked. 'You look a bit worried.'

A little desperately, she pounced on a different truth. 'Actually, Hugh, you've caught me out. I'm planning a little surprise. A surprise party for you.'

It wouldn't really matter about spoiling the surprise. Or, at least, she hoped it wouldn't.

Hugh's eyebrows lifted high. 'A party for me?'

'Yes, darling, for your sixty-fifth. It's a significant age, you know.'

'Yeah. I'll officially be a senior.' He pretended to wince and clutched at his back.

Jackie flashed him a bright, reassuring smile. 'The best-looking senior around these parts.'

She knew he would have his doubts about the party idea, and she rose from her chair and went to him, slipped her arms around him. 'It'll be a lovely party with our family and friends, and you deserve a little fuss, Hugh. It doesn't need to be a big do.' She kissed his jaw, enjoying the rasp of his day-old beard. 'This is something I want to do for you.'

Her husband's dark eyes mirrored the fond warmth she'd always felt for him. They'd been incredibly lucky. Throughout the ups and downs of the decades they'd shared, they'd always been best mates, drawing strength from each other's company.

Hugh's quiet sense of humour and common sense were like a steadying and reassuring anchor. In return, she knew he savoured the simple fact that Jackie was as in love with him now as she'd been when they met.

'You'll let me do this, won't you, Hugh?' she said. 'You know it'll be fun.'

'Oh, I've no doubt it'll be fun. I was thinking of you, love. Are you sure you want to load yourself with all the extra work?'

'It won't be too much. I'm not going to be silly. Not over the top, like I was with that sixteenth birthday party for Flora. I'll admit I went too far with that one, but I learned my lesson. Seth's twenty-first was much more low-key.'

'Yes, because Seth put his foot down.'

Jackie shrugged, then offered her husband a coy smile. 'You can put your foot down, too.'

He laughed indulgently, kissed the tip of her nose. 'I'll hold you to that.'

'Good. I'm glad you don't mind, because the Woods and the Kinsellas have already said they're coming. And so has your sister.'

'Deb? That's good. I don't see enough of her.'

And whose fault is that? Jackie wanted to ask. But she kept her mouth shut. She didn't want any tensions to spoil this party, even though she felt less than warm towards Hugh's sister. Deborah had made it clear that she thought Jackie had it easy, with nothing to do all day except 'play' with her house and garden and her wardrobe.

Deborah was so very busy, of course, with her painting, which was incredibly important and practically consumed her. But her house was chaotic and her ideas about parenting seemed very lax to Jackie.

'I think I'll hit the hay,' Hugh said now. 'We've got that appointment with Santino in the morning.'

Santino Cavallo was their accountant in Mareeba, and although Jackie had mastered basic bookkeeping and looked after most of the Ruthven Downs paperwork, they were both expected at the accountant's office for an annual review and to sort out their tax. It was a side of their business that always seemed to drain Hugh. An early night was probably a good idea.

He was about to leave, when he turned back. 'By the way. I noticed the top of the dining room sideboard's missing. What happened?'

With his mother's letter fresh in her thoughts, Jackie felt a zap of guilt but, somehow, she managed to reply quite smoothly. 'I took the mirror into Burralea to have it re-silvered. There's a new furniture restorer there. A girl called Alice Miller.'

'A girl restoring furniture?'

'Yes, Hugh.' When he looked surprised she couldn't help having a dig. 'Don't be so old-fashioned. You know very well women can do anything these days. Anyway, Brad Woods recommended her.'

Accepting this with a good-natured shrug, her husband headed off down the hall, and Jackie breathed a sigh of relief. She knew she couldn't hold off indefinitely in telling Hugh about the envelope, but she would worry about that tomorrow. Or perhaps the day after, as tomorrow would be busy.

Returning to her desk, she closed down the laptop, took her mug to the kitchen and turned out the lights.

Hugh was reading when she came to bed, bathed and moisturised, and wearing her favourite old blue gingham pyjamas. The curtains were still open, but she left them. The moonlight wasn't bright enough to keep them awake and they were usually up soon after dawn.

Hugh looked up from his book and smiled. 'You planning to read?'

Jackie shook her head. She'd finished a book last night and she hadn't quite decided what she was in the mood for next. 'I don't think I'll bother.'

'I've had enough.' He closed his novel and, once Jackie was settled, he turned out the bedside lamp.

They lay side by side in the darkness. Jackie watched the soft moonlight and listened to the silence, broken only by the faint buzz of insects and, in the distance, the soft, persistent call of a mopoke. She thought about the letter she'd started to read. Stella, nursing in Singapore during the war and meeting Tom Kearney.

Jackie's knowledge of World War II was hazy, but she did know that Singapore had fallen to the Japanese and there'd been horrific stories about the consequences. She wondered how Stella had escaped. And how had Tom Kearney's story ended?

More anxiously, she wondered how Stella's story was connected to Magnus's will.

But then there was the biggest question of all – why had Stella hidden the papers?

Jackie wasn't sure that she wanted to know.

It couldn't be good news, surely?

A worried sigh escaped her. She was beginning to wish that she'd left the mirror as it was. No one at the party would have minded about a few spots of wear and tear.

In the darkness, Hugh turned to her. 'You okay? You seem restless.'

'Sorry. I was just thinking.'

'Are you sure there's nothing bothering you?'

'No, not really.' What else could she say? And anyway, she might be worrying about nothing. But she couldn't dismiss those chilling words that Stella had written.

I have done a terrible thing . . .

She realised Hugh was still waiting for reassurance. She would have to make up something. Already, in one evening, this was becoming a habit.

'I do find myself thinking quite a lot about our trip,' she said. 'It was so much fun, wasn't it? I loved every minute. I could go back tomorrow.'

This, at least, was the truth. Over the past twelve months, Jackie had often caught herself in a reverie – once again strolling the cobbled streets of San Sebastián, eating *pain au chocolat* at a pavement café in Paris, visiting the Tower of London.

'Seeing all those new sights,' she said. 'It was just so stimulating and interesting. Such an eye-opener.'

'It certainly was.' Hugh sounded relieved. 'Sounds like you've finally developed a taste for travel.'

'Well, yes, I think I must have. I know I've been busy with Charlie this year, but maybe we should plan another trip. Or even several trips. Perhaps we should have a bucket list.'

'I'd like to try Italy.'

'Yes, I suspect we'd both adore Italy. And Greece,' Jackie added, warming to this topic. 'I know someone on Facebook who's just had the most amazing swimming holiday on a Greek island.'

'Mmm.' Hugh sounded so-so about this. 'There's South America,' he suggested with more enthusiasm. 'Machu Picchu, Lake Titicaca, the Canopy Walkway in the Amazon. A huge amount to see there.'

'Not to mention Asia,' added Jackie, who would happily visit any of these places. 'Apparently, Vietnam is very beautiful.' Her thoughts slipped to Stella's letter. 'And Singapore. That would be interesting, too. Actually, there are great deals on flights out of Cairns and we need only be away a few days. Tilda Howard was telling me that Singapore's *the* place to go to see Christmas lights.'

'Christmas lights? Is that a priority?'

'Well, no, not a priority exactly.' Jackie wasn't really sure why she was pushing for Singapore. 'But a little trip like that is worth thinking about.'

A small silence ticked by and then she said, 'We could do a lot more travelling if you were retired.'

'Yeah, I know.' Hugh stacked his hands beneath his head and lay looking up at the ceiling. 'I've been giving it some thought lately. But to retire properly and hand over to Seth, we'd probably need to move away from Ruthven Downs.'

Jackie nodded. 'Yes, that would be a wrench.'

'You'd miss Charlie.'

She smiled into the darkness. Her small grandson had certainly won a huge share of her affections.

Just the same, Charlie was totally mobile now, and getting into more mischief every day. There'd been times lately when Jackie had felt quite worn out after a full day of caring for him. Heaven knew how active he would be by the time he was a reckless two-year-old.

She was conscious of divided loyalties whenever she thought about the future. She wanted to support Seth and to spend time with Charlie, but she'd also been looking forward to spending more time with Hugh, which could only happen if he retired.

'We wouldn't have to move too far away,' she said. 'But I do understand how hard it would be for you to leave here. I'd find it hard enough and I haven't lived here all my life.'

Then again, Ruthven Downs meant much more to Jackie than she was prepared to admit out loud. Her feelings for the property were tied up with how she felt about Hugh, of course. Marrying him had been like a fairytale, a miracle. She'd been Cinderella, lifted from obscurity to a position of considerable standing.

The Drummond property had come to mean a great deal more than simply a place to call home. This vast, beautiful, successful cattle station was a vitally important source of security and status for her. Jackie had been damn proud of her role here and she'd worked hard at it, treating it seriously, like a career.

The management of the household was her area of expertise. She'd kept the homestead and its gardens in tip-top order, and she'd thrown herself with gusto into caring for her children.

What did young women call it these days? A stay-at-home mum? Jackie had relished that particular lifestyle choice, despite her sister-in-law's disdain.

She'd pushed herself beyond the household tasks, though – learning to ride a horse and working hard to get to know the cattle industry. In the years before Seth was born she'd enjoyed helping Hugh with the outdoor work, assisting him to muster or to draft the cattle, as well as learning how to cook on an open fire, so she could feed the ringers in the stock camps.

When it came to mixing with other grazing families, she'd felt completely at home. She'd found her tribe. Her sense of identity was now closely tied to this house and this land.

'Maybe I'm due for a change,' Hugh said suddenly, breaking the train of her thoughts.

Mildly surprised, Jackie turned to her husband. In the faint glow of moonlight, she saw his familiar, handsome profile and fancied she caught a resolute tilt to his jaw.

'I should talk to Seth,' Hugh said.

'Well, I'm sure he's more than ready to take over.'

'Yeah, I reckon he's dead keen, but he needs help with Charlie.'

'He can always hire help.' Jackie was surprised to hear herself saying this. She loved Charlie, of course she did, but she wasn't getting any younger.

'Actually, Seth should find himself a wife.'

'If it was that easy, I'm sure he'd have one by now.'

'He never gets out to meet anyone.'

'No.' She gave Hugh a dig with her elbow. 'Is that what you did? Decided it was time to get married and went out and found me?'

'Never,' her husband responded good-humouredly. 'You found me. When I walked into that salon, I didn't stand a chance. You barred the door, locked the windows and wouldn't let me out again.'

'Oh, for sure!' Jackie was laughing as she gave his arm a playful punch. 'But maybe you should give Seth some advice.'

'The last thing our son will listen to is advice from his old man about women.' Hugh rolled towards her. 'Anyway – why are we talking about Seth at this time of night?'

Jackie yawned. 'I can't remember.' Another yawn escaped.

Nestling closer, his body warm against hers, Hugh murmured, 'I suppose we really should get a good night's sleep.'

Jackie couldn't help smiling. She knew her husband well and she'd had a fair idea that this was how their cosy bedtime chat would end.

Sure enough, Hugh was already tracing a circle with his fingers on her hip.

'Mmm,' she murmured sleepily. 'Maybe I could manage to stay awake for a few minutes longer.'

She rolled over to him and their lips met in a lovely, long and lazy kiss as his hands glided deliciously over her skin.

10

The bell in the shop rang once, and was followed by a cheery, masculine voice. 'Knock, knock?'

Alice stepped away from the mirror glass she'd been cleaning with specially de-ionised water and a lint-free cloth.

'Coming,' she called, peeling off a pair of pink latex gloves and setting them with the cloth on the workbench.

She untied her apron as she crossed the workroom and hung it on a hook by the doorway to the shop. From here she had a view of her customer. He was standing with his back to her, his thumbs hooked loosely in the loops of faded jeans, apparently studying the Art Deco plant stand she'd acquired just yesterday.

Even from this back view there was no mistaking those muscle-bound shoulders.

Alice didn't welcome the silly reaction they caused. She needed a steadying breath before she spoke. 'Can I help you, Seth?'

Seth Drummond turned and his blue eyes flashed as he smiled at her. 'Hello, Alice.'

Taking another step into the shop, she eyed him cautiously. She couldn't imagine why he'd come.

'I was in town,' he said with an easy smile. 'And I thought I'd drop by. I hope you're not too busy.'

Alice was certainly too busy for idle chat, and she suspected that a man with a small son, who was quite probably also married, should not be 'dropping by'.

'Were you hoping to pick up the mirror?' she asked. 'I'm afraid I'm still working on it.'

Seth responded with another charming smile. 'I have to confess I called out of idle curiosity.' He nodded to the small collection of furniture and bric-a-brac on display, and then to the view through the doorway that opened into Alice's workroom. 'It's a nice set-up you have here.'

Alice stiffened. It was time to nip this in the bud. 'So where's Charlie today?' she asked coolly.

Seth Drummond didn't flinch. 'He's at day care. There's quite a good place in Mareeba and he seems to like it. He's fascinated by the other little toddlers.'

Alice's voice cooled to borderline frigid when she posed her next question. 'Does Charlie's mother work in Mareeba?'

A muscle jerked in Seth's jaw. His smile tightened and he didn't answer straight away, which confirmed her suspicions. Perhaps it was her imagination, but the air in the shop seemed to crackle with tension. Maybe Seth had realised he'd overstepped the mark.

Alice certainly hoped so.

He wasn't smiling when he spoke. 'Charlie's mother lives in England,' he said quietly. 'She was out here for a year, then she went home to marry her English boyfriend.'

'Ohhh.'

The shaky syllable was all Alice could manage. She was too stunned. Wrong-footed. She'd convinced herself that Seth Drummond was a married family man and she'd decided she was pleased about that. It gave her the perfect excuse to forget him, and to avoid thinking about her own failings with regard to small children.

But now, her thoughts churned dizzily. The mother of Seth's cute little boy was in England. Married to an Englishman.

And it seemed possible now that Seth Drummond was something of a hero. A heroic single father rather than a sleazy married man on the make.

This shouldn't have been a big deal, but to Alice it felt huge. Despite her resolve to forget the man, she'd spent a ridiculous amount of time thinking about him over the past few days.

Now she was rapidly reassembling her thoughts. He was still a man with a small son, but that didn't warrant her cold shoulder.

Seth was watching her cautiously, no doubt unsure of his welcome. 'Sorry if I've interrupted your work,' he said.

Alice found herself offering him an apologetic smile. 'I'm not terribly busy. I was working on your mother's mirror, actually. It's all cleaned and just about ready for the new coat of silver.'

At this, Seth's eyes flared with fresh interest. He glanced past her, through to the workroom. 'I've never met anyone who knows how to re-silver mirrors.'

It was hard to hold back a fully fledged smile, a small olive branch. 'Would you like to see the mirror? Although I should warn you, it just looks like any piece of bevelled glass at the moment.'

'I'd love to see it. I'm intrigued.'

To her annoyance, she felt quite warm in the face as she led him into her workroom.

He stood for a moment, hands resting lightly on lean hips, looking around at her workspace, at the bits and pieces of furniture, the workbench scattered with chisels, planes and sandpaper, the old enamel sink in the corner, the tins of glue and varnish stacked on the bare concrete floor, the wall of glass doors opening onto the sun-filled back garden.

'This is a great area, isn't it?' he said.

'I love it,' Alice admitted.

'And you live upstairs?'

'Yes.' But in case Seth had any bright ideas about investigating her living quarters, she pointed to the easel where the mirror glass was secured. 'So here's the work in progress.'

His eyes widened. 'That's our mirror?'

'That's it. I was just in the process of cleaning off any last smudges or fingerprints before I apply the new silver.'

He nodded, walking closer. 'I've never really given much thought to how mirrors are made. I guess you had to clean off all the old backing first?'

'Yes, that came off with paint stripper. Then I used nitric acid to take off the silver.'

'You'd want plenty of ventilation then. But I guess all you have to do is keep all these doors open.'

'Yes, there's loads of fresh air, but I'll be extra-careful with the silver. I have to mix it with chemicals, so I'll wear a mask for that.'

Seth's eyebrows lifted. 'Sounds almost as dangerous as catching a scrub bull.'

'Not if I'm sensible.'

Now he grinned. 'I usually say the same about catching bulls.' Again he turned to the clear sheet of glass. 'Do you spray on the silver?'

Alice looked at him with a puzzled smile. 'Are you really interested in this, or just being polite?'

'Of course I'm interested. As I said, I've never met anyone who does this line of work, let alone a woman.' Seth made a sweeping gesture and grinned. 'A place like this, you'd expect an old guy with glasses and grey hair in a greasy ponytail.'

Alice couldn't help smiling, but she continued her explanation in her most businesslike voice. 'Well, putting the silver on is actually my favourite part. The mix is clear when it first goes onto the glass, but then it turns silver as it dries.'

'That must be cool to watch. And what happens then? You add the backing paint, I guess.'

She nodded. 'First there's a coat of copper to seal the silver, and once that's dry, there's another coat of protective backing.'

'It's quite a process.' There was clear admiration in Seth's smile. 'And I'm thinking that maybe you need a decent lunch, before you tackle a job like that.'

He slipped this suggestion in so smoothly and charmingly Alice found it impossible to refuse. 'Sounds like a plan,' she said. 'Thanks.'

'Where would you like to go? The pub? The Lilly Pilly café?'

Alice's usual lunch was a quick cup of soup or a sandwich. She considered their options. Going to either the pub or the café would involve sitting in full public view for at least half an hour or so, and she knew that in this small village, eagle eyes would be watching. Tongues would soon be wagging and in no time gossip would be spinning about her and Seth Drummond.

'There's a new pie shop that's just opened,' she said. 'I haven't tried it yet, but I've heard rave reports. We could always grab a couple of pies and bring them back here.'

'Great idea.' Seth grinned and rubbed his flat stomach. 'I'm partial to a good meat pie. Haven't had one for ages.'

Alice washed her hands at the sink and they went out through the shop, leaving a sign hanging on the front door – *Back in five minutes*.

The pie shop was only three doors away, but walking even that short distance involved going past Tammy the hairdresser's plate-glass window.

The eyes and ears of Burralea, Brad Woods had called Tammy when Alice first arrived, and sure enough, the hairdresser grinned madly and gave an excited wave of her scissors when she saw Alice and Seth.

'She'll be into my shop later to find out all about you,' Alice told him.

He simply smiled. 'Joys of a small town.'

Sensational aromas greeted them as they entered the pie shop. The owner, whose name was Ben, according to the sign over the door, was a cheery guy with longish sun-bleached hair, more like a surfer than a cook. But the range of pies in heated glass cases looked and smelled divine.

Alice and Seth made their selection – two beef and red wine pies for Seth and a lamb and filo parcel for Alice.

'How about a drink as well?' Seth asked. 'I think I'd like a ginger beer.'

It was ages since Alice had drunk ginger beer, but now her taste buds tingled. 'Yes, I'll have one too, thanks.'

They carried their drinks and the pies, warm and fragrant in brown paper bags, back to Alice's place. Alice kept her eyes averted from Tammy's window.

Back in her shop, she said, 'I often have lunch on the steps right here.' She pointed to the extra-wide doorway at the back and the two broad, solid wooden steps that were almost like a small deck leading to the tangled garden.

'Suits me fine.' Despite his height, Seth lowered himself to the floor with athletic ease.

Alice tried hard not to notice how very hot he looked, sitting there with his broad shoulders propped against the door frame, his long jeans-clad legs sprawled comfortably. She sat on the other side of the wide doorway and it was very pleasant, with sun filtering through the weeping bottlebrush tree. Ben had supplied paper napkins and they used their paper bags as plates as they ate.

'Wow,' Seth said after the first bite. 'I'm glad I bought two of these.'

'Mine's yummy, too.'

They munched in companionable silence for a bit, enjoying the sunlight as they snapped the tops of their ginger beers and drank straight from the bottle.

Inspired by Burralea's street plantings, Alice had filled a wide-brimmed pot with alyssum and lobelia and a small yellow daisy, which she'd set next to another pot of herbs on the brick pavers at the bottom of the steps. Already the combination of vibrant blue, white and yellow was a pleasing contrast to the splash of green herbs. In a couple of weeks the display would be dazzling.

Seth, however, was looking back to the glass on the easel. 'So how did you get into this line of work?' he asked.

'My grandfather had a backyard workshop,' she said. 'And I lived with my grandparents from when I was ten, so I was always hanging around, watching him. Of course, I've done a couple of TAFE courses, but really, I learned almost everything I needed from my grandfather.'

'I'd believe that,' said Seth. 'You can't beat hands-on experience with a master.'

'I guess it's the same with learning how to manage cattle.'

'Pretty much. I did a degree in Applied Science at uni, though, and it helps to stay up to date with all the new info about cattle and land management and the various markets.'

Seth opened his second brown paper bag. 'Are you sure you wouldn't like to try a corner of this?'

Alice laughed. 'No, I'm fine, thanks. Mine's delicious. I'll make coffee in a minute.'

After he'd eaten a mouthful, Seth said, 'I don't want to sound too curious, but you said you lived with your grandparents. Does that mean that your parents are – elsewhere?'

Alice was used to this question, but it still wrought a painful clench in her chest. 'My parents were killed in a car accident when I was ten.'

She saw the instant flash of sympathy in Seth's eyes, heard him swear softly, almost beneath his breath.

'I'm so sorry,' he said.

She nodded. 'Yes, it was terrible.' She drew a deep breath, trying to stem the welling of emotion that talking about this could still evoke. 'But it was a long time ago,' she said next. 'And my grandparents were wonderful.'

'But still – to lose them both when you were so young.' Seth gave a slow shake of his head. 'That's tough.'

The rest of his pie sat abandoned on its brown paper bag, but eventually he picked it up again. He didn't ask her about brothers or sisters, so Alice didn't tell him about Daisy. Over the years, she'd learned that it was easier not to talk about her baby sister, even though the silence always left a sad empty space in her heart, almost as if she was denying Daisy's existence.

'Would you like coffee?' she asked to change the subject.

Seth looked pleased. 'Coffee would be great.'

She jumped to her feet. 'I'll be back in a tick,' she added in case he had any ideas of following her. Much as she liked Seth, she had to be cautious. He was a father of a cute toddler, after all. The kind of guy she could never get serious about. 'How do you like it?'

'Black with one, thanks.'

'I'll take those paper bags and the bottle.' She held out her hand for these and then hurried away.

————

Seth watched as Alice disappeared up the stairs. Watched her long legs in slim blue jeans, the neat curve of her butt, the fiery river of her hair, tied back loosely and hanging past her shoulders, a splash of autumn against the leaf green of her shirt.

Even from the back view she was beautiful. Face to face, she was gobsmackingly gorgeous.

He was glad he'd followed up on his hunch to call in. Alice had been in his thoughts almost constantly and now, seeing where she lived and worked, he was more fascinated than ever.

He had to be careful, though. After a year of living alone with Charlie, he was kind of desperate for female company, but he didn't want to frighten this girl off by being too eager.

In the past he'd had his share of success with women, but he was a man with baggage now. And a woman with Alice's looks could pick and choose.

Seth allowed himself to muse about Alice. Her oval face had a serious, bewitching beauty and her skin was pale with a soft, delicate bloom that made him long to touch her. But it was her eyes that totally captivated him. He'd never seen a redhead with such lustrous dark brown eyes, and he'd certainly never met a girl with such an endearing tiny fault in her right eye – an enchanting slice of gold at five o'clock.

Seth had thought that perhaps he'd imagined it last time, when she'd come out to the homestead, but now he'd seen her again, and there it was, like an embedded piece of amber. He thought it was adorable.

He found himself wondering about Alice's parents and felt another gut slug at the thought of their tragedy. But then he imagined them marvelling over their baby girl, fascinated by the unique speck of gold that emerged as her eyes deepened from the slate grey of a newborn to chocolate brown. He thought about little Alice moving in with her grandparents. Her story hit him harder now than it might have before he'd become a father with a lively youngster of his own.

In a reverie, still thinking about this, Seth realised with a jolt that Alice was coming back down the stairs, making her way carefully with two mugs of coffee and a tin tucked under one arm.

He jumped to his feet. 'Here, let me help you. Can I take that?'

'Thanks,' she said as he freed her of the tin. 'I remembered I still had some shortbread.' She smiled. 'Although maybe you don't have room for anything else.'

'I reckon I can always make room for shortbread.'

Seth set the tin by the top step and relieved Alice of his mug.

'I probably made these a bit too full,' she said. 'You might want to take a couple of sips before you sit down again.'

Obediently, Seth sipped. 'Good coffee. Is it local?'

'Yes. From Mareeba. I'm trying to buy as much local produce as I can. Low food miles and all that.'

'There's certainly an abundance on the Tablelands.'

They settled back on the top step.

'It's fabulous here,' Alice said. 'I love all the local yoghurt and cheese. And the range of fruit and veggies at the farmers' markets is amazing.' She opened the tin and offered it to him. The shortbread looked perfect. Pale creamy gold and crusted with caster sugar.

Seth took a piece. 'Thanks. Did you get this at the Burralea markets?'

Alice gave a little laugh. 'No. I actually made this with my own fair hands.'

'Wow. So there's no end to your talents.'

She turned a pretty shade of pink and Seth had to fight off an urge to forget the coffee and shortbread while he tasted her luscious lips.

'I'm no great shakes as a cook,' she said. 'But this shortbread is my grandmother's recipe and it's fail-safe.' She broke off a small corner and tossed it to a fat brown hen that had wandered into the yard.

They both watched the hen peck eagerly at the crumbs.

'That's the neighbour's chook,' Alice said. 'I'm thinking I'd like to get a couple of hens of my own. I love the idea of fresh-laid eggs.'

Seth nodded. 'Can't beat 'em.'

'I guess you have your own chickens?'

'Yeah. Well, my parents do. More than they need, fortunately, so there's plenty of eggs left over for Charlie and me.'

'Do you and Charlie live at the homestead?'

'No. I built my own place.'

Alice looked surprised. 'Built it? By yourself?'

He shrugged. He didn't want to give her the wrong idea. 'I'm no master builder. It's just a kit home.'

'Still. You must be handy.'

She shouldn't smile like that, especially when he was sitting down in tight jeans. 'You have to be handy, living on a cattle property,' he said.

'Yes, I suppose you wouldn't want to be calling a tradesman for every little thing.' Alice set down her coffee mug and wrapped her arms around her knees. 'So what's the average day of a cattleman like? Do you spend a lot of time riding horses, or do you mostly use a quad bike?'

'A bit of both. It depends on the terrain. We muster on horseback, especially in the hilly country, but we've put in some good roads, so I can get around the property in the ute for a lot of the jobs.'

'I've never ridden a horse.'

He felt his pulse quicken. Was this an opening? 'You'll have to give it a go.'

'Maybe.' Before he could respond again, Alice asked quickly, 'What do you love about your work?'

Perhaps she was keen to change the subject.

And Seth was busily trying to work her out. There was a definite vibe between them. He was sure he wasn't fooling himself about that. But every time he seemed to make headway, Alice retreated again.

'What do I love about my work?' he repeated, as he recalled her question. 'I don't think anyone's ever asked me that. But I guess I like being my own boss and I love being in the outdoors, working with the land, the cattle, keeping active.' He shot her a quick glance. 'What about you? What do you love about your work?'

She grinned. 'Touché. No one's ever asked me, either.' She thought for a minute, resting her chin on her up-drawn knees.

Seth watched, mesmerised by her profile, by the fall of her bright hair.

'I think I love the possibilities,' Alice said. 'I love bringing something old and neglected back to life. And I love wondering about the stories connected to old pieces of furniture. Who did they belong to? Who loved them? What could this chair or that mirror tell us if they could talk?'

Her eyes were shining as she said this and Seth felt a physical pain in his chest. No doubt about it, he was falling hard for this girl.

'That reminds me,' Alice said. 'Has your mother said anything about that envelope?'

Seth blinked, struggling to pay attention to her question. *What envelope?*

'Sorry.' Alice was watching him and she smiled awkwardly. 'It's none of my business. I shouldn't have asked.'

Bloody hell. The envelope she'd brought to the homestead. Of course.

He tried to reassure her with a shake of his head. 'No, of course you can ask. It was good of you to deliver it.' He shrugged. 'I suppose my parents have taken a look at it, but I never thought to ask. They haven't said anything.'

Alice nodded, gave a brief smile, then looked down at her empty coffee mug.

Seth got the message. He'd taken up enough of her time. 'I guess you need to get back to work,' he said, leaping to his feet.

'Yes.' Alice rose too.

He picked up the mugs. 'Can I take these upstairs for you?'

'No, no. Leave them here, thanks. I'll take them up later.'

Seth nodded, then glanced towards the easel. 'Good luck with the mirror.'

'Thanks. And thanks for lunch.'

'My pleasure.'

She walked with him through to the shop. At the front doorway, he hesitated.

'The mirror should be ready the day after tomorrow,' she said. 'I'll give Jackie a call to let her know.'

'Okay. Thanks.'

Alice didn't offer her hand as she said goodbye. In fact, she didn't quite look Seth in the eye.

It wasn't the farewell he'd hoped for. She was retreating, pulling down the shutters.

With a brief wave and a courteous smile, he left. He felt down, though, as he climbed into his ute and started the motor. He drove off down Burralea's main street, past the Woods' office opposite, past the hairdresser and the pie shop, to the intersection with the Lilly Pilly café on one corner and the big old pub on the other.

As he drove on, past the little white church that had been turned into an art gallery, his thoughts were all about Alice. He knew he wasn't going to give up on such a lovely girl, but he wasn't feeling madly confident. He came with baggage these days and, apart from asking where Charlie was, Alice hadn't asked any questions about his little guy. She seemed more interested in his cattle than his son.

Driving back towards Mareeba past newly ploughed paddocks where sarus cranes scavenged for grubs in the deep chocolatey furrows, Seth decided it made sense to resolutely shift his thoughts from

Alice's beauty to her question about the envelope she'd delivered.

Seth had dumped the enveloped marked *To the Drummond Family* on the desk in the homestead without really giving it another thought. But it was pretty odd to hide a document like that behind a mirror. Alice had clearly considered it important, or she wouldn't have gone to all the trouble of hand-delivering it.

Being a straight-up-and-down kind of guy, Seth found the prospect of family secrets unsettling, especially as his grandmother's name had been on the back of the envelope. He'd been very fond of his gran. When he was little he'd sometimes gone to stay with her in her cottage perched on an Atherton hillside.

She'd made the best scones in the world, which she'd served with homemade jam and thick dollops of cream, and she'd never scolded him for eating too many. She'd known cool things, too, like how to tie knots, and she'd bought him an ant farm. His mother hadn't been too excited when he brought the farm home, but Seth had been crazy about those ants and their mysterious underground life.

He remembered the time his dog got his paw caught in a dingo trap. His grandmother had known exactly what to do, and the vet had praised her to the skies. Seth had learned then that she'd trained as a nurse when she was young.

That news had been an eye-opener. As a kid, he'd never really considered the possibility that his gran had experienced a full and interesting life before she grew old.

11

War was on our doorstep and I had never worked so hard. All through December and January, the bombing of Singapore continued and the news of fighting in the north kept getting worse and worse.

Every room and corridor of the hospital was crowded with the wounded. Day after day, a procession of ambulances set off for the railway station to meet new trainloads of soldiers arriving from Malaya.

For Stella, the night at Raffles Hotel, when she and Tom had talked of 'toy soldiers' and of her eagerness to be part of the action, now seemed like a long-ago, childish dream.

These days she was frantically busy, giving morphine injections, cutting badly burned clothing from open wounds, changing dressings every hour. All the nurses were exhausted and frightened by the news of the enemy's relentless progress south.

Admittedly, the girls only confessed in private to being worried. Matron had reminded them to show a brave face in the wards; they had to keep their patients' morale up.

The weather was awful, with stifling heat and humidity broken only by drenching rain that forced the more mobile patients off the verandahs and into the already crowded wards. Perhaps the worst thing, though, was the smell.

When the men arrived from the Malayan jungles, very badly wounded, covered in blood and grime and sweat, the nurses struggled to find time simply to clean the wounds, let alone bathe their patients properly as they normally would.

Stella saw very little of Tom.

Occasionally, he got a message to her – an unexpected and carefully cryptic, handwritten note left for her at the nurses' quarters.

All's well here. Thinking of you always. Stay safe.

Stella was so busy on the wards and so exhausted by the end of each shift that she knew almost nothing about life beyond the hospital. News of the outside world came mostly via Freddy, who was now volunteering full-time, although she went home to Guy whenever she could manage it.

Freddy reported that anti-aircraft guns had been set up at the golf club and troops had moved into the clubhouse. Coconut Grove, Singapore's most fashionable nightclub, had closed down. Raffles Hotel had put up blackout curtains in the ballroom, but the orchestra still played from eight until midnight. Only a few stalwart souls ventured out, though. It was hard to find a taxi after dark.

Even so, many Singaporeans, including the British expats, seemed to carry on with 'life as usual'.

'The Smythe-Crowleys had a near miss at Raffles the other night,' Freddy told Stella as they were unpacking a new, much-needed shipment of bandages and dressings. 'They were in the dining room and they'd finished their soup and were waiting for their main course when the sirens went off. A few seconds later the whole building was shaking. The waiters bolted, but Giles and Bunny stayed at their table, cool as you please. Then Giles took himself off to the kitchen, found their steaks and brought them back to Bunny. They kept eating their steak and drinking French claret while everyone else ran around in a panic.'

Stella smiled at Freddy's story. She knew that Bunny and Giles would have put on a brave face, but she also found this attitude worrying. A crazy sense of unreality seemed to linger among the civilians. Despite the mounting death toll and clear evidence of impending doom, people still believed that the island couldn't fall. And although there was some talk of evacuating the women, the general feeling was that this was too much like running away.

After hearing Tom's grave concerns about Singapore's defences, Stella couldn't help feeling that these people were foolish rather than plucky.

Just once, in mid-January, Tom managed to see Stella when she was off-duty.

Such a thrill it was to be with him at last, to be reassured that he was fit and well. So lovely to see that wonderful smile and to hold his hand again, his fingers linked with hers. Even more wonderful to read the special message in his eyes. Just for her.

'I was able to get a car from a friend of a friend,' he said. 'I can drive you to Robinson's. At least they're still serving decent coffee.'

Stella had hardly ventured into the city and she was shocked by the extent of the devastation, with street after street lined by smoking buildings and burned-out cars. Robinson's was crowded with refugees who had nowhere else to go, but it was still open for business. Tom and Stella found a table in a corner.

They didn't talk about the war. It was too real, too horrifying, an ever-present reality now, and this was possibly their last chance to learn more about each other.

They talked about happy memories, the things they missed about home. They argued gently about their favourite things. Roast lamb or roast goose. Christmas in the snow or Christmas in the summer holidays.

Stella told Tom about her one and only birthday party, when she was eight and children had come from cattle stations more than fifty miles away.

'It was only cake and lemonade, sausage rolls and balloons,' she said. 'With Blind Man's Bluff out in the yard, and Pin the Tail on the Donkey, while our mothers drank Pimm's on the verandah. So simple, really, but to us it seemed like the most exciting event ever.'

She smiled as another memory stirred. 'Betty James gave me perfume for that birthday!' Pressing a hand to her heart, she sighed dramatically. 'Such amazing luxury! The perfume came in a little bottle shaped like a French poodle. Eau de cologne.'

Then her smile wavered and went out like a snuffed candle. 'I can't remember the last time I smelled French perfume.' These days her nostrils were filled with the scent of blood, or carbolic, or smoke.

Tom reached across the table and covered her hand with his. His skin was warm and his hand was broad and golden brown. Stella loved the way it enveloped hers completely. She wanted to imprint the shape of his hands on her memory. Wanted to remember every part of him. The fall of his dark hair. The shape of his jaw. The laughter lines around his eyes.

If only they had more time.

'I'll buy you perfume when all this is over,' he said. 'And we'll go to a tropical beach. Not Singapore. Somewhere in Australia, perhaps. We'll have a cabin among the palm trees right on the sand. We'll lie in bed and listen to the sea and watch the moon come up over the water.'

Stella was hot all over as she pictured it. The two of them in a cabin, lying together on a wide bed and looking out through open shutters. She could almost smell the sweetness of coconuts and frangipani, the salty tang of the sea. Could almost feel the night breeze, cool on her skin, and the potent warmth of Tom's naked body beside her.

He rubbed his thumb slowly over her knuckles and she wished he could hold her hand forever.

'We'll make it happen, Stella.'

His words and his touch awoke a violent yearning in her. She was suddenly breathless, wanting Tom and knowing it might never happen. This bloody war had brought them together, but it would also, almost certainly, tear them apart.

The Japanese might arrive any day now. How could they expect to survive?

Time was of the essence. She wanted Tom. Now. She was shocked and thrilled by the fierceness of her need. Anywhere would do.

'Stella.' His hand tightened around hers and his eyes were fierce. Burning.

Lifting her chin, she met his gaze boldly, let him read her message of impatience and desire.

'Let's go,' he said.

Outside, the air was hot and still, and the surrounding sea lay flat like a sheet of shiny metal.

Instead of driving back to the hospital, Tom headed in the opposite direction. Stella wondered if he was aiming for the swimming club. Or perhaps the East Coast Road? She didn't ask questions. She didn't want to break the magic spell that seemed to have swept over them. Every inch of her skin was acutely alive and aware.

The streets of the business district were as bustling as ever, and Tom was nudging past a badly parked oil tanker when they heard the roar of engines overhead. Then bombers appeared in the sky in front of them, looking for all the world like menacing silver sharks.

Tom reacted instantly, swerving the car into a clear space at the edge of the road and slamming on the brakes. 'Get in the drain!' he yelled.

Terrified, Stella wrenched her door open and tumbled out, diving for the smelly concrete ditch. As she landed, she felt the sting of scraped knees and elbows. Then she found herself lying in several inches of filthy water.

She couldn't see Tom, had no idea where he was, but before she could even look for him, a spine-chilling, whistling shriek sounded directly overhead.

Instinctively, Stella shrunk lower, covering her head with her arms as a deafening explosion blasted frighteningly close.

And then another.

The whole world seemed to shake. Then everything went very dark.

When Stella opened her eyes, she was buried beneath a heavy weight. She couldn't breathe.

Silence. Pitch blackness.

Panic flooded her. This was it. She was going to die. Buried in a Singapore ditch.

Where was Tom?

Blindly, she pushed at the heavy object on top of her. She didn't know if it was fallen earth, or timber, broken metal, or even a piece of concrete. To her surprise, her hands met fabric and warmth and then the unmistakable stickiness of blood. Oh, dear God. A body.

Not Tom. Please don't let it be Tom.

Desperate and fearful, Stella pushed again, harder, and there was no resistance from the body, which was even more frightening. With another horrified push, she felt the body slump away beside her and she managed to sit up.

Dazed and dizzy, soaked in drain water, she looked in terror at the figure she'd shoved aside. It wasn't Tom, but an Indian man.

Unconscious.

Several times she tried to feel his pulse, but there was nothing. Her ears were ringing from the blast and her throat was tight with tears as she looked down at the Indian's handsome, lifeless face. His staring dark eyes.

With shaking hands, she lowered his eyelids.

Fighting tears and coughing, she looked around her, peering through the swirling fog of dust and smoke as she tried to take in her surroundings. She saw Tom's borrowed Austin parked, as they'd left it, at an awkward angle, its doors hanging open.

Past it, she saw the gaping black hole of an obliterated shopfront and another body lying beneath the charred remains of the doorway. Nearby, three parked cars were now burning hulks. Shocked Indian women in bright saris huddled together beneath a rubber tree.

Frantically, Stella looked for Tom, but there was no sign of him.

Tears and smoke stung her eyes. 'Tom!' she cried weakly.

But then another voice, a man's voice, yelled hoarsely, 'The tanker! Get the bloody tanker away!'

Through the clearing smoke, Stella saw him, yelling in the middle of the road. He was European. Not Tom, but a fair-haired fellow, in a British military uniform. His right arm had been blown off and the stump was bleeding, dripping crimson onto his neat uniform. With his good hand, he was pointing past the burning cars to the tanker parked alongside them.

A group of Chinese and Indians, cowering on the footpath, were looking at him in a dazed kind of stupor.

'For Christ's sake!' the wounded man screamed. 'Someone do something. Get that thing moving. The keys are in there. It's going to blow up!'

Then he suddenly seemed to realise he was injured. He stared at his bleeding stump. And he collapsed.

Stella's nursing instincts kicked in and she hurried across the road to the unconscious man, kneeled quickly and felt for his pulse. It was there – just.

A fleeting movement caught her eye and she saw Tom. She had no idea where he'd come from, but he was racing out of the smoke, past the trio of burning cars towards the tanker, which was almost certainly full of highly flammable fuel.

Oh, dear God.

'Tom,' she called.

But he either didn't hear her, or was too focused on his mission to respond.

Before Stella could call again, Tom was clambering up into the tanker. She held her breath. She had no idea whether he knew how to drive such a cumbersome thing. All she could think was that, at any moment, it could explode.

Then she returned her attention to the collapsed man. If she wanted to save him she had to act quickly.

As the tanker's engine coughed and spluttered, she swiftly undid the narrow belt at her waist, slipped the strap through the buckle and pulled as tightly as she could around the poor fellow's bleeding stump. Then more tightly again.

The blood flow slowed, but what she needed now was a bandage.

She would have torn up her skirt and petticoat, but they were soaked with blood and dirty ditch water. There was a scarf in her handbag, but that was still in Tom's car.

It would have to do. As she hurried back to the Austin, she heard the screech and strain of the tanker's engine. Tom must be having trouble getting it to start. Another screech and sputter.

She sent up a frantic prayer. *Please, God, help him. Please don't let him die.*

Her thoughts were chaotic as she scrabbled for the scarf. She heard the tanker's engine whirr again and this time it grumbled and roared to life. As she hurried back across the road to her patient, the huge tanker began to lurch forward and then kangaroo-hopped drunkenly over the bitumen.

In a matter of moments the cumbersome vehicle was clear of the burning cars and it continued careering across the wide stretch of road. As she kneeled beside her patient, the tanker came to a slamming halt against an uprooted tree on the far side.

Thank you.

Blinking through tears of relief, Stella unfolded the scarf patterned with pink and yellow butterflies and began to wrap it around the bloody stump.

She was sitting in the gutter, with her patient's head in her lap, cradling his wounded arm in the crook of hers when Tom came back to her.

'Are you all right?' he asked, crouching quickly beside her.

'Yes, I'm fine.' Ridiculously, she began to cry.

'Hey, there.' His voice was gentle and, by a miracle, he found a clean handkerchief in his pocket. But it was no longer clean after he'd dried her grimy cheeks. 'How's your patient?'

Stella touched her fingers to the man's neck. He was young and suntanned with blond hair. Rather nice looking. 'There's still a faint pulse.'

'Good.' Tom didn't hesitate. 'Let's get him straight to the hospital then.'

Carefully, Tom supported the young man's shoulders while Stella held his legs. Between them, they lifted him into the Austin. He groaned as they eased him gently onto the back seat, but he was soon out to it again.

Together, they made a quick check of the devastated street to see if there were any other injured people in need of help. Most people were simply stunned and shaken, but they found four bodies, including the Indian.

'This man landed on top of me in the gutter,' Stella told Tom. 'I was terrified. I couldn't breathe, but I think he may have saved my life.'

Tom looked shaken and slipped an arm around her shoulders. He gave her a quick hug and then they drove back the way they'd come.

'You were very heroic,' she told Tom. 'I was terrified that tanker would catch fire.'

'Must admit I've never driven one of those things before. I had no real idea what I was doing.'

'I've never put on a tourniquet, not on a bleeding stump.'

'You were incredible,' he said quietly, and they shared crestfallen smiles.

The car sped along back streets pockmarked with the grim evidence of recent bombings. At one corner, water gushed over the road from a broken pipe. At another a Chinese man was trying to sweep away fallen bricks.

Stella found it hard to believe that only a short time ago her head had been filled with lust and longing. Instead of passion, she'd encountered a close brush with death and had come face to face with the reality of war. Tom was so blackened by dust and smoke that his teeth looked bright white by contrast, and she knew she had to be just as dirty.

Her dress, once a pretty shade of pale blue with darker blue flowers embroidered around the hemline, was now bright red with the blood of two men.

While the young man was being admitted, Tom waited at the hospital entrance. It was some time before Stella was free to speak to him, but the news was good.

'The doctors think he hasn't lost too much blood and he should pull through,' she said.

'That's wonderful.' Taking her hand, Tom drew her through the hospital doorway to the courtyard outside. It was late afternoon and the air was tinged with the orange light of the sinking sun. A flock of brightly coloured birds squabbled noisily in the mango trees by the gate. 'I'm afraid my time's up,' he said. 'I have to get back to the barracks.'

Stella nodded. 'And I need to change and be ready for my shift.'

He touched a dust-streaked hand to her cheek and she wondered how such a simple touch could feel so important. So perfect. She lifted her hand to hold his palm there, cradling her cheek. She wanted to make this precious moment stretch forever, wanted the war to stop, the world to stand still.

'I know the timing's all wrong,' Tom said. 'But I'm going to say it anyhow. I'm in love with you, Stella.'

Joy exploded inside her. 'Your timing's perfect,' she assured him.

'When this is over, I'm going to find you, and I'll ask you to marry me.'

'Oh, Tom.'

Heedless of the dirt and blood on her clothing, Stella slipped her arms around his neck. 'My answer will be yes.'

Then she kissed him. And when he kissed her back, her wish came true. The world stood still and she lost herself completely in the sweetest and most precious of kisses.

It was only when Tom finally released her that she heard the loud cheers and whistles from the group of curious patients watching from a verandah above them.

12

The one-armed soldier proved to be a young man from Devon called Alan Huntley. A former surveyor, just twenty-two years old, Alan had been working in Malaya at the time of the invasion, but then of course he'd been conscripted into the army.

'I'm told that you saved my life,' he said to Stella.

'And you saved a lot of other people's lives by warning us about that tanker,' she assured him.

Alan had a great sense of humour and was coping manfully with the loss of his arm, but as a right-hander, he struggled to write with his left hand. Stella offered to be scribe while he dictated a letter to be sent home to his family.

Stella had written several similar letters in the past weeks, courageous messages of love and hope to wives and families from wounded men who feared they might never see their homeland again. Her heart broke a little further with each letter. And her own letters home were even harder to write.

By the end of January the air attacks were unbelievably ferocious. All through the nights and well into the mornings, the Japanese bombers and Zero fighters strafed the length and breadth of Singapore Island. The RAF didn't have enough planes to fight them, and the worst attacks were on the docks, their approach roads now choked with convoys of army lorries racing to get military stores away from the wharves.

The black smoke of burning oil tanks hung over the city. Casualties were heavy and the clanging of ambulance bells was constantly in the background. Hospitals overflowed and private homes were being used to house the wounded.

In the midst of the frantic activity, a Chinese orderly found Stella.

'A phone call for you, Sister.'

Stella's heart was thumping as she hurried to the phone. 'Hello?' Clutching the receiver, she sank back against the wall, eyes closed, praying that it wasn't bad news.

'Stella?'

Tom's voice brought a rush of sweet relief. 'Oh, Tom, how lovely. How are you?'

'I'm fine, thanks. How are you?'

She was almost dropping with exhaustion. 'I'm fine. Terribly busy. Where are you?'

'We've been working in the north.'

This brought a fresh jolt of fear. 'You're not still up there? On the mainland?'

'God, no. Johore's on the brink of collapse. Our troops are retreating back across the Causeway as fast as they can. No, the engineers are building up the island's northern defences at last.'

'Oh, thank goodness.' Stella knew this was one of the hugely important tasks that Tom and his brigadier had been desperate to implement months ago. Until now, all the guns had been trained on the sea rather than the mainland.

'Good luck,' she said. 'I hope it goes well, Tom. You might save us all yet.'

'We can only hope.' After a pause, he said, 'I wish you could get out of here, Stella.'

Stella swallowed. She couldn't pretend she wasn't scared. All the army wives had been shipped out finally, ordered to leave the island, almost too late. 'But the nurses can't possibly leave,' she said. 'We have a job to do.' She thought of Alan Huntley and the others like him. 'Our patients need us.'

'Yes, of course.' Tom spoke gently, if sadly, and then in a more determined tone, 'As soon as I get back from here, I'll come to see you.'

'That would be wonderful.' She was smiling as she gripped the receiver. In a burst of giddy foolhardiness, she said, 'Let me know when you're coming and I'll have champagne on ice.'

It wasn't an idle boast. A friend of Guy Cornick's had hitch-hiked from up-country Malaya. Keeping one jump ahead of the Japs, he'd brought several cases of champagne with him and had generously shared them around.

'Can't leave good champagne for the Nips,' he'd said.

Now, Stella heard Tom's laugh on the end of the line and she pictured his smile, his handsome face creasing into laughter lines and his silvery grey eyes narrowing to sparkling slits.

She bit hard on her lip to stop herself from weeping.

'I'll look forward to the champagne,' he said.

Each day the news got worse. On the first of February, thousands and thousands of British, Australian and Indian troops marched across the Causeway that bridged the strait between the mainland and Singapore. The last men to cross were the pipers of the Argyll and Sutherland Highlanders. Stella had heard from some of the wounded Scots that they'd fought every inch of the way south from the Siamese border.

As soon as the men were safely across, the Causeway was blown up.

Word quickly spread. The Japanese were already in Johore on the other side of the strait and they'd opened artillery fire on Singapore Island. Now it was only a matter of time.

Freddy Cornick arrived at work looking pale and drawn.

'Our house was hit last night,' she told Stella. 'A blast blew the front door off its hinges and I dived under the dining table. Then there was a second bomb that landed on the verandah. Oh, God, I was sure I was going to die. It sliced the top clear off the sideboard and there's a great gaping hole in the ceiling now.' Freddy swiped away tears. 'Our phone's gone and the water system's had it.'

Stella slipped her arms around her friend. 'Will a hug help?'

For perhaps a full minute, the ever-strong Freddy clung to her, trembling, but then she straightened, wiped at her tears and pinned on a brave smile.

'I'm okay, really,' she said. 'It's poor Guy I feel sorry for. He's started destroying his precious stocks of wine.'

'So he knows there's no hope?' Stella was aghast. Guy, like many Singaporeans, had been certain that the moat around their fortress would keep them safe.

Freddy shrugged. 'I guess. He hasn't admitted to giving up hope, but it's taken him years and years to collect that wine, and last night he stayed up for hours smashing bottles of his best French claret. Today he's burning bank notes and destroying confidential papers.' Her mouth turned square as she struggled with tears. 'It's just so damn awful.' Then, with a touch of hysteria, she laughed. 'I had silk pyjamas hanging on a line on the verandah. And now they're in ribbons.'

'You should leave,' Stella told her. 'Go now while there's still a chance. You're a civilian. You don't have to stay here.'

Freddy wrung her hands. 'I'd feel such a deserter.'

'But think of the alternative,' Stella said gently.

'Oh, Stella.'

Neither woman dared to actually speak about the alternative, or the potential fate of the military nursing staff after the enemy arrived. Stella tried not to think about it. It was just too sickening to contemplate.

The hectic pace in the wards was a godsend, really. While she was on duty, doing twelve-hour shifts, she didn't have time to think about anything but the task at hand. Off duty, she was so weary she fell into bed. But before sleep claimed her, she did send up a prayer for Tom each night. And the bottle of champagne was safely stowed under her bed.

It was almost a week later that Freddy left. In true Freddy style, she gave all her nursing friends a parting gift – a piece of jewellery, or an item from her wardrobe. For Stella, there was a pair of exquisitely carved white jade earrings and the black and white gown she'd worn to Raffles.

The girls wept buckets when Freddy said goodbye. The whole world was unsafe now. No one knew their fate. Many ships weren't making it home.

Then, out of the blue, Matron called a meeting in her office. Standing stern and square-shouldered, she didn't beat about the bush. 'We have orders to evacuate,' she told them.

A collective gasp rose from the nurses.

'But we can't evacuate,' someone cried.

'What about our patients?' called another.

'I'm not leaving. They can't make me,' a tall, dark-haired sister announced stoutly.

Stella felt like weeping. She was so very confused – relieved at the thought of escaping from here, but fearful about the journey and, like the others, guilty about leaving patients behind. Only a handful of the men were well enough to face the ordeal of evacuation.

What would happen to the rest of them? How could they possibly abandon them to the enemy?

And Tom? What about Tom?

Conflicting emotions played in the matron's face. Clearly, she was as upset as anyone. 'I'm sorry, but you cannot disobey orders.' She spoke in the no-nonsense voice that always won the nurses' silence. 'The first contingent will leave on Tuesday the tenth, on a Chinese ship, the *Wah Sui*. I'll compile a list of names for the first group. It will be posted on the noticeboard and there'll be more lists and dates to follow.'

This news brought another cocktail of emotions, another cycle of relief, despair, fear and guilt. It was too much to digest. In the end, Stella simply felt numb.

Peg and Vera were to leave on the first day, and Stella's name appeared on the next list. She was to leave on the *Empire Star* on Wednesday, 11 February.

She tried to get a message by telephone to Tom. The young solider she spoke to sounded hopeful, but there was no response from Tom. She had no idea where he was. In bed she hugged her pillow, remembering his kiss. His arms about her, and sinking into the bliss of his lips on hers.

I'll buy you perfume when all this is over. And we'll go to a tropical beach.

On the night before Peg and Vera left, Stella opened the champagne. She'd managed to cool it by smuggling it into an ice box.

The cork popped loudly and the champagne fizzed. The girls drank it out of toothbrush tumblers and tried to be cheerful. They talked about home and the things they were looking forward to back in Australia. They drank a toast to Freddy. And to Guy's friend who'd supplied the champagne. And for Stella's sake they also toasted Tom.

They did their best to keep smiling, but perhaps, like Stella, they were thinking of all the civilian women now being recruited to fill their shoes. Despite their bubbling drink, the party fell a bit flat.

Back on the ward for the last time, Stella dressed Alan's arm. 'I don't want to leave here,' she told him.

Alan frowned. 'You have to.'

'But what can the army do if I refuse? They're too busy to arrest me.'

'Don't talk rubbish. You have to go.'

'I don't see why.'

'Then I'll tell you why.' Alan looked away for a moment and his Adam's apple rippled in his throat as he swallowed. 'Word's out about what the Japs did to the nurses in Hong Kong,' he said tightly.

'What?'

He kept his gaze averted.

'Tell me, Alan.'

'Gang rape. Murder.'

Stella flinched, went cold all over.

Alan turned to her. He looked so young and handsome and English with his fair hair and blue eyes. 'Don't stay here.' His eyes were suddenly glittering with tears. 'Please, don't stay.'

Stella, fighting her own battle with tears, pressed her lips together tightly. Her throat was too choked for words, but she nodded and gripped Alan's good hand.

He lifted her hand to his lips. 'Goodbye,' he whispered. 'Good luck.'

'You too,' she managed, and somehow, despite the tears, she squeezed out a smile.

At dusk, a brief, violent thunderstorm drenched the city. Stella knew she wouldn't sleep and she stayed on duty all night. To her dismay, throughout the night there was muffled hammering from guns to the north. She had no idea where Tom was. No idea what the gunfire signalled.

No one seemed to know. Apparently, communication lines were down.

In the morning, Stella said goodbye to her friends, including Jean, who were due to leave the following day on the *Vyner Brooke*. Carrying a small bag stuffed with Freddy's dress and her few possessions, she joined the other assigned nurses from Australia, Britain and India and climbed into the waiting ambulance.

Each nurse was given a backpack with rations of iron tablets, field dressings, morphine and other medical supplies. They were also given white armbands with red crosses.

'In case you're caught by the Japanese,' they were told.

It was a chilling reminder as they set off for the port, while enemy planes zoomed overhead.

Such a harrowing journey. The streets were littered with the hulks of burned-out cars. Bodies lay on footpaths, waiting to be collected, and buildings in the Chinese quarters were burning all around them. Driving past, Stella could hear the crackling flames and falling timbers.

Thick black smoke poured from the oil terminal, and the port and dockland were in chaos, littered with cars abandoned by panicking civilians hunting for a ship.

The *Empire Star* had originally been a cargo ship designed to carry twenty-four passengers. Today, two thousand people were crammed into its holds and berths and onto its crowded decks. Embarkation was a lengthy process, but despite the press of people, the mood was calm. Stella supposed they were all stunned as she was.

'In case of bombing, go below decks and take instructions from the officers,' they were told.

Stella helped mothers with fractious children and then, as the hot, suffocating day drew to a steaming close, she found a space at the railing on the deck. The sky over the Singapore waterfront glowed bright tangerine. The once-busy port was now almost deserted. She could see the tall rickety buildings of Chinatown, occasional clumps of trees or rows of palms, the more ornate buildings of the business district. Columns of smoke and the glow of fires.

She remembered the excitement of her arrival in this exotic port. The night at Raffles and the magic of meeting Tom. The next morning in Chinatown. Their spectacular kisses.

Tom's promise.

Whether it's tomorrow, next week, or at the end of this bloody war, I'll find you.

Watching the colour fade from the sky, Stella knew she had to believe this. It was the only way she could possibly keep going. She had to believe it would happen. This war would end.

And Tom would find her.

13

To: Jackie Drummond
From: Flora Drummond
Subject: Another opera season

Hi Mum,

Our rehearsals are about to finish and soon we'll be moving into the performance venue, so it's getting pretty exciting here. I always love the first dress rehearsal in the theatre. It's so different after seeing the singers in their everyday clothes. Something magical happens, even down in the orchestra pit.

To be honest, I'm in my element. Did I tell you we're doing *Turandot* this year? It's still my favourite opera, even though it's so grisly with beheadings and stabbings. The music is sublime. Mum, do you remember that summer we discovered 'Nessun Dorma' on ABC FM? The first time we heard it we just fell in love, and so we checked the program to see when it might be on again, and we got up at five-thirty just to hear it. Well, I'm finally playing it now, and the tenor is superb – no, not Oliver, but a guy called Jim Bones. Yes, that really is his name. He sounds like a pirate, doesn't he?

The soprano who's playing the princess is a total diva. Everyone's talking about her. She doesn't like anyone looking at her while she's singing – anyone from the cast, that is. She loves the audience, of course. According to Oliver she sweats something terrible under the lights.

Anyway, that's enough from me.

Love to you and Dad,

Flora xx

P.S. Oh, and by the way, the lease on my flat is coming to an end, and I'm moving in with Oliver. Colour me happy.

To: Jackie Drummond
From: Flora Drummond
Subject: Temporary promotion!

Hi Mum,

Glad you're okay about Oliver and thanks for giving your blessing. I do understand that you'd feel better if you'd met him before I moved in, but I hope it won't be too long before we can organise that. Don't worry, Mum, I know you're going to really like Oliver. In the meantime, I've attached a photo of us (as requested) at Captain Baxter in St Kilda. We look pretty happy together, huh?

In other news . . . I'm filling in as leader of the second violinists. It's my friend Amy Fischer's position, but she's having physiotherapy on her shoulder and can't play for a couple of weeks, poor thing.

I don't suppose this is really my 'big break', but it feels pretty damn important. I sat up all night marking the bowing on my music. Now I just have to make sure I follow it.

I'm waiting on my good bow to come back from being re-haired. I hope it'll be ready for opening night.

Can you tell me more news from home? How's Dad? How about

Seth and Charlie? Seth doesn't write. I know he's busy, but it would be great if he could Skype now and then. What about another photo or two? I'm Charlie-deprived.

Better dash.

xx

To: Seth Drummond
From: Flora Drummond
Subject: Thanks for the pics

Hi Seth,

Thanks so much for sending those pics on your phone! Charlie is gorrrrgeous!!!! My goodness, he's growing up fast. I feel like he'll be at school before I get to see him again. How are things with you, anyway? Are you getting out at all? Having a bit of a social life?

I know you're super-busy, so I don't expect lengthy emails. Just the occasional text would do. As one of my gay friends says, let's stay in textual intercourse :)

Lotsa love,

Floss xx

On a Friday afternoon at Ruthven Downs, four women sat around a white cane table in a corner of the verandah, shaded by lattice and lavender bougainvillea. They'd all brought notepads and pens. This was a party-planning meeting and the women meant business.

Jackie had called the meeting after three of her friends had telephoned, all asking how they could help with the party preparations. It seemed foolish to refuse these kind offers, so she had returned their calls and here her friends were.

Bless them.

The business of the party had gained such a head of steam that Jackie hadn't reopened the drawer in her desk with Stella's envelope. She told herself it had sat behind that mirror for all those years, so it could stay locked away until after the party.

She felt a bit guilty about it, but Hugh was really looking forward to the party now and she didn't want anything to spoil his special day. In fact, Hugh was so pleased she'd agreed to this meeting with her friends that he'd volunteered to collect Charlie from day care, while Seth carried on working on a recalcitrant bore pump and several fences that needed mending.

Now, the women were chattering and laughing as Jackie set down a tray with a coffee pot and mugs, milk and sugar, promising to be back in a moment with something to eat.

'I hope you haven't gone to too much trouble,' her neighbour Prue Hargreaves remarked. 'No home baking.'

Jackie's smile was sheepish. 'Just a slice and scones.'

Prue rolled her eyes behind her rather dramatic red-framed glasses. 'Jackie, for heaven's sake, bought bikkies would have been fine. We're here to *save* you work, not to make it for you.'

'Oh, well.' Jackie laughed. 'I suppose the CWA has a lot to answer for.' And she sent a wink to Maria Versace, a fellow Country Women's member.

'Well, I'm not going to complain,' said Kate Woods, who'd driven over from Burralea. 'I was busy with a client and I skipped lunch, so if it's your date slice, I'll be having double helpings, thank you very much.'

'You're in luck. The date one's so easy. It was done in a flash.'

Jackie hurried off to the kitchen and was back promptly with two platters. The women set to pouring coffee, to eating, and most importantly, to planning. Jackie had already organised the hiring of extra seating, glasses, cutlery and crockery, so they turned their attention to the food to be served.

As usual, it was Prue who spoke up first. The same confidence that prompted her to wear letterbox red spectacle frames carried into all areas of her life. 'My golden rule is simple,' she said as she scooped a dollop of cream onto a scone. 'Loads of food, loads of drinks, and loads of ice.'

'And not too many nibbles to start with,' suggested Kate. 'You want people to still have room for dinner.'

'Yes, keep the hors d'oeuvres simple,' agreed Prue. 'For my money, you can't go past chunks of parmesan cheese wrapped in prosciutto. It's so easy and the saltiness goes really well with champagne.'

'I like the sound of that.' Jackie quickly added this to her food list. Mareeba had a large Italian population and the local deli sold wonderful prosciutto. 'Maybe we could get away with the cheese and prosciutto and then bowls of nuts for the beer drinkers?'

'Yes, why not?'

There were nods all round and they happily moved on to discuss the mains. 'I was thinking I'd do roast chickens,' said Jackie. 'You know, with rosemary and garlic and lemon. I can cook them, plus roast veg, in the oven. And then my Greek Cypriot lamb in the crock pot. I'll do that ahead of time. It's easy to reheat.'

'Yum, that Cypriot lamb of yours is divine,' said Kate. 'I was wondering about my sticky pork ribs?'

'Absolutely, yes, please.' Jackie beamed at her. 'They'd be fabulous. We could keep them warm in the Weber.'

'And I could bring a couple of my big lasagnes,' offered Maria.

'Oh, yes,' cried a chorus. Maria was Italian and used to cooking for her huge extended family. Her baking-dish-sized lasagnes were mouth-watering.

Everyone agreed. This selection would be perfect. They talked quantities and then moved on to discussing salads.

Prue was famous for her mustard potato salad, so that was a definite.

'And Christy makes a wonderful Moroccan salad,' Prue said. 'It's sensational, with carrots and chickpeas and then lovely spices and almonds. I think there's orange, too. I know Christy would be happy to make up a couple of big bowls.'

'Oh, heavens, no,' Jackie protested. 'Christy must be far too busy with three little ones. She won't have time to cook for Hugh.'

The Hargreaves' eldest daughter had married a local school teacher and had produced three babies, including twins, in an astonishingly short space of time.

Prue waved Jackie's concern aside. 'Christy's incredibly efficient. She puts me to shame and you know how much she adores Hugh. The whole family does, of course.'

Jackie knew Prue was also remembering the occasion, many years ago, when the two families had been picnicking on the bank of the Barron River. Christy had been five at the time and she'd fallen into the water. The hole was deep and Christy couldn't really swim, but Hugh had promptly dived in and rescued her.

There'd been no doubt that his quick response had saved the little girl's life. The incident was hardly ever mentioned these days, but Jackie knew that the Hargreaves were eternally grateful.

'Well, Christy's salad will be a wonderful contribution,' she said. 'Please pass on my thanks. Actually, I'll be sure to phone her.' Jackie checked her notes. 'I'll throw in some leafy greens, but we probably have enough salads. The men aren't great salad eaters.'

'Don't I know it!' said Kate. 'You should hear Brad. "Give me a plate of salad," he says, "and you'll have to revive me with a piece of pizza under my tongue."'

Everyone laughed at this and Jackie thought how good it was to be able to relax with friends. Have fun.

'Speaking of daughters, as we were previously,' Kate went on, 'I'm really looking forward to seeing your Flora again, Jackie. We were away last Christmas when she came home. I really missed catching up with her.'

Jackie nodded happily. 'It'll be wonderful to have her home, even though she can only stay a few days.'

Kate helped herself to her second piece of date slice, and Jackie envied her ability to eat heartily and stay slim. But then, Kate was always jogging.

'And I understand we'll get to meet Flora's new man,' Kate said. 'Fancy our little Flora from Woop Woop snagging an opera star. What's his name again? Oliver?'

'Yes. Oliver Edmonds. We're all looking forward to meeting him.'

'So, she's bringing the boyfriend home to meet the family?' Maria's eyebrows lifted. 'That sounds significant.'

'Yes, I think it's a big step. Not only is he coming home, but Flora has moved in with him.' Jackie smiled as she said this. It was important to show every confidence in her daughter, although in truth, she did worry about Flora taking such a huge step with a man neither Jackie nor Hugh had met.

Just the same, it was lovely to know that their daughter had found a man who shared her love of music. Jackie suspected that her motherly pride in Flora's musical talents was a tad excessive. But after her own humble youth, she took secret delight in her daughter's success – and Oliver *had* looked rather handsome in the photo Flora sent.

Everything was turning out well. If only she didn't have those blasted hidden documents nagging at the back of her mind. Every so often she would remember them and Stella's words – *I have done a terrible thing.*

It happened again now and she felt a flash of panic.

'Jackie, are you all right?'

Prue, ever perceptive, was frowning at her.

Jackie swallowed. Good grief, how long had she been lost in her thoughts? She quickly resurrected her smile. 'Yes, sorry. I – I was just distracted for a moment. There seem to be so many things to think about.'

Prue patted her hand. 'Darling, that's why we're here.'

'Yes, and thank you.' She sent them all a sincere smile. 'Friends are so important. They really are.'

A small silence fell over the group, almost as if she'd embarrassed them. Jackie blushed. 'And I have a habit of stating the obvious.'

'But you're so right,' said Prue smoothly. 'We can choose our friends, but we don't get to choose our family. I can think of a few rellies I'd gladly disown.'

They all laughed again, even Jackie, although the mere mention of relatives caused another unhappy niggle. She quickly changed the subject.

'So, I think we just about have the food covered.' She flipped a page in her notes. 'I've already made the birthday cake and Dulcie Forest is icing it for me. As for dessert, I was going to stick with ice-cream and fruit salad. Hugh's never been one for really sweet things anyway, so I was planning something like watermelon and mint and ginger.'

This was met by vigorous nods and murmurs of agreement.

'It's something Flora can make on the day,' Jackie said. 'And Seth's looking after the drinks.' She grinned deliberately. 'So now we get to the fun part – the decorations.'

'And the music,' said Maria. 'You mustn't forget that. Music sets such a mood for a party.'

'That's Flora's department,' Jackie told her. 'She's been talking to her father by email and she's compiled a playlist. It's all in hand. She's bringing her iPod and a docking station, and I believe she's sorting out speakers with Seth.'

Prue clapped her hands in delight. 'Isn't it lovely when our children grow up and can actually be useful, instead of just costing us money?'

This brought another laugh, then they went on to talk about decorations. They quickly agreed that votive candles gave any venue a special ambience.

'You can set out lots of them,' said Kate. 'And it still won't look like a séance. I have a boxful I'd be happy to bring along.'

'Yes, they'll be gorgeous on your verandahs,' agreed Maria.

'And you could have – say – three groups of the candles on the big table in the dining room,' suggested Prue. 'And you already have those lovely solar lights in the garden.'

Jackie madly took notes. The place really would look lovely, and once again her excitement about this party took hold.

'So – what are your plans for greenery and flowers?' asked Kate. 'I have a mass of hippeastrums coming on. I know they're ordinary, but they still look good in a tall vase.'

'I'd love some,' said Jackie. 'They might be ordinary in Burralea, but I struggle to grow them out here. If we have yours in vases, I won't have to pick my few and I can leave them in the garden.'

'Pity it's too early for agapanthus,' mused Maria. 'I'll have hundreds soon.'

Kate laughed. 'Yes, thoughtless of Hugh not to be born in November.'

'But then he would have been a Scorpio.' Maria sounded doleful now. 'You wouldn't want that. My father-in-law was a Scorpio.'

At the mention of fathers-in-law, another ping of alarm twanged in Jackie's chest. Why did every conversation seem to lead back to her guilty secret?

'Well, I'm a Scorpio.' Prue sat up, dramatically straight-backed with her chest out. 'And I can't see anything wrong with me. There's no sting in my tail.'

Everyone laughed.

'No, darling, that's why we love you,' said Jackie, and she reached for the empty coffee pot. 'Will I make another pot? Anyone for refills?'

Her friends shook their heads.

'I'm sure we're all politely stuffed, thanks.' Kate slipped on her reading glasses and looked down at the notes she'd made. 'I was wondering if you wanted any party games.'

'Oh, I hadn't thought,' said Jackie. 'Games could be fun, I guess. I'm not sure that I know any good ones, though.'

'And perhaps they'd be hard to manage with lots of guests.' Maria could always be relied on to be sensible.

A mischievous sparkle had leaped into Kate's eyes, however. 'What about a round or two of Truth and a Lie?'

Truth and a Lie? Jackie frowned and tried to ignore the sudden spurt of panic. 'How – how does that work?'

'You make three statements about someone and everyone votes on which is the lie.'

'That sounds like fun,' said Prue. 'And it would still work even with your number of guests, Jackie.'

'We'd have to have statements about Hugh, of course.' Kate's enthusiasm was clearly gathering steam. 'Two true statements, plus a lie. I'm sure Brad knows all sorts of funny stories about Hugh from his uni days.'

'And Brad's a lawyer, so whatever he comes up with will be both clever *and* safe,' suggested Prue, who also seemed delighted by this idea.

'I – I don't know,' Jackie hedged. Of course she was thinking, *again*, of the envelope from Hugh's father that still lay unopened. Instructions pertaining to his will. 'I suppose if we kept it light. Nothing . . . too dark.'

'Well, yes, of course,' said Kate. 'That's a given. But I'm sure Hugh doesn't have dark secrets anyway.'

No, thought Jackie. *Not that he knows about.*

She realised her friends were all looking at her expectantly, waiting for her to reassure them.

She said, as calmly as she could. 'If Hugh has secrets, he hasn't shared them with me. But I'm not totally sure we need that game.'

'You're right,' said Kate, who'd been watching her carefully. 'Those things can sometimes get out of hand and Hugh's such a sweetheart, we'd hate to spoil his night.'

Jackie hoped her smile didn't look too desperately grateful. 'Thanks for pushing me to have this meeting, girls,' she said. 'I feel really confident about the party now.'

'It's going to be fab,' said Prue, rising from her seat. 'We all love Hugh and being here to share his birthday will be really special.'

Jackie hugged her, then hugged Maria and Kate. Their optimism was contagious and when she stopped thinking about that envelope, she felt as upbeat and confident as she had when she'd first come up with the party idea. It was going to be wonderful and she was foolish to be so fussed about the old bits of paper Alice had found behind the mirror. She would probably laugh about it later and real- ise she'd tried to make Mount Everest out of a molehill.

She was feeling much calmer when Hugh's Pajero appeared around the bend.

'Speak of the devil.' Prue was grinning as he drove up to the front of the homestead.

The women were ready to leave, but they gathered at the top of the steps and watched as Hugh got out of his vehicle and extracted Charlie from his special seat in the back. Jackie thought how good he looked – her handsome cattleman in his favourite blue shirt and jeans and RM Williams boots. His hair was silver, his face a little more lined, but his physique was as trim and athletic as ever, and to Jackie he looked perfect with his little grandson in his arms.

Of course, her friends wanted to fuss over Charlie and the little boy bore their attention gallantly.

'So how are the party plans?' Hugh asked them.

'Brilliant,' declared Prue. 'It'll be the social event of the year.'

'Yeah, right.' Despite his smile, Hugh looked mildly embarrassed. 'A lot of fuss for an old codger.'

Their friends dismissed this with laughter and waves of their hands and soon they were calling goodbye, and getting into their cars, driving away.

Hugh set Charlie down and kissed Jackie's cheek.

'You look happier,' he said, studying her with narrowed eyes.

'I am,' she said. 'You were right about getting help. I was silly to try to do everything on my own.'

She could see the relief in his eyes. Then he took Charlie inside while she went to gather up the afternoon tea things.

14

'Hey, Alice, are you almost finished for the day?' Tammy, the hair-dresser, put her turquoise-tinted head around the doorway to Alice's workroom.

'Yep, I reckon I'm done.' Alice had been sanding the last leg of an English oak side table and she sent Tammy a smile as she dropped the sandpaper onto her workbench.

'Fantastic.' Tammy produced a bottle and two wine glasses from behind her back and held them up with a gleeful grin. 'It's wine o'clock on a Friday, after all.'

Alice glanced at the clock on her wall. It was five o'clock and her official closing time was five-thirty. 'You usually work late on Friday nights, don't you?'

'I know. I can't believe I got to close early today.' Tammy waggled the glasses. 'That's why I need to celebrate.'

'And I'm not likely to get another customer at this hour.' Washing her hands at the sink, Alice told herself it was fine to enjoy a quiet drink on the back steps while she left the shop open till closing time.

It had rained for most of the morning, but the afternoon sun had left the broad timber steps warm and dry.

'Ooh, I love your floor cushions.' Tammy beamed at Alice's latest purchases, cushions in bright tropical aqua, pink and lime green stacked in readiness by the doorway.

'I found them at the markets.' Alice had bought the cushions after Tammy's last visit. Just as Alice had predicted, the hairdresser had popped into the shop to not-so-subtly probe her about Seth Drummond.

Naturally, Alice had assured the girl that she and Seth were *not* an item and, as compensation for the lack of gossip, she'd offered wine. The two of them had ended up chatting for ages about where they'd lived and worked and about moving to Burralea. About previous boyfriends – Tammy had a particularly colourful history. About Ben in the pie shop – Tammy was convinced he was a man with an interesting past.

'Why would a surfie type move to the mountains unless he was getting away from something?'

They'd even talked about their dreams for the future.

To Alice, chatting companionably with Tammy as the daylight faded, their conversation had definitely felt like the beginning of a friendship. And she'd decided that a scattering of floor cushions and a candle or two could transform her back steps into a congenial entertaining area.

Now, as Alice lit citronella candles and the pink glow of sunset settled over the back garden, Tammy lowered herself happily onto the top step with a cushion beneath her and another at her back. She wriggled her hips. 'Very comfy. You'd better be careful, or I might set up camp here.'

Tammy unscrewed the bottle of sauvignon blanc and poured it into the two glasses.

'Would you like some cheese to go with that?' Alice asked.

'Not really, thanks.' Tammy patted her trim waist. 'Once I start on cheese I can't stop. As it is, I'm going to have to run twice as far in the morning to work off this wine.'

'Really?' Tammy had mentioned running a couple of times now. Alice was more of a walker. 'Where do you run?'

Tammy shrugged. 'Nothing too serious. Down to the lake and back. You should come. It's fun. A great stress release.' She lifted her glass. 'Here's cheers.'

'Cheers.' The wine was crisp and cool. 'Very nice,' Alice said.

'Mmm. Not bad.'

'How's your week been?' Alice asked.

'A bit quiet. Ben said he's had a quiet week, too. I told him not to panic. All he needs is a couple of busloads of tourists to come through and he'll be run off his feet.'

Alice took another, deeper sip of her wine. She'd eaten very little for lunch and the wine seemed to slip into her veins quickly. She wondered if Tammy was keen on Ben the pie man. He was certainly rather cute. But before she could ask, Tammy leaned forward, her eyes narrowed with sudden purpose.

'Now tell me, Alice. You avoided giving me a straight answer last time. But I'm curious. For God's sake, why have you convinced yourself that you shouldn't see Seth Drummond again?'

Zap. The mere mention of Seth's name made Alice jump. She'd been working hard to erase him from her memory and she really didn't want to talk about him. But she suspected Tammy wouldn't give up easily.

Shooing at an insect that was trying to fly into her glass, she struggled to dredge up an answer that would satisfy the girl's curiosity. Unfortunately, she couldn't get past the bald truth.

'Seth's a single father,' she said, keeping her eyes on her glass.

'Yes, I know,' responded Tammy, who of course knew everything about everybody. 'So what?'

'That's not really my scene.'

Tammy frowned at this. Alice, needing fortification, took

another hefty sip of her wine.

'Isn't Seth's kid still just a toddler?'

'Yes, but he's pretty little. Sixteen or seventeen months.'

'And isn't his mother in England?'

'Yes, I don't know the full story, but I think she was out here backpacking.'

Tammy pulled a face. 'Is she coming back to Australia?'

'Apparently not. She's married.'

Tammy stared at Alice blankly. 'So you don't have a problem.'

Alice sighed. On the surface, her excuse sounded pathetic. 'I do, actually. I'm not very good with little kids.'

This was dismissed with an easy shrug. 'Jeez, it's not as if Seth would bring his toddler on a date.'

'No, but –'

'But the guy's red hot, Alice, let's face it.' Now Tammy flapped the neckline of her T-shirt to emphasise her point. '*And* he's obviously interested in *you*.'

'How would you know?'

'I saw the way he was looking at you.'

'You saw us for what, all of five seconds?'

'I saw enough. Christ, Alice, you'd have to be blind not to notice.' Tammy's expression was almost pitying. 'And it's not as if seeing a guy means you have to jump in and start caring for his offspring.'

'No – I know.' Alice rubbed an anxious finger around the top of her glass. 'But – as he hasn't actually asked me on a date, none of this is really an issue.' She didn't add that she'd more or less given Seth the cold shoulder for the very reason that she didn't want him to get too interested.

Needing to change the subject, she checked the time again. It was almost five-twenty. 'I think I may as well shut up shop.'

Tammy acknowledged this with a nod, drained her wine and

reached for the bottle to refill her glass.

'I'll be back in a tick.' Already on her feet, Alice hurried away.

The shop had old-fashioned double doors with three panes of glass in each panel and bolts at the top and bottom. She was slipping the top bolt into place when a ute swerved into the parking space directly in front of her. She sensed something familiar about the vehicle and her heart gave a crazy kick.

It kicked again as Seth Drummond climbed out of the driver's seat.

'Hey,' he called. 'Sorry I'm late. I meant to get here earlier.'

Alice drew a quick, very necessary breath. The smell of damp, hot bitumen reached her, combined with the jasmine that climbed her shop's awning. Dusk was falling quickly. Already the sky was turning purple and a flight of flying foxes swooped and darted overhead.

'I suppose you've come for the mirror,' she said as Seth rounded the ute. She'd phoned Jackie Drummond two days ago to tell her that it was ready.

'Yes. I meant to get here earlier, but I was delayed. I'll grab it now, if it's not too inconvenient.'

He was dressed in a crisp white business shirt, open-necked, with the sleeves rolled back, showing off his tan. His jeans were neat and deep blue, quite a change from the soft, battered and faded ones she'd seen him in previously. His boots were polished and he looked freshly shaved. Even his dark hair was neater than usual.

Regrettably for Alice, this tidied-up version of Seth was possibly even more attractive than his scruffy cowboy look. She knew Tammy would be agog when she saw him.

Needing a chance to regroup, she paid studious attention to undoing the bolt and reopening the doors.

'I was about to close up,' she said.

'I'm in luck then.' Seth came into the shop, bringing a drift of aftershave.

The scent whispered to Alice to close her eyes and breathe deeply. Damn. She had to get a grip.

'The mirror's still out the back.' She nodded towards the workroom. 'Do you want me to wrap it? I have some strong cardboard, but it might rain again before you get home.'

'I brought a tarp. It's in the back of the ute. And there's a tie-down cover as well.'

'Oh, well. You're all sorted.' Alice was doing her best to remain cool and together. The fact that Tammy was all ears in the next room didn't help.

Sure enough, when she and Seth went out the back, Tammy was no longer relaxing on the cushion with her glass of wine, but on her feet.

Had she been trying to eavesdrop?

'No need to get up!' Alice told her. 'This will only take a minute. A customer's come to collect his mirror.'

But Tammy was ploughing agitated fingers through her spiky turquoise hair. 'I'm so sorry, Alice. I'm a freaking idiot.' Her wide-eyed gaze took in Seth as she said this. 'I totally forgot I'm supposed to be washing and setting Audrey Ryan's hair this evening. The poor old girl's not well. She can't come in to the salon any more and I've been calling in at her home.'

Alice narrowed her eyes. She was sure Tammy had come up with this sudden excuse as soon as she'd heard Seth's voice, but she could hardly accuse her friend of lying.

'That's a pity,' she said carefully. 'I was looking forward to finishing our drink.'

Tammy, however, was already halfway to the door. 'So sorry to leave you high and dry. We'll have to make it another time.'

'What about your wine?' Alice called after her. 'You should take it.'

'No, no! I bought it for you.' The smile Tammy offered them was borderline coy. 'Enjoy.' Then she gave a careless shrug. 'Or save it till next time. Byeee! Must dash.'

With a waggle of her fingers and a flash of mischievous eyes, Tammy was gone.

Alice let out her breath in a tense huff. 'Well,' she said. 'That was my new friend Tammy. She runs the hair salon a few doors down. I would have introduced you if she'd given me a chance.'

Seth was smiling and she was suddenly aware all over again of just how very blue his eyes were. She switched her gaze to the abandoned wine and glasses and cosily arranged cushions. Her certainty deepened. Tammy was deliberately giving her and Seth 'space'.

I'll have to have a word with that girl.

At least Seth hadn't picked up on the blatant ploy. He was too busy checking out the restored mirror.

'It's perfect,' he said, crossing to the easel. 'You've done a great job. Brilliant.'

'Yes, I'm pleased. You can hardly see the scratches.'

'I can't see any at all.'

'I hope Jackie likes it.'

'She will. She'll be stoked.'

Alice smiled. She'd worked hard to produce a good finish and she'd been very satisfied with the result. 'Shall I help you to carry it out?'

'I'm sure I can manage.'

Seth made it look easy, of course, and no doubt it was supereasy compared with almost any job he tackled on a daily basis. In no time, he had the mirror safely wrapped and stowed, and the back of the ute covered and secured.

Alice, standing on the footpath in the light coming through her shop's doorway, tried not to be too impressed by his economy of movement.

With the task completed, Seth faced her with his hands propped lightly on his hips. Night was falling quickly. Already, the evening star was peeping over the patch of rainforest at the end of the street.

'So, your girlfriend stood you up?' Seth said.

Alice shrugged. 'It was only an impromptu thing. A Friday drink.' She wondered if Seth was expecting her to invite him in.

'I was thinking of something impromptu myself.' He smiled again and, despite the gathering darkness, his blue eyes glowed. 'Dinner at Quinn's, perhaps?'

Alice swallowed. She knew there had to be a reason for his neat attire, and she wasn't completely surprised by the invitation.

It was tempting. Quinn's was one of Burralea's most popular restaurants, run by an Irish chef and his French wife.

All reports had been excellent and Alice had thought about trying the place out, but she'd never really fancied dining alone, sitting there in silence, fiddling with her phone, or reading a book while other diners chatted intimately over candlelight. Besides, since arriving in Burralea, she'd been busy with other kinds of social events.

She'd started going to fortnightly quiz nights, and just last week she'd been invited to an exhibition by local artists raising money for the rural fire brigade. These nights been fun, but the thought of a restaurant meal was very alluring.

Problem was, going to Quinn's with Seth would most definitely count as a date, and she'd just finished telling Tammy why that wasn't a good idea.

'I'm sure Quinn's would be booked out on a Friday night,' she said.

Seth was already reaching into his pocket for his phone. 'I'll give Kieran a call.'

'Kieran Quinn? You know him?'

Seth grinned. 'If you live in this district long enough, you get to know most people.'

He stood before her in all his wide-shouldered, blue-eyed gorgeousness, phone in hand, one questioning eyebrow raised, waiting for her response.

It was her chance to send him packing.

Heaven help her, the last thing she wanted was to watch this man drive away. Before fresh doubts and warnings raised their ugly heads, Alice nodded. 'Okay. I guess it's worth a try.'

Then she listened to Seth's end of a very matey phone conversation, with the result that Kieran Quinn could indeed squeeze them in.

Alice glanced down at her dusty work jeans and smock. 'I'll need to shower and change.'

'There's no rush,' Seth assured her.

But this left her with a new dilemma. She could hardly leave Seth alone downstairs with nothing to amuse him but Tammy's wine and a citronella candle. She had no choice but to invite him up into her private domain, where he could at least listen to music or watch TV while she got ready.

'Bring that wine and come on up,' she said, trying to sound casual and offhand about showering and changing with only a thin wall between her naked self and this sinfully attractive man.

15

It was only a date and not an especially important date, Alice told herself, but she selected a new bar of handmade soap for her shower. The soap was another find from the local markets and the scents of fragrant patchouli and sweet mandarin would linger on her skin long after she was dry. She didn't ask herself why this should matter.

Stepping out of the shower into the steamy bathroom, she heard the slow sensuous notes of a saxophone coming from the next room, slipping under the door like smoke. At the thought of Seth there, drinking wine and listening to music on her iPod, anticipation danced inside her.

In the bedroom, she opened drawers and made selections. And deliberately reminded herself that Seth had a son. Charlie.

She remembered the little boy's golden hair, his soft, baby-smooth skin, the warm weight of him in her arms. His wriggling body as he struggled to be free. She remembered him running away from her, one foot in a thick sock and the other bare.

Then her mind went slightly crazy. She saw Charlie toddling into danger, disappearing into a muddy pool, falling under a bus, out of a window.

In an eddy of despair, Alice sank to the edge of her bed while her mind flashed back to the bleak autumn afternoon all those years ago when she'd waited for her parents and Daisy to pick her up from soccer practice. She must have been a forlorn little figure as she stood there on the footpath, waiting and watching as all the other kids' parents arrived and took off again. For home.

Rain had threatened and the wind blew dry, crackly leaves at Alice's bare legs. Eventually, Sara Halliday's mother saw Alice standing there alone. Mrs Halliday took pity on Alice and she and Sara had waited with her.

Sara had complained. She was missing her favourite TV show, but her mother had given them lollipops. Alice could still remember the sweet and sour flavours mingling on her tongue. After they'd waited for almost an hour, Mrs Halliday had tried to ring Alice's home.

A neighbour had answered. The police were there . . .

Stop it, for God's sake.

Not now. Not tonight.

Alice couldn't believe she'd let her thoughts spin so far out of control. Was she crazy?

She'd never talked to anyone about this issue, but her discomfort around little people had become a source of embarrassment that only deepened as she grew older.

She hadn't wanted to see a shrink. Didn't want to have to talk about it. She knew avoidance was cowardly, but she hated the thought of exposing her inner self to a stranger, and until recently, she'd found it easy enough to cover up.

Surely she could handle a simple dinner invitation without having a meltdown about Seth's cute and vulnerable son? This was a date, for God's sake, not a long-term commitment. If Seth knew she was agonising over a potential role as mother for his boy, he would probably run a mile.

Going out with him should be a cinch. She was a practised hand at short-term relationships.

Except she was beginning to suspect that Seth was the nicest, hunkiest man she'd ever met and short term with him might not be so simple.

How naïve she'd been to think that by travelling north she could run away from her troubles! The world over, nice, hunky guys expected to marry and produce sons. She should have run to a nunnery, not a country town.

But I've already said yes. I can't back out of tonight. Not now.

Alice stood and scowled at her reflection in the wardrobe mirror. She was over-thinking this whole situation. Again. She really had to learn to cool her jets. Relax and enjoy herself.

Taking a deep breath, she continued to get ready, choosing a matching bra and knickers – demure mauve rather than lacy black – and her favourite dress, a silk sheath in moss green.

She pulled off the scrunchie that held back her hair and shook her curls free, combed them lightly. Carefully but quickly, she applied cinnamon and smoke to her eyelids, a coppery gloss to her lips, a subtle bronze blush beneath her cheekbones. With the addition of gold earrings, black high-heeled sandals and a black and gold wrap, she was done.

When Seth saw her, his eyes shone in a way that made her skin tingle all over.

The atmosphere at Quinn's was rustic and romantic, with walls painted in a rich terracotta and floors paved with local stone. On every table small candles glowed in frosted glass. Pots of lush ginger and ferns filled the windows.

Enticing aromas wafted from the kitchen as Alice and Seth were shown to a table in a secluded corner. It was very pleasant, mulling together over the menu, discussing favourites, making choices, selecting a bottle of French shiraz.

They decided to start with two entrées to share, and as Alice spread pâté on a slice of locally sourced ciabatta, she could feel herself sinking under the seductive spell of the atmosphere, the food and wine, and the handsome man sitting opposite her.

But before she got too carried away, she dived in with the all-important question. 'So who's minding Charlie tonight?'

'My parents,' Seth said. 'I'm lucky. They love having him.' He smiled. 'I don't like to overdo it, though. To be honest I haven't been out like this in quite a while.'

Alice told herself this wasn't significant. Of course it wouldn't be easy, living out there at Ruthven Downs, some distance from town, and shouldering the responsibilities of fatherhood.

'What's it been like for you?' she felt compelled to ask. 'Figuring out how to care for a baby? I guess it was a steep learning curve.'

'Too right.' Dropping his gaze to his wine glass, Seth's expression was thoughtful, as if he was recalling the endless nappy changes, the floor pacing and sleepless nights. 'It certainly makes you grow up in a hurry.'

A pang of guilt spiked in Alice's chest. No doubt her avoidance of small people showed a marked lack of maturity. 'Was there anyone to help you?'

'My parents, of course, but I was pretty stubborn about wanting to do it myself.' Seth's smile was shrewd. 'We don't have to talk about Charlie, you know. That's not why I asked you to dinner.'

Alice swallowed quickly. 'Right.' Could he see right through her?

Seth topped up her wine glass. 'So what made you decide to move up here?' he asked.

She told him half the truth. 'After my grandmother died, I was a free agent and I felt like I needed a change. Gran used to tell me about a holiday she had up here on the Tablelands, a long time ago. She talked about the lakes and the rainforest and how beautiful it was.' Alice gave a smiling shrug. 'I guess she made it sound all very perfect and *over the rainbow*.'

'And now you're here, what do you think?'

'Well, I'm still settling in, but I really like it. It's certainly very beautiful and I love how much cooler it is here in the mountains. It's quiet, of course.'

'Not too quiet for a city girl?'

'I don't think so. Not so far. There's always someone popping into the shop.' Alice helped herself to some of the French tomato salad. The tomatoes were local, vine ripened and succulent, the herbs and vinaigrette the perfect, finely balanced accompaniment. 'What about you? Do you enjoy living in the bush?'

'Yeah, I love working in the outdoors.' Seth grinned. 'I can't imagine getting into a suit and tie and catching a train to work. Mind you, my sister lives in Melbourne.'

'Really? Is she working there?'

Seth nodded. 'She plays in an orchestra. Violin.'

'Wow, she must be good.'

'Yes, she is.' Seth helped himself to the salad and Alice found herself fascinated by his workmanlike hands wielding the dainty silver servers. 'Flora's talented and conscientious, and she had a brilliant teacher at boarding school who really helped her and pushed her.'

'Boarding school? Did you go there too?'

'I did. Charters Towers.'

'Oh, wow!' Seth looked puzzled, so she explained. 'When I was a kid, I was desperate go to boarding school. I used to pretend that my bedroom was actually a dorm filled with my school friends.'

He smiled momentarily, but then his blue eyes seemed concerned. 'Were you lonely as a child?'

'Not really. There were moments, of course, when I missed

my – my family. But I think the boarding school obsession came from reading too many Enid Blytons.' She grinned to reassure him. 'All those secret passages and midnight feasts.'

'Well, we didn't manage many midnight feasts at my school.' Seth topped up their wine glasses. 'But we certainly got up to stupid pranks.'

'Tell me about them.'

He hesitated and gave an uncomfortable shrug. 'Just stupidly juvenile boys' stuff.'

'Come on,' she urged. 'I was prank-deprived. I went to a Catholic girls' school.'

She sent him a playful, pleading look and, with a slight grimace, he gave in.

'Stuff like stealing a guy's clothes when he was in the shower. Putting toads in kids' beds. Decorating some poor sucker's desk with pics from a porn magazine.' He rolled his eyes at this last admission.

Perhaps it was the mention of porn. This time, when their gazes met across the small table, the friendly vibe between them lingered and changed subtly. All sorts of sparks went off inside Alice. She hoped she wasn't blushing.

She broke off another piece of bread and slathered it with pâté. After a mouthful or two, she said, 'Your life has been almost the opposite of mine.'

'Because of your school-prank deprivation?'

'No. I was thinking more about our families. You've grown up on your property with your family, and you're still there, living close by your parents, working with your father every day. And now you even have three generations there, with Charlie.'

'That's true, but all that closeness has its downside, you know. I find myself chafing at the bit at times.'

'The old bull and the young bull?'

Seth grinned. 'I guess.'

'But you must also feel very secure.'

He'd been helping himself to the last of the tomato salad, but he paused, watching her, and his eyes shimmered with unmistakable sympathy, as if he'd sensed her inner battles. 'Yeah. I guess I shouldn't complain.'

'And I wasn't trying to suggest you've had it easy,' Alice amended. 'I'm sure it's impossible to judge other people's lives from the outside.'

The waiter came to take their plates and return with their mains. A prawn risotto for Alice and slow-cooked duck for Seth. Again the courses were delicious and, for Alice, everything about the meal and her companion kept her senses humming.

As they ate, they talked on about their work, about the places they'd been to. They were amazed to discover that they'd both spent the same Easter break enjoying a camping holiday on Fraser Island, and they couldn't believe they'd missed seeing each other. Throughout the meal, their glances seemed to grow more sizzling. At times, Alice felt such an intense connection with Seth she could scarcely breathe.

She'd never shared a meal with a man who had such a devastating effect on her. Had never spent an entire evening wondering, imagining . . . and it was almost impossible to remember why this was unwise.

Despite the delicious menu options, they agreed they had no room for coffee and dessert. When Seth paid the bill, he ducked his head around the doorway to the kitchen and Kieran Quinn appeared, round-faced and jovial, wiping his hands on his white apron.

'Very pleased to meet you,' the grinning chef said, as Seth introduced Alice and he shook her hand. 'Although I should warn you,' he added with a cheeky wink, 'you're asking for trouble going out with this guy.'

'I'm sure that's good advice,' Alice replied.

The problem was, primed by wine and their very pleasant evening, she didn't feel inclined to follow it.

Outside, beyond the restaurant's awning, rain was falling in a fine mizzle.

'You wait here,' Seth told Alice, 'and I'll get the ute.'

'No, no.' She shook out her wrap and pulled it around her, tossing a long black and gold tail over one shoulder. 'The rain's only light. I'll be fine.'

Seth hesitated. 'Are you sure?'

'Of course.' It was only a couple of hundred metres to her shop.

So they set off together, over the road and through the park filled with pretty flower beds, with Seth's warm arm protectively around her shoulders. The scent of night jasmine drifted on the fine misty rain. In the darkness ahead of them a curlew scurried on long skinny legs before disappearing into a clump of ginger.

At the corner of Alice's street, the rain began to fall in earnest and they ran now, heads ducked against the drenching needles. Alice was a little breathless by the time they reached her shop, but the breathlessness wasn't merely from running.

Seth's white shirt was almost transparent and the wet fabric was clinging to him, outlining his taut, athletic frame. Water droplets gleamed silver in his thick dark hair.

She managed to open the door without fumbling and turned on the light.

'I can't send you home like that,' she said. 'Come up and I'll get a towel.'

She saw the flash of an unreadable emotion in his eyes, and she turned quickly before her own feelings showed. Her heart pumped hard as he followed her up the stairs.

When they reached her small living room she turned on a lamp, shed her sodden wrap, draping it over a wooden chair, then headed quickly for the linen press, where she found a couple of thick, man-sized towels. She handed one to Seth.

'Thanks.' He didn't immediately start to dry himself.

He stood in the middle of her lounge room, staring at her. His mouth quirked in a happy-sad smile. 'You know, you're even more beautiful when you're half-drowned.'

It wasn't the first time Alice had been told she was beautiful, but the praise had never mattered in the way it did now, had never made her feel so emotional, so close to the tipping point.

Stepping forward, Seth lifted the towel to her face, wiped the splashes of rain from her nose and her lips. Her eyes were level with the dark column of his throat and she could smell the faintest hint of his aftershave and the damp cotton of his shirt.

She looked up and met his gaze, and the message in his blue eyes was burning. Inescapable. In that moment, she knew for certain where this evening had been heading from the moment he'd stepped out of his ute.

Their first kiss was incendiary. A blaze of passion exploding like a starburst, leading quickly to the shedding of damp clothes.

They left a soggy trail behind them. His shirt, her dress, his belt and jeans, falling in rapid succession as they made their way to the bedroom, stopping only for impatient nibbles and kisses.

She'd left a lamp on and the bed, with its colourful Indian throw rug, looked inviting.

'You're shivering,' Seth murmured as he slipped his hand beneath the elastic of her panties.

'Not from cold,' she assured him.

He pushed the wispy fabric down, letting it fall silently to her ankles. As his fingertips brushed a teasing path over her stomach, desire tugged and licked deep inside her. She wound her arms around his neck, pressed close and kissed him again.

She heard him groan, and pulled back. 'You okay?' she whispered.

He gave a soft chuckle. 'Yeah, of course, but it's been a while.'

'Me too. Maybe we should calm down.'

'Never,' he said, slipping her straps from her shoulders and dipping his head to her breast.

16

Soft lamplight outlined their bodies as they lay, catching their breaths, like exhausted swimmers who'd finally made landfall.

Seth knew he should probably say something meaningful to Alice, but he was afraid he might sound way too enthusiastic, like some dickhead who'd finally scored after an entire year of abstinence.

Truth was, this night with Alice Miller had been beyond amazing. Seth hadn't been sure she would even come out with him and he'd left the dinner invitation till the last minute, to give her fewer chances to back off.

Now, he'd not only shared a thoroughly enjoyable dinner with her, but *this* . . .

He'd never expected such spontaneity and passion. Had never experienced such satisfying pleasure. Everything about this girl was damn off-the-charts perfect.

Thank God he'd come prepared, even though he hadn't expected this to happen. That was one life lesson now indelibly imprinted on his brain, although as it turned out, Alice was on the pill. She'd even joked that she would have taken two pills a day if she thought it would make her less likely to get pregnant.

Seth might have continued to ponder this, but a movement beside him caught his attention. Alice was brushing tears from her eyes.

His heart stilled in his chest. 'Alice?'

'I'm sorry,' she said, sniffling. 'I'm okay. Honest.' She reached for the sheet that was pooled at their feet and dragged it up to cover herself, used a corner of it to dab at her eyes. 'I just didn't expect –'

She left the sentence dangling.

'No,' Seth said softly. 'Neither did I.'

She looked at him, her brown eyes glistening. She smiled, but the smile seemed slightly bewildered, and he had a feeling his might seem that way too.

'I'm sorry,' she said next, as she dabbed at her eyes again. 'I know guys hate girls who cry.'

'Tears are okay,' he assured her. 'As long as you don't say, "Now you'll think I'm awful."'

She gave a soft giggle.

'And girls with brown eyes and a golden fleck have special immunity anyway,' he added.

She sighed. 'You're so damn nice.'

Seth feigned shock. 'I've been called a lot of names. Never nice.'

'Well, I could be more accurate, but I don't want to give you a swelled head.'

She sat up, tugging the sheet around her, holding it over her breasts. Her auburn hair glowed in the lamplight, tumbling in soft curls to her shoulders, and Seth now had a view of her pale and perfect back. He longed to touch her skin again, touch her hair. Touch her.

'The thing is, I don't want to give you the wrong impression,' she said.

Seth had been reaching towards her, his hand in mid-air. Now he drew back. 'What wrong impression?'

Alice gripped the sheet more tightly, bunching it in front of her. 'I – I know this was –' She stopped and seemed to be hunting for the right words. 'I just felt I should warn you – that I'm not really ready to start a relationship.' She turned to him sharply. 'I know I'm probably jumping the gun. You – you might not even be thinking about long-term or anything. But I – I just wanted you to know.'

Seth needed a minute to take this in. He hadn't really had a plan beyond hoping to see Alice tonight. Now he was certainly interested in seeing her again. And again.

He'd never met a girl quite like her before. So serious and conscientious and yet so unbelievably sexy.

But he felt concerned for her too. He wasn't sure what had upset her, but losing her family at such a young age must have been hell. The emotional fallout was bound to be complicated.

'Well, you can rest easy,' he said. 'I'm not looking for a long-term relationship either.'

Alice blinked as if he'd surprised her. 'I see.' Her shoulders relaxed a little. 'That's – that's good. I wasn't sure. I thought maybe – you know – because of Charlie –' With a groan she pulled the sheet right over her head. 'Oh, God, just tell me to shut up, will you?'

Seth leaned over and pulled the sheet down. Her eyes were tightly closed, her mouth pulled into a tight grimace.

He touched her cheek with his fingertips and she opened her eyes.

'I get where you're coming from,' he said. 'My mum's always telling me I need a woman to help look after Charlie.'

'Don't you want one?' she asked, looking surprised.

'Not at the moment.'

It was more or less the truth. Seth couldn't pretend he wanted to remain a bachelor forever, and it wasn't as if he hadn't thought about finding a girlfriend who'd be happy to step in as a mother for

Charlie. But he had enough on his plate just now with looking after his son. Inviting a woman to move into their household would be a huge step and would bring a host of other responsibilities – like worrying about whether she enjoyed the bush life, or fitted in with his family, or wanted another kid of her own.

'I'm not in any rush,' he said.

'Oh.'

Alice's response was so soft it was hard to tell if she was pleased by his answer or not.

Seth touched her hair, as he'd been longing to do, and let his fingers thread through the silky curls. 'That doesn't mean I'm not hoping to see you again.'

She smiled now, and dropped her head to one side, letting her cheek rest against the back of his hand. 'I'd like that too, Seth.'

'There you go.' He was relieved and happy; things were turning out fine. 'We're in total agreement.'

And he wanted her again. Now.

Luckily, she put up absolutely no resistance when he ran his hand over her thigh, over the super-smooth curve of her hip, and rolled her on top of him.

17

When Jackie woke, the sun was already up and streaming brightly across the bed. She turned and saw Hugh lying with his back to her, and she remembered it was Saturday. He would head out later to check on his pregnant and newly delivered cows, but there was no urgency. They could lie in for a bit.

She settled back against the pillows, wriggled comfortably and closed her eyes. She might have drifted back to sleep, if a sound hadn't reached her from the room down the hallway. A soft gurgling laugh.

Jackie's eyes flashed open. Good heavens, she'd almost forgotten that Charlie had spent the night with them. He was obviously awake and playing in his cot. He wasn't too bad at entertaining himself, but the laughter would turn to tears if she left him there for too long.

She swung out of bed, put on her slippers and the green and pink silk dressing-gown that Hugh had brought back from a business trip to Indonesia. Not wanting to wake her husband, she tiptoed down the hall and greeted Charlie quietly.

Her grandson's grin was ecstatic, and he held up his arms to her with such endearing glee that her heart did a small somersault of joy. 'Hello, darling. How are you this morning, my happy little boy?'

After a lovely hug and a kiss, she gave him his favourite rabbit to play with while she laid him on the spare bed and changed him. Then she took him through to the kitchen and set him in the high chair with a mug of milk and a biscuit, before turning the kettle on.

From the window over the kitchen sink, she could see to the east where the sun was already quite high above the gum trees. It had rained during the night. Hugh would pleased. With luck, the dams would hold out till the proper wet season arrived after Christmas.

Her garden, at least, looked refreshed.

Honeyeaters greeted each other noisily as they feasted on the last of the bottlebrush flowers. Jackie was sorry to see the end of the bottlebrush season, but with spring, new flowers were arriving. Several varieties of ginger were sending up colourful spikes and the day lilies had promising fat buds. They should be open in time for Hugh's party.

Jackie looked beyond her garden to Seth's cottage and saw his ute parked beneath the big African tulip tree. She wondered what sort of night he'd had. She certainly hoped he'd enjoyed himself.

The kettle came to the boil and she made two mugs of tea. Hugh was awake when she took them through to the bedroom, with Charlie toddling behind her, clutching his half-eaten milk arrowroot biscuit.

'Pum-pa!' the little boy squealed.

'Hey there, Bruiser,' Hugh greeted him.

'I don't know why you call him Bruiser,' Jackie complained. 'He's the gentlest little fellow, aren't you, Charlie boy?'

Hugh merely chuckled. 'If he can call me Pum-pa, I can call him Bruiser.' He gave Charlie a helping hand to clamber up onto his side of the bed.

Jackie set Hugh's mug on the bedside table. The boy was already bouncing on Hugh's knees and she was reminded of their early years, when they'd had their little ones in bed with them on the rare mornings that Hugh slept in.

Now Hugh wriggled his toes beneath the quilt and Charlie giggled as he tried to grab at them. She thought of Seth living alone without an adult companion to share this kind of fun and she felt a motherly pang of regret. More than anything in the world, she wanted her children to be happy.

At least Flora seemed very content with her life and her boyfriend in Melbourne, and perhaps Seth would find someone soon. Jackie was glad he'd started going out again.

'Seth's home,' she told Hugh.

'Daddy!' piped up Charlie, instantly recognising his father's name.

'Yes, darling, Seth's your daddy.' Jackie reached over with a tissue to wipe biscuity dribble from Charlie's chin. 'Now come to Nan and let Grandpa drink his tea.'

Obediently, Charlie allowed himself to be cuddled, and Hugh reached for his mug and took a deep, appreciative sip. 'I heard Seth arrive home,' he said. 'It was pretty late.'

'How late?'

Hugh chuckled. 'Just before sun-up.'

Jackie's eyes widened. Seth had been rather vague about his plans for last night. 'Well, we've both been saying he needs a social life.'

'Indeed we have. Let's hope he enjoyed himself.'

'I've had my fingers crossed,' Jackie admitted. 'But I hope Seth also remembered to collect the sideboard mirror for me while he was in town. I don't really have time to get over to Burralea.' She smiled at Hugh. 'By the way, the acceptances for your party are rolling in. At last count we were up to forty-five.'

'Forty-five guests?' Hugh looked stunned. 'I thought you weren't going over the top.'

'I'm not. But you have a lot of friends, Hugh, and people will be insulted if they're not invited.'

Her husband didn't look convinced. 'Where are we going to put them all?'

'Oh, we've got it all sorted. It'll be easy enough to rearrange the lounge and dining rooms to make more space, and there are all the verandahs. And hopefully, the weather will be kind to us and people can spill out into the garden as well.'

'Hmmm.' Hugh was frowning. But the frown quickly morphed into a grin as he tickled Charlie's tummy. 'Forty-five party guests. What do you think of that, Bruiser? Soon it will be sixty-five. One for each year.'

Jackie didn't like to tell Hugh that yes, there were bound to be many more acceptances. 'I was wondering about asking the mayor,' she said as Charlie's delighted squeals died down. 'Do you want to invite him?'

This time Hugh looked totally appalled. 'No, I bloody well do not want to invite the mayor. Why would I want him at my birthday party?'

She gave a defensive shrug. 'You did serve a term on the shire council.'

'That doesn't mean I want politicians at my birthday party.' Ignoring Charlie for a moment, Hugh regarded Jackie sternly. 'Please be sensible, love. You know how I feel about these things. We don't want this party to be bigger than Ben Hur.'

'All right,' she said contritely.

'And I don't want you wearing yourself out either. I know the girls are helping with the food, but you'll still be cleaning the house from top to bottom, won't you? Manicuring the lawn with nail scissors and scrubbing the ceilings with a toothbrush.'

'Oh, for heaven's sake, there's no need to exaggerate.'

'Well, you do get carried away.'

'I just want the place to look nice.'

'You should at least hire someone to help you.'

'You know why I won't,' she responded a little tersely.

'Because you're a control freak?' Her husband said this without bitterness, but the comment still stung.

The problem was, he was partly right. Hugh had suggested years ago that Jackie should have household help.

'I don't hesitate to hire people to help with the mustering or the fencing,' he'd said.

But Jackie knew that housework was a poor comparison. The thing was, she'd never felt comfortable about hiring a woman to help clean her house. Yes, it was true that her mother's work as a cleaner had kept a roof over their heads after her father died, but it was the memory of her mother's nightly exhaustion after long days cleaning other people's homes that stopped her.

The memories were still painful now, all these years later. Even though there'd been times Jackie really could have done with help, she hadn't been able to take that step.

But this party was all about Hugh and she didn't want any aspect of it to upset him. As she took Charlie back to the kitchen to make his breakfast, she mentally crossed off five other possibles from her invitee list.

Hugh was showering and shaving in the bathroom and Charlie was messily trying to feed himself porridge when Seth appeared at the kitchen door.

'Hello, darling,' Jackie welcomed him. 'I didn't expect to see you up so early.'

Seth shrugged. 'It's after seven.'

There was an edge of challenge in his voice, but Jackie didn't back down. 'You had a late night, didn't you?'

Seth merely shrugged again.

She couldn't help feeling curious, but of course she wouldn't press him.

'Charlie hasn't quite finished his breakfast,' she said. 'Come on in.' She went to wipe Charlie's porridge-smeared face. 'Look, Charlie, here's Daddy. Would you like a cuppa, Seth?'

'I can get it.'

'Of course. I'll just put the kettle on.' She was never happier than when she was fussing over her family.

'That sideboard mirror's in the back of the ute,' Seth said as he helped himself to a mug and spooned in coffee.

'Oh, that's great, thanks.' Another job Jackie could cross off her list. 'I'm so glad you remembered. How's Alice?'

'She's fine.'

Jackie noticed a guarded look in Seth's eyes and she was struck by the pleasing possibility that he might have been with Alice Miller last night. Till the early hours?

She was surprised by how much the thought delighted her. 'Alice is a lovely girl,' she couldn't help adding.

'I'll get the mirror for you now,' Seth responded without looking her way. 'While Charlie's finishing his breakfast.'

The kettle came to the boil, but Seth ignored it and took off. By the time he arrived back with the carefully wrapped mirror, Charlie was banging his spoon against his empty porridge bowl and Jackie had made Seth's coffee and set it on the counter with a plate of toast and her homemade cumquat marmalade.

'Where would you like this?' Seth asked. 'In the dining room? I can reattach it to the sideboard, if you like.'

'That would be great,' Jackie told him. 'But don't worry about it now. I've made your coffee.' She pointed to a spot on the floor, clear of cupboards, where the mirror could be propped against the wall.

'Just leave it there.'

'Down!!' wailed Charlie, and he tossed his spoon onto the floor.

'I'll take care of him,' said Seth as soon as the mirror was safely stowed.

Jackie would have liked Seth to enjoy his toast and coffee, but he was always fiercely independent about Charlie.

She wandered to the mirror and peeled away a corner of the canvas wrapping. 'Oh, it looks lovely, doesn't it?' She pulled a bit more of the canvas away. 'All the scratches and spots are gone. It's as good as new.'

'Yeah, Alice did a great job.'

There was still a cautious note in her son's tone, and Jackie quickly looked up, trying to judge his mood. Unfortunately, Seth was busy wiping Charlie's hands and she couldn't see his face.

But as she continued to check out the mirror, her imagination had a lovely time, getting quite carried away, conjuring a future with Alice Miller as her daughter-in-law.

'By the way,' Seth said suddenly. 'Whatever happened to that envelope?'

Whack!

Jackie's happy musings came crashing back to earth and guilt rushed in to take their place. 'Envelope?' she hedged.

'The one Alice found behind the mirror.'

Of course she knew what he was talking about.

'Gran's name was on the back,' Seth said. 'What was it all about?'

'Oh, it's – it's like a diary,' Jackie said quickly. 'It's a bit rough, only in note form really, but it's quite interesting. It's about when she was a nurse during the war in Singapore.'

'Singapore?' Seth looked surprised.

'Yes, she never talked about it, did she? I hadn't even realised she was over there.'

'Singapore was overrun by the Japs, wasn't it? They set up Changi Prison.'

'Yes, but I think Stella got out just before then.' Jackie hoped Seth wouldn't probe too deeply. She hadn't read the rest of Stella's notes.

'If it was just a diary, I wonder why Gran bothered to hide it,' Seth said. 'Seems a bit weird. Was there some kind of secret?'

'I – I don't think so.' But Jackie couldn't be sure, and of course she was remembering the other envelope inside the bigger one with Magnus Drummond's instructions to his lawyer. 'I must admit I got busy and I haven't finished reading it.'

'Reading what?' asked Hugh, coming into the room.

Jackie froze. She was thinking again of his mother's words – *I have done a terrible thing.*

She had planned to find out what this terrible thing was before she told Hugh about the envelope. But she'd hoped she could leave it until after the party – just in case it was in any way upsetting. It had been hidden away for so long now. Another couple of weeks shouldn't hurt.

She glanced quickly at Seth, who was watching her expectantly, clearly waiting for her to answer his father.

Instead, she frowned at Seth and shook her head, warning him to remain silent as she frantically struggled to find a safe answer. But before she could speak, Charlie rushed forward with his little arms outstretched to Hugh.

'Pum-pa!' he cried and Hugh swept him up high, called him Bruiser and seemed to totally forget he'd ever asked a question.

Jackie let out a huff of relief, but she had seen the puzzled, unsettled look in Seth's face. She knew he would ask his question about the envelope again and next time he would expect answers.

———

It was Sunday afternoon before Jackie found the time and the privacy to take another look at the contents of Stella's envelope. Hugh was having an after-lunch nap, and instead of lying down with him as she sometimes did, she headed for the office, telling him she had emails to deal with.

She felt a little sick as she unlocked the drawer in the desk. It was silly. She was probably being melodramatic, but she couldn't shake off a sense of dread. She wished now that she'd dealt with this when it had first arrived.

She'd been foolish to dither. She should have given the envelope straight to Hugh instead of trying to protect him. Hugh would have promptly handled whatever issues these papers raised. The whole matter would have been done with by now.

Resolutely, Jackie pulled the drawer open and found Stella's notes and Magnus's instructions just as she'd left them. Anxious to get to the heart of this quickly, she put the closely written sheets of Stella's diary aside and turned her attention to Magnus's envelope.

There was a letter inside it, written in a strong spiky script on blue-lined paper. There was a brown stain suggesting that something had been spilled by Magnus when he wrote out his instructions. Jackie took a deep breath as she began to read.

Ruthven Downs
19 November 1970

Dear Kenneth,
I am instructing you to change my will. The Drummond family estate must be passed on to my daughter, Deborah.
This must be confidential and I am not prepared to discuss the details with you. My instructions are clear and I want it all, including Ruthven Downs, to go to Deborah.
I am being specific in totally excluding my wife Stella

and her son Hugh. I know you will try to talk me out of this, as you are a family friend, but I have gone through hell recently and this is my decision. My wife knows about this change.

It is all because of Stella that I have been forced into this unhappy situation and she can take responsibility for her son when I am gone. She can survive on the bank account and investments we set up for her after our marriage, but the Ruthven Downs property and estate funds must remain with Deborah and the Drummond family bloodline.

Do not call me or try to discuss this, just proceed to change the necessary documents.

Magnus H Drummond

Jackie read this with a hand clasped over her shocked mouth. Oh, dear God, it was unbelievable.

She read it again, just to be sure, but the message was still just as terrible. Magnus was more or less implying that Hugh wasn't his son.

He hadn't declared this outright, but it was glaringly obvious, reading between the lines.

My wife Stella and her son Hugh . . . she can take responsibility for her son when I am gone . . . the Ruthven Downs property . . . must remain with Deborah and the Drummond family bloodline.

Jackie was shaking so badly she almost tore the letter. The implications of its message were terrible. Hugh should never have inherited Ruthven Downs.

It was almost impossible to contemplate.

She set the distasteful letter down beside Stella's notes and then stood, too upset, too *appalled* to remain seated.

But what on earth should she do? She was too stunned to think straight. She couldn't go running to Hugh with this terrible news, not until she'd thought about it properly.

She began to pace, her arms tightly folded, her shoulders hunched, sick with fear. Now she understood Stella's claim to have done a terrible thing. She'd hidden these instructions.

Obviously, they'd never reached the lawyer. Hugh certainly knew nothing about this letter. He believed he was Magnus's son. And on his father's death Ruthven Downs had passed to him as the only son.

But, dear God, this wasn't what Magnus had wanted. Hugh shouldn't be living here as proud owner of Ruthven Downs. *She* shouldn't be here. Nor Seth and Flora. Or Charlie.

All of this – the homestead, the property, the cattle, their good standing in the district – should never have been theirs in the first place. It should all belong to Deborah.

Oh, God.

Jackie's knees almost gave way. She sagged against a timber filing cabinet. The beautiful life she'd enjoyed here was suddenly completely spoiled. She felt as if her marriage and her happy family life were based on a lie.

Closing her eyes to hold back tears, she tried to picture Deborah's reaction to this sudden revelation. Would she be shocked? Upset? Smugly triumphant?

Jackie couldn't be sure. She'd never really got to know the woman properly. Deborah had always been so aloof and fiercely independent, living as a single mother with that strange son of hers in their hippie-style house in the rainforest at Cape Tribulation.

They hadn't seen enough of each other to get over the hurdles of their differences. It wasn't just the fact that visiting Deborah involved close encounters with pythons and green tree frogs. Jackie had never really felt welcome, and there'd been times when she'd been sure that Deborah resented her comfortable lifestyle here with Hugh.

But she also knew Deborah had rejected Hugh's offers of

financial assistance. Somehow, the woman had scraped together a living for herself and her son by selling her paintings and pottery in local galleries and at tourist markets, which was rather clever of her, really.

Meanwhile, Jackie had been a kept woman, living very contentedly in the family homestead – with two of Deborah's paintings hanging in the dining room and the thousands of acres that should have been hers, not Hugh's.

Oh, Stella, what have you done?

Jackie dashed back to the desk and grabbed Stella's diary pages. She knew Hugh would soon be up, and she had to hurry, so she skipped the rest of Stella's wartime chronicles and turned quickly to the last pages, hoping they might hold a clue to Stella's fateful decision.

Scanning the lines quickly, Jackie couldn't see any mention of hiding the letter. Stella was still writing about Tom Kearney – something about searching for him after the war, and then a secret meeting with him in Cairns.

So perhaps there had been an affair, but there was no mention of Hugh's birth. No suggestion that he was Tom Kearney's son.

Jackie almost groaned aloud with frustration. There were important gaps in this story. Who was Hugh's real father? Why were Magnus's instructions hidden?

How could they ever know the truth, and what on earth should she tell poor Hugh?

He'd devoted his whole life to running this property. Almost every day, he'd risen early and, like all men of the land, he'd worked long hours outdoors in all kinds of weather, dealing with cyclones and floods, as well as drought and bushfires.

Pacing the room again, Jackie thought about the nights Hugh had spent in frosty paddocks, nursing a cow through a difficult labour, and the long sultry days of drought when he'd carted stock feed from one end of the property to the other. She remembered the times he'd worried about falling beef prices, and the time the government had dropped a particularly bad bombshell by suddenly closing down a profitable Asian market.

Hugh had weathered each storm with his customary calm resilience and he'd put every ounce of his being into making this property a success. It would be so unfair to reveal this terrible news to him now, especially with his birthday party so close. She wanted it to be a celebration at the pinnacle of his career as a cattleman.

This last thought brought Jackie to a sudden halt. She knew avoidance was a character fault, but she couldn't tell Hugh about this with the party looming. It would be too cruel. She couldn't bear it.

Jackie couldn't help feeling annoyed with Stella for having left this disturbing puzzle without supplying enough clues. Admittedly, she'd skipped through the final pages very quickly, so she might have overlooked a vital snippet, but it was too late to double-check. She could hear Hugh up and about.

There were still so many questions. Was Tom Kearney involved? Hadn't he promised Stella that he'd find her once the war was over? Stella had known that and she loved him, so why had she married Magnus Drummond?

18

It was only by a miracle that I arrived safely in Australia. Our ship, SS Empire Star, *was heavily attacked by Japanese bombers, but despite massive damage and terrible loss of life, we limped safely to Batavia. Eventually, after repairs, we reached home. I was dreadfully worried about Tom and about the fate of my fellow nurses on the other ships, but the only way to cope was to carry on nursing. I was posted to Townsville, which is where I met Magnus.*

Stella found it hard to adjust to being 'back home'. It didn't help that Townsville was overrun with Americans looking for a good time, while she just wanted to lie low, to live quietly.

At least at the hospital she could throw herself into her nursing, and she was happy to spend her time off quietly reading or sewing, or writing letters. She wrote to Tom's family in England, using an address he had given her, and she asked if they had any news of him. There was an unnervingly long wait before she finally received a rather formal reply from Tom's mother, informing her that her son was alive and imprisoned in Changi.

Stella was so relieved to know Tom was alive that she was

floating on that happiness for days. But as the first relief wore off, she began to worry about the conditions in the gaol and the Japanese treatment of the inmates.

It was impossible to put the Singapore experience behind her. Her new nursing friends found her reluctance to join them at parties and dances quite strange, although they weren't without sympathy. They did understand that she'd been through a very grim time in Singapore and again during the voyage home, and they knew she was very worried about the fate of her fellow nurses on the other two ships that had not yet made it safely back to Australia.

Just the same, they were convinced that she needed 'jollying up'.

'Come on, Stella,' some of the nurses urged. 'The dance halls are full of poor fellows who just need someone to dance with.'

Other girls tried a different tack. 'If you're feeling patriotic, you can dance with the Aussies. We'll take care of the Yanks.'

'Give it a go, Stell. You're such a looker. You'll make some poor soldier's night.'

Stella did go to dances once or twice, just to please them, and she had a pleasant enough time, but she couldn't stop thinking about Tom and the night they'd met at the exotic and glamorous Raffles Hotel. In many ways, she felt as if she was holding her breath now till the war was over and she could see Tom again.

She felt better on the wards, where the routine and discipline of nursing kept her from thinking too much. All the hospitals in Townsville were busy with casualties streaming in from New Guinea and the islands.

Stella worked in a huge, six-hundred-bed tent hospital set up at Pallarenda and she spent long hours on the malaria wards. At other times she went with the ambulances down to the wharf, or to Garbutt Base to greet the incoming patients who came by air. All these men were quickly sorted to determine who would be evacuated south on hospital trains.

But although the hospitals were busy and the wounded still suffered, the conditions in Townsville were close to nursing paradise compared to what Stella had experienced in Singapore and aboard the *Empire Star*.

At least her experiences had given her confidence, not only in her nursing skills, but also in her ability to mix with people and to hold her own in conversations. She realised she was a far more mature person than the excited girl who'd first stepped ashore in Singapore, and she felt as if she'd reached the point where she could handle just about anything the war could throw at her.

She met Magnus Drummond on the malaria ward.

He was a very tall and rather handsome officer, a young lieutenant who'd been fighting in the New Guinea jungles. He had a neat moustache and piercing dark eyes, and a dignified bearing that seemed to suit his name. But he wasn't stuffy. He was typical of the Australian soldiers she was nursing – he never complained and seemed more concerned about the condition of the other members of his unit, who were also being treated, than he was about himself. As far as Stella could tell, he was very friendly and popular with the other men. He was older than them, in his late twenties, while they were barely out of their teens. He was given the affectionate nickname of Old Man.

Once he was well enough to walk around, Lieutenant Drummond would visit the other patients. He wasn't a joker, exactly, but he seemed to spread good humour through the ward, and Stella had seen him reading a newspaper to a young soldier who'd been blinded by a Japanese sniper.

Just the same, Stella might not have taken any special notice of Magnus if she hadn't been on night shift and heard him sobbing in his sleep.

This wasn't uncommon, of course. Several of the men had woken and been disoriented, with no idea they were in a hospital, sure that they were still in the jungle, with the enemy only yards away, skulking about in the dark.

But one night Lieutenant Drummond's distress was worse than anything Stella had previously encountered.

She was sorting out medicines and checking dosages when she heard the yelling and screaming. The commotion was even louder than the aircraft roaring overhead and when she hurried into the ward, Magnus Drummond was sitting up in bed, his hair dishevelled, his dark eyes wild and staring.

'Contact front!' he yelled. 'Contact front!'

Stella spoke calmly as she approached him. 'Lieutenant Drummond, it's all right. You're safe. You're in Australia.'

He turned to her, staring blankly.

'I'm Sister Murray,' she said. 'You're in Australia, in Townsville. In the hospital.'

But he continued to stare at her without any sign of comprehension. And although he was clearly agitated, the expression in his eyes wasn't fear, but quite the opposite. His eyes blazed with a fierce anger that made her step back, suddenly afraid.

His whole body was vibrating with fine tremors, and he seemed to be poised on the edge of some dreadful, violent act.

'Lieutenant Drummond,' she said again as calmly and soothingly as she could.

He turned in her direction, but she knew he wasn't seeing her. He just crouched in the bed, completely disoriented and confused, preparing to launch vengeance on an imaginary enemy as he gripped the steel frames on either side of him so tightly his knuckles were white.

It was very disturbing to see such a normally calm, dignified and friendly man so greatly transformed and deranged. Stella knew there was only one thing she could do. She fetched a doctor, who didn't hesitate to calm the poor man by injecting a sedative.

At the end of her shift, Stella lay awake thinking about the terrible experiences that the men on her wards must have endured, wondering how long this dreadful war was going to last.

And of course, she worried about Tom.

The next day she made a point of visiting Lieutenant Drummond. She thought he might not remember the horrors of the night, but when she found him sitting outside the tent, smoking a cigarette, he looked embarrassed.

'Please forgive me,' he said. 'I believe I terrified you last night.'

Stella shook her head. 'Not at all. I wasn't really frightened, but I was certainly worried.'

There was a chair beside him and she sat. 'I'm no psychiatrist,' she said, 'but I understand it can be good to talk about these things and I'm a very good listener. I'm not easily shocked either. The soldiers in Singapore told me all sorts of horrors about the Japs in Malaya.'

But Magnus shook his head. 'I can't. I certainly can't talk about New Guinea to a woman.' His face was suddenly hard, and his gaze, as he tapped ash from the end of his cigarette, was stony.

Stella took a different tack. 'So, what part of Australia do you come from?' she asked. 'Where's your home?'

'Our place is further north,' he said. 'A family cattle property called Ruthven Downs. In the Cairns hinterland.'

She smiled. 'That's a bit of a coincidence. I grew up on a North Queensland cattle station too.'

His dark eyes lit up with obvious delight. 'Whereabouts?'

'Black Watch Station out west of here, near Hughenden.' She hastened to add, 'We don't own the property. My father's the manager.'

Magnus nodded and she could see the tension in his body begin to ease. 'I miss the bush,' he said quietly. 'Do you?'

'Sometimes.'

He bent down and crushed the stub of his cigarette in the dirt, and when he looked up again his expression was much calmer. 'I miss it badly,' he said quietly. 'I miss the smell of gum leaves in a billy fire. And I miss riding. The rush of air past my face. The movement of a good horse under me.'

He was smiling now, and he really was quite handsome when he smiled. 'I miss the early mornings. The mist along the river, the gentle chatter of finches in the bottlebrush.'

Stella nodded. 'I think it's the peace and quiet of the bush that I miss,' she said, remembering how she'd longed for that peace during the whining of bombs and the terrifying explosions in Singapore. 'I sometimes fantasise about a campfire down by the river. The smell of a good stew cooking in a camp oven on the coals.'

'Ah, yes,' he agreed. 'You can't beat the breathless hush of a camp beside a paperbark creek with that clear green, still water. Or the red glow of an ironbark campfire under a starry sky.'

Stella was used to men from the bush and she'd found many of them to be shy around women, almost tongue-tied. Yet the way this man talked was almost poetic. She supposed his eloquence was the result of a good education.

Now, his chest rose and fell as he drew a deep, steadying breath and let it out again slowly. 'When this is over I'm going home and I'm staying there, for good. I didn't realise how important a patch of scrubby country and an old homestead could be until I thought I'd never see them again.'

These were sentiments Stella could easily relate to and she couldn't help feeling a deep stirring of sympathy.

'That's something to look forward to,' she said.

'I'm certainly sick of travel.' He gave a wry chuckle. 'I should never have left home in the first place.'

She knew he was joking – or half-joking.

'So, were you like the fellows in that Fred Astaire song?' She sang a line or two. '*We joined the navy to see the world. And what did we see? We saw the sea.*'

'Yeah,' said Magnus. 'Except all I saw was desert and jungle.'

'Well, at least you've had variety,' she teased. 'I only saw Singapore.'

'There you go. Proves my point. All those miles and nothing worth seeing.'

He lit another smoke, letting it hang loosely from the corner of his mouth. 'And I won't be leaving North Queensland again. If I make it home, I won't even stray beyond the home paddocks.'

'That's a bit excessive,' she suggested gently.

'Okay. I'll drive down to the front gate to pick up the mail, but I won't leave the district unless there's a very good reason.'

'Such as?'

His eyes flashed with a warmth that surprised her. 'Visiting you out at Hughenden.'

She smiled to cover her surprise, then stood and smoothed down her uniform. Unexpectedly, she remembered the innocent remark she'd made to her mother before she embarked for Singapore.

I'll come home from this war and marry a grazier and have six strapping sons.

How naïve she'd been then, with no knowledge of the life-changing force of real love. Had she honestly thought it would be easy to pick out a suitable husband?

Now, it wasn't an Australian grazier, but a British civil engineer who she desperately hoped would share her life.

19

When the phone rang, Seth was reading Charlie his favourite story about a brown bear. The two of them were together on a beanbag and Charlie, freshly bathed and fed, was nestled between Seth's thighs. This was their nightly ritual and they both knew this story by heart. Charlie took great delight in stabbing the page with his finger whenever he saw Brown Bear.

Now the phone's shrill bell interrupted them and Seth scowled. He was inclined to let it go to voice mail until he remembered that it might be Alice, getting back to him about a planned date for Friday night.

'Hang on a sec, mate,' he told Charlie as he heaved himself up. 'You look at the pictures. I won't be long.'

Charlie looked up with big blue eyes as Seth crossed the room. The kid was so damn cute Seth felt his heart twist.

He was smiling as he lifted the phone. But the caller wasn't Alice. It was an unidentified number.

'Hi, Seth, it's Joanna.'

Joanna?? Fuck. Seth went cold all over.

When Joanna had dumped Charlie, she'd been adamant that there'd be no further contact. About a month after she'd left, Seth had tried to formalise some kind of agreement with her – he had her home address on their employment records. Her reply had been brief and unambiguous.

I am not in a position to be part of your son's life and I will not make any claims on either of you, now or in the future.

Even so, Seth had lived in dread of hearing her plummy English voice again. He'd even had nightmares where she'd turned up at Ruthven Downs to tell him that she'd changed her mind and wanted Charlie back.

'Are you still there?' Joanna said. 'We need to talk.'

Fury surged through Seth. More than anything, he wanted to hang up on her. 'How can I help you, Joanna?'

She gave a nervous little laugh. The sound set his teeth on edge. Why would she be ringing him now, other than to tell him that she'd changed her mind and she wanted Charlie after all?

'Nigel and I are coming out to Australia,' she said. 'And I was hoping to see you.'

'Why?' There wasn't a shred of warmth in his voice. He couldn't help it. He was too shit-scared to think about manners, and before she could answer he jumped in with a challenge. 'Joanna, you promised.'

'I know,' she said in a very small voice that gave him no comfort. 'But let me explain, Seth. You see, I found that I had to tell Nigel about Charlie. It was just too big a secret to keep to myself. It was eating away at me. And then, in the end, when I did tell Nigel, he was amazing. Much more understanding than I'd expected.'

Bully for Nigel, Seth thought uncharitably. He looked across to Charlie who was still sitting innocently where he'd left him, trying to turn the pages of the book and babbling happily to himself about Brown Bear.

'I'd just like to see him,' Joanna said, and Seth could have sworn there was a wobble in her voice. 'I'd like Nigel to meet him too. Just once. And Nigel would like to meet you, Seth. We'd both like to thank you for everything you've done for Charlie.'

'Jesus.' Seth couldn't hold back the profanity. He was sick to the stomach. 'And then what?' he snapped. 'You're not going to ask to have him back?'

'No,' Joanna said. 'I'll keep my promise.'

Seth wished he could believe her. 'So when are you flying over here?'

'We'd like to come next week, if that's okay.'

Seth bit back another swearword, but hell, talk about short notice.

'We'll just make it a very quick visit,' she said. 'We don't need to come out to your farm. I don't think I could face your whole family. Would it be too inconvenient to meet in Mareeba? At a coffee shop, perhaps?'

Seth was damned angry when he disconnected. Against his better judgement, he'd agreed to meet Joanna, but his blood was boiling. Hell, she made it sound so simple and cosy.

How crazy was that? This girl had been ultra-cool about dumping her kid and returning home to the other side of the world. And when she'd left, she'd been convinced that this Nigel bloke wouldn't have a bar of her if she turned up with another man's child.

Now they wanted to have a cosy cuppa, and according to Joanna, Nigel was so sensitive and understanding that he wanted to thank Seth for taking care of his wife's child.

Bullshit.

Seth didn't believe a word of it. That pair wasn't crossing hemispheres and travelling to a remote part of Australia just to sit down and have a cup of coffee and a comfy chat.

Seth was so scared he could hardly breathe.

Charlie was asleep, a miracle that happened more and more easily these days. Some months back, Seth had read a couple of books on managing kids and they'd claimed that having a bedtime ritual helped. So he kept the whole bath, dinner and story routine going in the same order every evening.

It seemed to work.

Now he looked down at his son lying so innocently in his cot and he felt his chest tighten. He thought of the many months that he and the little guy had put in together. It was true he couldn't possibly have managed without the support of his parents, but Charlie wasn't their mistake and Seth had wanted to shoulder the bulk of the burden.

After the stresses and strains of the early weeks, when the crying and feeding had been exhausting and endless, there'd been all kinds of rewards. Charlie's first proper laugh, the first time he'd rolled over, and then when he'd learned to crawl and walk. More recently, the first time he'd said 'Dad'.

Life was so much easier now. Seth found it hard to remember the bad times, like when Charlie was teething, when he would have cheerfully boxed the kid up and posted him off to his mother in England. His son had miraculously morphed from a tiny pink and squirming creature into a proper little bloke with personality in spades. Seth loved his little boy so much now. He couldn't imagine his life without him.

Damn Joanna. Her phone call had left him shaken and hollow inside. All year, the possibility that she'd renege on her deal had nagged at him, but he'd kept telling himself she was too selfish to bother much about Charlie.

Now, it seemed her maternal instincts had caught her out. Problem was, Seth understood that. The whole parenthood thing could creep up on you. For him, the knowledge that he'd unwittingly created another human being had brought overwhelming guilt and a huge sense of obligation. The love and caring had come later.

But how much stronger must those feelings be for the woman who'd actually carried the child, given birth to him and nurtured him through those fragile early weeks? Obviously, Joanna had tried to fight her maternal instincts, but the ties were deep.

And hell, how would Joanna react when she actually saw her kid? Charlie was such a great little guy. His mother was bound to fall for him hook, line and sinker. And this husband of hers was clearly more reasonable and supportive than she'd made out, or he wouldn't have agreed to come out here.

But for pity's sake, what was their plan?

Seth could so easily imagine the pair of them putting all kinds of pressure on him to hand his son over. Nigel's family was aristocracy or something. He was probably used to getting his own way.

Seth looked again at Charlie lying in the glow of a rabbit-shaped night light. Leaning down, he touched his son's soft, warm cheek and suddenly his eyes and throat were stinging.

He turned and left the room quickly.

———

Alice was rather shocked by the leap of excitement she felt when she picked up the phone and heard Seth's voice. She'd been trying to stay calm, to put her feelings for the guy into perspective. They'd both agreed that their relationship should be casual, which obviously meant she should not be thinking about him every spare second. Day *and* night.

Yet Seth had barely said hello before she was grinning from ear to ear and feeling all warm and glowing.

'I was wondering how busy you are next Thursday afternoon,' he said.

Alice calmed down a notch or two. Thursday afternoon was a strange time for a romantic date. What was he planning? 'I have the shop, Seth. I usually don't close until five-thirty.'

'Yeah, I know it's a big ask. But something's come up, a kind of emergency. I could really use your help.'

She could hear the urgency in his voice, but his request was puzzling. It was only Monday now. What kind of emergency could be predicted in advance?

Then again, her shop wasn't exactly busy. She supposed she could put up a sign in her window warning customers ahead of Thursday. 'I could probably help,' she said cautiously. 'Why? What's happened?'

'Charlie's mother wants to see him. She's flying out from England with her husband.'

'Oh.' Alice frowned. 'I thought she wasn't interested in Charlie.'

'Yeah, that's what I thought too.' Seth sounded nervous. After a brief pause he hurried on. 'Look, I know this will sound pretty crazy, but I was wondering if you could help me. Maybe pose as my girlfriend.' He made a small throat-clearing sound. 'Like a serious girlfriend.'

Alice stiffened, suddenly on high alert. 'You mean you want to present me to Charlie's mother and her husband as –' she had to stop to swallow the lump of dread that had lodged in her throat – 'as Charlie's potential stepmother?'

She heard the nervous huff of Seth's breath, as if he'd sensed her resistance.

'Just for one afternoon, Alice. That there'll be two of them against one of me and I don't really trust Joanna to play fair.'

'Oh, God.' She hadn't meant to say that aloud. Seth already seemed stressed and he was asking for her help. But he had no idea how hard this would be for her. 'So, I assume you don't want to give Charlie up?'

'Hell, no.' He sounded shocked that she could even suggest such a thing. 'Look,' he hurried on, 'I'm really sorry to dump this on you. The problem is, I've been out of circulation these past twelve months, and I can't really think of anyone else to ask.'

Alice was remembering the only other time she'd been with Seth's little boy, when he'd squirmed to be out of her arms. She'd felt so inadequate. How on earth could she convince another woman that she was good with small kids? 'But Charlie hardly knows me,' she said.

'I don't think that will be a problem. He's a good little fellow and very friendly.'

Alice winced. She could feel herself slipping into quicksand. Sinking deeper and deeper.

She should have trusted her original instincts and stayed well clear of this man. Seth was gorgeous, but there were always going to be complications involving his son, and she was the wrong woman for him. She'd known that from the start, and yet she'd gleefully gone out with him and then even more gleefully jumped into bed with him.

Whether she liked it or not, she was involved. And Seth was in trouble. The unfairness of his situation was undeniable, and he'd been awesome in the way he'd almost single-handedly cared for Charlie. The thought that Charlie's mother might suddenly swan back in and demand her rights was appalling.

How could she not agree to help him?

'Look, I'll do this,' she said. 'But I can't promise I won't be nervous. I'm really not very experienced with little people.'

'That's fantastic, Alice.' He sounded so relieved. 'I really appreciate it. I know it's a bluff and a bit underhanded, but it's the best I can come up with at short notice.' After a brief pause, Seth said, 'It might help if you could send me a photo. I'll show it to Charlie and talk you up.'

'Right.' Alice might have laughed at the craziness of this, if she hadn't known it was deadly serious for Seth. He was scared. She was scared too. 'What if Joanna wants to push for custody?'

There was a heavy sigh on the other end of the line. 'She reckons she won't do anything like that. And I'm probably overreacting. I just don't want to take any risks.'

'Okay. Fair enough. I've got your mobile number now, so I can send the photo.' Alice tried to sound businesslike to cover the nervous flutters in her stomach.

20

Had she really agreed to Seth's request? Alice couldn't quite believe it. She was always so cautious and she'd only just met the man, and yet here she was, telling him she'd pose as his intended life partner. And yet, despite the bizarreness of the situation, she found herself preparing for the meeting with Charlie's mother with the same conscientious care she might have given to an important job interview.

First, she took the promised selfie and forwarded it to Seth's phone, and then she went through her wardrobe searching for the right clothes. Her natural tendency was towards a slightly hippie-gypsy look, but if she was posing as a potential grazier's wife – yikes, the very thought caused an unexpected flip in her belly – she needed the conservative, casual chic worn by women in country style magazines.

Eventually, she settled on a dusty pink linen shirt and blue jeans and, for jewellery, a simple gold chain and the diamond stud earrings her grandmother had given her for her twenty-first birthday.

Her shoes were more of a problem.

Alice tended to wear flimsy ballet slippers, or delicate sandals, or velvet boots.

In the end she drove over to Atherton in her lunch break and bought a pair of plain brown leather ankle boots. She told herself it wasn't a complete waste of money. Now that she lived in the bush there were bound to be other occasions when she could wear these.

On impulse, she added a neat brown leather handbag with a shoulder strap. It matched the boots and would look much more authentic than her usual drawstring velvet.

When it came to choosing a hairstyle, however, Alice decided to leave her curls free and flowing. Seth seemed to like them, and if she was to be part of his ammunition, she needed to make the most of her assets.

The meeting place was rather more than a café. It was set in an attractive garden in a back street of Mareeba and included a tasting section for local coffee varieties, as well as a chocolate shop, and an extensive area filled with gift items as bright and alluring as Aladdin's cave. A little swing, perfect for Charlie, stood in the shade of a tall bottlebrush tree.

Seth looked surprised when he saw Alice. He gave her a kiss on the cheek and his customary warm smile, but she could see the bemusement in his eyes as he checked her out.

'What is it?' she asked nervously. 'Are my clothes all wrong?'

He grinned. 'No, of course not. You look great. Just – different.'

'I tried to dress like a country woman, a wannabe grazier's wife.'

He smiled crookedly. 'Well, I guess that makes sense, but I didn't realise there was a uniform.'

'Oh, Seth, of course there is. Think about the way your mother dresses.'

He grinned. 'Okay, point taken, but it's not compulsory.' He ran his deliberate blue gaze over her and smiled again. 'You look fabulous, and you're sure to impress Joanna.'

'Well, that's the main thing.' Alice might have felt self-conscious if she hadn't seen the tension in Seth's eyes. 'How are you feeling?'

'All the better for seeing you.' This time his smile did ridiculous things to her insides. Proximity to this man was dangerous. She had to remember the seriousness of this exercise.

She turned her attention to Charlie, who was looking super-adorable, like a miniature man, in denim shorts, a navy polo shirt with green stripes across his chest and very smart sneakers. The clothes were crisp and clean and looked brand new. No doubt Seth had gone to as much trouble with his son's wardrobe as she had with hers.

Ignoring the sudden tightness in her chest, Alice kneeled down to Charlie's height. 'Hello, Charlie.'

He looked at her with big blue eyes that were so much like his Daddy's.

'This is Alice, Charlie,' said Seth. 'The lady in the picture on my phone.'

Comprehension dawned in the little fellow's face. He smiled. 'Alee!'

'That's right,' she said, returning his smile. 'My name's Alee. Clever boy.' The old fears threatened, but she knew she had to ignore them. There was no room for her hang-ups today; she was doing this for Seth, for a higher cause. 'Would you like a ride on the swing?'

Charlie grinned and began to toddle towards the play equipment. Alice glanced at Seth, who nodded his approval, before she lifted Charlie into the swing seat with a safety belt for toddlers. As she buckled him in, the little boy giggled with delight and she began to push gently.

She caught Seth's expression as he stood watching the two of them. Dear heaven, the man was gorgeous. Dangerously so. She concentrated on Charlie, and pushed gently, joining in his excited little squeals.

She was concentrating so carefully on her task that she didn't notice Seth's approach until he was right behind her. Then he slipped his arms around her waist and hugged her from behind, drawing her back against his powerful chest and sending rivers of heat over her skin.

'Just practising,' he murmured close to her ear. 'I guess this is how we should behave if we're madly in love and planning to be married.'

'Married? Oh, yeah, right,' she managed breathlessly. 'I – I guess.' But the images his words created made her head swim. Marriage. In bed with Seth every night. Waking at his side each morning.

'Oh, there you are,' called a very English voice.

Alice turned in Seth's arms to see a smartly dressed young couple loaded with gift-wrapped parcels. Joanna Fox-Richards was blonde and reed slim, with straight hair to her shoulders and blue eyes that were possibly even more like Charlie's than Seth's were. She and her husband were both smiling cautiously.

This was it. Show time.

Alice felt a spurt of pure panic. She only hoped she would be able to give Seth the support he needed.

To her surprise, Seth gave her another quick hug and a kiss on the cheek before he released her. She knew this was for Joanna's benefit, but when he stepped away, she felt instantly bereft. Good grief, for a moment there, Seth's hug had seemed incredibly significant.

She realised now that she'd miscalculated when she'd prepared for this event. She'd been focused on her role with Charlie, but if she wasn't careful, her role as his father's 'intended' could really mess with her head.

It was too late for doubts, though.

As Seth went forward to greet Joanna and Nigel, Alice tried to help Charlie out of the swing.

Of course, he didn't want to cooperate.

'No!' he yelled, scowling and clinging fiercely to the chain handles.

So *not* a good start.

'Come on,' she pleaded gently. 'Come and meet Joanna.'

'No!'

Seth was politely kissing Joanna's cheek and offering Nigel his hand. Alice kneeled down beside Charlie. 'Look!' she whispered. 'The nice lady's brought you presents. All the way from England.'

Perhaps Charlie caught the intentional excitement in her voice. Despite a stubbornly protruding bottom lip, he stared with more interest at the strangers.

And now his father was beckoning to him.

Taking advantage of this momentary distraction, Alice slipped her hands beneath Charlie's armpits and lifted him swiftly out of the swing.

He might have protested, but she hurried to the waiting adults, announcing brightly, 'Here we are. Here's Charlie!'

'Oh!' Joanna's voice broke on the single syllable and Alice's preoccupation with Charlie was suddenly eclipsed by his mother's stricken face.

Joanna's facial muscles were working overtime as she struggled not to cry.

'Oh,' she said again, and her mouth trembled and her eyes shone as she stood there, trying to smile as she stared at her son.

Seth was also watching Joanna's face carefully, his expression stern, almost wooden, his shoulders tense. He was clearly braced for a battle, but he remembered to introduce Alice.

'This is Alice Miller,' he said, placing a possessive arm around her shoulders.

'You must be Seth's girlfriend?'

'She certainly is.' There was a hint of triumph in Seth's voice as he gave Alice a one-armed hug.

'How – how lovely.' Joanna sent a swift glance to her husband, as if she were seeking his support.

Nigel Fox-Richards smiled benignly. He was only a little taller than Joanna, and he was stockily built with a round, ruddy face, a slightly crooked nose and a thatch of thick, tawny hair. To Alice he looked like an affable farmer rather than the snooty Lord of the Manor Seth had claimed him to be.

As Alice shook Joanna's hand, the English girl's gaze zeroed in on her ring finger, which was, of course, lamentably bare. Alice resisted the temptation to rub at the tell-tale patch of skin.

'No ring yet?' Joanna remarked.

Alice gulped and sent a quick glance to Joanna's ring finger, which was impressively stacked with platinum, sapphires and diamonds. 'We haven't had time, have we, Seth?' she said.

Seth blinked.

'The engagement ring, sweetie?'

'Ah, yes. I mean no.'

Alice hoped Joanna didn't notice that Seth was obviously scrambling to adapt to the sudden elevation of their status.

But then he flashed one of his trademark smiles. 'We've only just made the big decision and we're waiting till we can get down to the jewellery shops in Cairns.' He shot Alice a quick glance. 'We're looking forward to it, aren't we, darling?'

Alice nodded. 'There's a much better selection in Cairns.' She managed to keep her smile in place and hoped it didn't look too strained.

Wisely, Seth quickly changed the subject by scooping Charlie into his arms and settling him comfortably on his hip. 'And this, of course, is the star of the show.'

Now, as Joanna looked at her son, her mouth twisted again, and Alice couldn't help feeling sorry for her.

'Hello, Charlie.' Joanna's voice was cracked and squeaky as she clutched at her parcels.

'Say hello to Joanna,' Seth prompted.

Charlie smiled shyly. 'Huwwo.' And then he buried his face in his father's shoulder.

Tears shone in Joanna's eyes and she looked helplessly down at the parcels in her arms.

'You need to offload.' Alice pointed to the round picnic table that she and Seth had earmarked. 'You can put everything here.'

'That's great, thanks.'

Tension lingered as Joanna deposited her parcels, then found a tissue in her pocket, wiped at her eyes and blew her nose. Everyone took a seat. There was a high chair for Charlie, and Alice was relieved when Seth took over strapping him in. She would have fumbled for sure. Then Seth asked for their coffee orders and went to the counter to place them.

Alice, alone with the enemy, so to speak, had at least come prepared. Reaching into her new leather handbag, she found the tiny tractor she'd bought and gave it to Charlie to play with. To her relief, he immediately made growly noises and pushed the toy around the tray of his high chair.

'You obviously know what Charlie likes,' Joanna said.

Alice smiled. 'He's pretty easy to please.'

And now, for the first time, Nigel spoke up. 'He's a very handsome little chap.'

'Yes,' agreed Alice. She almost added that Charlie looked a lot like Joanna, but somehow it felt disloyal to Seth.

'How long have you known Seth and Charlie?' Joanna asked next.

Alice hated lying, but what choice did she have? She could hardly say two weeks. 'A few months.' She glanced over to Seth at the counter, willing him to hurry back, but the pretty waitress was laughing at something he'd said and taking her time in giving him his change.

Meanwhile, Charlie sent his tractor over the edge of the high chair's tray and looked down with amazed delight as it crashed onto the concrete below.

Nigel obligingly reached down and picked it up for him. 'There you go,' he said kindly as he set it back on the tray.

Charlie grabbed the toy and, with a chortle of delight, immediately dropped it over the edge again.

Oh, Charlie. Clearly this was a new game.

This time it was Alice who bent down to get the toy, and she was deliberating whether to give it back to Charlie when Seth returned and Joanna took the opportunity to push her presents across the table.

'They're all for Charlie, I'm afraid. I couldn't resist bringing him a few little things.'

At Joanna's urging, everyone became involved in unwrapping the gifts, and the 'few little things' proved to be a mountain of toys – wooden puzzles, a take-apart plane, a giant fire truck, a set of prehistoric animals, even a knife, fork and spoon set.

Joanna kept apologising. 'I'm sorry. I couldn't help myself.'

Seth's smile had a fixed quality. 'Wow, Charlie. Christmas has come early this year.'

Of course, their coffees arrived in the middle of this and, with paper and toys scattered everywhere, the waitress had trouble finding space on the table for their mugs and the platter of pastries Seth had ordered.

Alice collected the paper and found a bin and by the time she returned, Joanna had taken her place beside Charlie and was showing him a dinosaur and making roaring noises.

'I knew you wouldn't mind,' Joanna said, offering Alice a coy smile.

'No, of course not.' Alice couldn't quite bring herself to return the smile though, and as she took the seat next to Nigel that Joanna had vacated and swapped their coffees, she caught Seth's eye.

He was giving nothing away, but she could tell that he was more tense than ever, as if he was waiting for a time bomb to detonate. She wasn't surprised when he decided to tackle Nigel.

'So what are your plans while you're in Australia?' he asked.

'This meeting was pretty much the sole purpose of our visit.' Nigel nodded towards Charlie and his wife, who were giggling together as Joanna broke a piece of shortbread into small chunks and began to feed them into Charlie's willing mouth. 'Joanna was desperate to see Charlie.'

Seth nodded, but he didn't smile and the muscles in his throat worked as he swallowed. 'When Joanna left last year, she assured me that she didn't want Charlie to be any part of her life. I've been working on that basis.'

The temperature around the table seemed to drop several degrees, and Alice held her breath.

Joanna opened her mouth, but before she could speak, her husband jumped in.

'We understand that, Seth, and Joanna and I are both very grateful to you for taking such good care of Charlie.'

'Grateful?' Seth glared from one to the other. 'I wasn't doing it for you two.'

Alice longed to reach out to Seth, to give his hand a reassuring squeeze, but she was now on the far side of the circular table and he wasn't looking her way.

'You've obviously done a wonderful job,' Joanna said. 'Charlie's so happy and he's positively glowing with good health.'

'And Seth's done it all, almost entirely on his own,' Alice felt compelled to add. 'He even built a cottage, so he and Charlie could have their own home.'

Joanna looked suitably impressed and ever-so-slightly stunned. 'How – how have your parents reacted to Charlie?' she asked Seth.

'They love him,' he told her simply. 'Mum helps with baby-sitting. They've both been fantastic. Supported me every step of the way. Couldn't have been better.'

'Right.' Joanna nodded and, for the first time, looked a tad uncomfortable.

Seth handed her a plastic mug with a lid for Charlie's juice, and Alice was surprised by how isolated she felt on the far side of the table. She was supposed to be demonstrating her motherly skills and Joanna had trumped her. As she watched Joanna pour juice into the mug and offer it to Charlie, she felt as if she'd let Seth down.

'So,' said Nigel, sounding suddenly important and serious, as if he realised the time had come to talk turkey. 'I should explain what Joanna and I were hoping.'

Alice held her breath and she saw Seth's jaw tighten.

'We would very much like to continue to see Charlie from time to time,' Nigel said.

Seth frowned. 'You mean, you want to visit him here?'

Nigel looked to Joanna. 'We'd be happy to come out to Australia once a year or so, but we thought that perhaps, in time, when Charlie's older, he might like to visit us in England too.'

Seth didn't respond at first.

'We'd love Charlie to come to England,' Joanna added anxiously. 'We'd look after him beautifully, Seth.' She fixed him with huge, beseeching blue eyes. 'What do you think?'

'I don't know,' Seth said stubbornly. 'You wouldn't start pushing for him to stay with you full-time, to go to school over there?'

Joanna gave a slow, sad shake of her head. 'Not if you didn't want it.'

'He's an Australian,' Seth said. 'He goes to school here.'

'All right.'

Seth still looked doubtful.

'I never dreamed I'd miss him so badly,' said Joanna.

This brought a rolling of the eyes from Seth. 'I did try to warn you, but you were dead-set certain you could leave him behind.'

'I know.' Tears gleamed in her eyes as she stroked Charlie's soft, golden hair. 'But I couldn't help missing him. I'm his mother.'

'*Jesus.*' A low groan broke from Seth and his hands tensed into fists.

'Joanna,' Alice jumped in quickly, desperate to try to help Seth. 'I don't think you realise what a truly *huge* effort Seth's put into caring for Charlie.'

'Yes, I'm sure –'

'Sorry,' Alice interrupted hotly. 'But I suspect you don't have a bloody clue. You dumped your baby and swanned off to England, knowing full well that Seth was on his own with a whole cattle property to run –'

Seth held up his hand. 'Alice, it's okay,' he said, just as she was getting a full head of steam.

'No, it's not, Seth. Not if –'

She saw the warning in Seth's eyes and stopped, but she didn't appreciate being cut short when she was only trying to stick up for him.

Nigel turned to her with a sympathetic smile. 'We do understand, Alice. I'm not sure I could have coped anywhere near as well as Seth has.'

'But it's not just a matter of coping.' Alice could feel her own emotions churning. She hated to think how Seth must feel. 'Seth's poured his heart into fathering Charlie.'

'I know!' cried Joanna. 'I do understand.' Now her tears spilled, making tracks down her cheeks.

Alice looked again to Charlie, wondering how long it would be before he started to fidget.

'Just tell us what you want,' Joanna said to Seth.

'What I most definitely do *not* want is a custody battle somewhere down the track.'

'That won't happen,' intervened Nigel. 'I give you my word on that.'

'Right,' Seth said carefully.

'But it might be worth drawing up a proper legal agreement, just so everyone's clear,' Nigel added.

Alice let out the breath she'd been holding. This sounded fair, but she could see that Seth was taking his time, letting this new proposal sink in and no doubt trying to look at it from every angle.

The tense silence that hovered over the group as they waited for him to speak was suddenly broken by Charlie.

'Swing!' he demanded, struggling to be free of the seatbelt that held him into his high chair. 'Swing, Ali, swing!'

Seth shot a scant smile to Alice. 'Sounds like he's learned a new word. Would you do the honours?'

'Yes, of course.' Standing quickly, she hurried to Charlie's side. Conscious of Joanna watching her with sharp-eyed attention, she was grateful that she managed to undo the high chair's seatbelt without too much fumbling.

Once free, Charlie almost leaped into Alice's arms, which was rather gratifying, but then she caught a whiff of an ominous smell. 'I think Charlie needs changing.' She tried not to sound too despairing.

Joanna jumped to her feet. 'I'll come and help you.'

Alice quaked. Was she about to be revealed as a fraud? She'd never changed a nappy, not even on a helpless little baby, let alone a squirming, vigorous toddler.

Seth jumped to his feet as well and held his arms out for his son. 'I'd hate you to spoil your afternoon tea. I'll take care of this.'

Alice longed to hand the boy over, but she was supposed to be Charlie's intended stepmother. Wasn't this her supreme test?

'We'll be right, thanks,' she told Seth bravely. And then to Joanna, 'Charlie's very wriggly. It might be worth bringing a couple of toys to distract him.'

Seth looked a tad worried as he handed Alice a small knapsack. 'You should find everything you need in there.'

'Thanks.' She tried for a smile and couldn't quite manage it.

Joanna's smile was wry as they left with Charlie for the parents' room. 'Seth's such a together chap. You've done well.'

'Yes,' Alice said faintly.

21

Seth frowned as he watched the two women leave. *Hell.* He had no idea how Alice would handle this challenge, especially with Joanna hovering over her. He shouldn't have let Alice try to do this. He should have insisted, should have taken charge.

'I know this is tough for you.'

Seth blinked. Joanna's husband was offering him a sympathetic smile. 'Thanks,' he said tightly.

'I must admit I wasn't looking forward to this meeting,' Nigel added. 'It was rather a daunting prospect to be here with my wife, sitting next to my wife's former lover, and with her son being brought up on the far side of the planet.'

Seth was in no mood to sympathise. He gave an offhand shrug. 'It was Joanna's call.'

'I know that, Seth. And the poor girl's poured her heart out to me. She's full of guilt about this. She even admitted that she was the one who hit on you, not the other way round.'

This was a surprise. Carefully, Seth asked, 'Did Joanna also tell you that she left Charlie here because she was scared you'd reject him?'

'Yes.' Nigel sighed. 'She shouldn't have felt that way. I'm in no position to point the finger. For those eighteen months, when we went our separate ways, we agreed we were both free agents.' He shrugged and his mouth tilted in a rueful smile. 'It seemed like a good idea at the time.'

He dropped his gaze to his coffee cup and his ears reddened. 'The thing is, I love her, Seth. I really do.'

This certainly took the wind out of Seth's sails. He'd been braced for a patronising aristocrat, even a bully, but Nigel Fox-Richards was quiet and well-meaning. A regular bloke. Sincere, too.

To Seth's surprise, he liked the man.

'Look – if I were in your shoes,' Nigel went on, 'I'd probably have a barrage of lawyers and a barbwire fence around Charlie.' He reached out his hand to Seth. 'I swear we're not going to try to take him away from you.'

'Thanks.' Seth felt as if a brick had lodged in his throat as he clasped Nigel's hand firmly. 'I must admit I was pretty fired up about this.'

'That's perfectly understandable.'

They looked each other in the eye.

'I can tell just by looking at you, you're a man of your word,' Seth said.

Nigel's eyebrows rose. 'How?'

'You've got a rugby broken nose, mate.'

They laughed together then, a clear declaration of peace, and they might have settled into a discussion about rugby if the girls hadn't reappeared.

Seth wondered how Alice had managed. At least she looked quite relaxed, and Charlie seemed happy enough as he hurried ahead of them.

'All good?' he asked as they arrived.

'Fine.' Alice smiled as she caught his eye. 'Charlie's mum did the honours.'

'Ah,' Seth said with a knowing grin.

It was time to say goodbye. Joanna bade Charlie a tearful farewell, but the little fellow submitted dutifully to her hugs.

'Obviously she's really going to miss him,' Nigel said as they walked to their hire car. 'I don't suppose you two would consider coming to England?'

'Well –' Seth glanced towards Alice, who was studiously avoiding his gaze. 'We'll certainly think about it,' he said. 'Won't we, Alice?'

'Sure,' she muttered.

'I've only travelled in Asia,' Seth added. 'So it's probably time I broadened my horizons.'

'And perhaps we could set up Skype?' said Joanna, when she'd finished wiping her eyes.

'Yes, sure.'

There were more goodbyes, Charlie waved with gratifying enthusiasm, and the Fox-Richards drove off, heading for Kuranda. Joanna lowered her window, shot out a slim arm jangling with silver bracelets and waved. The car disappeared around the corner and Seth felt a huge weight roll from his shoulders.

The rendezvous had gone a hell of a lot better than he'd expected. They'd reached the best possible outcome.

Such a relief.

He got to keep his son. Charlie would grow up knowing his mother and developing an ongoing relationship with her, and Nigel's lawyer would draw up an agreement that could only be finalised when everyone involved, including Seth's lawyer, Brad Woods, was happy with the terms.

It was also good to know he'd been wrong about Joanna. He

could see now that she'd been more confused and scared than cold and heartless, and she'd made the mistake of not trusting the man she loved to stand by her.

He drew a deep breath and let it out slowly, only now realising how very tense he'd been. All week.

Alice took Charlie over for a final swing and he thought how great she was, even going to the trouble of dressing for the part and then sticking up for him. He could have kissed her. Hell, he longed to kiss her now, to tell her how much it had meant to have her at his side.

Damn pity they'd been lying about their relationship.

It wasn't a big lie, but he'd asked a lot of a girl he'd only dated once. Yet they'd worked as a team and it had felt right. Unexpectedly so.

As if she knew he was watching her now, Alice turned from her task at the swing and sent him a smile. 'You must be so relieved to have that behind you. I thought it went well.'

'Yeah, couldn't have been better.' He walked over to her. 'Thanks for your help. I'm sorry I put you through all that, but you were wonderful.'

She didn't look so sure. 'I stuffed up when I threw that in about being engaged. Sorry. Joanna was staring at my ring finger and I said the first thing that jumped into my head.'

Seth couldn't believe she was still stewing over that. 'You're not still worrying about it, are you?'

'Aren't you? Joanna and Nigel will be expecting an engagement announcement. A wedding.'

Seth shrugged. 'It's not really any of their business.' Then he offered what he hoped was a reassuring smile. 'Anyway, we've got plenty of time before we see them again.'

'But don't they want to Skype almost as soon as they get back?'

'To talk to Charlie. Not to grill us about our relationship.' If

Seth hadn't been feeling so relieved and upbeat, Alice's panicked expression might have bruised his ego. But of course, he knew this particular girl had issues. She'd hinted at them last time they'd been together, but he didn't want to open that can of worms now. He'd already had enough tension for one day.

It was late afternoon. Almost all the patrons and tourists had left the café and the gift shop and Seth was looking forward to heading for home, getting Charlie sorted for the evening and unwinding over a beer.

There was only one thing that could improve on that scenario.

'Why don't you come back to my place?' he said. 'I'll cook you dinner to say thank you.'

Alice hesitated, which was no real surprise to Seth. So far, this girl had treated every step of their acquaintance with caution. Except when it came to sex, and then she'd been terrifically spontaneous.

He found the contrast between her carefulness and her passion intriguing. And incredibly addictive.

'Come on,' he urged gently, glad that he had his own place now. A man nudging thirty shouldn't be still living at home, but it had taken Charlie's arrival to kick him into action. 'You've got an hour's drive back to your place and then you'd to have start cooking. Give yourself a night off.'

Alice definitely looked interested, but she didn't say yes.

'I cook a mean steak.'

This time she grinned and she was more gorgeous than ever.

'All right. You've won me. Thanks.'

———

As Alice drove west, following Seth's ute, she wrestled with her usual second thoughts about the wisdom of her decision. Going home with Seth would be totally appropriate if she really was his girlfriend, but their relationship was supposed to be ultra-casual. Absolutely no strings.

But then, she knew how huge this day had been for him. After a week of tension and worry, he was probably experiencing a sense of anticlimax, especially at the thought of going home alone, tending to Charlie, and then sitting down to his dinner on his own. This should be a night for celebration and it was only natural that he might want a little company.

Given her involvement in the day's minor coup, she was the logical person to invite.

Okay, she told herself. *So turn off the stress-o-meter. Relax. Enjoy.*

They veered away from the main road and onto the dirt track that led to the homestead. The sun was a dazzling orb in Alice's line of vision and she lowered the visor against its glare, following at some distance behind the dust thrown up by Seth's ute. When she reached the cattle grid, she slowed down carefully, remembering the other time she'd come here, when she'd been so flustered by meeting Seth.

He still had a brain-melting effect on her, she reminded herself as she pulled up beside his ute under a big old tree. Common sense and self-restraint were needed this evening. Which meant she certainly wasn't going to stay the night, not with his parents living so close.

Ralph the blue cattle dog rushed forward to greet them, tail wagging madly.

'I think he remembers you,' Seth said. 'He likes you.'

'How do you know?'

'He didn't bark.'

Alice was surprised by how much this pleased her. She could almost imagine she was becoming a proper country woman.

Seth unbuckled Charlie, who was tired and grumbling, and slumped with his head on his father's shoulder as they went into the cottage.

'He fell asleep on the way home, so I need to get him fed and into bed quickly before he gets his second wind,' Seth said.

'Sure. What can I do to help?'

He flashed her a grateful grin. 'Would you mind scrambling an egg while I give him a quick bath?'

'Not at all. With toast?'

'Yeah. Toast fingers with a little Vegemite.'

'Yum. Lucky Charlie.'

'And grab yourself a beer from the fridge.'

Alice wasn't really a beer drinker and she still had to drive home, so she made do with a glass of tonic water before finding an egg, milk and butter and settling to her task.

Seth's place was simple, with an L-shaped area for the kitchen, dining and lounge, then two bedrooms and a bathroom. Uncurtained sliding glass doors opened onto a small deck that overlooked the gum-tree-shaded creek.

It was all rather pleasant and homely with Charlie's toys in a basket on the floor beside a brightly coloured beanbag. These items looked new and modern, but the rest of the furniture was clearly second-hand. Alice supposed they were pieces from the homestead. She couldn't imagine that Seth shared her favourite pastime of scouring second-hand shops.

To her surprise, everything seemed to be dust and clutter free. Even more surprisingly, the fridge and the cupboards, although not immaculate, were in pretty good order. It made a nice change from the bachelor pads she'd encountered in Brisbane, where sinks overflowed with a week's worth of dirty dishes and the coffee tables were littered with empty beer stubbies. But then, those guys hadn't had a baby to care for.

Seth's baby.

Alice's breathing faltered, but she fought off the flutters of fear. Everything had gone extremely well today. She'd managed fine in her small role with Charlie and now he was safely back in his father's care.

Relax.

As she whisked egg and milk and added it to a little melted butter in a saucepan, she could hear laughter and splashing from the bathroom. Cosy and comforting sounds as the daylight outside turned to the purple of gathering dusk.

She allowed herself to let go, to shrug aside any fears of catastrophe – Charlie wasn't going to drown in the bath, or slip and smash his head. She even found herself fantasising about living here with Seth and his child. For a heady moment, it felt ever so remotely possible.

There was something very steadying and reassuring about Seth. Perhaps it came from growing up in the bush. Alice suspected that cattlemen had to be capable and resourceful, managing the land and their stock, as well as maintaining structures like fences and buildings, and keeping an eye on the business side of things. Seth was probably good at most things he turned his hand to.

He was blissfully good in bed.

With that breath-robbing thought, she gave the egg mixture an extra stir and took it off the heat, and she was cutting a slice of toast into fingers when there was a knock at the door.

Alice hadn't heard anyone arrive on the verandah, but there was a man on the deck. Tall and broad-shouldered like Seth, he was older, with a pleasantly lined face, silver-grey hair and dark eyes.

'Hey there,' he said, sliding the screen door open. 'I'm Hugh, Seth's father.'

Before Alice could answer, Seth came out of the bathroom with Charlie in his arms.

The little boy, damp and glowing and wrapped in a towel, gave an excited squeal. 'Pum-pa!'

'Dad,' Seth said. 'Thought I heard your voice.'

There was an embarrassed tilt to his father's smile and the glance he sent Alice was almost apologetic. 'I saw the extra ute outside and thought it was Jim Lang's. I wanted to speak to him about rigging up some extra lighting for this damn party next week.'

Seth shook his head. 'I haven't seen Jim in ages. I think he's working out at the mines these days, but if he's in town, I'm sure he'd be happy to help you.' Then he nodded to Alice. 'This is Alice Miller. She fixed up that sideboard mirror for Mum.'

Hugh Drummond's smile was warm. 'Hello, Alice. I'm very pleased to meet you.'

'Yes, it's lovely to meet you.'

'Jackie's thrilled with the mirror,' Hugh added as they shook hands.

'That's great.'

'I – er – ran into Alice in Mareeba,' Seth said. 'We got chatting and . . . ' He gave a shrug, and left the sentence unfinished.

Alice hoped her surprise didn't show. She'd assumed Seth's parents would have known about Joanna's visit.

'I'm sorry I've intruded.' Hugh was already diplomatically retreating to the open door. 'I'll be off.' He gave Alice a quick smiling wave. 'Catch up with you in the morning, Seth.'

'Yeah, okay. I'll be taking another look at that bore at Big Bend. I think the pump's still playing up.'

His father nodded. 'I was meaning to speak to you about that.'

'Pum-pa!' Charlie cried again, clearly disappointed to see his grandfather leaving so soon.

Hugh gave his grandson a wave. 'See you in the morning, too, Bruiser.'

Then he disappeared.

Now it was Seth's turn to look apologetic as his father left. 'I wasn't expecting that. I know you're trying to stay under the radar. Mind you,' he added with a smile, 'it's almost impossible when you live in a country town.'

'I'll cope,' Alice said. She was actually surprised by how unfazed she felt. Some of Seth's cool must have rubbed off on her. 'How do you want to serve Charlie's egg?'

Seth grinned, clearly relieved. 'There's a plastic Humpty Dumpty dish in the cupboard next to the sink. I'll just throw his pyjamas on, and we'll be back in two ticks.'

He was as good as his word. In no time Charlie was dressed and in his high chair, seriously concentrating as he scooped the scrambled egg and steered it precariously towards his little mouth.

'I should probably save his bath till after his dinner, now that he's feeding himself,' Seth said. 'He ends up in such a mess, but I've got this bedtime routine happening that seems to work.'

'If it works, I guess you should probably stick to it. Not that I'm an expert. I know next to nothing about little kids.'

'I suppose I shouldn't get too hung up on routine.' Seth shrugged. 'We'll work something out.'

'You're wonderfully relaxed with him.'

'He's broken me in.' Seth chuckled. 'You should have seen me at first. Scared shitless.'

'I don't doubt it. How on earth did you manage at the start?

Seth shot her a boyish grin. 'I've nursed a baby wallaby and plenty of orphaned calves, getting up to feed them at all hours, so I had a vague idea. And there's all kinds of info on the internet.'

'I'm not sure I could have done it.'

But Seth, having no idea how seriously she meant this, merely waved her comment aside. 'Course you could. Anyway, it comes naturally to sheilas, doesn't it?'

Fortunately, he grinned, as if he didn't expect her to answer this, and as Charlie munched on a finger of Vegemite toast, Seth went to the fridge. He held up a beer. 'Like a cold one?'

Alice shook her head. 'I'm okay, thanks. I had a tonic water.'

'Hell, I guess you prefer wine. I should have stopped at the bottle shop.'

'It's okay, Seth. Honestly. You have plenty of tonic water and I love it, and I still have to drive home tonight.'

The flash of disappointment in his eyes surprised her. Had he expected her to stay?

He was probably quite at ease about having a girl sleep over within sight of his parents' place, but for Alice it was too much like announcing they were 'serious'.

'Your father doesn't know about Joanna and Nigel,' she said, needing to change the subject. 'Didn't you tell your parents?'

Seth shook his head. 'I thought about it, but I knew they'd want to rally around me. Show their support. They probably would have expected to come along to the meeting today.'

'You don't want their support?' As a girl without a family, she found this surprising.

'I knew it would freak Joanna. That's why she wanted to meet in town and not out here. Anyway, it's my problem, not theirs. And Mum's got enough on her plate at the moment with this party for Dad. She's running around like a headless chook. Invited half the district.' He sent Alice a lopsided grin. 'You watch. You'll probably get an invite tomorrow.'

A reaction somewhere between alarm and pleasure rippled through her. 'Would you want me to come?'

He didn't hesitate. 'Of course.'

Dinner was as delicious as Seth had promised.

While he put Charlie to bed, Alice peeled sweet potato, then drizzled it with olive oil, sprinkled it with salt and pepper and wrapped it in foil before popping it in the oven.

She found fresh beans in the fridge and prepared them for steaming with a dab of butter, and by the time this was done, Seth had reappeared without Charlie.

'Fingers crossed,' he whispered.

He nodded towards the deck, and they took their drinks outside and sat on the deck's edge, watching as the dusk deepened the shadows between the white-trunked gums along the creek bank, and the evening star appeared.

It was very quiet and peaceful, with no sound from Charlie, and only the occasional distant bird call. Alice thought how comfortable and happy she was. Here. In this setting. With this man.

She searched her memory, trying to recall a time when she'd felt this same pleasant mix of calmness and excitement, and she knew this evening's happiness was different from anything she'd felt before. Deeper. Sweeter. So close to perfect it was scary.

As darkness fell, they went back inside. Seth had dipped their steaks in a mix of Worcestershire sauce and mustard and now, while he seared the meat and then finished it off on the small barbecue on his deck, Alice set the beans to steam. They ate outside by candle-light, with Ralph sprawled at their feet.

It was wonderfully quiet, with only a background buzz of insects. Alice encouraged Seth to tell her more about his life here on Ruthven Downs, and he told her about his dream to breed stud bulls.

'I can't really interest Dad in my breeding schemes, though.' He looked frustrated as he told her this. 'But I reckon the market is ripe. Buyers are getting really picky and there's a strong interest in really top-quality bulls.'

'I take it you don't mean buyers like me choosing beef at the butcher's?'

'Well, yes, you're important too.' He smiled across the table, his blue eyes sparkling. 'And now you've eaten this beef, you'll be much more choosy.'

'I believe I shall be,' Alice rejoined with a sparkling smile of her own. 'I don't think I've ever eaten steak quite so delicious.'

'But if I had a cattle stud,' Seth continued more earnestly, 'I'd be selling to other cattlemen who were looking to buy bulls with a high breeding value. The local beef producers want cattle bred in the north that have already adapted to our conditions – ticks and buffalo fly and the tropical heat.'

Alice could see this was something that really mattered to Seth, and she was surprised by her own flare of interest. There was something extra-attractive about a guy with ambitions.

'So I guess you're looking forward to when your father retires and you can do your own thing,' she suggested carefully. 'Is that likely to happen any time soon?'

'Mum's busily planning his retirement for him.' Seth smiled. 'I reckon she'd get Dad back to Europe in a flash if she could, but I'm not sure that he's actually ready to let go of the reins.'

Perhaps he's waiting for you to get married, Alice thought, and then she hastily switched her thoughts elsewhere. Anywhere . . .

'Anyway . . .' Seth reached across the table and briefly touched the back of her hand.

So ridiculous the way a simple brush of his fingers could set off hot flashes all over her skin.

'There's no hurry,' he said softly.

She supposed he meant there was no hurry to get the cattle business sorted, but already her mind was rushing on a completely different tangent and she was thinking about his rather marvellous, unhurried lovemaking skills.

Perhaps it was just as well that a large moth chose that same moment to dive-bomb their candle flame, snuffing it out.

'A kamikaze moth,' Seth said quietly and, without a hint of flirtatiousness, he rose and began to gather up their plates.

Alice followed him inside.

'Your veggies were great,' she said as he put the dishes in the sink. 'I'll have to remember to bake the sweet potato in foil.'

She smiled and stood a little awkwardly in the middle of his living room, looking around as she tried to remember where she'd left her phone and car keys.

'Coffee?' Seth asked. 'To keep you alert for the trip home?'

Alice was sure she should leave now, before she had more errant thoughts about staying. And yet, she nodded. 'Yes, coffee's a good idea.'

'Plunger? Instant? I don't have a fancy machine.'

'Instant's fine.'

Crazily, she found herself watching his every move as he filled the kettle, selected mugs, spooned in coffee. His hands were big, squarish and tanned. Outdoor hands. And she was helplessly fascinated by the sight of them performing simple kitchen tasks.

'Do you take sugar?'

Alice blinked. 'Sugar? Um – no – thanks.'

Seth's smile was quizzical and she hoped he couldn't guess that her thoughts had taken off again.

There were only two armchairs, beautiful old, upholstered things, with carved silky-oak arms and cane inserts in the sides. They took a chair each and Alice told herself she was grateful there wasn't a sofa.

She sat rather demurely sipping her coffee, while Seth sprawled, legs comfortably apart. They talked about safe topics like Burralea, and the people she'd met. Tammy, Ben in the pie shop, Brad Woods and his wife. Her customers. They discussed the possibility of a walk together with Charlie, following the rainforest track around one of the lakes. *Some time.*

They didn't talk about taking Charlie to England. Well, of course they wouldn't.

Alice finished her coffee and rose, holding out her hand for Seth's mug.

'Thanks.'

She set his empty mug with hers on top of the plates in the sink. 'I can stack the dishwasher.'

'Don't you dare.' Seth was still in the armchair, supposedly relaxed, but the guarded watchfulness in his eyes couldn't quite hide the smoulder of desire.

He wanted her.

A thousand tiny wings fluttered in Alice's chest. He wanted her. She didn't want to leave. She spied her keys and phone beside the fruit bowl on the kitchen counter. 'I'd better get going,' she said, but she made no move.

Seth smiled a little sadly.

She felt a little pang.

Go, Alice. Get out of here. You're not right for him.

As her hand closed around the car keys, he said, 'All week I've been checking your photo on my phone, to make sure I didn't just dream how lovely you are.'

She felt suddenly as fragile as a soap bubble, pretty and shiny, suspended in the moment before vanishing into thin air. In the next heartbeat, she was crossing the room to him. Another beat and she was astride his thighs.

She saw the surprise in his eyes and knew it was the same surprise reflected in her own. She'd never done anything remotely this brazen before, not even at a drunken party, and now she was stone-cold sober. Her heart was thundering as she felt his solid denim-covered thighs beneath her. He lifted a hand to a curling tendril of hair, let his fingers trace a shiver-sweet trail down her cheek to her chin. At last, he leaned in and by the time his lips touched hers, she was already lost to reason and common sense.

To her relief, he didn't ask if she'd changed her mind about leaving. He knew her answer and he rose from the chair, bringing her with him, her legs locked around his waist, his strong arms wrapped around her. And he didn't stop kissing her lips, her jaw, her throat, as he carried her down the short hallway.

The lights in the homestead were out when Alice left around midnight. At least there were no barking dogs and she prayed that the sweeping arc of her headlights didn't reach the window where Seth's parents slept.

As she made her bumpy way down the track, moonlight painted the paddocks bright silver. She saw the distant silhouette of a row of huge pine trees. Closer, she saw owls with big white faces perched on fence posts, no doubt on the lookout for mice. She saw the moon hanging in the sky like a shiny metal plate, and she thought how special it was to see all these secret midnight things. So different from driving home in the city.

For half an hour or so, she drove happily, wrapped in the warm afterglow of making love with Seth. It was only as she turned onto a back road that skirted the little village of Tolga that she came back to earth and remembered how foolish she'd been.

She'd let the day's success go to her head, and somewhere in the mix, she must have convinced herself that she could handle a relationship with Seth, and with his son. But of course, caring for Charlie had been easy today with Seth there to back her up every step of the way.

In reality, she'd done little more than push the boy on a swing and scramble an egg. She hadn't actually fed him or bathed him or read him a story. She hadn't even been required to change his nappy. Joanna had happily taken care of that.

And yet, if she continued to see Seth on a regular basis, the day would surely come when she would have to mind Charlie on her own.

Then she would panic.

Just thinking about it brought hot flurries of terror now, so much so that she forgot to dip her headlights from high beam, causing the driver of the truck coming towards her to flash his bright lights in her eyes and give a loud blast of his horn.

Alice jumped and almost swerved off the road into a ditch. Her heart raced and her palms were damp as she drove on, super-carefully.

She was still on edge when she reached home, and she took ages to get to sleep. When she did, she dreamed about Charlie, but somehow he became Humpty Dumpty and he fell off a wall and the doctors couldn't save him. She woke at dawn in a cold sweat.

22

Jackie was up early, pottering in the garden, pulling a few weeds and doing a little pruning before it got too hot. She loved the cool quiet of the mornings with only the bird calls for company. She noticed a couple of pot plants that needed watering and attended to them, filling a watering can from the side tap.

By the time she'd pulled off her gardening gloves and stowed them with her secateurs on a shelf in the laundry, Seth and Charlie were in the kitchen. Seth was accepting Hugh's offer of coffee, and pouring Charlie a tumbler of milk.

Jackie beamed at them. She'd been thrilled last night when Hugh had come home to report that Alice Miller was in Seth's kitchen, scrambling an egg for Charlie, no less. However, she refrained from mentioning this immediately. 'Dad says that bore pump's still playing up,' she said instead.

'Yeah. I'm going to take another look at it.' Seth touched his coffee mug to his father's. 'Cheers, Dad. Might need you to cast your expert eye over it.'

Hugh grinned. He'd always been better with mechanical issues than Seth. 'Yeah, that's okay, son, but I might get you to do something for me.'

'What's that?'

'Bring that nice girl of yours along to my party to brighten the place up a bit.'

'Yeah, sure.' Seth concentrated on setting his mug on the table and helping himself to a little extra sugar.

Jackie remembered that Seth had been guarded and offhand when she'd previously raised the subject of Alice. She was sure it meant he cared, and he didn't want his family stuffing things up for him.

As Seth finished stirring his coffee he sent her a sharp, searching glance. 'Have you managed to take another look at those things Alice found behind the mirror, Mum?'

Jackie felt a flash of sharp panic. She'd been meaning to warn Seth against raising this subject.

'What things?' asked Hugh.

Seth shrugged. 'Some sort of diary that Gran kept during the war.'

'Excuse me? A diary? My mother kept a diary?' Hugh frowned as he turned from his son to his wife. 'Did you know about this, Jackie?'

Jackie wished she could disappear. Sink through the floorboards, go up in smoke, or at the very least, faint like a heroine in an old-fashioned romance novel. Instead, the floorboards stayed solidly beneath her and she remained inconveniently upright, while her husband and son stared at her. Waiting for her answer.

What could she say? She couldn't tell Hugh everything. Not now, in front of Seth. Her heart hammered so loudly it seemed to be banging in her ears.

'I – I've only glanced at it,' she said, avoiding Hugh's puzzled frown.

'But – you've found a diary of my mother's?'

'Alice found it,' Jackie corrected. She knew she was splitting hairs, but she was fighting for time, trying to *think*. 'Alice found it when she re-silvered the sideboard mirror. But it's not a proper diary, just a few pages of notes.'

'So? Why didn't you tell me about it?'

'I'm sorry. I've been distracted. You know – with the party and everything.' This was *almost* true.

Hugh didn't look the slightest bit convinced. 'You obviously had time to tell Seth.'

'*No*. Alice told Seth – when she brought the envelope out here –' Jackie stopped, knowing she was digging a deeper and deeper hole for herself.

Hugh had set his mug on the kitchen table, as if he'd lost all interest in drinking it, and he stood facing Jackie squarely with his arms crossed over his chest. His expression was uncharacteristically wary and watchful, his eyes narrowed.

Jackie could tell that he was thinking hard, trying to work out why she might keep such a significant find to herself.

The silence in the kitchen was thunderous. Somewhere outside a distant cow bellowed.

At last, very quietly, Hugh said, 'What's going on?' His dark eyes were intense. 'It's strange enough that my mother would hide her diary, or whatever it is, in the first place. But now – if you're hiding it too –'

He gave a slow shake of his head. The muscles in his throat worked. 'You're not trying to protect me from bad news, are you?'

Jackie's heart slammed. What on earth could she say? She could feel tears welling behind her eyes and prickling her throat. She knew she was on the brink of telling him.

But she couldn't lift the lid on this problem now. Not when the party was so close, with everything planned and steaming full speed ahead. She had to bluff her way through it. To somehow try to stop Hugh.

'I've only read bits,' she said. 'I know you should have been the first one to read it, Hugh. But the thing was – I – I was actually saving it for you.' Suddenly she had a brainwave, the only solution possible. 'I was saving it for your birthday. It was going to be part of your present. A surprise!'

Seth, who'd been staring from one parent to the other with puzzled interest, now looked abashed. 'Sorry, Mum. You never said.'

Jackie ignored him. She was too busy holding her breath, waiting for her husband's response to this unforgivable lie.

Seth must have realised that Charlie was no longer in the room, and he went off to find him, calling his name.

Hugh's smile was uncertain. 'That's – a nice thought to surprise me.' But he still didn't look totally convinced. His smile faded and the puzzlement lingered.

From down the hallway came the sound of Charlie's giggles as Seth caught up with him.

Hugh switched his gaze to the view through the kitchen window. He seemed to stare way off to a distant paddock where eagles had nested in a dead tree. Last week Jackie had joked with him about this precarious home for the noble eagles' offspring, a haphazard handful of twigs shoved into the tree's fork. Last week, their own world had been safe and secure.

Seth popped his head around the kitchen doorway. He had Charlie propped on one hip and he eyed his parents cautiously. 'If you guys don't need me, I might head off to start working on that bore,' he said.

Jackie and Hugh spoke together.

'All right.'

'Yes, sure.'

'I'll mind Charlie,' Jackie said, holding out her arms for her grandson.

'I'll be out there shortly, son,' said Hugh.

Seth hesitated a moment, watching with a baffled smile as if he was waiting for his parents to say something else.

'Say bye-bye to Daddy,' said Jackie, just a little too brightly, as she gave Seth a wave. 'See you later.'

As soon as Seth left, Hugh rounded on her. 'So what's this diary about?'

Jackie's heart took off again, but somehow she kept her voice steady. 'It seems to be mostly about the war. When Stella was a nurse in Singapore.'

His eyes widened. 'That sounds interesting. I'd like to read it.'

'Now?'

He shrugged. 'Well, we've kind of spoiled the surprise, haven't we?'

'I guess.' But Jackie was thinking of those fateful opening words in Stella's diary.

I have done a terrible thing . . .

If ever there were words that raised questions, these did, especially when they were part of a message from a mother to her children. As soon as Hugh read this, he would want to know everything. He would scour Stella's diary, reading much more closely than his wife had.

Now Jackie wished she'd read those last few pages carefully to make sure there was no mention of Magnus's instructions to his lawyer.

'Seth wants you to check the bore and I need to give Charlie his breakfast. I'll have it ready for you when you get back,' she said, setting Charlie down.

'Where is it?' Hugh asked.

Jackie stared at her husband, stunned by his uncharacteristic firmness.

'It's in the office.' She went to the pantry cupboard to get Charlie's porridge. 'Why?'

'Obviously, I'd like to read it.' Hugh spoke with excessive patience. 'And I'd like to see it now.'

'But the bore –'

'Forget the bore. It can wait.'

'And Charlie needs his breakfast.'

'Jackie, for heaven's sake.'

'Oh, all right,' she snapped, slamming the pantry door closed. 'Sit tight and I'll bring it to you.'

Hugh blinked, clearly surprised by her tone. *Damn*. She was only making things worse by letting him see that she was rattled.

She drew a quick breath, trying to calm down. 'If you'll keep an eye on Charlie, I'll be back in a moment,' she said quietly. And with eyes demurely downcast, she left the room.

By the time Jackie had reached the desk, she'd hatched a new plan. She took out Stella's closely written pages and smoothed them with shaking hands.

Then, carefully, she removed the top page and the last three pages and put them back in the drawer. She was confident that these middle pages weren't especially problematic and, with luck, they would keep her husband happy for now. No, not just for now, but until after the party.

She couldn't quite believe she was being so duplicitous. These hidden documents were a serious threat to Hugh's, and the entire family's, happiness. And yet, she'd let a birthday party take priority.

Was she really so dreadfully shallow? It was only a party, for heaven's sake. She'd let the whole thing get out of hand.

If she was honest, she knew she should seriously consider cancelling the party while they attended to this problem. After all, it had the potential to upset the entire family.

Standing in the middle of the study, the diary pages in her hand,

Jackie pictured ringing her friends, ringing everyone on the guest list and telling them the party was off, telling Maria not to bother with the lasagnes, telling Christy Hargreaves they wouldn't need her Moroccan salad. Telling Flora – oh, dear, if there was a crisis, perhaps Flora should still come home. But she shouldn't bring Oliver, should she?

Jackie's mind spun. She imagined going out to the kitchen to Hugh, handing him all the documents and telling him that the party would have to be cancelled. She pictured his face, and felt her mouth pull out of shape as tears threatened.

Calm down.

She took several deep breaths and tried to think clearly. Perhaps her original plan was okay. Perhaps she should stick to it.

Yes, she should give Hugh these few pages, and then they'd deal with everything else later. Straight after the party. Squaring her shoulders, she felt better. She left the study.

In the hallway she checked her reflection in the mirror and was alarmed to see how pale and strained she looked. She pinched her cheeks and practised smiling and, after several tries, decided she looked marginally calmer.

Okay, let's get this over with.

She found Hugh in the kitchen feeding Charlie pieces of banana. 'Here you are,' she said. 'I'm afraid it's not in a book. It's just pages – more like a long letter. I hope it's in order.'

'Thanks, love.' Hugh accepted the folded pages without examining them. He set them on the table and reached for Jackie's hand. 'Sorry I got stroppy.' He rubbed his thumb affectionately over the back of her hand. 'It's just that the whole business seems strange. I'm puzzled about why Mum would hide something like this.'

'I know.' Jackie gave what she hoped was a nonchalant shrug. 'You might find out if you read it properly.' Bending down, she kissed his creased forehead. 'And try not to worry. We need to aim for a lovely, smooth lead-in to your party.'

Hugh grinned. 'Yeah, right,' he said dryly.

He stood, folded the pages and put them in the button-down pocket of his work shirt. As he left the room, Jackie wished she could follow her own good advice about trying not to worry. But first, she had to read those last pages of Stella's properly.

23

I waited so long for the end of the war, never dreaming it would bring me the greatest heartbreak of all.

So many times during the long years of the war, Stella had tried to imagine her homecoming. She'd longed to see her parents, to feel the warmth of their welcoming hugs and to know that she could stay at home for as long as she wanted to.

She'd imagined quiet afternoons on the verandah, chatting with neighbours over a cuppa, playing cards perhaps. She'd dreamed of riding her horse along the river bank, joking with her brothers and listening to their stories – it was years since she'd seen them.

When the war's end finally arrived, however, her return home was different from her fantasies in almost every way possible.

To begin with, her little brother Mark, who'd been old enough to enlist for the last year of the war, was killed in Borneo just a few weeks before the Japanese surrender. This tragic news was a dreadful blow, made harder to bear by the fact that Stella's other brother, Stephen, was still in Japan as part of the Occupation Force. He was waiting for a troop ship and had no idea when he would be home.

To make matters even worse, Stella now knew that her friends and many others who'd left Singapore on the other two ships, the *Vyner Brooke* and *Wah Sui,* had lost their lives. This news weighed extra-heavily on Stella's heart.

But there was yet another blow – the cattle property that she had always regarded as her home had been sold. The owner, referred to by everyone in the district as Young Mr MacArthur, had been a bomber pilot with the RAAF, and when he was killed during the fighting in Europe, his aged parents had arranged for the property to be sold quickly.

Stella's parents had been left with no choice but to move, to manage a new place, much further west. The country was dry and inhospitable, and the new homestead was little more than an ugly fibro shed, so very different from the rambling, verandah-wrapped Queenslander of Stella's childhood. There were no shade trees here, and the yard was bare and stony with straggling weeds instead of a pretty garden.

Sadly, Stella's mother was so grief-stricken and dispirited after losing Mark that she hadn't the heart to brighten the place with her usual home-making touches. Stella did her best with the garden, but it was the middle of the dry season and she couldn't achieve much.

Of course, she never stopped worrying about Tom, but given her parents' grief, her concerns for a man she'd met briefly at the beginning of the war felt rather self-indulgent. She kept her worries to herself, but she scoured the newspapers that eventually reached them, hunting for information about the British Army in Singapore, and she wept over the dreadful photos of the emaciated prisoners.

Stella also wrote to Tom's family again, asking after Tom and informing his parents of her change of address. Each week dragged as she waited for the post, but there was no response from the Kearneys.

Then, the most surprising thing happened.

She was sitting at the kitchen table with her mother, slicing onions for a beef stew, and wishing they had carrots or beans to add to the pot, when they heard the sound of a vehicle.

'Car coming,' her mum commented, without looking up from the potatoes she was peeling.

A visitor was a complete novelty. Stella, being curious, went to the kitchen window to watch the cloud of dust bowling towards them over the flat, treeless plain.

She wondered what they had to offer a guest. She'd made a batch of Anzac biscuits a few days earlier, and she tried to remember how many were left. If the visitor stayed long enough, she might have time for a hasty batch of scones.

'I hope it's not someone wanting to see your father,' her mum remarked dolefully. 'He's way out riding the boundaries, won't be back till sundown.'

'You never know, it could be Stephen.'

Her mother frowned, gave a doubtful shake of her head, but then she must have reconsidered this possibility. She paused in the middle of her peeling, and hope flared in her tired blue eyes, showing a brief glimpse of the pretty women she'd once been.

Stella bit her lip, wishing she hadn't spoken the thought aloud. There was every chance the caller wouldn't be Stephen, and the last thing she wanted was to cause unnecessary disappointment for her mother.

'Better get these things into the stew, so we can tidy up,' she said.

Quickly, she slid the onions from the chopping board into the pot and helped her mum to finish the potatoes. She put the potato peelings into the chook bucket, then wrapped the onion skins in newspaper and took them to the bin outside the kitchen door. While her mum wiped the tabletop, Stella washed her hands at the sink, and watched through the window as a truck emerged from the dust cloud.

There was little time to check her appearance. The truck was already pulling up at the rusty front gate. The dogs barked, straining on their chains. Stella hated having them tied up, but it was necessary here at this new place. There were dingoes about and her father hadn't yet managed to mend the fence around the house.

'Quiet!' her mother yelled at the dogs as she hurried to open the front door.

Stella stayed at the kitchen window, watching as a tall, manly figure climbed down from the truck. His dark hair was cut short, back and sides, and he had a neat moustache. Even in civilian clothes – dark trousers and a white shirt – there was no mistaking his military bearing. The shock-wave of recognition made her gasp.

Good heavens. It was Magnus Drummond.

Stella was so surprised, she had to cling to the edge of the sink. How on earth had he found her?

It was eighteen months since she'd last seen him in Townsville. At the time, he'd been on leave and had sought her out at the hospital. He'd persuaded her to have dinner with him and to walk with him in the moonlight along Townsville's Strand. She'd known he was keen on her – she would have needed to be blind not to have seen that. Nevertheless, there was no 'understanding' between them.

Now, her stomach knotted with a bewildering mix of excitement and dismay. Magnus Drummond had come all this way, and her mother had taken off her apron and hurried down the hall. Already, she was opening the front door to him.

Slightly dizzy, Stella kept her grip on the sink as she drew calming breaths. She heard his deep voice.

'Good morning. Are you Mrs Murray?'

Her mother responded politely. 'Yes, that's right. How can I help you?'

'I was hoping that Stella might be home.'

'Oh? Oh, yes. Yes, she is. Oh – oh, just a minute, I'll get her.' Her mother's quick footsteps pattered down the short hall. 'Stella!' she called, her voice high-pitched with excitement.

When she came into the kitchen her eyes were huge and shining. Small spots of pink showed in her cheeks. 'You have a visitor,' she said, in a stage whisper.

Stella nodded.

'I'll put the kettle on,' her mother said next, motioning for Stella to go to him.

'I can look after making the tea.'

'For heaven's sake, girl, don't be silly. Go and entertain your visitor.'

Stella wished the hallway were longer, wished she had more time to compose herself, but suddenly she was there in the small ugly lounge room, crammed with the furniture her parents had brought from their old house.

The tall man standing in the middle of the room made the space feel even more crowded.

He smiled when he saw her. 'Stella, hello. How lovely to see you again. It's been such a long time.'

She held out her hand to him. 'This is a surprise, Lieutenant Drummond.'

He smiled. 'You'll have to call me Magnus now. I've been demobbed.'

'You must be so pleased about that. You seem fit and well.' She knew she was talking too formally, like a nurse to a patient. She couldn't help herself.

If Magnus noticed, he didn't show that he minded. 'Yes, I'm completely recovered.' He favoured her with another smile. 'You look well, Stella.'

'I'm very well, thank you. I – ah – I imagine you've been home to your property? I hope you found it in good condition.'

'Not in too bad a shape, thank goodness. I'd de-stocked before I enlisted, so there were no cattle to worry about. Grass a mile high in places.'

'Really? So there's no drought up your way?'

'No, quite the opposite. We're harvesting stock feed to send south.' Again Magnus smiled, and he really was quite handsome when he smiled. 'It was a huge relief to see the old place again.'

Now he looked about him at the empty armchairs, and Stella, whose mind had been racing in several directions at once, remembered her role as hostess. 'Please, take a seat. You've come such a long way. My mother's just making us some tea.'

'How kind. Thank you.'

Stella sat rather stiffly, while Magnus seemed completely relaxed, crossing one long leg easily over the other. She had to admit that his commanding demeanour gave their shabby lounge room a certain touch of class.

'How did you find us?' She had to ask. 'My parents moved here only recently.'

'It wasn't hard,' he said. 'Most people I asked seemed to know your father. He's a highly respected cattleman.'

Stella couldn't help being pleased to hear this. 'So you're out this way on business?'

'In a manner of speaking, but my business is purely social.' Another smile. 'You must know, Stella. I came to see you.'

She couldn't think how to respond to this. Back in Townsville, Magnus had told her that he would come to find her after the war, but she hadn't really believed that he meant it.

Tom Kearney had made the same promise, and her head and heart had remained filled to the brim with her longing to see *him*.

Now, she felt a stirring of panic, almost as if she was falling into a trap. *Where are you, Tom? Please, please write.*

She was rather grateful that her mother appeared just then,

carrying a tray loaded with the tea things, including the plate of Anzacs.

Immediately, Magnus leaped to his feet and Stella's mother, who wasn't used to such gallant manners, actually blushed. Stella was glad for the distraction of pouring the tea and enquiring whether he took milk or sugar, offering the biscuits.

As the three of them sipped their tea, she explained to her mother that she'd met Mr Drummond in Townsville.

'How nice,' her mum said, beaming at them both.

'Your daughter's a wonderful nurse, Mrs Murray.'

Her mother nodded enthusiastically. 'We always knew Stella would make a good nurse. You should have seen her with sick animals when she was little.' She turned to Stella, her eyes wide with excitement. 'Remember that time you raised the baby bandicoot using powdered milk in a fountain-pen filler?'

'Mum, I don't think Mr Drummond wants to hear –'

'Indeed I do,' Magnus interrupted. 'It sounds like a charming story.'

'Well, perhaps I should let Stella tell you,' her mother said next, and she swallowed her tea so fast she was in danger of scalding herself. 'You two young people can have a nice catch-up chat. But I'm afraid I can't sit around all day. I have outside chores to see to.'

Stella knew this wasn't true. The chickens had been fed and the washing was pegged out, but she could hardly argue with her mother. In no time at all, she heard the back door open then shut, and she was alone in the house with Magnus Drummond.

Unmistakable fondness shone in his dark eyes. 'Stella, I'm sorry I couldn't warn you I was coming.'

'I – I understand. It's not easy when we don't have a telephone.'

'Are you living here alone with your parents?'

'Yes. One of my brothers was killed at Balikpapan and the other is still in Japan.'

'I'm so sorry.' Magnus spoke with evident sincerity. 'I wish I'd known. I would have offered my condolences to your mother.'

'It's all right,' she said. 'Sometimes it's easier not to talk about the war.'

For the first time since he'd arrived, his face tightened. 'I won't argue with that.'

Stella remembered his night-time terrors. Since then, she'd nursed a lot of men who'd been similarly affected. It was more than likely that Magnus would never want to talk about his wartime experiences. The memories were simply too horrendous.

Magnus carefully set his teacup and saucer back on the tray, and then he sat a little straighter.

'Stella,' he said, 'I know this is awkward. I would have liked time to court you properly, to show you Ruthven Downs.'

'Ruthven Downs sounds Scottish. I guess Drummond is a Scottish name?'

Stella knew she was asking these questions partly to distract Magnus from the subject of courtship, but she couldn't deny that she was also interested in his property. It sounded very fine.

'That's right,' Magnus was saying. 'My father came out from Scotland as a young lad. He was quite a pioneer.' Now he rose to his feet and came towards Stella. She was still sitting and he seemed to tower above her.

'Stella, you must know why I've come.'

Her chest tightened and she had difficulty breathing.

Magnus bent forward, reached down for her hand, which she was sure must be icy cold, but he didn't seem to mind. Clasping her hand firmly, he drew her towards him with surprising gentleness. She felt slightly mesmerised as she rose from her chair.

His dark eyes glowed with a fierce new light. 'You're a wonderful woman,' he said. 'You're beautiful, and you're clever and kind. I can't think of any woman I regard more highly.'

Magnus swallowed. It was the only sign that hinted he might be nervous. Meanwhile, Stella felt strangely numb all over.

'I'm hoping that you might do me the huge honour of becoming my wife,' he said.

'Oh . . .' Her mind went blank.

How dreadful to be tongue-tied at such an important moment. The poor man. Stella tried again. 'I'm the one who must feel honoured, Mr Drum– I mean, Magnus.' She tried to look into his face, but she couldn't quite meet his hopeful gaze. 'But you are right. This proposal *is* very sudden. And – and quite unexpected. I really do feel that I need time to – to –'

To wait till I hear from Tom.

A picture of Tom's face swam before Stella. She saw his sparkling eyes and his lovely, face-crinkling smile. She remembered the wonderful night at Raffles, the way her heart had seemed to *know,* right from the very start, that Tom was The One. And, of course, she was remembering his kiss beneath the poinciana tree on Orchard Road. She could still recall the exact sweet and perfect pressure of his lips on hers. Then his kiss goodbye at the hospital.

Magnus held her hand a moment longer before releasing it. 'Of course, I should have known you're too sensible to rush into anything impetuous. I'm happy to give you time to consider this, Stella. Not too long, mind you.' He added this last comment with a charming smile.

Stella nodded. There were moments when she felt she really could like this man. He was faultless, really.

'Perhaps you'd also like to make the trip north at some point, to see where I live?' he said.

She gave another nod. 'Perhaps – yes, thank you.'

'I have your address now, so we can keep in touch. I'm assuming you don't mind if I write to you?'

'No. No, of course not. I'd like that.' Although it was a letter from a certain Englishman that she wished for with all her heart. Thank heavens Magnus wasn't a mind-reader.

As he turned towards the door, Stella felt bad that he assumed he must leave so soon after coming such a long way over the rough beef roads.

'You'll stay for lunch, won't you?' she asked, wishing she had more to offer than cold corned beef and tinned beans.

Magnus hesitated, clearly considering this invitation, but then, with a hard-to-read glance around the shabby lounge room, he shook his head. 'Thank you. That's very kind, but I'd better head off. I'd like to get back to Charters Towers by this evening.'

Stella accepted this. Under the circumstances, she supposed that even if the food had been sumptuous, their lunchtime conversation would have been strained. She walked with him to the rusty front gate. Fortunately, the dogs didn't bark this time, and Magnus kissed her gently on the cheek.

'Thanks for coming all this way, Magnus.'

He smiled. 'It's been my pleasure.'

He really was the perfect gentleman. She felt she had to give him some hope. She said, 'I'll look forward to your letter.'

Was that relief she saw in his eyes?

'I'll certainly write, and we can work out the best time for you to visit Ruthven Downs. I know you'll love it.'

She nodded and managed a faint smile. Reaching up, she returned his kiss, her lips brushing his jaw. She saw a stirring flash in his eyes and then he climbed into the truck. He started up the motor and they waved. She was relieved that he seemed happy as he drove off.

'Stella, what's happened? Why is Mr Drummond leaving?'

Stella hadn't reached the front door before her mother came storming around the side of the house.

'He wants to reach Charters Towers by tonight.'

Her mother's jaw dropped and she stood with her hands on hips, her bosom heaving, as if she'd been running. She was squinting in the bright sunlight, but Stella could still see the dismay in her eyes. 'Surely you didn't send him away?'

'No, of course I didn't. I invited him to join us for lunch, but he didn't have time to stay.'

'Oh, for Pete's sake, Stella, what do you think this is? Bush week? A man like Mr Drummond doesn't come all this way just to pass the time of day.'

When Stella didn't answer, her mum's eyes narrowed. 'Did he pop the question?'

'Now you're jumping to conclusions.'

'Logical conclusions. He did ask, didn't he?'

Stella sighed. 'Yes, but don't get your hopes up.'

She turned and went into the house. It was too hot to stand in the sun arguing. She continued through to the kitchen and made a business of checking the stew pot simmering on the stove. Her mother came up swiftly behind her.

'Stella, don't tell me you turned him down?'

'No – not exactly. But I couldn't say yes when I hardly know him.'

'But you could have –'

'I've only really known him as a patient, Mum. Apart from meeting on the hospital ward, we've been out once. I can't marry a man I hardly know.'

'Sometimes, one night is all it takes.'

Now it was Stella's turn to be surprised. 'Was that how it was for you and Dad?'

Her mother smiled shyly. 'I knew the first night I met him that I wanted to marry him.'

And, of course, Stella was thinking again of Tom.

'Mr Drummond's obviously had enough time to make up his

mind, Stella.'

'Well, he was a patient with time on his hands. I was busy with a whole ward of men to care for.'

'But you must think he's handsome?'

'Yes, I'll admit he is quite good-looking, but there needs to be more – doesn't there?'

Her mother didn't answer at first. She stood in the kitchen, disappointment written all over her face. Then she sank heavily into a chair at the kitchen table and gave a weary shake of her head. 'I don't want to rush you, love. But believe me, you're not going to meet a man like Mr Drummond out here.'

'Mum,' Stella said more gently. 'I can't really stay here forever.' She had planned to stay till Stephen was safely home again. 'I'll need to get a job.'

Her mother shrugged. 'You'll find it's not like it was before the war. So many young men, good men, have been killed.' Her mouth trembled and tears shone in her eyes. 'I hope you're not making a mistake, love. Anyone can see that Mr Drummond's a very fine style of a man. I was so looking forward to giving your father some good news when he got home.'

The comment found its mark. Stella sighed. Her mother had suffered so much recently and she would have loved to bring a little joy into her life.

'We're going to write to each other,' she said. 'And Magnus is planning to invite me to see his property at Ruthven Downs.'

'Oh.' This news perked her mother up. 'Well, that's something to look forward to, isn't it?'

Stella nodded. She would have liked to confide in her mum, to tell her about Tom Kearney, but she was sure it wouldn't be wise. Not yet, when she still had no news of him.

It was in the steaming week before Christmas, when the dry, dusty plains shimmered with heat haze and the entire landscape sweltered and thirsted for rain, that a letter finally came from England.

Stella collected the mail from the letterbox, which was made from an oil drum nailed to a post, and brought it inside. There was a letter from Magnus as well, the third letter he'd written in as many weeks, and about half a dozen Christmas cards.

But it was the English stamp and postmark that made her heart leap. Hastily, she slipped the envelope into the pocket of her apron. She wanted to make sure that she had complete privacy when she read this all-important message.

Leaving the rest of the mail on the kitchen table, she took the precious letter from England outside to the toilet in the backyard. Locking the door from inside by sliding the bolt across, she sat on the closed wooden seat, keeping the unpleasant smell confined to the deep pit under the seat, and took the envelope out of her pocket with shaking hands.

The sender's name on the back was Mrs RJ Kearney.

Not Tom.

Stella drew a deep breath, trying not to panic just because his mother had written. It didn't mean bad news. Tom was still alive. Stella was sure of it. He had to be. But she was sick with nerves as she slid her fingernail under the flap and tore the envelope open.

It was stiflingly hot in the confined space and the tiny window offered only just enough light.

Be well, Tom. Please, please, be safe and well.

She drew out the thin, neatly folded pages and held them unopened in her lap as she closed her eyes and tried to pray. But it was no use. She was too anxious and her mind wouldn't stick to the task, so instead, she quickly opened the letter and read.

Richmond, UK
November 1945

Dear Miss Murray,

Thank you for your letter enquiring about our son Tom. He is safely home again, after spending three years in Changi Prison. According to our family doctor, Tom was lucky to have survived the wounds he received in the final battle before his capture. Since then he has become malnourished and has suffered from beriberi and dengue fever. His condition was only made worse by the brutal treatment from the Japanese guards.

As a nurse, I'm sure you will understand that after everything my son has been through, he is still in a bad state physically and mentally. Being reminded of his wartime experiences will not assist in his recovery, which will take many months yet.

For this reason, my husband and I have decided that we will not pass on your letters to Tom. It's for the best. We do not believe that putting Tom in touch with an Australian nurse who shared some of the horrors of Singapore can be of any use to him now.

You're so very far away in Australia and the poor boy has only just arrived home. He needs the peace and quiet of England now and the company of his old friends.

As you are someone with his best interests at heart, I'm sure you will understand, and you will not to write to us, or to Tom, again.

Tom needs to put the terrible war experience and all its unpleasant memories behind him and to get on with his life in this blessed time of peace. Eventually he will take up with friends who can remind him of his happy life here before the war.

I extend to you and your family my very best wishes
for a happy, holy and peaceful Christmas and I wish you a
healthy and prosperous New Year.

Kindest regards,
Eileen Kearney

24

Seth waited till Charlie was asleep before he rang Alice.

'Hey,' he said, when she answered. 'How's it going?'

'Seth, hi.' The mellowness in her voice and the warmth of those two short words made him smile, bringing instant hot and happy memories of their latest night together.

'I had a phone call from your mother this morning,' Alice said.

'Yes, she told me she'd called you.' He felt compelled to add, 'I did warn you.'

'Yes, I'm glad you did. I suppose Jackie also told you I accepted? I'm coming to the big party?'

'Yeah, I'm really pleased. It should be a good night.'

'I'm sure it'll be fabulous.'

Seth drew a quick breath. He'd heard the subtlest change in Alice's voice, and he braced himself for a 'but'.

'But I must admit I *am* a bit worried,' she said next.

'You're not having second thoughts?'

'Well – yes, kind of.'

Just in time, Seth bit back an urge to swear. Instead, he waited, giving her a chance to explain.

'I'm just a little worried that we might be sending the wrong message to your family,' she said. 'You know, that we're serious. This party is such a significant family event.'

Seth was standing on the deck, looking out into the dark bush, but now he sighed, let his head drop back as he stared up at the night sky littered with stars. So far, he'd played along with Alice's request to keep their relationship casual, but after just a few times together, he knew he was more than ready to get serious about this girl.

He'd had enough girlfriends over the years to know that everything about being with Alice was different. She was perfect for him. He was crazy about her.

'I'm sorry,' he heard her say. 'I know it's not fair to tell you this now, after I've already accepted your mother's invitation. I must be driving you mad.'

'Kinda,' he admitted.

But perhaps he should have known that ambivalent Alice would have doubts and second thoughts. Hadn't this been the pattern of their relationship so far? Alice was gorgeous, in almost every way his dream woman, but she had more complex layers than Maria Versace's lasagne.

'The thing is,' she said. 'I do have my reasons. I – I'd like to explain.'

Seth forced himself to ask, 'Do these reasons involve Charlie?'

A small silence. Seth gripped his phone harder.

'Yes,' Alice said at last. 'It's complicated. It's to do with how my parents died and –'

'Hold it, Alice.'

'Excuse me?'

Seth felt bad about interrupting her just when she was about to open up, but this sounded like heavy shit, too important to leave to a phone conversation. 'I'll come over to your place.'

'Are you sure? Isn't Charlie already asleep?'

'Yeah, but he should be okay to move.' Seth had never disturbed Charlie at night before, but he was sure he needed to be with Alice while she talked about this. Last thing he wanted was to just let this girl slip away because he wasn't paying attention.

If there was any chance she *was* trying to back away from him, he needed to be there on the spot, watching her facial expressions and body language, reading her mood.

'Charlie will drop back to sleep while I'm driving to your place,' he said. 'I can be there inside the hour.'

'All right.'

It was hard to gauge Alice's response to this. Seth could only hope she would be happy with his sudden intrusion.

Charlie grizzled as Seth lifted him from the cot, along with his favourite stuffed rabbit, but the boy lay sleepily in Seth's arms as he carried him to the car. The business of buckling him into his seat upset him, of course, but as Seth had hoped, the hum of the motor and the rhythm of wheels spinning over bitumen soon lulled him back to sleep.

Burralea was in darkness when he arrived, with only a few house lights glowing through lounge room curtains. When he drew up outside Alice's shop, everything seemed to be dark, but then she came to the front door carrying a torch.

'Do you have a power outage?' he asked.

'No, I turned the lights out. I thought they might wake Charlie.'

Seth was surprised that she'd gone to so much trouble, but he quickly hid his reaction. 'Good thinking.' He dropped a grateful, quick kiss on her cheek, then went back to unbuckle his sleeping son.

'Let's go upstairs,' she said softly, as he nestled Charlie's heavy head against his shoulder. 'You can put him on my bed.'

Her hair was caught up in a casual knot and she was wearing floral green and purple tights and an oversized purple T-shirt. She looked bloody sensational.

Now, using the torch to light the way, she led Seth through the shop that smelled of furniture polish and then through the workshop that smelled of wood shavings, then finally up the narrow staircase. A lamp glowed softly in the corner of her bedroom, and the scent of lavender wafted from pale grey sheets as Seth lowered the little boy onto the bed.

They made a nest of pillows around him and tucked the rabbit close. Charlie wriggled and squirmed a bit, but he didn't open his eyes, and it wasn't long before he was stroking the silky lining of one of the rabbit's ears and settling back to sleep.

Seth and Alice stood together, still as statues, watching, waiting in total silence. Soon Charlie's ear-stroking stopped. His plump little hand lay relaxed and soft.

'Well done,' Seth whispered to her. 'Thanks.'

Together, they backed out of the room and closed the door gently, retreating to Alice's small, lamp-lit living area, which, like Seth's, comprised a kitchen, dining and lounge.

'Take a seat.' She waved towards a red velvet armchair. 'What would you like? Coffee?'

Seth could see that she already had the mugs, coffee and spoons ready beside a lit candle on the kitchen counter. 'Yes, sure. Thanks.'

'Instant okay?'

'Of course.'

As he lowered himself into the chair, he wished he felt calmer about this impending discussion. He had no idea what Alice was going to tell him about her parents' accident, and he couldn't imagine how the hell it involved Charlie. He'd driven himself crazy on the trip over here, trying to guess what her problem might be.

It was hard to tell if she was tense too. Her face was a picture of concentration as she spooned coffee into mugs and poured the boiling water. She brought him a steaming mug and set it on the chair's broad arm, and he tried not to stare at her legs in the floral tights as she made herself comfortable in a chair opposite him.

She smiled shyly, crossed her gorgeous legs, then tucked a stray curl of flaming hair behind her ear, but despite the casualness of her actions, he could see now that she *was* nervous, as nervous as he was.

Seth sipped the coffee. It was rich and aromatic. 'This is great, thanks.'

Alice flashed another quick, awkward smile, then looked worried again.

There was no point in prolonging the agony, so he dived in. 'You were going to tell me about your parents' car accident.'

'Yes.' Alice took a sip from her mug. 'The thing is,' she said, keeping her gaze fixed on the square of cream fluffy carpet, 'it wasn't only my parents who died. There was a baby in the car, too.' She looked up then, and her dark eyes were already too shiny. 'My little sister, Daisy. She was a toddler, actually, not much older than Charlie.'

'Bloody hell.' Seth's gut clenched at the mere thought.

Alice looked down again to the mug in her hands. 'Daisy didn't die straight away in the crash. She was in hospital for a week. My grandmother used to take me to visit her every day. She –' Her mouth trembled. 'She was unconscious. She never woke up.'

Seth couldn't think what to say. He tried to imagine the horror of it. Alice, at the age of ten, losing her parents and then, on top of that, a baby sister lying helpless in hospital, no doubt swathed in bandages.

Then losing her.

'I'm afraid it's scarred me,' Alice said.

Seth nodded. 'I daresay it would be hard to get over.'

'I still get nervous around little people,' she said. 'They're so cute and sweet and vulnerable.'

'You mean, you're actually scared of them? Of kids?'

'I have all these hang-ups and phobias about what might happen to them.'

'But you were so good with Charlie the other day.'

'That's because you were there too. If I'd been on my own . . .' Alice gave a sad shake of her head. 'I'm afraid I would have freaked.'

Seth sat very still, trying to take this in, to understand. He figured that Alice was close to his age, which meant that almost twenty years after she'd lost her family, she still hadn't come to terms with her loss. He felt appalled for her, and desperately sad. But what did this have to do with *his* father's birthday party?

Something wasn't adding up.

'My problem is,' she went on, as if she sensed his confusion, 'if I allow myself to get serious about you – or about any man, for that matter – sooner or later, one way or the other, I'll eventually run into the problem of kids.'

'You mean, you don't want to have anything to do with them? Ever?'

Alice looked miserable as she shook her head.

Fuck. Seth stared at her in dismay, his mind whirling as he tried to take this in. He felt dazed. Totally side-swiped.

He knew he should probably be more sympathetic, but he was remembering his own fears when he'd been landed with a tiny baby. He'd been scared witless when Joanna dumped Charlie on him, but somehow he'd copped it on the chin and just got on with the job.

Now, here he was, finally getting over the shock discovery that he'd fathered a beautiful child with a woman who seemed to show no maternal instincts. And he'd hooked up with a girl, a gorgeous girl he was crazy about, who was too scared to wipe his kid's nose, or give him a cuddle if he fell over.

Seth was trying to stay calm, but he could feel an emotion that might have been anger gathering steam. 'I must be your nemesis,' he said. 'Why would you even date a guy who already has a little kid? It's a wonder you gave me the time of day.'

Alice opened her mouth to respond, then closed it again and simply sat there, clutching her coffee mug and looking contrite, almost as if she'd expected his tirade. Then she uncrossed her legs and shifted her position. And damn it, even now when he was angry as hell, those skin-tight floral leggings made him horny.

With a burst of impatience, he jumped to his feet and strode to the other end of the room. From there, he looked out through a window to the dark street below. He saw the faint gleam of his ute and remembered that night when he'd pulled up at Alice's door, determined to persuade her to have dinner with him.

And that answered his question, didn't it? He couldn't pretend he didn't know how they'd ended up together. The chemistry between them had been amazing. Right from the start, he'd been a goner, blind to anything except the fact that Alice, by some lucky miracle, was as keen as he was.

Unfortunately, the memories of how great they'd been together made tonight's bitter reality so much harder to accept.

A host of questions clamoured for answers. How could she live like this?

Seth was battling anger and disappointment in equal parts as he turned to her. 'So how do you plan to live the rest of your life? Have a series of one-night stands? Or perhaps one-month stands, with birth control as a top priority?'

He threw his arms wide. 'Will you put an ad on an online site – *Wanted, a husband – must be sterile*? Or maybe you'll manage to draw up a pre-nup that rules out pregnancy?'

Alice glared at him. 'Why don't you just come right out and suggest I find a married man? A family guy who wants to keep his mistress a mile from his kids?'

Seth shrugged. 'That would work.'

Now she let out her breath in a heavy, fed-up sigh. 'I thought you might be more understanding.'

He knew he'd been too harsh. The poor girl obviously had a major problem. 'Sorry.' He returned to his chair and sat down. Reached for his coffee mug, which was barely warm now, took a sip. 'I really am sorry,' he said again.

More calmly, he asked, 'Have you tried to get help for this? Talked to a shrink? Some kind of counsellor?'

Alice grimaced as she shook her head. 'I know, I know. I should have seen someone by now. It's cowardly to just go on avoiding a situation, instead of facing up to it and dealing with it. But – but I hate talking about it. I never do talk about it, if I can help it.'

Seth supposed he should be flattered that she'd cared enough to tell him as much as she had. Not that it solved anything.

Grimly, he said, 'So I guess this boils down to the fact that you plan to steer clear of any long-term relationships.'

'Yes. I'm afraid so.' She looked thoroughly miserable as she said this. Miserable but unyielding.

A chill sliced through Seth as he considered his options. The last thing he wanted was to call it off with Alice. But this business of keeping their relationship casual and under wraps was harder than it had seemed at first glance. He couldn't deny that Charlie was a complication.

And if all Alice wanted was short-term sex, then she'd had it.

'I guess it's just as well you've told me this now.' He wasn't proud of the brutal edge to his voice, but he couldn't help it. Walking away from this girl wasn't easy. 'I think you're right,' he said. 'You shouldn't come to the party.'

Out of the corner of his eye, he saw Alice flinch, but although the small movement stabbed at his heart, he knew he couldn't back down.

'If we went as a couple it probably *would* send the wrong message,' he said. 'My parents – well, my mother at least – is pretty desperate to see me settle down with a nice girl to help with Charlie.' He put air quotes around 'nice girl'. 'We need to set her straight, before she starts planning an engagement party to follow straight on from Dad's birthday.'

Alice nodded. 'I'll ring Jackie first thing in the morning.'

'No. Don't you worry about it. I'll let her know you aren't coming. It might be awkward for you to explain and she still might try to persuade you. It could get tricky.'

'What will you tell her?'

Seth swallowed what felt like a fish bone lodged in his throat. He forced himself to look Alice in the eye. 'I'll tell her that it didn't work out between us. That we've broken up.'

Then he stood quickly and carried the mug through to the kitchen, poured the last of his coffee into the sink and rinsed the mug with cold water. 'I'd better get Charlie,' he said.

———

Alice wasn't sure that her legs would support her as she pushed herself out of her chair. She felt completely hollow inside, as if she'd scooped out her heart and handed it, bleeding, to Seth on a plate.

She'd never dreamed it would be so hard to break up with him. He was the nicest guy she'd ever met and the sexiest, most tender lover on the planet. The chemistry between them was a rare and special thing, but she had to do this. He would be so much better off without her and her hang-ups.

At least, that was what she'd told herself. But then she saw the pain in his eyes, she nearly lost it. She was within a hair's breadth of bursting into noisy tears, and her body felt as frail and stiff as a ninety-year-old's as she went to open the bedroom door.

Little Charlie was still lying just as they'd left him, with one hand resting on the stuffed rabbit and his wheat gold hair glowing in the lamplight.

Seth leaned down and whispered, 'Come on, little mate.' Then he gently lifted Charlie.

Briefly, the little boy whimpered and squirmed.

'Ssh,' Seth soothed, cradling his son's head against his bulky shoulder.

'I'll bring the rabbit,' Alice said.

Seth nodded. 'Thanks.'

Once again, she used the torch to light the way down the stairs, but Charlie was fussing. As they made their way through the shop, he began to cry loudly, and louder again as Seth shifted Charlie's position while he felt in his jeans pocket for his car keys.

'I'll open the door for you,' Alice offered, but it didn't help.

Charlie screamed when he realised he was being put back in the car seat. Seth, however, continued with the task manfully.

'Perhaps he'd like a drink,' Alice suggested. 'Milk? Water?'

'Maybe a little milk,' Seth said over his shoulder as he wrestled with the wriggling toddler and the seatbelt buckles.

By the time she'd hurried back with a plastic tumbler of milk and a shortbread biscuit, Charlie was buckled in, but still roaring. A window opened down the street and a head popped out.

'Here's a nice drink.' Alice leaned in through the ute's open door and offered the milk to Charlie.

To her amazement, just like that, Charlie stopped bawling. She could see his little face in the glow of a streetlight, pink and puffy from crying as he blinked big blue eyes at her.

'Ali,' he said, and he actually smiled. Smiled while tears still trembled on the ends of his lashes.

A sob welled in Alice's throat and she had to hold her breath to stop it from bursting noisily out.

'Drink some milk, Charlie.' Seth's voice, coming from behind her, sounded a little frayed around the edges.

Obediently, Charlie drank some of the milk and then he smiled at her again, this time with a white milky moustache.

She handed him the biscuit.

'Ta,' he said softly as his little hand closed around it.

'See? You do have the knack,' Seth told her, but he sounded weary and he certainly didn't smile.

Alice stepped back and stood, holding the tumbler, while Seth closed the door on Charlie and walked around to the driver's side.

He looked at her over the bonnet. 'Goodnight, Alice. I – ah – good luck with everything.'

'Thanks.' She forced the words past the raw tightness in her throat. 'Goodnight.'

He slipped behind the wheel, closed his door, started the motor. Took off.

Somehow, Alice made it inside and back up the stairs. She left the tumbler on the kitchen counter and hurried into the bedroom, where she threw herself onto the bed that still smelled of baby talcum powder, and she wept.

25

'What's the matter, Jackie? Can't you sleep?'

When Hugh walked into the kitchen, Jackie was sitting in semi-darkness. The only light was the one over the stove, and she was in her nightdress with a mug of warm milk and honey on the counter in front of her.

Hugh glanced at the clock on the wall. 'It's three o'clock.'

'I know,' she said, yawning. 'I'm dead tired, but I just can't sleep.'

It was so annoying. She'd been tired after a full day of minding Charlie and had gone to bed early. Hugh had stayed up reading the diary, his day having been filled with helping Seth to fix the bore and then mustering a mob that had strayed into a rocky gully. Jackie had fallen asleep quickly enough, only to find herself wide awake in the early hours, worrying about Hugh's reaction to his mother's story about Tom and Singapore.

'I suppose it's all this party planning,' Hugh said.

'Yes, I guess it's got my mind going.' Jackie was unwilling to talk about the diary now, in the middle of the night. Hugh might launch into awkward questions that would lead to showing him Magnus's letter as well.

That was the last thing she wanted. They needed to enjoy the party first, get it safely behind them. At least, this was what Jackie had tried to tell herself, but in her heart of hearts, she knew she was plain scared and she was using the party excuse as a delaying tactic. It was a damn flimsy excuse, though.

'I'm not sleeping too well, either,' Hugh said.

Jackie avoided asking his reason. 'Would you like a mug of hot milk and honey?' she asked instead.

'Yes, but you stay there. I'll get it.'

Hugh, in striped pyjamas and bare feet, moved efficiently between the cupboard and the fridge, fetching a mug and milk, pressing buttons on the microwave.

Jackie pushed the honey jar across the counter towards him.

'Thanks.' He rummaged in the drawer for a spoon. 'That's a fascinating story of Mum's about Singapore.'

Okay, there was no avoiding it. A cold shiver shimmied over Jackie's skin, but to her surprise there was also a glimmer of relief. Lately, she'd felt as if she'd been hanging on to her mother-in-law's secret for years. The strain was really getting to her.

Wrapping her hands around the comforting warmth of her mug, she said, 'I didn't even know Stella was in Singapore during the war, did you?'

'She probably mentioned it once or twice, but neither she nor Dad talked much about the war.' Hugh dropped a generous spoonful of honey into his mug of hot milk. 'I guess it's strange, really, considering that's how they met.'

'Really?' Jackie watched his workmanlike hands as he stirred his drink, then set the spoon on the drainer. 'I don't think I knew that.'

'Mum was nursing in Townsville when Dad was shipped back from New Guinea. He was one of her patients.'

'How – romantic.' Jackie wasn't a very good actor and she was a bloody hopeless liar. She knew she sounded ridiculously nervous.

Hugh's eyes narrowed, watching her as he sipped. 'I don't suppose meeting Dad in the wards in Townsville was nearly as romantic
as meeting this Tom Kearney fellow at Raffles in Singapore.'

'Maybe not.'

'But it's pretty strange, don't you think, the way she wrote
about that and then hid it? I suppose the wartime romance had a
big impact and she needed to get it off her chest, but then she didn't
want Dad to find out.'

'Well – yes.' Jackie stared at the counter top, trying to keep her
face impassive. 'It's quite a mystery.'

'I might be able to make more sense of it if I could read the whole
thing. Did you know there are pages missing? I don't seem to have
the beginning or the end.'

'Oh?'

'You must have noticed.'

Jackie knew she couldn't keep avoiding Hugh's gaze, but when
she glanced up, she was confronted by a suspicious glint in his dark
eyes. She flinched. 'Those pages were damaged when they were
crammed into the sideboard,' she said quickly.

'I'd still like to take a look at them. Where are they?'

'I – I can't really remember.' Oh, good grief. Had she really said
that? Had she sunk this low, just for the sake of saving a party?

But deep down, Jackie knew this was no longer just about the
party. This gathering of their family and friends had become more
than a birthday celebration for Hugh. It was a recognition of the life
she'd forged here, a celebration of the hard work she'd put into running this homestead, the work she, Hugh and Seth had all put into
the property. The property that was now at risk.

She drained her mug, getting a sweet mouthful of honey at the
very bottom.

'What's going on, Jackie?'

'You shouldn't be stressing about this now,' she said, a little desperately. 'It's the middle of the night, Hugh. We should both be trying to get back to sleep.'

But her usually amenable husband stubbornly shook his head.

'Sorry,' he said, 'but I didn't come down in the last shower.'

Jackie clutched her mug tightly in both hands. 'What are you talking about?'

'I know you didn't want me to read this diary. That story about keeping it for my birthday was a furphy, wasn't it?'

Jackie wished she was a quicker thinker. As she hunted madly for an answer, she probably looked as guilty as a child caught with her hand in the biscuit tin.

And Hugh, unfortunately, didn't take his eyes from her. 'Jackie, don't try to pretend that you have no idea what happened to the missing pages.'

She imagined him reading those opening words. *I have done a terrible thing* . . . 'I told you, Hugh. They were damaged when they were in the back of the sideboard. They're almost impossible to read.'

'That's a pity, but I'd still like to take a look at them,' he insisted quietly. 'Where are they now? In the drawer in the office desk that just happens to be locked for the first time since we've been married?'

He's noticed.

Jackie let out the breath she'd been holding. Eventually, contritely, she gave up the fight. 'Yes.'

'Good. Could you unlock it, please?'

'Now, Hugh? At this time of night? If you start trying to read it now, you'll never get to sleep.'

Her husband shrugged. 'The alternative is to lie awake wondering what it's all about.'

Jackie knew when she was defeated. All this time, she'd been trying to protect her husband, to make this party a joyous celebration for him, but she knew she couldn't prolong this battle, especially at ten past three in the morning. She had no choice but to hand it all over and see what Hugh could make of the mystery his parents had left behind.

'I wanted to save this till after the party,' she said quietly. 'But all right, if you insist, I'll get it for you.'

As she slid off the kitchen stool, her sprigged cotton nightgown floated about her ankles and the timber floorboards were cool beneath her bare feet. Hugh followed her into the office, where she switched on the light and tipped the little key out of the crooked clay pot that Flora had made many years ago in preschool.

'There's a document here from your father, as well,' she said as she fitted the key to the lock and slid the drawer open. 'But it might be best to read all of Stella's notes properly first.'

'Something from my father?' Hugh looked worried now. 'Have you read it?'

'I –' Jackie didn't quite answer as she handed Hugh the envelope. To her surprise, she felt strangely relieved.

As she began to back towards the door, Hugh looked inside the envelope and frowned. She wondered if he'd already seen his father's bold handwriting and the rather startling heading – *Instructions pertaining to the will of Magnus H Drummond*.

'I might go back to bed,' she said, which was probably cowardly, but Hugh was taking out the rest of the pages and lowering himself into the chair at the desk, and she longed to escape to the sanctuary of their bedroom.

She took another step.

'Just a minute,' said Hugh. 'What's this here about my father's will?'

Jackie swallowed. 'I think – it seems to be instructions for his lawyer. For Brad Woods's father. What was his name? Kenneth?'

Hugh looked incredulous. 'And it was hidden behind the mirror in the sideboard?'

'Yes,' she said softly.

'Good God.'

Hugh was opening the envelope with his father's instructions now, and panic curdled the milk in Jackie's stomach. She felt it rise in a hot tide, reaching all the way to her throat. Her legs were suddenly weak, and she had to lean back against the bookcase near the door for support. But she couldn't take her eyes from the dawning horror on Hugh's face as he read his father's preposterous claims.

In the short time it took Hugh to read the page, he seemed to age ten years. He sat slumped in the chair, his eyes stricken, his skin pale, his mouth hanging open with shock.

Then he lifted his gaze to her, and he looked like a man who'd been given a death sentence. 'You've read this?' His voice was quiet. 'You know what it says?'

Reluctantly, Jackie nodded. 'But I think it must be a terrible mistake.' The fear and worry that had been hounding her for weeks rushed back now in full force. She had to dash a hand at the sudden tears in her eyes. 'Otherwise, why would Stella have hidden it?'

'I don't know. I can't believe my mother would –' Hugh didn't finish the sentence. He looked up at Jackie with an expression of heartbreaking helplessness. 'He wanted to disinherit me. What are we going to do?'

'I – I'll put the kettle on. You need tea. Or maybe a good stiff scotch.'

'No, I don't want tea. Or scotch. I need a clear head for this.'

'Magnus must have been mistaken,' she said again. 'It has to be some kind of misunderstanding. This happened not long before he had that stroke.'

'But there's also a chance it could be true.'

'That you're not his son?'

'Yes. Wait, will you, while I see what's here. Christ almighty. There might be some kind of terrible confession.'

Leaning unsteadily against a bookcase, Jackie waited while Hugh read through the other pages his mother had written, his eyes ferociously scanning the closely written lines.

Then, with a despairing groan, he gave the pages a disgusted slap. 'It's more than possible.' Hugh looked both shocked and defeated. 'Tom Kearney came out here to Australia. He and Mum met up again after she'd married Dad. They had an affair and it's all here in the bloody diary.'

26

My decision to marry Magnus wasn't desperate. By the time I visited him at his beautiful property Ruthven Downs, I'd already decided to set aside my heartbreak over Tom Kearney. I had no choice, really. It was a case of getting on with my life or pining for Tom forever. I honestly never expected to see Tom again. I'd closed the book on that chapter of my life, or rather, his parents had closed it for me.

Stella enjoyed the gentle rhythm of the days at Ruthven Downs. She loved the beautiful old homestead and, within eighteen months of her marriage, she had a sweet little daughter to love and care for. She felt fulfilled and happy, managing her family, raising chickens and growing vegetables which she pickled and preserved, painting rooms inside the house and making new curtains.

Sometimes she even helped Magnus with the cattle, especially at calving time, when a cow had a difficult labour, or when a newborn calf had a health problem that needed extra attention.

She appreciated every aspect of her new life. Magnus was a generous and considerate husband, and he took great pride in her as his wife, and in their daughter, Deborah. He'd even chosen Deborah's name.

'You can't beat a good Old Testament name,' he'd claimed. 'And Deborah goes well with Drummond. When we have a boy we'll call him Adam or David.'

Stella hoped she might have a say in naming their next baby, but she kept the thought to herself. She didn't want to upset Magnus. While he was pleasant company most of the time, he still suffered from nightmares and occasional bouts of depression. At these times, he would become brooding and uncommunicative and would sit for hours in his study drinking scotch.

She knew something unbearable had happened in New Guinea and she hoped that some day he might trust her enough to talk about it.

Most of the time he was fine, though, and on the whole, Stella's life was smooth sailing.

Until a letter arrived from Tom Kearney.

Stella was sitting at a table on the homestead verandah. A willy-wagtail was singing prettily in a wattle tree nearby and little Deb, as Stella liked to call her, was within reach, in the playpen. At nine months, Deb was a chubby little thing with a mop of dark curls. She was good at entertaining herself, and on this morning, she was solemnly taking wooden pegs out of a bucket and then putting them back again, over and over, while Stella went through the mail, separating out the bills.

By now Stella was familiar with the handwriting of most people who wrote to her and Magnus, but today there was a script she didn't recognise. And the envelope was addressed only to Stella.

She sent a fond smile and a wave to Deb before she casually turned the envelope over. And saw Tom Kearney's name.

Shock ripped through her like a bullet, making her cry out so loudly that Deb looked up and frowned at her.

How could he write now?

After all this time?

Stella felt as if she'd fallen from a great height. At first she was too stupefied to think. She sat with her eyes tightly shut as memories and longing and a thousand regrets crashed over her like an ocean pounding at a sea cliff.

It was some time before she felt strong enough to read Tom's letter. She knew that Magnus was miles away, working with stockmen on the far extremities of the property, but she still looked around and back over her shoulder, as if she needed to be sure that no one was watching while she read what Tom had to say.

It was a very brief note.

Exchange Hotel
Cairns
13 April 1949

Dearest Stella,

I hope this letter finds you in good health. I know it will come as a shock, and I apologise, but I did promise that I would find you. It's taken me a long time, but here I am at last in Cairns.

Is there any chance that we could possibly meet? I believe Mareeba is the nearest town to you. If you'd like to name a suitable time and a place, I could meet you there.

Stella, I know that you are married and this will be difficult for you, but my search has brought me such a very long way, and I can't go back to England again without at least seeing you one more time.

I will remain in Cairns for one month, hoping to hear from you.

With my sincerest good wishes,
Tom

Stella read the letter over and over. She read it with tears, with smiles, with terrified alarm and with joy, and finally she read it in utter desolation. She didn't think it was possible to feel so broken, so completely cut in two. One moment she was thrilled at the thought of seeing Tom again, the next she was in total despair that this good news had come too late.

One thing was certain, however.

She had to see him.

Over the next few days, she plotted and planned and schemed.

Magnus was to begin mustering soon and he and his stockmen would be away, camping out in the bush for several days. Stella knew from previous musters that her role was to send the men off with supplies – home-baked bread and fruit cakes and a hefty mountain of corned beef. Once they were gone, she would normally sit at home alone for the rest of the week.

She knew how to drive Magnus's truck, and she wrote to Tom telling him that she would meet him in Cairns. Then she lived on pure adrenaline in the week leading up to the muster, almost bursting with excitement as she went about her everyday chores.

On the night before Magnus left, he made love to her and, for the first time ever, Stella pretended he was Tom. She couldn't help herself. Her head was completely filled with thoughts of Tom.

Lying together afterwards, Magnus seemed a little surprised. 'You were very passionate tonight, my dear.'

'It must be because you're going away,' she said.

'Will you miss me?'

'Of course I will.'

But the small untruth lay heavily on her heart, and she took ages to get to sleep.

Two days later, dressed in high heels and her best summer linen, Stella walked up to the reception desk at the Exchange Hotel in Cairns, carrying Deborah and a small suitcase.

'Mr Tom Kearney is expecting me,' she said, holding her chin high as she addressed the young man behind the desk.

But before the fellow could respond, a deep voice spoke her name. 'Stella.'

Her heart thudded. She turned and there he was.

'Tom.'

'Hello, Stella.'

She stood, trembling, drinking in the sight of him. It really was Tom. Her Tom. After all this time, when she'd given up all hope, here he was. The same dearly remembered face. The same tanned skin and longish jaw, the same adorable smile creases at the corners of his friendly grey eyes.

Tom, no longer in uniform, was dressed like any other holiday-maker in an open-necked white shirt and trousers, without a coat or tie.

Stella wasn't sure how long they just stood there looking at each other and smiling with tears in their eyes.

Then Tom held out his hand for her suitcase. 'Let me take that.'

'Thank you.'

As he stepped closer to relieve her of the suitcase, he leaned in to kiss her cheek and she couldn't resist turning her head so that their lips met. It was the merest fleeting brush of their mouths. His skin against hers.

For Stella, it was as devastating as a fireball.

Tom seemed to have the same reaction. They stood stock-still, staring at each other, stunned. And in that moment they knew. Nothing had changed.

'I hope it wasn't too difficult for you to get away?' Tom said.

She told him about the muster.

'How long can you stay in Cairns?'

'A day or two. Three at the most.'

Tom gave a slow, thoughtful nod as he digested this news. 'I was thinking that perhaps we could go to another hotel.'

Stella guessed the direction of his thoughts. They could book in at another hotel as husband and wife. Her heart leaped at the chance and she didn't hesitate.

'Yes.' She spoke a little breathlessly. 'Let's do that.' She nodded towards the sun-bright tropical street outside. 'I have a vehicle.'

Tom searched her face. 'You're sure?'

He was asking her to commit adultery, but he was also giving her the chance to back away.

As she tried to think calmly, she remembered the day in Singapore, when they'd been on the brink of making love, and devastation had erupted all around them.

Surely now, they were owed this second chance? If this wasn't meant to happen, she reasoned, Fate wouldn't have allowed Tom to find her. This might not be the right time, but Fate couldn't always get the timing right.

'Yes,' she said. 'I'm sure.' She looked down at Deborah in her arms, placidly sucking her thumb. 'As long as you don't mind an extra companion.'

'Of course I don't mind,' Tom said politely.

Under the circumstances, she knew politeness towards her offspring was probably as much as she could expect from him.

But to her surprise, he asked, 'Are you going to introduce us?'

'This is Deb,' she said. 'Deborah.'

'Hello, Deborah Drummond.' Tom held out a finger and Deb's plump little hand closed around it. Of course, she then tried to get his finger into her mouth.

Tom laughed. 'She's strong and she has teeth.'

'Yes, three.' Stella was grinning as he delicately extracted his finger, and before the awkwardness of the situation could spoil the moment, she said quickly, 'Right, let's go then.'

Tom's face was alight with unmistakable happiness as he took her hand firmly in his.

Their room was simple but clean, with a double bed covered by a white chenille spread and a wooden cot set in the corner for Deb.

They didn't speak about Singapore, about Changi or its aftermath, or whether Tom's mother had ever told him about Stella's letters.

And he didn't ask her about Magnus.

Stella had weaned Deb a month earlier and getting her to sleep wasn't as easy as it used to be. Stella gave her a bottle and tried to pat her to sleep, but Deb must have sensed her mother's impatience and kept wriggling and squirming.

'I think I'm upsetting her. I'm too tense,' she said.

In the end, Tom offered to carry Deb for a bit. He settled her over his shoulder like a pro, then he patiently paced back and forth, and began to sing 'Danny Boy' very softly and slightly off-key. Deb immediately stopped squirming and whimpering. After another soft, crooning verse, the baby's eyes were closed.

'You have the knack,' Stella told him in awe. She couldn't have imagined Magnus doing anything like that.

She settled the baby in the cot and went to join Tom, who was standing in the doorway, one shoulder propped against it as he looked out at the limited view.

'Here, hold out your hand,' he said as he extracted a small but very glamorous bottle from his trouser pocket. 'I promised I'd bring you perfume.'

He placed the bottle in the palm of her hand.

'Oh.' Stella stared at its fluted sides and gold lid. 'Fancy remembering that.'

'I remembered everything about you, Stella.'

The perfume was called Shalimar, and the names *Guerlain* and *Paris* were written with a flourish on the lid.

'Thank you,' she said and she unscrewed it. 'Oh, my goodness.'

It smelled exotic, like something from the *Arabian Nights*, very sensual and forbidden. She pressed a little to her wrist and held it up for Tom to smell.

He smiled. 'It suits you.' Then he nodded to the view outside of hot bitumen and shiny black cars and shopfronts. 'I'm afraid it's not a hut right on the beach, with palm trees and the moon rising over the sea.'

Remembering the other promise he'd made in Singapore, Stella felt close to tears, but Tom was smiling and she forced herself to be brave. 'If we stand on the bed we can probably see the sea.'

He laughed. 'Shall we find out?'

'Why not?'

Grinning like children, they kicked off their shoes and held hands as they climbed onto the bed. The mattress sagged and swayed beneath them as they stood together, still holding hands, laughing softly so as not to wake the baby.

Stella pointed to the narrow strip of blue just visible over the tops of the buildings. 'I told you. There's the sea.'

'Yes, and there's even a palm tree.'

'Two palm trees!'

They laughed. And hugged. Then tumbled together in a happy heap on the chenille spread.

Now the room was quiet apart from the baby's soft snuffling sounds, and Tom and Stella lay, suddenly serious as they looked into each other's eyes.

For a terrible moment, the knowledge that this miracle was forbidden and temporary overwhelmed Stella. She thought they might both give way to unspeakable sadness.

Tom touched a finger to her lips. 'Let's not talk about this,' he said. 'Not now.'

She knew he was right. There was so much to talk about. Too much, and talking would spoil the happiness of seeing him again. She nodded, pressing her lips tightly together, the way a child might when making a vow of silence.

Tom kissed her then, teasing her lips open, and as his tongue touched hers, Stella shivered happily and closed her eyes. But then she opened them again and pulled back just for a moment, because it was so perfectly wonderful to see Tom, *her* Tom, up this close, his eyes inches from hers, shining with emotion.

Here they were, setting aside their dreams and despair, wanting only this. Now. And now there was no war to stop them.

Tom kissed her again and, as his lips worked their magic, he began to undo the buttons on her dress. An overwhelming longing bloomed, first in her heart and then, as he caressed her skin, skimming the lacy edges of her underwear, the longing spread like fire to her breasts and between her thighs.

At last.

With a little burst of impatience, she tugged his shirt free from his trousers, then undid the buttons. She was smiling shyly as they wriggled out of their clothes, letting them fall to the floor on either side of the bed.

Reaching for her again, he kissed her nose, her chin, her mouth, teasing her breasts with gentle caresses and tweaks.

'Ohhhh.' The soft syllable slipped from her as sensation claimed her. She'd never felt like this before, so relaxed yet needy, like ripe fruit trembling on the branch, ready to fall.

Now she knew without doubt that this was where she belonged, in this man's arms, in his bed, sharing his love, his life.

'I love you.'

They lay together afterwards, beneath a slowly circling ceiling fan, and the words that filled Stella's heart had to be said.

'I'm so sorry, Tom, I should have kept waiting. I should have known you would come.'

He lay very still and silent, staring at the cracked paint on the far wall.

Needing to see his face, to read his expression, Stella propped herself onto one elbow. The pain in his normally sparkling grey eyes said it all. He'd endured years of cruel hardship, privation and torture in Changi, but he'd never given up hope of finding her again.

She'd let him down. So badly.

Unshed tears choked her throat and it was some time before she could speak. 'I don't suppose your parents showed you any of my letters?'

Tom flinched as if he'd been shot. 'You wrote?' It was barely a whisper.

'Of course I wrote. I kept your address and I sent several letters to your parents.'

'In Richmond? They moved back there in 1943.'

'Yes, I sent them to Richmond. I even told them about our new address when my parents moved to another property.'

Tom sat up, letting the white sheet fall to reveal his long, lean torso, the dark hair on his chest and the shiny scars on his back. His eyes were wide with dismay and something deeper, perhaps horror.

'They never said a word.' He looked stunned as he shook his head slowly. 'Why would they do that?'

'Your mother told me you were in a very bad way. She said they were worried that I'd stir things up. I think they were scared you might never recover.'

'I memorised your address. In Changi I used to repeat it to myself all the time, so I couldn't forget it, but when I finally got home, my letters to you were all returned.'

He looked so upset Stella didn't like to add to his misery by telling him how badly the final dismissive letter from his mother had hurt her.

'I tried the usual channels to find you,' she said. 'But the army was too busy trying to bring our boys home. They didn't have time to worry about a nurse looking for her English boyfriend.'

Tom's lips betrayed the saddest of smiles.

'What are we going to do?' she said.

He glanced towards the cot. Deb was still asleep, but Stella knew it wouldn't be long before she woke.

'We're going to make the most of what little time we have.'

As he reached for her again, she was already melting towards him.

27

When Deb woke they went for a walk. The afternoon was hot and still, and they found a park on the waterfront and spread a tartan picnic blanket beneath a cassia tree.

'It's almost as hot as Singapore,' Stella said.

Tom shook his head. 'Nowhere's as hot as Singapore.'

As if to prove this, a cool breeze wafted in from the sea, dampening their heated skin and bringing the tang of salt and coral. Deb laughed and rolled happily on the rug between them, dexterously sucking her bare pink toes.

They munched on apples and shared a chocolate bar. People walking past smiled at them, no doubt pleased by the sight of a happy family enjoying some well-earned relaxation. Stella donned sunglasses and turned her face away. She was only an hour or so from home and she'd taken a risk by being with Tom in broad daylight.

But as they sat there, sedately talking about the past, about the baby, about Freddy Cornick and other people they'd known in Singapore, Stella's head was filled with sensory memories – of Tom's kisses, of her body loosening beneath his touch, of him being inside her.

They bought grapes and bread and cheese and a bottle of wine and took these things back to their hotel room. The bathroom was down a hallway and they took it in turns to use it. Stella bathed Deb and changed her into a smocked cotton nightdress. This time, after their outdoor excursion and another full bottle of milk, the baby went to sleep easily.

They made love again hungrily, with the urgent anticipation of lovers now familiar with the pleasures awaiting them. They ate in bed, naked with a thin sheet draped over them, nibbling grapes and cheese and drinking ruby red wine from tumblers.

The baby slumbered on and the night was theirs. A night for leisurely, slow lovemaking, a night of tangled limbs and a thousand wandering kisses. A night of precious intimacy, of exquisite ecstasy to imprint on their memories, to hold close to their hearts as a talisman against the unknown future.

In the cold grey light of dawn Deb stirred. Stella tended to her quietly, trying not to disturb Tom. He was awake, though, and he sat, propped against pillows, watching as Deb lay in her arms, greedily sucking the rubber teat. And he asked the questions that had not yet been voiced, the questions that had to be asked.

'What are we going to do, Stella?' A painful pause. 'Would you consider leaving your husband?'

Oh, yes, she would consider it. Stella knew now with a terrible certainty that she'd made a dreadful mistake by marrying Magnus. But had she the courage to break her wedding vows? To leave her husband?

She thought of his midnight terrors and shivered. How would he react to the pain and humiliation of having his wife walk out of their marriage? How would her family react? Their friends?

Thinking about it, imagining the tears, the anger, the outrage and the condemnation, she felt the colour drain from her face, saw the hope fade from Tom's eyes. Her stomach churned. She couldn't bear to hurt him any more than she already had.

'I don't want to lose you again,' she said.

'I love you so much.'

'I know.' A tear spilled down her cheek and dripped onto Deb. 'I know.'

'I could come with you when you spoke to him,' Tom offered. 'Stand by you.'

Stella shook her head. 'Thanks, but I'm not sure that would work.' She had no idea how Magnus might react. Given his violent outbursts, she was terrified that he might even try to kill Tom.

She would have to go about this very methodically, be very calm and sensible. 'I'll talk to our lawyers,' she said. 'I'll get their advice and – and their help, if I need it.'

That night, after another day of walking, talking, playing with Deb . . . she traced the scars on his back with her fingertips, felt the ridges and the soft, new, reddened skin.

'I used to dream of you,' Tom told her.

'I wish I'd been able to stay there to nurse you.'

'I'm glad you weren't there. You don't want to know how badly they treated the women prisoners.' He reached for her, pulling her on top of him. 'I dreamed of you like this.'

Stella laughed. She still couldn't quite believe how abandoned and reckless she felt with Tom. Leaning forward, her breasts brushed his chest as she kissed him confidently, nudging her tongue past his lips.

This was meant to be, she thought. *The war got in the way and*

I lost direction, but I belong with this man. He is my destiny.

All she needed was to stay strong and she could make it happen.

They smiled bravely when they parted the next day. They'd both agreed Tom shouldn't hang around. It would only create an undue sense of pressure. Patience was what they needed now. Patience and hope. Tom gave Stella an address in New Zealand and she promised to set up a special post-office box for his mail. He would shake off his restlessness by exploring the South Island and wait till he heard from her.

With a final embrace, he kissed her brow. 'I hate leaving you to cope alone.'

'It's best this way. Magnus isn't an easy man.'

Tom drew back, frowning as he searched her face. 'He wouldn't hurt you?'

'No.' She tried to sound confident. 'I'll be fine, but I'll need to choose the right moment.'

'Oh, Stella, I'm asking so much. Too much.'

'You're not asking, you're giving.' She hugged him close. 'You're giving me what I want.'

Reassured, he walked with her to the car, and watched as she strapped Deb into a basket on the back seat. Deb wailed, but she stopped when Tom reached in and waggled a finger in her face. 'Till we meet again, little girl,' he said with a sadly lopsided smile.

Two months later Stella wrote to him.

Ruthven Downs
9 June 1949

Dearest Tom,

I'm so sorry to tell you this, but I have dreadful news. Tom, we can't be together. I know I promised I'd speak to Magnus, but the most unexpected thing has happened. I'm pregnant again. I didn't know at the time, but I must have already been pregnant when I went to Cairns to see you.

I know the baby has to be Magnus's because you used protection and we were so very careful. I'm so sorry. I can't believe the dreadful timing. I've been quite weak and ill with morning sickness, and I simply haven't had the strength to face up to the battle that divorce would entail.

Darling Tom, my heart is breaking as I tell you this, but I fear I must let you go. I have no choice. I've had a quiet word with a lawyer friend and he has warned me that, as the guilty party in a divorce, I have very few options.

It's not fair to you to hold out hope, or to make you any kind of promise. I couldn't walk away from my children, and I know that's what Magnus would demand, especially if this baby is a boy.

I'm weeping oceans as I write this, but you need to forget me now. I love you, Tom, and I will never stop loving you, but Fate has yet again conspired against us. Be free, my beautiful, darling man. I will never forget you. I will never forget our wonderful nights in Cairns.

In my heart, you will always be mine and I yours, but I want you to get on with your life, as I must get on with mine.

All my love,
Stella

It was ten months, ten long, sad months before Tom replied. By then, baby Hugh was already smiling.

Her son had his father's dark eyes, but he looked on the world much more gently than Magnus ever had. Such a placid, sunny little fellow Hugh was.

Stella couldn't help but be happy with her little family, and she had all but given up hope of ever hearing from Tom again. Then, during a trip to town to have Hugh weighed at the clinic, she found a letter waiting in her special post-office box.

Villa Carmen Maria
Calle Defensa
San Telmo
Buenos Aires
Argentina
20 April 1950

Dear Stella,

By now your pregnancy should be behind you, and I sincerely hope that both you and your new baby are well and thriving. I hope little Deborah is well too. I daresay she's running around by now and getting into all sorts of mischief. You must have your hands full.

As you can see from the postmark, I'm in Argentina. I've taken a job with Ferrocarriles Argentinos working on building railway bridges. It's quite demanding work, but very satisfying, and there's nothing like having a brand-new job in a new landscape, with a new culture and language, for jolting a man out of a rut.

The scenery is breathtaking, but I won't go into details. You're a busy mother and you don't need a travelogue. I wanted to reassure you, though, that I'm enjoying the life here very much. As you've no doubt discovered for yourself, hearts do have a way of healing.

Keep well, Stella. I'll write to you at Christmas.
Fondest wishes,
Tom

Hearts do have a way of healing.

Stella wept when she read this, sitting in the car on the side of the road on the way back to Ruthven Downs. She tried to be unselfish, to be glad for Tom, and she *was* glad that he hadn't been hanging about miserably in England. He was having adventures, just as he'd had in Malaya before the war. He was getting on with his life, as she'd begged him to do.

She tried to be strong. She would keep the post box and she would write to Tom at Christmas, and perhaps at other times, but she wouldn't allow herself to wonder about anyone else who might be living in Villa Carmen Maria with him. She wouldn't think about beautiful girls in Argentina, girls with flashing dark eyes and curving bodies and long, black silky hair. But she knew for sure that her heart hadn't healed. At best, she'd thinly papered over the cracks.

Now, in spite of her very best efforts, those cracks split wide and deep.

28

'Hugh, we shouldn't worry about this now. We should go to bed.'

Hugh was still sitting at the desk, elbows propped, staring gloomily at the pages in front of him, but now he turned to Jackie and reeled back in shock, as if she'd grown a second head. 'How can I go to bed after reading this?'

Jackie groaned. 'I wish I'd burned it. I wish Stella had burned it instead of hiding it away, only to cause problems for someone else.'

Earlier, she hadn't been able to sleep, but she felt desperately exhausted now, as if the strain of recent weeks had finally flattened her. She sank onto the only spare chair in the room, a spindly thing, rarely used, with a seat upholstered in delicate needlepoint. 'I just don't understand why Stella did this.'

'Neither do I.' Hugh gave an agonised sigh. 'You know what it means. You'll have to call off the party.'

'No! No way! That's crazy.'

'I'm sorry, Jackie, you have to. How can I have a party now? How can I celebrate turning sixty-five, when I've been living a lie all these years? Enjoying a property that shouldn't have been mine? I have a wrong to set right. A man's life doesn't amount to much if he doesn't follow his conscience.'

'But you're not thinking straight, Hugh.' He was reacting exactly the way she'd feared. He'd always been such a stickler for doing the right thing. There was every chance he would want to rush straight to Deborah to tell her the whole sorry story.

If it wasn't for this ungodly hour, he would probably have rung his sister straight away and offered her Ruthven Downs lock, stock and barrel.

'What would Deborah do with a cattle property?'

'Who knows?' Hugh threw his arms into the air with a melo-dramatic gesture that was completely out of character.

'Deborah's an artist, Hugh, not a grazier.'

But Hugh – her calm, sensible, reasonable Hugh – would not be comforted. 'Deb never had the chance to find out, did she? Her whole life might have been different if she'd inherited this place.' His eyes widened, as if he'd come to another realisation. 'The fellow who fathered her son might have hung around. That son of hers might have actually put in a solid day's work.'

Jackie almost snorted. 'Imagine Xavier running a cattle station.' She tried to picture Deborah's long-haired, guitar-twanging, sleepy-eyed son rounding up a mob of runaway cleanskins, or leg-roping an uncooperative steer. Impossible.

'Xavier never got a proper chance either,' Hugh said quietly.

'Oh, darling.' Jackie rose from the chair and crossed the room to slip her arms around her husband. 'I knew you'd take this to heart.'

For the first time in all their years of marriage, Hugh shrugged away from her. 'There's no other way to take this, I'm afraid. My father wanted to disinherit me. God, I don't even know if he *was* my father.'

Soundly rejected, Jackie crossed her arms and tried not to panic. It was hard to reassure Hugh about his father's claims. She'd never met Magnus Drummond – he'd died before she met Hugh – so she'd only ever seen photographs.

'You have Magnus's dark eyes,' she suggested, still trying to be helpful. 'Stella's eyes were blue.'

'Half the population has dark eyes.'

Despite the stubborn tilt to Hugh's jaw, there was a haggardness to his face now that frightened Jackie. He might give himself a heart attack if he didn't calm down. She said quickly, 'There is a way to ease your mind about the paternity question.'

'How?'

'You and Deborah could have a DNA test. They're pretty simple these days.'

Hugh turned to her, his brows meeting in a frown as he searched her face. 'How do you know so much about it?'

She would have preferred not to tell him, but she was ready to do just about anything to ease his mind. 'I had a test done. I wanted to make sure that Charlie was Seth's son. I never said anything at the time. I was a bit ashamed of myself.'

It was hard to gauge Hugh's reaction as he stared at her. 'Does Seth know this?' he asked, at last.

Jackie shook her head. 'I sent samples of his and Charlie's hair. They were easy enough to find. And it works. It just takes a bit longer than the mouth swabs, but –'

'For heaven's sake, Jackie. What was the result?

'Charlie is Seth's son. There was no doubt about that. Although, if there was ever a custody battle, it might not hold up in court without the mouth swabs. But the results were still quite clear.'

'Well, I'll be damned.' Hugh gave a dazed shake of his head. 'I can't believe you would –' He left the sentence unfinished and stood staring at the far wall as he digested this latest news. Then he shot Jackie another questioning glance. 'What would you have done if Charlie hadn't been Seth's boy?'

'I don't know. I don't think I would have said anything, actually.

By the time the results came back, Seth was already so committed to the boy, I realised it wasn't that important after all.'

To her surprise, Hugh smiled. Perhaps he was thinking of the way their sweet little Charlie had so easily stolen their hearts and become part of their lives.

'Maybe that's how your mother felt, Hugh. She might not have known who your father was for sure, but perhaps she decided it didn't really matter.'

'Or perhaps, like you, she was just responding to the natural urge of a mother to protect her son.' Hugh spoke more calmly now and there was even a hint of a smile. 'A lioness guarding her cub.'

It was so strange to be talking about all of this now, in the office of all places, in the middle of the night. Jackie was aware of the precious hours of sleep they were losing and she longed for bed. But there was an important point she couldn't leave untouched.

'Speaking of cubs,' she said, 'have you thought how this is going to affect *your* children? If you're going to start stirring things up with Deborah, Seth and Flora also have a right to know. Seth especially needs to know what he's in for. After all, we're okay, really. We're on the brink of retirement, but Seth's grown up expecting to take over the running of this place. Out of all the family, he has the most to lose.'

'I know, I know.' Once again, Hugh looked worried and exhausted. 'And the cruel irony is that Seth loves this life even more than I do. He has a real affinity for the land and the cattle.'

'And he has all sorts of plans,' Jackie agreed.

'Whereas, if I'd had a choice when I was young, I probably would have been an architect.'

Jackie's jaw dropped. 'Really?' She found it impossible to believe that Hugh might have wanted a different life. He'd been such a conscientious cattleman. It was like discovering that Mozart would have preferred to be a goatherd.

All this time and Hugh had never said a word.

'I think that's why I kept up the friendship with Ian Kinsella all these years,' Hugh said. 'It means I get to talk to him about his work from time to time. To live the architect's life vicariously.'

'But you've worked so hard at being a cattleman.'

'Well, yes, of course I have. I had no choice. It was a huge responsibility.'

'But you didn't hate this life, Hugh.' She couldn't help the pleading note in her voice. Being a grazier's wife had meant so much to her. She couldn't bear to think that Hugh had been unhappy.

'Well – no, I didn't hate it.' Hugh's smile was rueful. 'Sorry, I shouldn't have said anything about architecture. I suppose it was just a pipe dream, and it's all a bit heavy for this hour.'

It certainly was. Jackie wasn't sure she could take any more surprises. 'It's almost four now,' she said. 'And you're only going to make yourself sick if you spend the rest of the night pacing the floor. Let's go back to bed. We should try to get a bit of sleep, at least. You'll be able to think much more clearly then.'

To her relief, Hugh didn't argue this time. Together they left the office, turned out the light and went back down the hallway to their bedroom. It wouldn't be long before a faint glimmer of dawn showed at the edges of the curtains, but they settled comfortably enough in bed together, spoon-style, as they had so many times before.

With Hugh's body warm and reassuring at her back, Jackie felt comforted at last. Surely if they supported each other through this, everything would turn out all right?

But there was one question she still needed to ask. 'We can have the party, can't we, Hugh? I couldn't bear to call it off now.'

'Yes, yes,' he murmured softly against her neck. 'You know how I hate to disappoint you.'

When Jackie woke, the sun was shining so brightly through the curtains she had to squint against its glare. For a blissful moment her world seemed perfectly normal, until she remembered Hugh's discovery and his middle-of-the-night reaction.

Rolling over quickly, she saw that he was already up and had left a mug of tea for her on the bedside table. When she touched it, it was cold.

She wondered where he was, and then, more anxiously, wondered what he'd been up to while she was sleeping. That thought jolted her out of bed. She thrust her feet into slippers, found her silk kimono and pulled it on – anyone might be in the kitchen at this hour – then dashed a comb through her hair and went through to the kitchen to find her husband and make a fresh cuppa.

Hugh was at the kitchen table, calmly eating boiled eggs and toast. He smiled when she came in, so the news couldn't be all bad.

'Did you get some sleep?' Jackie asked as she refilled the kettle.

'Yes, I haven't been up long. Maybe twenty minutes.'

She glanced at the clock. It was ten past nine. She couldn't remember the last time she'd slept so late. 'Have you made any phone calls?' she asked more cautiously.

'Yes. All done.'

'All?' It was hard not to panic. 'Already?'

'Yes, Jackie, keep your hair on. I rang Brad Woods first, and I asked him to check the family records to see if they ever received a copy of Dad's letter.'

'Right.' Jackie took a quick breath and told herself to calm down. 'That's sensible, I guess. They might even be able to explain why the will was never changed.'

'I hope so. At least they'll be able to give me good advice.' Hugh dipped his spoon into the second egg. 'And I rang Deb.'

'Before you've heard back from Brad?

'Yes. It didn't feel right to keep her out of the loop.'

'I – I suppose.' An anxious weight settled in Jackie's chest. 'How did she react?'

'Rather strangely, actually. She seemed to think it was hilarious.'

'Really?' Jackie's sense of relief was short-lived. The doubts soon rushed back. 'Do you think Deborah might have been too surprised to think straight? She might think differently when she gets over the shock?'

'Maybe.' Hugh was annoyingly unconcerned as he tipped a spoonful of egg onto the corner of his toast. 'I asked her to come a day early, before the party. Flora will be here then and we can have a proper family meeting.'

'Oh, Hugh, that's a terrible idea.'

'I think it's eminently sensible.'

'But I'll be up to my ears in preparations.'

His eyes narrowed. 'I thought you had a team of helpers now.'

'That doesn't mean –' Jackie stopped. If she made out that the party was a huge load of work, Hugh might still want to call it off. 'I was looking forward to having Flora and Oliver to ourselves for a day,' she said instead.

Which was true. Having Flora come home with Oliver was so exciting. 'They're going to be here for such a short time and we won't have much of a chance to get to know Oliver.'

'Well, I'm sorry, Jackie, but I think there are bigger issues at stake right now than getting to know Flora's latest boyfriend.'

'Except I think this pair might be quite serious,' Jackie muttered almost under her breath as she rinsed out her mug with freshly boiled water and reached for a teabag.

If Hugh heard her, he didn't let on, and she felt a spurt of annoyance. But she quickly suppressed it. There was enough justifiable tension in the air without her adding to it. However, this latest development meant there would be two more for dinner on the night before the party. She hoped the chicken casserole she'd already prepared and frozen would stretch.

'I'm going to check my emails,' she said, over her shoulder, as she headed down the hall to the office, carrying her tea.

Over the past few weeks, she'd thoroughly enjoyed turning on her computer each morning and checking her emails, seeing the party acceptances roll in. Today, to her delight, there was a new email from Flora. She clicked on it quickly.

From: Flora Drummond
To: Jackie Drummond, Seth Drummond
Subject: Dad's party

Hello, my lovelies. I'm afraid I have some disappointing news. Oliver's not going to be able to make it for Dad's party, after all. Something's come up, an important gig he can't really get out of.

I'm sorry, of course, but nothing will stop *me* from coming home. I'm so looking forward to seeing you guys and to giving Charlie a big special hug from Aunty Flo. BTW Seth, I saw a little girl the other day who is only two years old and she has a 1/32nd-sized violin. I didn't know they could make them smaller than 1/8th. It was SO cute, but I promise I won't bring one home for Charlie. Not this time, at any rate.

Mum, are there any special goodies you'd like me to bring from Melbourne? The delis down here are *amazing*. What about those divine Haigh's chocolates I brought home last Christmas?

Love to you both and to Dad,

Flora x x xx

Jackie stared at the screen in dismay. Something felt wrong about this message, but she wasn't sure what. It was like one of those silly fears that lingered after waking from a bad dream. Perhaps it was the vagueness of Flora's excuse about Oliver – the brevity and the things she hadn't said. Her daughter's emails were usually so chock-a-block with details.

As she closed the screen, she drew a deep sigh. She'd been so looking forward to this party, but now she was feeling more worried with each passing hour.

What else could go wrong?

29

On Monday evening, Tammy settled onto her favourite cushion on Alice's back step, ready for a chat.

'So what's news?' Alice asked, handing her a steaming mug of homemade chai latte and hoping to steer the conversation well away from her own sorry situation with Seth.

Tammy grinned. 'My news is all about Ben the Pie Man. We're seeing each other.'

'Wow!' Alice feigned surprise, although this wasn't really unexpected. Tammy had been eyeing Ben off for ages. 'When did this happen?'

'Oh, a few days ago.' Tammy's grin would have outshone the Cheshire Cat's.

Alice made herself comfortable on a cushion facing her friend, and settled back. After a shitty weekend, she willed herself to relax on this beautiful warm evening. She'd turned out the main lights and had lit candles, and their glow was soft and enchanting as their scent mingled with the aroma of the two women's spiced drinks. Down among the lilly pillies along the back fence, the tiny lights of fireflies darted and blinked.

'Well, you certainly look happy,' she told Tammy.

'Oh, I am. Very. Ben's –' Tammy paused as if she was searching for exactly the right word, but then she gave a shy shrug. 'What can I say? He's simply lovely. And that's not a word I'd usually use to describe a guy – but he's sexy and fun and just plain nice.'

'That's wonderful.' Alice raised her mug in salute. 'Here's to you and Ben.' She took a sip of her drink and tried not to think about another man who was 'simply lovely'.

'So have you found out why a surfie type has moved to the mountains of Far North Queensland?' She couldn't help asking this. Tammy had mentioned once before that she suspected Ben was running away from something and, as Alice had made a similar move, the question was close to her heart.

Tammy nodded. 'Ben was surprisingly open about it.'

'That's the Tammy factor.' Alice smiled. 'I'm sure you have a way of getting people to open up.'

'I've certainly heard some doozies from my customers. Then again, they're victims in my chair and I have a pair of scissors in my hand.'

Tammy laughed at her own joke and Alice joined in, but she wished she felt happier. She'd had the most miserable weekend, even though she'd tried really hard to distract herself from thoughts about Seth. On Saturday morning she'd gone to the Burralea markets and had bought several early Christmas presents for the offspring of friends in Brisbane. Then in the afternoon she'd gone to a singing workshop held in the village hall.

It was a lot of fun and although Alice wasn't a marvellous singer, she could hold a note, and she'd enjoyed blending her voice with others. Kate Woods had been there, and other friendly locals, and Alice had felt quite uplifted for a couple of hours.

Afterwards, though, she'd returned to her flat and remembered little Charlie lying in a nest of cushions on her bed, remembered

Seth sitting in her lounge room, staring at her in pained disbelief as she explained her sad story. And the reality of never seeing Seth or Charlie again hit low and hard.

Yesterday she'd driven down to Cairns, ostensibly to check out the second-hand shops, but mainly because she'd just needed to keep busy.

'I can tell you Ben's story,' Tammy offered. 'I know he won't mind.'

'Well, only if you feel comfortable.' Alice couldn't pretend she wasn't curious and she knew Tammy was dying to tell her.

'We were right about the surfing. Ben lived on the Gold Coast.' Tammy even managed to sound like a storyteller now, adding a once-upon-a-time tone to her voice. 'He grew up there and he was a mad-keen surfer, and he had a job as a plumber for one of the big construction companies. But he also managed to get himself tangled up in the party-drug scene.'

Tammy shot Alice a significant glance. 'He did time.'

'So he was dealing?'

'More like supplying friends.' After a beat, Tammy hurried on. 'Anyway, while he was on the prison farm he worked in the kitchen and he started to learn about baking. He really liked it. Liked it much better than plumbing. And anyway, he wanted to make a fresh start, break away from the old gang. So once he was out, he got a job in a bakery and finished his apprenticeship. And as soon as he could, he got away from the coast. He says there are too many people down there who know him, who keep trying to lure him back to the dark side.'

'Or bully him into it?' suggested Alice.

'Possibly, although he wasn't with that heavy bikie scene.' Tammy shrugged and smiled. 'Anyway, he loves it here, and that's music to my ears. He says he plans to stay. The rent on his shop's reasonable, the locals are so friendly and word's starting to spread that his pies are great.'

'They certainly are.' Alice smiled. 'And I love a story with a happy ending.'

'Well, it feels more like a happy beginning than an ending at this point. But you never know.' Tammy drained her mug and set it down. 'That was so yummy. You'll have to give me the recipe.'

'Happy to.'

Tammy eyed Alice curiously. 'So how are things with you? How's your business going?'

'Oh, it's chugging along okay. Luckily, I don't have a lot of competition from any big furniture stores, and the people up here and the tourists seem to like hunting for second-hand bits and pieces.'

'Especially the lovely things you seem to find. I've been checking out that tall green vase in your window. It's gorgeous.' Before Alice could respond to this, Tammy asked quickly, 'How's Seth?'

Thud.

'He's fine.' Alice hoped she sounded convincing.

Perhaps not. Tammy rolled her eyes.

'You know what I mean, Alice. How are *you* and Seth?'

'We're –' Alice looked away, out into the dark night beyond the reach of her candles. 'There's no me and Seth. We've broken up.'

'No!' Tammy sounded truly horrified. 'God, no, Alice, I don't believe it.'

'Well, I'm afraid it's true. It was my decision,' she added quickly before Tammy got the wrong idea.

'But how could you break up with him? He's gorgeous. *And* well off. He owns a cattle property, for God's sake.'

Alice hit straight to the heart of the matter. 'He also has a son.'

Tammy stared at her, a deepening frown creasing her brow. 'I know you're not mad about kids, but I thought you weren't going to let yourself worry about it. You wanted to date Seth anyway.'

'Yeah, I did, and it was okay at first, but now he's invited me to a party for his father's birthday. A major family affair.'

'And?'

'I didn't think I should go.'

'Are you crazy, Alice?'

'It's sending out the wrong message. Makes it look as if we're serious.'

Tammy was still frowning as she chewed this over. 'So you really can't get serious about Seth because he has a cute little kid?'

Alice knew it sounded pathetic, maybe even heartless and selfish. 'I don't really want to talk about it.'

Why not? a small voice suddenly whispered in her ear. What was the harm? Ben had been brave enough to tell Tammy that he'd been to jail and she hadn't turned a hair.

Perhaps it was the balmy night and the scent of the candles, but as Alice played with the idea of offloading her worries, something felt different about this evening. When she looked at her friend with her aqua hair and her rows of ear studs, her ready smile and her willingness to talk about herself and her new boyfriend, Alice's own reticence to spill seemed rather pointless and silly.

Here was someone who was not only willing, but also eager to listen to her. Someone who was used to listening to other people's woes.

Quickly, before she lost her nerve, Alice said, 'My hang-up about little kids started when I was ten, when my little sister Daisy died.'

And she found herself telling Tammy the whole story, about the accident and her parents, and going to the hospital with her grandmother, seeing fragile Daisy lying helpless every day for a week.

Tammy listened in silence, her eyes brimming with sympathy and even the shimmer of tears. 'That's so tough,' she said softly, when Alice finished. 'Oh, my God, you poor thing.'

'But I should have got over it after all this time,' Alice said.

This brought a slow, careful shrug from Tammy.

'The thing is –' Alice began, and then stopped as she realised she was on the brink of telling the rest – the part that she'd never let out before.

But now with Tammy, her fear of talking about this wasn't half as horrible as the misery that had plagued her all weekend after she'd let Seth walk out of her life.

'The thing is, I still feel guilty about what happened to my family.'

Tammy frowned. 'But you were only a child. You weren't even in the car.'

Alice swallowed the painful lump in her throat, then dived in again before she had time for second thoughts. 'On the afternoon of the accident I had soccer practice. It was after school and I was supposed to get a lift home with our next-door neighbours – Robbie Graham and his mum.' She smiled weakly. 'I was a little snot about it. I didn't want to go with them. Robbie was always teasing me, telling me I was hopeless at soccer, and I knew he was going to keep on teasing me all the way home.'

She gave a sad shake of her head. 'I wouldn't get in the car with him.'

Remembering it all, Alice felt her lips begin to tremble. She couldn't go on.

'What happened?' Tammy asked gently. 'I suppose the neighbour went home and told your parents, and your parents had to come and get you.'

Miserably, Alice nodded, remembering the cold afternoon and the other mum, Mrs Halliday, who'd kindly waited with her, remembered the sweet-and-sour lollipop. The phone call.

'And on the way to get you, your parents had the accident,' said Tammy.

This time, as Alice nodded, tears stung her eyes. She struggled not to cry as Tammy watched her, and she knew the poor girl was probably struggling to come up with an appropriate, warm and fuzzy response.

'I think you should be telling this to Seth,' was all her friend said.

This was so not what Alice had expected, and at the mere mention of Seth, she gasped. Within seconds she was sobbing and Tammy was kneeling beside her, with her arms around her, no doubt wondering what on earth she'd said wrong.

The next morning, Alice was hanging a pair of antique lanterns in her shop window when she saw Jackie Drummond and her husband coming out of the solicitor's office across the road.

Balanced on a stepladder, Alice considered making a swift retreat, but Jackie had already seen her. She smiled and waved and Alice had no choice but to wave back, although she quickly returned her attention to her task. Out of the corner of her eye, though, she saw Jackie crossing the street, heading straight for her.

Okay, stay cool. Alice had no idea whether Seth had told his mother about their relationship status, and she still felt rather fragile after last night's heart-to-heart with Tammy. It was all very well for Tammy to tell her she should talk to Seth, but Alice had already told him 'goodbye' and she knew he wouldn't appreciate being messed around.

She felt ridiculously nervous as she slipped the lantern's handle over a hook, then climbed down.

'Hello there, Alice,' Jackie Drummond called warmly as she entered the shop.

Alice climbed out of the window and managed to smile. 'Hi, Jackie, how are you?'

'To be honest, I've been better.' Jackie fanned herself with a well-manicured hand, making her gold bracelet jangle as she rolled her eyes theatrically. 'Has Seth told you about our latest drama?'

'I don't think so,' Alice replied cautiously.

'About the documents you found behind the mirror?'

Alice gulped, shook her head. But her stomach sank. Had the Drummonds had been visiting their solicitor because of the documents? Right from the start, she'd had a bad feeling about those papers, but when she'd heard nothing from Seth, she'd assumed all was okay. 'Have they caused problems?'

'Alice, you have no idea.'

'Oh, dear.' Alice was remembering the morning she'd taken the back off the mirror. If only she'd left those documents safely in place instead of racing straight out to Ruthven Downs. She would never have met Seth or Charlie, and she could have saved herself and Seth and the entire Drummond family several truckloads of trouble.

'I'm so sorry,' she said.

'Oh, it's not your fault, Alice.'

Jackie gave another dramatic eye-roll. 'Can you believe it? I'm up to my eyes in planning this party and now Hugh is insisting that we have a family meeting. A Drummond summit – on the night *before* the party.'

Alice glanced through the doorway to the footpath across the street. There was no sign of Jackie's husband.

It shouldn't have been possible to feel more miserable than she had over the last few days, but Alice was a past master at feeling guilty, and she felt utterly wretched now.

'I hope it's not going to spoil his birthday,' she said.

Jackie let out a noisy sigh. 'So do I, my dear, so do I. For a while there, I thought Hugh was going to call the whole thing off.'

Stepping closer, she gave Alice's hand a reassuring pat. 'I like that colour on you. It's one of those shades of brown that only red-heads look good in.'

Alice blinked, thrown by the sudden change of subject.

'At any rate, the party's still going ahead,' Jackie said next. 'And despite all this fuss and carry-on, I'm determined to make sure it's a lovely evening.' To Alice's surprise, she actually beamed. 'We're really thrilled that you will be there with Seth.'

Oh, God. Alice opened her mouth, ready to set Jackie straight, and then swiftly shut it. Obviously, Seth hadn't said anything about their breakup to his mother, and Alice had already caused enough trouble with the documents. She wasn't prepared to burst this particular bubble for Jackie. She managed to smile, but it was a rather self-conscious effort.

Fortunately, Jackie didn't seem to notice. 'Thank heavens you and Seth aren't giving me any headaches,' she said. 'I've almost given up on the rest of my family. Even my daughter, Flora, has problems. She was supposed to bring her new boyfriend from Melbourne, but something's come up at the last minute. He's an opera singer, rather in demand, and Flora will have to come home on her own. It's so disappointing. We were really looking forward to meeting him. Such a pity.'

With another warm smile for Alice, Jackie reached out again and squeezed her hand. 'Anyway, enough of my moaning. It's lovely to see you again, Alice. And there's always a bright side. You wouldn't have met Seth if it hadn't been for these documents.'

Again, Alice opened her mouth to explain the truth, but then she saw the emotion in the woman's eyes. Until now she'd assumed that Seth's mother was very confident and together, but this morning she sensed a surprising vulnerability in Jackie Drummond, and she couldn't bear to cause the woman any further distress.

Then Seth's father rounded the shop's doorway carrying two delicious-smelling brown paper bags, and his smile of greeting for Alice was jovial.

'There's a new pie shop in town,' he said with a grin, as soon as he'd greeted her. 'And I couldn't resist giving them a taste test.' To his wife, he said, 'What say we take these down by the lake?'

Jackie gave a resigned sigh. 'There goes my chance for a nice salad and coffee in Tolga on the way home.'

'I don't think you'll be sorry,' Alice assured her. 'Ben's pies are fab.'

'Well, I'll take your word for it.' Jackie was smiling again as she linked her arm through her husband's. 'See you Friday night, Alice.'

30

Seth was on the back verandah, staring out into the darkness, when the phone rang. It was the way he'd spent several nights lately, sunk in moody thoughts rather than relaxing in front of the TV.

He'd been scraping the bottom of the emotional barrel these past few days. Letting Alice go had been hard, a huge kick in the guts, way harder than he'd expected. And now there was a family drama on the boil. A problem with his grandfather's will, raising unsettling questions about who the hell was supposed to own the property. Crazily scary stuff that had his parents well and truly stirred.

For all these reasons, Seth assumed the phone call was from one of the oldies, probably his mum, checking again that he was okay. She was worrying about his future.

Seth was worried too, even though the legal situation had been checked out with their family solicitors and there was no argument – Ruthven Downs belonged to Seth's father. The problem was, that hadn't eased his dad's conscience.

It was all rather bizarre, though. Who else but his dad could have run Ruthven Downs? And who else but Seth should take over? He couldn't imagine that his artistic Aunt Deb would want the responsibility of a cattle property, and his cousin Xavier was even less likely to be interested.

Seth could remember difficult school holidays, when Xavier had been sent up from the coast to visit them. His cousin had rejected all the usual activities on offer, like riding horses or quad bikes, or canoeing down the creek. He hadn't even wanted to go swimming in the waterhole.

All Xavier had wanted to do was play *Minecraft*, but the Ruthven Downs internet connection had been dodgy back then, which had pissed the kid off no end.

For Xavier, Ruthven Downs wouldn't be a prize, it would be more like a millstone around his neck, like going to gaol for life, with hard labour.

Seth, on the other hand, loved this life. He knew the property like the back of his hand and he loved the land, loved every aspect of working with cattle, whether he was helping to deliver a newborn calf or chasing down a wild bull through the scrub.

He enjoyed working with machinery too, apart from that recent hassle with the bore pump. He was happy fencing, grading firebreaks and building new stockyards. More recently, he'd become fascinated by the science behind breeding quality beef cattle.

He didn't know what he'd do if he couldn't be a cattleman. It would be like being told he could never walk again.

So . . . as he drew the phone from his pocket, he steeled himself for more bad news from one of his parents.

The caller ID, however, showed an entirely unexpected name.

Alice Miller.

Seth's breathing snagged. Why would Alice be calling?

She was the last person he wanted to talk to. He was still too damn angry. And sad. He'd experienced harrowing moments lately when letting this girl go had felt even worse than the prospect of losing Ruthven Downs.

The phone had almost rung out when he tapped on the screen to receive her call. He swallowed, ordered himself to stay calm.

'Hi, Seth.'

Fuck. Just the sound of her voice made him want her. He waited a beat before he answered. 'Alice, what's up?'

'I – I just needed to talk.' She sounded nervous. 'I saw your mother today. She called in at the shop.'

'Hell.' Seth grimaced. He could just imagine how awkward the conversation must have been. 'Sorry, I haven't spoken to her yet,' he said. 'Not about us. Something else has come up, a bit of family drama.'

'Yes, so I gathered. Jackie said it's to do with those documents I took out to your place.'

'Yeah.' Seth scratched the back of his neck, a dead giveaway that he was nervous, too. He took three paces to the edge of the deck, stared out into the night-dark bush. 'My mother's got herself all worked up, stressing about these documents, plus the party, and now my sister's boyfriend can't come, so she's upset about that as well. I was waiting till the air cleared before I told her our decision.'

'Yes, I realised Jackie had no idea about – us. And I didn't want to cause more hassles for her – for any of you, actually. That's why I'm ringing.'

'Okay,' he said. Then, cautiously, 'Sounds like you have a plan.'

'Well, I guess I mainly wanted to sound you out – see if you thought it might be better to hold off –'

Seth frowned. 'Hold off telling my family that we've broken up?'

'Well, yes.' Her voice sounded shaky. 'But only if you think it's a good idea. I don't want to stuff you around, Seth, but if you thought it might help the situation –'

'Hold off till after the party?'

'It's just a thought.'

Seth spun one-eighty degrees, looked back into his light-filled house, saw the living area strewn with Charlie's toys, the dirty pots and plates waiting to be loaded into the dishwasher. This mess was his life, the life of a single father, not the life of a responsibility-free bachelor, the life Alice required.

'So are you saying you'd be prepared to come to the party as if we were still a couple?'

She gave a self-conscious laugh. 'We've done it once before.'

Seth sighed. 'Yeah.' At the time it had seemed a smart idea to fool Joanna in order to protect Charlie. Unfortunately he'd also fooled himself. He'd started to think that maybe –

With Alice there were no maybes.

'Look, I'm not pushing for this, Seth. I know it wouldn't be comfortable for either of us, but Jackie seemed really on edge.'

'She is. She's super-stressed.' Seth had first become aware of this two evenings ago when he'd arrived back at the homestead close on sunset, having just finished vaccinating a pen of poddy calves that he'd recently separated from their mothers. Both his parents had cornered him, looking deadly serious and wanting to 'talk'.

'I think it's a good idea,' he told Alice now. 'There's enough going on here without us adding to the drama.'

'Okay.'

Okay. One little word.

He hadn't realised how tense he'd been until he felt his shoulders relax. He pictured Alice, curled in one of those armchairs in her flat, her auburn hair aflame in the lamplight. He would have given anything to be there again, helping her out of her clothes and –

'It seems I started this in the first place when I found the envelope,' she said. 'So I'd like to help.'

That was his problem. Alice wasn't just a beautiful and sexy girl. At heart she was also thoughtful and generous, wanting to help.

'Actually, if it's not stretching the friendship too far, there is something else you could help with on Thursday –' Seth stopped.

'Whoops, sorry, no, scratch that.'

'What? What were you going to say?'

He shook his head, annoyed by his faux pas. He'd been on the brink of asking Alice if she could mind Charlie, keep him out of his hair, while they had this family conference on Thursday night. It was going to be tricky, combining dinner and a meeting at the homestead with trying to get Charlie to sleep.

He'd already lined up a friend of a friend to babysit for the night of the party. Asking that girl to come on Thursday night as well would be stretching things.

He wasn't sure who he could turn to. He'd kept himself socially isolated this past year and it had paid off. He had the fatherhood thing pretty well sorted. The downside was he no longer had a wide circle of people he could call on at short notice.

Still, that was his problem, not Alice's.

'Sorry,' he said. 'It was a slip. For a moment there I forgot Charlie's a no-go zone for you.'

This was met by silence and then a heavy sigh on the other end of the line.

Reality check.

'It's okay,' Seth said, wanting to let her down gently. 'As I said, scratch that.'

'Okay. Sorry.'

'I'll see you here for the party on Friday. Around six? Okay?'

'Yes.' Her voice was very subdued now. 'See you then.'

Seth disconnected, let out a heavy breath, went inside. He tossed Charlie's toys into the basket, filled the dishwasher with the dirty dishes, threw some of his and Charlie's clothes into the washing machine, snagged a beer from the fridge and took it back onto the deck.

Tipping his head back, he took a long draught of icy lager. Talking to Alice had stirred him, but he had some serious thinking to do.

Once this party was over, he and Alice would be finished, once and for all.

After that, he really needed to get a life, start seeing people again. Seeing other women. Hell, yeah. The world was full of other women. Women who didn't run a mile at the first sight of an adorable toddler.

Twenty minutes later Seth's phone rang again and he was tempted to ignore it. He'd left it on the kitchen bench, and he was comfortable where he was on the back step. But then came the guilt trip. It was probably someone from his family, so at the last gasp he reluctantly relented and raced inside to answer it.

'Hello.'

'Seth, sorry to disturb you again.'

Alice. The hitch in Seth's breathing was not caused by the rush to the phone.

'I'm feeling bad that you can't ask me for help with Charlie.'

'But you –'

'I know what I told you, but I can't go on living like this. I know it's – it's irrational.'

Phobias usually are, he nearly said.

'What kind of help were you looking for?' she asked.

As yet, Seth didn't have a clear plan for handling Charlie while his family had their meeting. Now he weighed up the pros and cons of getting Alice involved.

The cons were obvious, Alice had outlined them in vivid detail, but there were plenty of reasons why he should grab this chance. Emotions would probably be rife during the family confab and it was hardly a suitable place for Charlie.

Even more importantly, Seth knew how much courage Alice's offer had taken. He wasn't sure if it was possible for people to change, but Alice sounded like she was willing to try, and the last thing he wanted was to belittle her efforts.

He told her about the meeting. 'It's scheduled for Thursday evening,' he said. 'The night before the party.'

'I could be there.'

'Well, thanks. That would be great. I'll be close by in the homestead if there are any dramas.'

'Yes, of course.'

'With luck, Charlie might already be asleep. But he's been going to bed later and later.'

'I've seen how you handle his bedtime.'

'Yeah.'

Seth stopped himself from asking Alice if she was sure about this. He knew she wouldn't have made the offer lightly and he could hear the determination in her voice.

'Thanks,' he said again, injecting as much sincerity into his response as he could. 'That would be very helpful.'

'Good.' It was hard to tell if she was scared or excited. 'I'll be there, Seth.'

'Fantastic. I'll text you a time before Thursday.'

'That sounds like a plan.'

Seth was smiling as he downed the rest of his beer. Maybe, just maybe, there was still a slim chance with Alice. But as he went back into the house, he found himself thinking about the potential drama that might erupt on Thursday night. He thought about his sweet, gentle grandmother again, and wondered what on earth had possessed her to hide those documents in the first place.

31

Call us foolish, but Tom and I continued to write to each other. It was an important way of keeping in touch, and Tom's letters became my lifeline. Of course, I was clinging foolishly to a lost hope.

The signs of Magnus's deterioration were subtle at first. During the years when his children were young he seemed fine, and he showed every outward sign of being perfectly content with his home life and his work as a cattleman on Ruthven Downs. He enjoyed the changing rhythms of the seasons, and he rose to the challenges of a grazier's lifestyle, coping with impressive equilibrium with the weather extremes of droughts and cyclones. He even rode the market fluctuations calmly when other farmers around him were quite desperate with worry.

Their children, Deb and Hugh, were a huge source of pride for Magnus. Hugh seemed to thrive on the outdoor lifestyle. At a very young age he became an expert horse rider, swam like a fish, and was a keen observer of nature. When he was old enough, he was happy to help Magnus with mustering and yarding the cattle, or any other work around the property. Deb had a more artistic temperament, preferring to paint the outback landscape than to ride around in it, but that didn't bother her father. She was a girl, after all.

It was when the children grew older and travelled away to boarding school that Magnus began to deteriorate. His nightmares from the war years returned with increasing frequency.

As Deb and Hugh progressed through high school and then moved to Brisbane to go to art school and university respectively, Magnus seemed to be more and more on edge. He began to have increasing problems with sleeplessness and then he returned to drinking whisky in copious quantities several evenings a week. To Stella, it seemed he'd lost interest in almost all of the things he normally enjoyed.

When they'd first installed a television, he'd been thrilled, watching endless cricket matches, documentaries and old movies. But as he grew more and more depressed, none of these shows pleased him. Instead they made him angry. He found the news stories about the Vietnam War especially upsetting.

When Stella tried to talk him into seeing a doctor, he snapped at her.

'I'm perfectly fit and well.'

'Physically, yes, you're fine, Magnus, but I think you might be depressed, or suffering from anxiety.'

'And why would I see a doctor about that?'

It was a losing battle. Like many men of the bush, he was fiercely independent, couldn't bear to show any hint of weakness to the outside world.

Then came a night when Magnus woke from a nightmare, sobbing helplessly, and he couldn't continue with the bluff and bluster any longer. Stella brought him a hot drink and a sedative that her own GP had prescribed.

'You can't go on like this,' she said gently, as she plumped his pillows and sat on the bed beside him in her dressing-gown. 'You need help. You need to speak to someone. The war keeps coming back to haunt you, doesn't it?'

He couldn't look her in the eye, but his face was drained and tortured as he sank back against the pillows.

Stella knew he was ashamed of the weeping. She understood that it was incredibly painful for this once-tough soldier to be revealed as a broken man.

'It must have been terrible in New Guinea,' she suggested gently. 'Having to fight the enemy in that jungle with all the mud and the mosquitoes and those dreadfully steep mountains.'

Magnus's chest rose and fell as he drew a ragged breath.

'I'm sure the rest of us have no idea what it was like,' Stella went on.

'The terrain wasn't the problem,' he said suddenly.

Stella sat very still, holding her breath as she waited for her husband to continue. He was half-sitting, supported by the pillows, looking out into the darkness beyond the pool of lamplight, his eyes wild with horror.

She tried to imagine what it must have been like for him in the jungle, with the threat of an unseen enemy lurking behind every tree. How many men had he seen die? How many men had he killed?

'The fighting must have been terrible,' she suggested. 'Watching your own men die. Having to kill Japs.'

Magnus gave an agitated shake of his head. 'But it wasn't only Japs I killed.'

It took a moment for the implications of his words to sink in. When they did, Stella pressed a hand to her mouth to hold back a shocked gasp. Tears stung her eyes and she could feel a pulse begin to pound in her neck. What on earth had he done?

Staring bleakly ahead, Magnus said, 'You should have seen what those bastards did to our wounded. We always tried to get the wounded men down the line to safety. The native bearers, the Fuzzy

Wuzzy Angels, were amazing. But if the Japs got to them first, they'd hack off their arms and legs and just leave them there to bleed to death. We'd do anything not to leave a wounded mate behind.'

'Oh, dear God.'

Magnus closed his eyes. 'We were on a forward patrol. Six men. And our sergeant copped it. He was a mate of mine, Jim Gregory from Half Moon Station over in the Gulf. He was shot in the spine. He couldn't move.'

Her husband's Adam's apple jerked in his throat as he swallowed. 'We were outflanked by a large Jap force, and we had to fight our way out of there.'

'You couldn't fight and carry a man at the same time.' Battling tears, Stella slipped an arm around his bowed shoulders. 'Not in that terrain.'

'No.'

She gave his shoulders a comforting squeeze.

'I had to think of what was best for the rest of my men. I needed to get them back alive.' Again, Magnus shook his head as he stared into the darkness. 'Jim knew he was a goner. He pleaded with me not to leave him there for the Japs. We all knew what they would do to him.'

Magnus's lips trembled, pulled out of shape. 'Jim begged me to shoot him. Said he would have done it himself if he could have used his arms, but he was paralysed.'

'Oh, Magnus.'

'I tried to carry him . . .'

Tears streamed down Stella's face, and Magnus was so distraught he couldn't finish his story, but he didn't need to. She knew what he'd done. He'd had little choice. But oh, what a terrible burden for the poor man to live with.

No wonder he was still so troubled.

For some time after that midnight confession, Magnus seemed calmer. He never referred to the breakdown again and Stella respected his need for silence, but she was pleased that he was less irritable. And the drinking eased.

Any progress that Magnus had made fell to pieces, however, on the day he arrived back from town, seething with a dark and dangerous fury.

His eyes were blazing, his jaw granite hard as he dumped a box of groceries on the kitchen table and turned on Stella.

'Who's Mary Davison?' he demanded.

Stella froze. For long, heart-thumping seconds, she stared at him. 'Why do you ask?'

A cruel, menacing smile titled his thin mouth. 'I went into the post office to pay a bill and the new post master was very friendly and helpful. He was also rather curious about a post office box being held for someone called Mary Davison. He seemed to think I was responsible for it, but he'd made a mistake. The account has always been paid for by SJ Drummond, hasn't it?'

'Oh.'

'Oh?' Magnus roared. 'Is that all you can bloody say?' He pulled an envelope from his shirt pocket. It was torn open and empty, but as the thin airline paper edged with red and blue fluttered helplessly onto the table, she could see all too clearly the address in Tom's handwriting.

'The poor, deluded new guy wasn't clued up. He thought I might want this.' He waved the letter in her face. 'You've been signing off as Mary Davison and exchanging letters with an Englishman for twenty fucking years!'

'There's no need to swear.' Stella was thinking of the man she'd hired to help in the garden, who was working just outside, but as the words left her lips, she knew how foolish she sounded.

'Don't you dare lecture me about swearing after what you've

been up to.' Magnus had gone very red in the face. 'My sweet little wife wouldn't say "shit" for sixpence, but she can quite happily
commit adultery.' He yelled this so loudly the gardener, who was
pruning the acalyphas, *must* have heard him.

'Magnus, for heaven's sake.'

A cold, bitter laugh escaped him. '"Magnus, for heaven's sake,"'
he mimicked in a tinny voice. Then he roared again, 'Will you get
off your fucking high horse?' Stabbing the tell-tale envelope with a
solid brown forefinger, he glared at Stella. 'Who's Tom Kearney?'

'He's a soldier I met in Singapore during the war.' Lifting
her chin, Stella refused to be cowed. 'But writing letters is hardly
adultery.'

'What about stealing away to Cairns to stay with a man in a
seedy hotel?'

Stella was so shocked she couldn't answer at first. How on
earth could Magnus know about that? After all this time? Twenty
years . . .

'I don't know what you mean,' she lied.

'Don't try to deny it, whore.' He was shaking with anger now,
and for the first time Stella felt frightened of him. 'I didn't listen to
Derek Briggs all those years ago when he tried to tell me that he saw
you down in Cairns with your fancy man. Not my Stella, I told him,
even though I knew I'd been out bush on a muster at the time. Like a
fool I trusted you, and I sent him off with a flea in his ear.'

Magnus lifted a hand as if he wanted to strike her. His fingers
curled into a fist, which he shook in her face, but before he connected, he drew his hand back and kept it tight against his chest. 'I've
always been honest with you. I've even shared my darkest secret, but
all this time, you've been cheating behind my back. You've probably
cheated on me dozens of times.'

'No, Magnus, no.'

'For all I know, my son's not even my own kid.'

'No!' Stella cried. 'That's not true.'

He wouldn't listen. With a snarl of disgust, he whirled on his heel and stormed off to collect the case of whisky he'd bought in town. Taking it to his study, he slammed the door behind him.

Several times, Stella knocked at the door to the study and pleaded with him to listen to her, but he wouldn't answer. She didn't see him again until evening and by then he'd also written a letter – to his lawyer.

32

On the day before the party, Deborah and Xavier arrived at Ruthven Downs just before lunch. Jackie was in the dining room, arranging long stems of red flowering ginger in a tall vase. Hugh was in an armchair in the adjoining lounge room. He was reading the paper somewhat restlessly, having been obliged to hang about the house, instead of taking off for far-flung corners of the property to inspect his cattle, his pasture, or the water levels in his dams.

'Here they are,' Jackie called as the unhealthy rattle of a vehicle on the track signalled the approach of Deborah's ancient Kombi van.

The only response from her husband was the rustle of his newspaper.

'Hugh,' Jackie called again. 'Deborah's here.'

Deborah was *his* sister, after all, and although Jackie had never achieved the bond with the woman that she might have hoped for, she knew that Hugh was very fond of her.

Today, however, Hugh was also extremely tense about the possible outcome of his sister's visit. Jackie wondered if he'd finally realised how impetuous he'd been to instantly share his father's preposterous letter with Deborah.

Now it was too late to change his mind. The rattling van had come to a standstill. A door slammed. Deborah Drummond was here.

Jackie hurried along the verandah and down the front steps, and at last, Hugh's footsteps sounded behind her.

'Ahoy!' Deborah called as she rounded the side of her van, and she looked, as always, like an ageing hippie in a blue and green kaftan, with her long grey hair falling from a centre part to hang limply past her shoulders. Her face was completely free of make-up.

Over the years, Jackie had played with the idea of styling Deborah's hair – a jaunty bob cut in at the nape, or something layered and wispy, but of course she'd never dared to suggest it.

'Lovely to see you,' she said now as she reached Deborah.

'You too.' Deborah kissed her, European style, on both cheeks. 'And don't look so worried, Jackie. I come in peace.'

Jackie laughed nervously, and stepped back to let Hugh and Deborah hug. Then Xavier emerged from the van, long and lean, bearded and scruffy in holey jeans and a faded grey T-shirt, smiling sleepily from beneath a full head of dreadlocks.

Dreadlocks, goodness. He'd had long hair his whole life, but this was a new statement of non-conformity.

Another round of greetings ensued and Jackie caught a whiff of whatever Xavier had been smoking.

'Charlie's not with you?' Deborah asked, as she looked around, frowning at the sweep of newly mowed lawns, the carefully weeded beds and pruned shrubbery.

'Seth's gone down to Cairns to collect Flora from the airport,' Jackie explained. 'And he's taken Charlie with him. Flora's desperate for a cuddle.'

'Aren't we all? I'm sure Charlie's grown heaps. It feels like ages since we've seen him.' Deborah slid open the door on the side of the van. 'Xavier, be a darling and grab our bags, will you?'

Inside the van, there was a jumble of art easels and boxes with tubes of paint, but Xavier dutifully unearthed a scuffed navy duffle bag and a drawstring patchwork affair that Deborah had almost certainly made with her own clever, crafty hands.

'I'll bring the esky,' Deborah said.

'Esky?' Jackie was so surprised she forgot to hide her reaction and her eyebrows shot high. In all the years she'd known Hugh's sister, Deborah had never contributed food or drink to any party. Not that Jackie had ever expected her to, but why the sudden change?

'Just a few bits and pieces,' Deborah said as she slid the van door shut with a slam. She beamed triumphantly. 'I thought we'd better bring a few supplies seeing that we're vegans now.'

Vegans? Jackie caught Hugh's eye. He looked as helpless as she felt.

'I know what carnivores you two are,' Deborah added airily.

Jackie thought of the party food she and her friends had planned so carefully – Maria's lasagne and Kate's pork ribs, her own Greek Cypriot lamb, not to mention the chicken casserole she'd cooked for this evening's family gathering.

And lunch? What about lunch? She'd been thinking of salmon and salad. She wasn't even sure what vegans ate. 'Can you have fish?' she asked.

'No, no fish. No animal products whatsoever.' At least Deborah looked matter of fact rather than smug as she announced this. 'No eggs, butter, honey or cheese. But don't worry. We love our salads and fruit and I've brought plenty of tofu and quinoa.'

As they entered the homestead, Jackie clung to a rather comforting thought. A vegan was hardly likely to want to take over the running of a beef cattle property.

———

Flora arrived off the flight from Melbourne looking like a proper city chick, with a trendy new, lopsided haircut, an equally trendy little black dress, a violin case dangling from one shoulder and a classy leather overnight bag in hand. She was even wearing a cardigan, an item of clothing that was practically unknown in Cairns, certainly at this time of the year.

Seth, watching her arrive through sliding doors, felt an unexpected lump in his throat. His kid sister had grown up, moved away, thrown off all visible signs of the horse-mad country tomboy he'd once so mercilessly teased.

She saw them and waved. 'Helloooo!' A small squeal escaped her as she hurried forward, her eyes excited, her arms outstretched. 'Charlie boy. How are you, you gorgeous little man?'

Charlie was a little shy, clinging to Seth while Flora kissed him and gushed.

'He'll soon thaw out,' Seth assured her. 'He's just a bit overawed at the moment.'

'Well, yes, there's so much to see in a busy airport, isn't there, Charlie? Wait till you see the lovely presents I've brought you.'

'And how about a hello for me?' Seth said.

'Of course. Sorry. It's so good to see you, big brother. I've missed you.'

Dropping her bag, Flora embraced him enthusiastically. Her blue eyes were sparkling as they separated again, and Seth thought, momentarily, that the sparkles might have been tears – and not happy tears, either. But Flora was smiling, so he must have imagined that flash of sadness. Perhaps she was just a bit emotional about coming home after almost a whole year away. And it was probably the make-up that made her eyes look so extra-bright.

He held out his hand for her bag. 'So, I guess this is it? You only have carry-on luggage?' She was home for only a few days, after all.

'No, actually, I do have a suitcase.' Flora looked a tad guilty about this. 'You know me, couldn't decide what to wear, so I brought the lot.'

Seth heaved an exaggerated sigh as he followed her to the luggage carousel.

'Now here's something that's fun to watch,' Flora told Charlie. 'Look at all the suitcases having a ride.'

Charlie wriggled in Seth's arms. 'Roun'n'roun,' he said, pointing to the carousel.

'Yes! Round and round. Wow, aren't you a clever boy?' Flora held out her arms again, and Charlie went to her willingly this time, submitting to a cuddle, before squirming to watch the bags trundling past on the conveyor belt.

Charlie continued to wave and exclaim over the circling luggage, but brother and sister were silent for a bit as they watched and waited. Then Flora tilted her head to scrutinise Seth. 'So how's the new girlfriend?'

The simple question shouldn't have caused a painful jolt in the centre of his chest.

'She's coming to the party, isn't she?' Flora persisted. 'I can't wait to meet her.'

Seth kept his face deadpan. 'Sounds like Mum's been spilling the beans.'

Flora shrugged. 'Mum hasn't had a lot to say. I'd reckon Alice Miller only scored a mention in every second email.'

She grinned as she told him this and Seth managed a crooked smile that he hoped didn't look too awkward.

'It's nothing serious,' he assured her. *And it will be all over within forty-eight hours.*

'That's a pity. I reckon you and Charlie could do with a little ongoing female company.'

Ignoring this unwanted advice, Seth couldn't resist getting his own back. 'Pity your bloke couldn't make it for the party. How is he? Everything okay?'

'Yes, he's fine.' Flora flipped her response over her shoulder, while she paid studious attention to the approaching luggage.

Then her phone pinged and she shifted Charlie onto one hip while she retrieved the phone from the pocket of her cardigan. 'Speak of the devil. Oliver's checking that I've arrived.' She quickly tapped a reply.

'Why couldn't he come, Floss? Last-minute hitch?' Seth was keen to keep the conversation well away from his own relationship issues, and for the past few months, Flora's emails had seemed to be almost all about Oliver. 'Did he score a new singing gig or something?'

Flora nodded, and bent to kiss the top of Charlie's head, without shifting her gaze from the luggage. 'Oh, there's my bag.' She pointed way down the line. 'Can you grab it, Seth. The silver one with the red bow.'

Within half an hour, the airport parking ticket was paid for, the luggage stowed, and Charlie, protesting, was re-buckled into his car seat, distracted by a brightly coloured toy monkey that Flora produced from her bag. They were heading back up the rainforest-clad range to Kuranda before Seth raised the subject of the family meeting. To his surprise, Flora knew nothing about it.

When she demanded an explanation, he had to hedge. 'Dad thought it would be a good idea to have a meeting while you and Aunt Deb are both home. To make a few decisions about the property.'

Flora wrinkled her nose. 'I can't imagine that I'll have much to contribute.'

'Why not? You're part of the family.' And there'd been a time, albeit quite some years ago now, when Flora's dream had been to grow up to be a cattlewoman. 'Are you a total city girl these days?'

At this, Flora frowned and looked out through the windscreen to the lush vegetation that arched overhead and crowded close to the sides of the winding road. Green tree ferns and palms abounded, along with clumps of flowering ginger and towering trees with thick trunks wrapped in snaking vines and creepers.

'I don't know,' his sister said in a small voice. 'When I'm down there in Melbourne I feel totally immersed in my work and the city lifestyle, but as soon as I set foot in the north again, I begin to feel a deep tug. It's weird.'

'I guess the north will always be home,' Seth said gently. 'And you never know, a different perspective from you could be useful in the family meeting Dad's organised.'

'Maybe.' Flora's phone pinged again and she took it out of her pocket, looked at the caller ID and sighed.

Seth noted that she dismissed it without bothering to respond this time, but she kept the phone in her lap, almost as if she expected more calls.

Again, he had the uneasy feeling that all wasn't quite right in his sister's world. Or was he transposing some of his own disappointment and confusion? He was on tenterhooks about Alice coming to the party, not to mention her offer to babysit Charlie this evening.

He knew the babysitting agreement was some kind of challenge that Alice had set herself, but he wasn't sure why this was suddenly important to her. They were supposed to be stepping back from each other, but this felt like a step closer.

Seth couldn't deny that her belated offer had been handy, but he wasn't going to be messed around. There was already enough drama with his family, without relationship hassles. And he really had no idea how well Alice would cope with his son.

Checking the rear-vision mirror again, Seth saw that Charlie had nodded off, still clutching the monkey. He always looked angelic and vulnerable when he was asleep, and Seth hoped all would go smoothly for the little guy and Alice. At least she wouldn't be far away, and he supposed she could always sing out if there was a drama.

Just the same, he would be relieved when this evening and the party, plus their charade, were behind them. Then he and Alice could say goodbye once and for all, and his life could get back to normal.

If only he knew what the new normal would be after the family's meeting.

33

By mid-afternoon, Jackie was starting to feel calmer. Lunch had proved pleasant enough, as their salad was deemed to be an acceptable accompaniment to Deborah's quinoa.

Deborah could still drink wine, Jackie noted with mild amusement, and Hugh opened a lovely cold South Australian white, which helped to mellow things nicely. Actually, with Xavier joining them in a drink, it wasn't long before a second bottle was needed.

They managed to keep their conversation to safe topics – the weather, old friends, the latest gossip from Deborah's art world, and Xavier's rather vague plans to launch a music career. When Hugh rather cautiously alluded to the sticky question of the Ruthven Downs inheritance, Deborah laughed.

'What a storm in a teacup, Hugh. Why on earth would I ever want this place?'

Jackie tittered at this with nervous relief.

Hugh looked more relaxed too. 'I suppose Mum must have had good reasons for not taking Dad's letter to the lawyers,' he said.

Deborah nodded. 'Dad was drinking heavily back then, if you remember. It was around the time he had his stroke, and I think he was starting to have memory lapses. There was a chance he might have written that letter one night in a drunken fury and then – who knows? The upset might have even brought on the stroke.'

Emboldened by this, Jackie added her two cents' worth. 'Well, I don't believe Hugh is Tom Kearney's son.'

'Of course he isn't,' responded Deborah emphatically. 'Hugh has Dad's dark hair and eyes after all, and you only had to see them standing together to notice the similarities. It was obvious,' she said with an expressive wave of her hand. 'Their height, the breadth of their shoulders, the shape of their jaws. Even the way they held themselves was the same.'

'Well, there you go,' Hugh said with a bemused smile. 'I never realised we had so much in common.'

Jackie refrained from clapping her hands in delight, but she was certainly thrilled with this happy resolution. 'It takes an artist's eye to spot details like that,' she said generously, and her gaze lingered on a painting that Deborah had given them that hung on the dining room wall.

She'd always liked this particular work, despite her reservations about her sister-in-law. It was an oil painting of a rainforest track with towering trees on either side, and it seemed to perfectly capture the magical beauty of the twisting vines, the lush green palm fronds, the thick buttressed tree trunks, while offering glimpses through the canopy to a bright blue tropical sky.

Even more interesting, and painted in careful, loving detail, was the back view of a hiker on the track. A man, tall and lean, in a khaki shirt and shorts, thick socks and hiking boots. He had sandy-coloured, curly hair and tanned, muscular legs, and Jackie had often wondered if he was Xavier's father. Deborah had always been tight-lipped about that subject.

Did all families have so many secrets?

Jackie was relieved that at least she could breathe much more easily now. She and Deborah were getting along famously, and Deb even helped her to clear the lunch things.

They had only just finished this task when Seth and Flora arrived. The travellers, having stopped at a café in Kuranda, weren't hungry, but more cups of tea – including herbal tea for Deborah – were served on the verandah. This, amid joyous greetings and hugs and major fussing over Charlie, as well as commiserations with Flora over her boyfriend's last-minute change of plans.

Then it was time for Charlie's nap and Seth carted him off. Hugh declared that he could do with a nap too.

'An excellent idea.' Deborah was a little flushed and animated after several glasses of wine at lunch. 'I find the drive from Cape Trib rather tiring these days. I might take that diary of Mum's to read while I have a lie-down.'

Peace reigned as Hugh and Deborah retreated to their rooms. Xavier, who hadn't been allocated a bedroom, would be sleeping on the day bed on the verandah. He announced that he'd go for a bit of a wander.

Left to themselves, Jackie and Flora opted for a second cuppa and the chance for a proper mother-and-daughter chat.

'You might like to do a little unpacking first,' Jackie suggested to Flora, as she refilled the electric jug. 'You must be hot in those clothes.'

'Mmmm.' Flora glanced down at her dress and black cardigan and shrugged. 'I guess.'

She came back in denim shorts and a long-sleeved white cotton top, looking almost like the country girl Jackie remembered, although in the past Flora's nut-brown hair had been long and usually tied back in a careless ponytail, and she'd practically lived in singlet tops.

Looking at her daughter now, Jackie thought she seemed paler, but that was probably to be expected after eighteen months in Melbourne.

'Are you tired?' she couldn't help asking. 'You've had a long journey. Feel free to have a rest, too, if you want to.'

Flora shook her head. 'I'm fine, Mum. I won't sleep tonight if I have a rest now.'

'I really like that asymmetrical bob,' Jackie added. 'I would have loved to try something like that when I was young. It makes you look very trendy and sophisticated.'

'Thanks.' Flora grinned, clearly pleased.

She'd brought her mobile phone back to the kitchen, and she checked it again now. Jackie had seen her checking it several times since she'd arrived. She supposed her daughter was now one of those young people who couldn't bear to be separated from their phones.

Jackie had seen them in cafés, young people sitting at tables in groups, every head bowed as they each madly scrolled through Facebook, or texted someone miles away, instead of talking to the friends they were actually dining with. She found this behaviour bizarre, but knew it was probably a sure sign that she was growing old.

'I suppose Oliver's missing you,' she couldn't help suggesting as her daughter frowned at the small screen in her hands.

'Um . . . yes, he likes to keep in touch.' Something about the way Flora said this bothered Jackie, but then the girl surprised her by coming close and dropping a warm kiss on her cheek. 'Thanks for the flowers in my room, Mum.'

'Oh.' Jackie shrugged at the unexpectedness of this. 'You know me, always fussing with flowers.'

'Yes, but it's wonderful to come home and see things looking so lovely and just the way they've always been. When I was a kid, I never really appreciated what a great job you did, keeping the place always looking so nice.'

'Gosh, thank you, darling.' Jackie's flush of pleasure was somewhat marred when she remembered how uncertain the future of this home was now, even though Deb had been so reassuring at lunch. She wasn't going to relax yet. That might have been the wine talking.

But she didn't want to talk about the property now with Flora.

This evening's meeting would come all too quickly.

Once they were back on the verandah, the conversation with her daughter wasn't quite as cosy and close as Jackie had hoped for. Flora chattered happily enough about Melbourne, about the orchestra and the friends she'd made, but now that Jackie was face to face with her, the enthusiasm that had sounded so real in emails seemed a bit forced.

Jackie remembered the strange sense of foreboding she'd felt when she'd read Flora's last email about Oliver's sudden change of plans.

She didn't want to spoil her daughter's homecoming by asking probing questions too early in the piece, but at some point over the next couple of days, she needed to satisfy herself that Flora really was happy.

Flora was asking a few questions of her own, mostly about Seth's girlfriend, Alice Miller, when her attention was caught by something in the distance. She paused in mid-sentence.

Looking out across the lawns, she frowned. 'Look, Mum. What's up with Xavier?'

Jackie followed the direction of her daughter's gaze, past the boundary of the homestead gardens to the cluster of sheds. Xavier seemed to be coming from the sheds and his normally dreamy demeanour had vanished. Instead, he looked agitated and was moving towards them with unusual speed.

Even as they watched, he broke into a jog. Jackie frowned. She could see Xavier's face more clearly now and he looked as if he'd seen a ghost. 'I wonder if he's seen a snake,' she said.

Flora shook her head. 'I reckon he'd be used to snakes, living at Cape Tribulation.'

'Tree snakes, yes, but probably not brown snakes.' Jackie was on her feet now, as Xavier raced up to them. If he'd been bitten he shouldn't be running. He should have stayed where he was and used his phone, like any other person his age.

Chances were, though, that Xavier was like his mother and didn't bother with mobile phones. Already Jackie was planning a frantic dash to their first-aid cupboard. She could grab a tourniquet and apply it while Flora dialled for an ambulance.

'What the hell's going on?' Xavier shouted as he leaped up the verandah steps with uncharacteristic energy, before he came bearing down on them, wild eyed and red-faced.

Jackie stared at him, totally perplexed. Clearly it wasn't a snake bite that bothered him. She spoke calmly. 'What are you talking about, Xavier?'

He waved his arms dramatically. 'What are Mum's paintings doing in a shed out there?'

'Her *paintings*?' Jackie felt her jaw drop so fast it probably dislocated. 'For heaven's sake,' she said. 'Which shed? Where?'

When Xavier continued to glare at her, she added defensively, 'I have no idea what you're talking about.'

'Like hell you don't.' Xavier, habitually undemonstrative, was extremely expressive now. He gave another theatrical fling of his arm and pointed back to the sheds. 'There's a pile of them over there. What are you lot up to? I'm getting Mum.'

Before Jackie could make any sense of this, Xavier strode off down the verandah towards the bedrooms. As he passed her, she caught another whiff of cigarettes. She didn't really know what marijuana smelled like, but this was certainly a different aroma from normal tobacco.

She realised then what this was all about. Deborah and Xavier had always been rainforest hippies and Xavier had snuck off to the sheds to have a quiet smoke. He was probably hallucinating. Deborah would just laugh.

Xavier, meanwhile, was now yelling at the top of his lungs. 'Mum, come quick. Mum! You gotta see what I've found.'

Surely he had to be seeing things? On some kind of trip? How could they possibly have any of Deborah's paintings in one of their sheds?

Jackie looked helplessly to Flora. 'Do you think he might be on drugs? Having a trip?'

Flora looked equally perplexed. 'Maybe. He smells like he smokes cigarettes not generally available to the public. And his pupils are dilated.'

'That's what I thought. He must be seeing things, surely?'

'It certainly sounds weird.'

They could hear Xavier's and Deborah's voices now, coming from within the house.

'What's the matter?' Deborah demanded. 'What paintings? What are you talking about??'

'In the shed. Mum, a heap of your favourites. You gotta come and see.'

Then Hugh joined in. 'What's going on? What's the problem?'

'Xavier seems to think he's found some of my paintings in one of your sheds.'

An ominous silence followed.

Jackie glanced Flora's way again and this time they exchanged anxious shrugs. Jackie hadn't a clue about the contents of the sheds. The buildings were rather ancient and shabby, made of corrugated iron. They were Hugh and Seth's domain. Mostly they housed machinery and stock feed, tins of petrol or cattle dip. In one shed, as far as she could remember, there were bits of old vehicles, saved for spare parts, but she hardly ever went near them and couldn't remember the last time she'd been inside one.

She was still puzzling through this when Deborah appeared on the verandah, followed closely by Xavier. Then Hugh came some paces behind them. Jackie could see straight away that he looked distressed.

Alarm shot through her. Why wasn't her husband his usual placid self, calming everyone else down? What on earth was this about? Surely Xavier was mistaken.

But Hugh's nephew was absolutely determined as he set off, back down the steps and across the lawn, his mother hurrying close behind him, her rubber thongs flip-flopping over the grass.

Frowning, shaking her head in confusion, Jackie turned to Hugh. 'What's this about? Is Xavier off his rocker?'

Hugh's face contorted in a pained grimace. 'Unfortunately, no he's not,' he said unhappily.

Goosebumps broke out on Jackie's arms. 'But –'

'I never thought he'd start nosing about in the sheds,' Hugh added tightly.

'You mean –?'

Her husband didn't wait to answer any more of her questions. For the briefest moment, impatience and despair warred in his usually gentle dark eyes, but then he took off after his sister and his nephew, his long legs striding to catch up.

With a helpless shrug, Jackie followed him. Flora, looking equally puzzled and worried, was close behind her.

Xavier was right. There were paintings in one of the sheds.

They were at the back of the least used shed, behind a pile of old broken furniture that should have been burned or taken to the dump years ago. Carefully stacked, the paintings had obviously been covered with tarpaulins and packaged in thick cardboard, but Xavier had stripped these away. Now the tarps were heaped haphazardly in a corner, and the jagged and torn pieces of cardboard lay curling on the concrete floor like tresses fallen from a hairdresser's scissors.

Exposed, the framed canvases glowed with the bright hues of oil paint.

Deborah took a step towards them, before a terrible wail broke from her and she crumpled at the waist, covering her appalled mouth with a trembling hand.

Hugh, standing nearby, closed his eyes, his face a picture of pain.

Jackie felt ice water pool in her stomach. None of this made sense.

'It's unbelievable, Mum,' Xavier cried, as he pulled one of the paintings out to show the vivid blue head of a cassowary poking through the lush green fronds of a licuala palm. 'I recognised the first package as soon as I saw the name of the Cairns Gallery stamped on the cardboard. So many of your favourites are here.'

His wild glare took in Jackie and Hugh and Flora, who remained near the door.

'To think I was feeling guilty about hunting for somewhere to keep my stash,' he said. 'I knew you lot were sniffing me like drug dogs at the airport, but you're the ones who've been exposed now.' Again Xavier gestured to the paintings. '*This* is the crime. Not me smoking a bit of ganja.'

As Deborah whimpered and the others stood stiffly in stunned silence, Xavier, like some kind of crazed art dealer trying to impress potential buyers, pulled out painting after painting, all in Deborah's typically vibrant style. First, a still life of a timber bowl filled with brightly coloured exotic fruit. Next, a scene of intricately twisted mangrove roots reflected in the surface of a glass-smooth creek. A delicate painting of native orchids followed, then another of rainforest pigeons, and a beautiful scene of a forest-fringed tropical beach.

The paintings were good; even Jackie, who knew almost nothing about art, could see how beautiful, original and skilfully executed they were. And Deborah's love of her subject matter came shining through, capturing the true essence of the tropical north.

With so much evidence before them, Jackie had to speak, to ask the obvious question. 'What on earth are these paintings doing here?'

Xavier and Deborah stared at her as if she was stupid, then they turned to Hugh.

With an unhappy shrug, he said simply, 'I bought them.'

'*You?*' There was so much emotion in Deborah's crestfallen cry. 'You *bought* them? For God's sake, Hugh, why?'

'You were struggling, but you wouldn't let me help you. You wouldn't accept any money.' Hugh lifted his hands in a gesture of helplessness. 'This was the only way I could think of to help.'

For a long moment, Deborah stared at her brother, her eyes wide and doubtful and glistening. Then, as she assimilated what he'd told her, her expression grew despairing, her mouth sagged.

She gave an agitated shake of her head. 'So how did it work? You had an arrangement with the gallery in Cairns?'

'With – a few places,' Hugh admitted.

'And as soon as my work arrived in their galleries, they were to be earmarked for you?'

'No, not straight away –' Hugh stopped, as if he realised he was making this worse.

Deborah blinked. Her mouth worked as she fixed him with a wild-eyed stare. 'So you only took the paintings if they didn't sell within a certain time frame?'

Silence fell until, reluctantly, Hugh nodded.

Tears shimmered in Deborah's eyes. 'Oh, God, Hugh, how could you?' A sob broke from her. 'Have you any idea what you've done? What this means?'

It meant you had bread on your table, Jackie wanted to tell her. She was desperate to defend her husband, even though she was angry with him, and shocked that he could do this without confiding in her. He must have paid for the paintings out of his personal account and he must have also had an arrangement with the post office in Mareeba. This was hardly the right moment to voice her own questions, though, so she kept her mouth firmly shut.

Hugh didn't speak either. And Flora – poor Flora, who'd only just arrived home – was still standing near the door, with her arms folded across her chest, looking as if she'd have given anything to jump on the next plane back to Melbourne.

Then, cutting through the silence, Deborah let fly. 'I've always believed that my paintings were sold to genuine art lovers. All these years, I've imagined them in people's homes, hanging on their walls, becoming part of their lives, and –'

Her mouth turned square, but somehow she managed to finish what she wanted to say. 'And all this time they've been hidden away in your bloody shed, like – like a dirty fucking secret.'

Deborah's tears fell now, streaming down her face, but instead of looking old and ugly, Jackie thought her sister-in-law looked rather like a courageous child as she swiped at the tears with the heels of her hands.

Poor Hugh looked pale and distraught. Tentatively, he touched Deborah on the shoulder. 'I'm sorry, Deb. I should have talked to you about this – I should have found a better way to help.'

'I didn't need any help.'

'I know that's what you always said, but there were times when you struggled. I – I couldn't bear to see how hard your life was – going without, while I had everything.'

'I'm an artist!' his sister cried, shrugging away from his hand, so that it fell uselessly to his side. 'That's what we artists do. We struggle. Our satisfaction comes from creating, from sharing the work we produce in the hope it will bring pleasure to others. Enrich their lives. Payment is a form of recognition, an unfortunate necessity, but we don't need all the trappings.' With this, she shot a venomous glare in Jackie's direction. 'I've never needed to live the high life.'

Somewhat desperately, Jackie found herself trying not to look guilty. It wasn't easy, when she knew she hadn't merely enjoyed the *trappings* Deborah referred to so scathingly, she'd also relished them. The lovely homestead, the social status of being a successful grazier's wife, the boarding schools for her children, the luxurious holidays. These things had meant everything to her. Too much.

'I suppose you knew these paintings were here,' Deborah snapped.

Jackie couldn't think of an answer. There was so much hostility in the woman's gaze and voice. If she responded honestly, claiming ignorance, she would leave poor Hugh high and dry.

'No one else in my family knew anything about it,' Hugh cut in, gallantly. 'This was my idea, and mine alone. My foolishly mistaken idea, it seems, and I take full blame.'

For the first time, his jaw stiffened and a hint of annoyance flared in his eyes. 'Take the paintings back, Deb. Just take the lot of them. You should sell them again.'

'Of course I should. In fact, I damn well *will* sell them, and probably for a good deal more than you paid for them.' She sniffed. 'My reputation has grown quite a bit in recent years.'

Hugh nodded and let out a heavy sigh, possibly a sigh of relief.

'But don't think I'm going to let you off lightly, Hugh.' Deborah's head was high now, and her shoulders were back, her eyes fierce, ready for a fight. 'Have you any idea how much you've hurt me? Do you realise how small you've made me feel? Can you possibly understand how much it galls me to know that all the work, all the heart and soul I poured into these paintings was pointless?'

'Deb, you shouldn't feel –'

'Don't tell me how I should or shouldn't feel.'

Hugh's eyes narrowed. 'There's no need to –'

'There's every need.' She stamped her foot. 'I can't believe you're so one-eyed about this. You haven't once tried to put yourself in my shoes.'

'That's not true.' Jackie had to jump to Hugh's defence again. 'Can't you see, Hugh only did this because he cared about you?'

'No, that's not how I see it at all. Hugh was more worried about his own guilty conscience, because he's been sitting pretty on this property all these years.'

Triumph gleamed in Deborah's eyes as she said this and, as she turned back to Hugh, her mouth curled in an unpleasant, almost cruel smile. 'And you know what? I'm going to help ease your conscience, little brother. I take back what I said at lunchtime. I've changed my mind. After this –' she flung an arm towards the paintings – 'I do want what's morally due to me and my son. I'm going to stake my claim on Ruthven Downs.'

34

'Hey, Charlie, look who's here.'

Alice tried to ignore the giddy rush of pleasure caused by Seth's welcoming smile. It was important to stifle her instinctive reaction. Their relationship was all but over. She was only here this evening to help Seth out.

She'd told herself it was the whole Drummond family that she'd come to help. It had seemed the right thing to do, given that she'd become unwittingly involved when she found their documents. But after this evening, and tomorrow night's face-saving exercise at Hugh Drummond's party, she and Seth would go their separate ways.

No point in dwelling on that cheerless prospect now, though. This evening Alice had to focus. She couldn't afford any distractions. She needed to apply total concentration to the task of caring for Charlie, while she faced down her personal demons.

Unfortunately, distractions abounded, starting when Seth's dog Ralph came rushing to greet her with flattering eagerness and a madly thrashing tail. Then there was Seth himself. An old grey T-shirt and battered jeans should not look so heart-stoppingly masculine. And, despite everything, Seth's smile could still send her spinning.

Then Charlie, more adorable than ever, with his floppy blond hair and bright blue eyes, already in his pyjamas and radiant with that special toddler after-bath glow. To Alice's surprise, he ran forward to her with his arms outstretched.

'Aleeee.'

She had prepared for this babysitting task with the conscientious attention to detail of a Special Forces soldier preparing for a secret mission against Al-Qaeda. During her research, she'd read that the 'Fake it till you make it' attitude really did work, so she'd decided to behave as if she was a different woman. This evening she would be someone who was calm and relaxed with small folk, someone sensible and phobia-free.

Psyching herself up to succeed was half the battle. She'd worked hard at it and she felt surprisingly calm as she kneeled to Charlie's height and held out her arms. 'Hello there, Charlie.'

Gleefully, the little boy accepted her hug and she caught the scent of strawberries. 'Oh, you do smell nice.'

'He had a bubble bath tonight as a special treat,' said Seth.

'A bubble bath. How lucky are you?'

It was working. Alice felt fine, like a nice, warm and friendly nanny type. As she straightened, Seth stepped closer to speak to her in a low voice. 'I'm afraid I need to get cracking.'

Alice frowned. 'I thought I was early.'

'You are,' he said. 'But unfortunately, there's been a new development on the home front. Things are hotting up and the meeting's been brought forward.'

'Is – is everything all right?'

Seth shrugged. 'Doesn't sound like it.'

'Are you worried?' she couldn't help asking.

For a moment Seth's expression was bleak, as if he was indeed very worried, but then he cracked a smile. 'Not much point in worrying till I know all the facts.'

'That's sensible.' His steady strength was reassuring and she had to fight an urge to lean in to him, to draw a little of that strength for herself. 'And don't worry about anything here,' she said. Tonight she had to stand on her own two feet. 'Charlie and I will be fine.'

Seth nodded. 'I'll have my phone and I'm only a couple of minutes away, so don't hesitate to call me if you're worried about anything.'

'I won't.'

He showed her where the tea and coffee things were, told her to help herself to anything from the pantry or fridge, showed her the mug Charlie drank from, the pile of Charlie's favourite bedtime books, the night light in his bedroom, the cupboard where the disposable nappies were kept.

'I hope he behaves for you,' he said when the tour was completed. 'Normally he's in bed by half past seven at the latest, but don't panic if he's not tonight. With any luck, I'll be back soon after then.'

'Okay.' Standing in the middle of the bedroom, Alice could feel Charlie's small hand linked trustingly with hers. 'We might take a look at one of these storybooks, hey, Charlie?'

Alice and Seth had already agreed over the phone that it would probably be best not to draw attention to the fact that Charlie's father was going away. So now, selecting a couple of books, she sat on the edge of the bed and Charlie scrambled up beside up her. She opened the pages of a picture book about a little boy who lived on a farm, and she was aware of Seth leaving quietly.

Charlie was exclaiming over a picture of a shiny red tractor, patting the page and making *broom-broom* noises, when the faint click of the front door sounded. Luckily, he didn't seem to hear it.

Alice let out a small huff of relief. Seth had slipped away without a problem. *Over the first hurdle.*

———

Now to face the family. Or possibly, Armageddon.

Seth was relieved that Alice and Charlie seemed okay, but his gut tightened when he considered his own future. There was every chance that his life would be forever changed during the next hour.

If the frantic text message from his mother was correct, dinner had been postponed and the meeting brought forward. Apparently, Aunt Deborah planned to stake her moral claim on Ruthven Downs after all. And given the way his father had been carrying on lately, Deborah would probably succeed.

Which would narrow Seth's options considerably – or broaden them, depending on how you looked at it. Right now, he had no idea whether he would end up homeless and penniless, or managing the Ruthven Downs property for his aunt, or, God help him, teaching bloody Xavier how to be a cattleman.

A glance across to the homestead showed his mother on the verandah, beckoning to him frantically, before running back inside. She was in a flap, of course. She loved this place, possibly more than any of them. This was her worst nightmare.

It was only a couple of hundred metres to the house, the only home Seth had ever known, but as he broke into a jog he felt as if he was running clueless into a lethal battle. An ambush?

———

Halfway through the third storybook Charlie grew restless and climbed down from the bed.

'Okay,' Alice said, taking her cue from him and setting the book about frogs and ponds aside. 'What would you like to do now?'

The little boy looked at her blankly, then headed for the bedroom doorway. Suddenly nervous, Alice hurried after him. Would he realise Seth was missing and begin to cry? Was the peace about to be shattered?

Charlie stopped in the middle of the lounge room, looked about him, looked at the sliding glass door and the bush beyond. Alice held her breath. He looked at the cane basket brimming with his toys.

She scanned the toys, hoping to see the rabbit, which she knew was his favourite, but she had no luck. A niggle of nervousness started in her stomach.

Stop it. Just do what any other sitter would do. Play a game with him.

What game? Alice picked up a little blue and yellow truck from the top of the pile. 'Would you like to play with this?'

Charlie looked at her strangely, as if this was the weirdest suggestion he'd ever heard. She took a deep breath. *Don't lose it, girl.*

Dropping to her knees, she pushed the little truck over the floor and tried to make engine noises. Charlie watched politely, but without any real interest.

'Dad,' he said, looking towards the door.

Desperate now, Alice grabbed a green and white striped cushion from a nearby armchair and dropped it over the truck. 'Oh, goodness,' she said, feigning huge surprise. 'Where's the truck? What happened to the truck, Charlie? Is it hiding?'

At least she had his attention again. Squatting beside the cushion, with his dimpled hands resting on his round pink knees, the little boy stared at the cushion for a moment, then pushed it aside.

'Oh!' Alice exclaimed with mock excitement. 'There it is. Clever boy. You found your truck.'

Seeing that she'd held his interest, she added, 'Will we hide it again?'

Charlie nodded and smiled. Alice covered the truck with the striped cushion.

The little boy looked up at her in eager anticipation. 'Truck?' he said.

'Where is it?' She lifted a corner of the cushion and Charlie gasped with excitement. 'Is it under here?' she asked.

He didn't seem sure, but he was riveted.

Alice pulled the cushion away. 'Oh!' she exclaimed again. 'There it is!'

'Truck!' Charlie crowed, his face alight with excitement. Then he grinned at Alice. 'Again.'

It became a game, a wonderful game. Over and over they hid the truck and then found it again, and with each rediscovery Charlie became more excited and squeally. Alice knew it was silly to feel such a huge sense of achievement, but she'd never expected such instant success. Somehow, instinctively, she'd hit on a way to entertain Seth's son. She could do this. She really could.

She was hiding the truck for the umpteenth time, and Charlie was hauling the cushion off again with an ear-splitting squeal that could have brought his father running, when she realised he was over-excited.

It was time to call a halt, or she would never get him to bed.

'Okay, I think it's time to calm down, Charlie boy.' She reached to draw him to her for a cuddle.

He wriggled to be free of her. 'More! Truck!'

'No, it's time we put the truck away to sleep in the basket.'

Slowly but deliberately, Alice picked the truck up and placed it in the basket. Charlie stared at her, the delight and excitement in his little face fading, replaced by trembling-lipped disappointment.

What now? she wondered. She'd been so pleased with herself. She'd been doing so well at this baby-sitting gig, but perhaps she'd peaked too early.

Her mind raced. 'Would – would you like a drink?'

To her relief, Charlie gave this some consideration and then nodded, and together they went into the adjoining kitchen. 'What would you like? Water?'

He pointed to the fridge. 'Juice.'

Alice wasn't prepared to argue, so she opened the fridge and found a bottle of apple juice.

'Ooh!' Charlie exclaimed, also spying a punnet of blueberries on a lower shelf. 'Berries!!'

'You like blueberries?'

This brought a nod and a rapturous grin.

Seth hadn't mentioned giving Charlie anything more to eat, but she supposed a few blueberries couldn't hurt, and as she was keen to keep the kid happy and calm, she rinsed a few and found a little plastic bowl for him.

'Here you are.'

'Ta,' Charlie said with endearing politeness as she offered him the bowl, but instead of taking the bowl from her, he gleefully chose a plump blueberry and popped it into his mouth, laughing as he did so.

Gosh, he was a cutie.

A split second later the laughter died as a desperate look of fear suddenly appeared in Charlie's eyes.

Oh, God.

'Charlie?'

The little boy was panicking. He flapped his arms madly, and a flaming sword of fear sliced through Alice. Charlie was going red in the face.

Was he choking?

No, no, no. This can't be happening. Not now. Not to Charlie. Not to me.

As he struggled to breathe, the worst kind of terror gripped Alice. She couldn't believe this was really happening. Unfortunately, it wasn't a crazy conjuring from her overwrought imagination. It was real! And worse than anything she might have dreamed up. *Kids can't choke on blueberries, surely?*

'Charlie,' she begged.

The poor little kid couldn't answer. He didn't seem capable of making even the smallest sound. Alice felt as though her heart had stopped.

She wanted to die, to run away. But she knew she couldn't. Charlie needed her. Now. This instant.

There was no time to grab her phone and call an ambulance. No use calling Seth at the homestead. Charlie's face was turning a deeper and deeper shade of scarlet with every passing second. Time was too precious. It was up to her.

Alice had never felt a sense of panic like this. It was hard to think straight, but she knew she shouldn't put her fingers down Charlie's throat, as she might push the obstruction further into his windpipe. She'd read that during the past week, when she'd been swatting up on babysitting first aid.

With a sob of terror, she scooped Charlie into her arms, grabbed a chair and sat with him slung over her knees. Then she thumped his back. Weeping, she thumped him again and again.

Charlie, come on, please, please cough it up.

Oh, Seth, oh, God, I'm so sorry.

She should never have volunteered to mind Seth's son. She should have known better. She was hopeless at this. Charlie – perfect, adorable little Charlie – was going to die.

She knew there was a first-aid action called a Heimlich manoeuvre, but she couldn't recall the exact details. As she thumped Charlie again, she felt totally inadequate, the very worst kind of –

Then she saw it. A small round blue fruit, perfectly formed, lying on the floor.

Oh, my God.

Alice looked at Charlie in her lap. His bright colour was fading. She sat him up and he gazed up at her in puzzlement, his eyes huge, his lower lip trembling. But he wasn't struggling to breathe!

The crisis was over?

'Are you okay, darling?'

He didn't answer, and Alice thought he might burst into tears and cry for his father, but instead he cuddled in to her and took several sobbing breaths.

'Oh, Charlie,' she whispered. 'Oh, darling.' Cradling him in her arms, she cherished a moment of total and utter relief, and Charlie clung to her, as if he somehow sensed that he'd been in mortal danger, but was safe with her.

Undone by his simple trust, Alice lost it. In a heartbeat she was weeping softly. She didn't want to scare Charlie, but she couldn't stop the tears. She was weeping with relief, but she was also weeping for all the years of tension and guilt, for the emotions she'd kept bottled deep inside for far too long.

35

The Drummonds were stony-faced as they gathered in the lounge room. Jackie had a supply of tissues tucked behind a sofa cushion. She hoped she wouldn't cry in front of her family, but if things turned nasty, she knew there was every chance that she would give way to tears.

Knowing Hugh's need to do the right thing, which would be even stronger after this afternoon's drama, she realised he was quite capable of handing Ruthven Downs over to his sister.

Now, the moment she'd dreaded for weeks had arrived. A final decision was about to be made.

From her position on the sofa, Jackie looked around her at the elegant rooms. She'd vacuumed this oriental carpet so frequently she knew its pattern by heart. She looked at the stately, old-fashioned furniture, thinking of the countless times she'd polished the arms, the carved backs and the solid round feet of these Rosenstengel lounge chairs that had been Stella's pride and joy.

Five years ago, Jackie had had these chairs reupholstered. Such care she'd taken over choosing the fabric.

Over the decades of her marriage she'd grown to love this house and each piece of furniture was like an old friend. She'd put down deep roots into this place. Her sense of self and her sense of security were closely tied to this house and its lands.

Now, facing its loss, Jackie felt once again vulnerable and uncertain, like the under-confident child she'd been all those years ago, when her father had died so unexpectedly, leaving her and her mother penniless.

It was a disturbing realisation. At this age, she was sure she should have developed more inner strength, more resilience – more *gumption*, her mother-in-law Stella would have called it.

It didn't help that Jackie had no real idea what Hugh was planning to do at this meeting. For the past hour, she'd been fielding phone calls from her friends about last-minute party preparations. In the brief few minutes they'd had to talk, Hugh had thrown up his hands in a gesture of helplessness.

'I'm afraid we'll just have to play it by ear,' he'd said.

Now, here they were here with a decision to be made. A huge decision.

Flora, at the other end of the sofa, was paying more attention to her phone than Jackie would have liked, but she'd been stressed enough when Jackie filled her in about the family's situation and she didn't want to stir the girl, so she held her tongue now. Hugh, sitting opposite, looked resigned and grim, and when he gave up his favourite armchair by the window for Deborah, Jackie almost protested. The gesture was far too symbolic for her liking.

Xavier, in a holey T-shirt and a pair of limp, striped, flared trousers that looked like pyjama bottoms, chose to sit cross-legged on the floor with his back against the bookcase. At least he seemed calmer now.

In the far corner were neatly stacked white Styrofoam boxes holding glassware, crockery and cutlery for tomorrow's party. Another thing to worry about. It would be a disaster if, after this evening, the family hadn't the heart for a celebration.

The last to arrive was Seth.

'Evening, all,' he said, bringing a warm smile to the sombre gathering. 'Sorry I haven't been more engaged with you guys today.'

'At least you could join us now, Seth,' said Jackie. 'Is Charlie happy with his babysitter?' She added this question loudly, wanting to make it quite clear that Seth had gone the extra mile to make himself available.

Seth nodded. 'Charlie's fine, thanks. So, what have I missed?'

A bitter laugh escaped Deborah. 'You haven't missed a thing.' Her voice dripped with sarcasm. 'Only the complete slaughtering of my artistic ego.'

Jackie sighed and fancied that Hugh might have sighed too, but he didn't flinch from quickly explaining to Seth, succinctly and calmly, about the paintings in the shed and Deborah's subsequent change of heart about her inheritance rights.

Seth frowned as he listened, and Jackie was interested to see that everyone in the room was waiting for his response.

Seth addressed his aunt. 'So we're not talking about your legal rights to this place. The issue is more about your moral rights?'

'Exactly.' Deborah lifted her chin. 'I was desperately disappointed when I discovered my work ferreted away in a dirty old shed, when I'd foolishly believed it was being enjoyed by art lovers in their homes.'

Seth nodded sympathetically. 'But the paintings you found here – I imagine they're only a small sample of your work.'

'Well, yes,' Deborah admitted reluctantly. 'But that's not really the point. I –'

'Deb has a right to feel aggrieved,' Hugh cut in. 'I should have been more open right from the start. I was trying to offer her a helping hand, but it was a ham-fisted way to go about it.'

The poor man looked so rueful Jackie wanted to launch across the room to hug him.

'So now you'd like to make amends?' Seth asked his father. 'You want to divvy up this property more fairly?'

Jackie tensed. This was the big question. Everyone had been watching Seth, but now they turned to Hugh for his answer.

Hugh nodded. 'You all know now about my father's letter. In my opinion, it makes the inheritance question more important than ever.'

'I certainly agree,' Deborah said hotly. 'Given what's happened,' she added, directing another glare to her brother.

Seth frowned. 'That's all very well for you, Aunt Deb, but I must say I'm surprised you feel that way. You were always so keen to remain independent. You kept your distance too. It's not as if you've been cracking your neck to spend time here.'

Oh, well said, Seth. Jackie almost applauded.

Deborah looked put out. 'Well, obviously, things have changed. And – and I –' She seemed to be floundering now. 'And I have Xavier to thank.'

It occurred to Jackie that Deborah's outrage was focused entirely on her art and had little to do with any emotional links she might feel towards Ruthven Downs. She hadn't even seemed moved by the touching story revealed in her mother's diary, which she'd almost certainly read by now. The sole source of her distress was the paintings in the shed. She was simply using Magnus's letter as a vehicle for revenge.

Jackie wished she could take Hugh aside to point this out, but he wasn't stupid. He'd probably realised this for himself. And he'd opened this conversation about the fairness of their inheritance as soon as he'd seen his father's letter, so he was unlikely to retreat. His sister's motivation was probably irrelevant.

'So let's proceed.' Deborah thumped the arm of her chair. 'I believe I've made *my* position quite clear.'

'But you're not going to demand the lot, are you, Mum?'

Everyone stared at Xavier, who'd been quiet until now.

His mother's mouth pursed in a self-righteous little pout. 'I'm certainly entitled to it all,' she said. 'For starters, I could make a fair claim solely on the basis of my father's letter. But now with the disappointment of finding those paintings – you know how upset I was. You were upset, too.'

Xavier fiddled with a loose thread hanging from the seam of his striped pants. 'Thing is, I'm feeling a bit uneasy about this now I've had a couple of hours to calm down. I know I stirred things up. Sure, I was upset for you, but I'm also remembering your first reaction when Uncle Hugh told you about Granddad's letter.'

Deborah's mouth gaped as she stared at her son, clearly shocked by his sudden disloyalty.

'The last thing you wanted was a cattle property.'

'But that was before.' Deborah swallowed and sat even straighter in her chair if that were possible, her hands tightly clasped in her lap. 'What are you trying to do, Xavier?'

He shrugged, and looked around the room with a shy, slightly rueful smile. 'I don't want to make enemies here. This lot are the only family we've got.'

'Yes, and you're important to us, too,' Hugh reminded him gently.

'I just want justice,' Deborah said, but there was meekness in her voice now, and Jackie sensed that she was backing down.

Xavier fiddled with the beaded end of a dreadlock. 'I know I was calling it a crime,' he said to Hugh, 'the way those paintings were stowed away and everything, but I can see you were trying to help.' Slowly he switched his careful gaze to his mother. 'And your sales have been fine lately.'

At this, Deborah nodded. 'They've been good.'

'And if Uncle Hugh's handing the paintings back, you'll be able to make more money from them. There's nothing to stop you selling them again. I reckon with your reputation now, they'll make quite a splash.'

'They should, yes.' Deborah sounded less sure of her ground now.

Jackie could have hugged Xavier. He was almost a different fellow this evening.

Now Seth spoke up. 'So, if we need to come up with a strategy moving forward, wouldn't the fairest thing be a family trust or some kind of shared company?'

'Of course.' Hugh shot a direct glance at Deborah. 'It should have happened years ago.'

Deborah shrugged.

'You wouldn't object to discussing this now?' Hugh asked her.

Another shrug.

For the first time at this meeting, Flora spoke up. 'I think it sounds like a very sensible idea.' She'd even put her phone away, completely out of sight. 'But we'd need to put a fair amount of thought into the way everything was shared. For example, we'd have to take into account the big effort Mum and Dad have put in here over a working lifetime. And then there's your involvement, Seth.'

Flora sounded so grown up. Perceptive too. Jackie knew she shouldn't be surprised, but it was certainly unexpected. It seemed the younger generation were coming into their own.

'Yes, you're a very important consideration, Seth,' chipped in Hugh. He looked around at everyone, as if to include them in his statement. 'Until now, I guess we've all assumed that Jackie and I will eventually retire and leave Seth here to run the place. If we go ahead with a family company or a trust fund now, it would probably be best to sell Ruthven Downs. So it's Seth who stands to lose the most. We'd have to compensate him for that.'

'Sounds fair to me,' said Xavier.

Jackie had been watching Seth closely, but he'd kept his

expression almost deadpan. 'How do you feel about it, Seth?'

Before he could answer, footsteps sounded on the verandah. And then, Alice Miller appeared at the door with Charlie in her arms and Seth's blue cattle dog at her heels.

Quite a picture the girl made, framed in the doorway, with the last rays of the setting sun behind her, lighting her bright hair to a flame.

'I'm so sorry to interrupt,' she said, looking embarrassed. 'I'm afraid Charlie's had a bit of an upset. Can I speak to you for a moment, Seth?'

Jackie almost leaped to her feet. What on earth could have happened? Just in time, she remembered that Seth could deal with this, of course, and she forced herself to remain seated as Seth took Alice out onto the verandah. French doors gave Jackie a clear view, though, and she couldn't help watching them.

Alice was explaining something to Seth, something rather dramatic, judging by the way she was flapping her hands about and shaking her head. And Seth, calm and steady like his father, slipped his arm around her shoulders. He seemed to be reassuring her.

Jackie knew she shouldn't keep watching, but she was entranced. They made such an appealing group – the dark-haired man and the auburn-haired girl, the little blond chap between them, and dear old Ralph, the blue heeler, looking up at them so attentively. She glanced around at the others and everyone exchanged wide-eyed, questioning expressions and shrugs.

Finally Seth returned, with Charlie and Alice, who was looking rather pale, Jackie realised now. At least Seth was smiling.

'There's been a spot of drama at the cottage,' he said. 'Charlie choked on a blueberry.'

'A blueberry?' Jackie gasped. Who would have thought? She'd often fed Charlie blueberries.

'He swallowed it whole while he was laughing –' Seth gave a

slight shake of his head. 'I guess it was one of those fluke things, but it got well and truly stuck. Poor Alice got a hell of a fright.'

'How awful,' cried Flora, who was already on her feet, and there were cries of sympathy all round.

Soon everyone was leaping from chairs, wanting to console Alice, and to make sure that Charlie was all right.

'Oh, Alice, you poor thing,' Flora was saying. 'I'm Seth's sister, by the way. Nice to meet you. But boy, what a terrifying thing to happen. That would be my worst nightmare.'

'What did you do?' Xavier wanted to know. 'How did you save him?'

Alice, blushing to find herself the centre of attention, told them about thumping Charlie over her knee.

'But he's okay now.' Seth was holding Charlie, and he proved his claim by tickling the little boy's tummy and inducing squeals of delight.

Eventually, it was Hugh who said, 'I think this is an appropriate moment to take a break. I'd say we've all earned a drink.' His suggestion was greeted with unanimous enthusiasm. 'You'll join us in a drink, won't you, Alice?'

The girl looked worried again. 'I really should be getting Charlie to bed.'

'Oh, come on,' said Seth. 'Just one.'

'But I interrupted your meeting.'

Hugh brushed this aside. 'I'm confident we can fine-tune the details over dinner – or after dinner.'

So then it was a matter of fetching glasses, of Hugh taking orders – wine, whisky or beer?

A bowl of nuts appeared. Flora had hunted them down.

'Don't let Charlie near them,' warned Deborah, lifting the bowl onto the sideboard out of reach.

Jackie, coming back from the kitchen after checking Deborah's spiced couscous and the chicken casserole that she was reheating, stood for a moment, looking at the family scene. Deborah and Flora had their heads together, deep in conversation. Xavier was on the floor, playing Hide and Seek behind an armchair with a delighted Charlie. Hugh was perched on the arm of the sofa, talking to Alice and Seth.

Everyone looked relaxed and happy, except perhaps Alice, who still looked a little uncertain and shy. The rest of them truly seemed to be enjoying each other's company. Not at all like a family in crisis, not even like a family on the brink of huge changes.

Jackie took a deep breath. She still didn't like the idea of selling this place, but at least it now seemed that tomorrow's party might not be a disaster after all.

36

Alice didn't sleep well. She dreamed about Charlie, about his father, about the entire Drummond family. One minute they were all in a lifeboat being rescued from a wild and choppy sea, the next they were driving wildly in a car down the wrong side of the highway. Then, just as crazily, Seth and Alice were alone, and he was pulling her into his arms for a kiss that promised to be the longest and love-liest kiss in all history.

She woke early the next morning, feeling groggy, but she rose quickly and took a steaming mug of coffee downstairs. Her workshop was filled with the pearly grey light of a new day, mist lingered in the garden, all was peaceful and quiet, and Alice felt strangely different.

Emotionally drained after the previous night's scare, she also felt calmer, certainly calmer than she would have expected.

Perhaps the calmness was part of the 'Seth effect'. He'd been so incredibly sympathetic last night.

She'd felt compelled to take Charlie over to the homestead to confess what had happened and to ask if he should see a doctor, but to her surprise, Seth had been more concerned about her ordeal than his son's. With his entire family watching, Seth had put his arm around her shoulders and hugged her close, and he'd been wonderfully understanding, his eyes filled with genuine concern.

For her.

Of course, by then Charlie had completely recovered, but Seth's reaction was still unexpected. Alice was touched, probably more deeply moved than was wise. After all, they were supposed to have broken up.

It was all rather confusing and she had no idea what to expect from Seth at his father's party tonight.

Now, though, sipping coffee, she deliberately shoved her concerns about her relationship and the Drummond family aside, and turned her thoughts to planning her day. She enjoyed using the hours before the shop opened to work on restoring bits and pieces of furniture. Her current project was an old desk she'd found at a garage sale in Herberton.

Scratched and covered in an ancient coat of the most dreadful liver-coloured paint, the desk had been stuck in a dusty back corner. For Alice, it had been love at first sight. She'd admired its lines and had been gripped by an urge to restore it to beauty.

Over the past week, she'd completely removed the ugly paint, using scrapers and a long-bladed knife rather than a chemical stripper that could damage the timber's fibres. Beneath the ugly layers, she'd struck gold. The desk was made from flame oak, a truly beautiful timber, native to the far north, that she'd only learned about recently.

This morning, she was ready for the second-best part of this task – sanding the desk's surface. Her aim was to make the mahogany-toned timber as smooth as glass before she applied the varnish.

A happy tingle of anticipation zinged through her as she finished her coffee and selected a fine-grade wet and dry sandpaper. Using soapy water as a lubricant, she folded the dampened paper over a wood block and began to sand, rubbing lightly to avoid making fresh scratches or clogging the sandpaper with wood dust.

After her years of experience, the movements felt familiar and instinctive and, almost immediately, the beautiful flame oak rewarded her. Flecks shaped like candle flames appeared, dark red and chocolatey brown, as attractive and exotic as leopard skin.

She would have loved her grandfather to have seen this timber. He would have been so excited.

As she worked, her thoughts drifted back. She remembered him working in his shed in the backyard in Ashgrove, remembered the smell of wood and turpentine, the tendrils of a passionfruit vine creeping over the window sill, the curling wood shavings on the concrete floor. She remembered her grandfather's age-spotted hands lovingly sanding a turned oak table leg.

One of the most satisfying things about her job was knowing that she continued the work he'd begun. Now, she tilted the desk-top into the light, till she found the angle that would show up any irregularities on the surface. She was aiming for a mirror finish and the desk would be beautiful. With a new lease of life, it could last for another hundred years.

Alice wondered who would be around to see it.

Charlie?

And just like that, pictures of the previous night slammed back. She was in Seth's cottage, reliving the horror, the heart-blistering ter-ror of Charlie's choking, and her stunned relief when she realised he was okay and looking quite pink and normal again.

The relief had overwhelmed her. She wasn't sure how long she'd wept. Poor little Charlie must have been quite bewildered, but he'd simply sat silently in her lap, watching her with his big blue eyes. When she'd stopped at last, she'd wiped her eyes on her shirt sleeve, and then she'd hitched him onto her hip and carried him to the sink where she'd left his cup of apple juice.

'Ta, Alee,' he'd said as she handed him the cup and his voice hadn't been the slightest bit husky.

She'd never in her life felt so incredibly grateful.

Thank you, thank you, thank you.

It was almost dark by then. In tune with the deepening light, an unexpected sense of peace had settled inside her.

She'd done it. She'd faced her very worst fear and Charlie had survived.

Her legs had been shaky, though, as she'd carried him back to the lounge room and sunk gratefully into a chair. Charlie had still been a little subdued and he'd seemed happy to stay in her lap. She'd explored the pile of toys in the basket beside her and found his rabbit, which he cuddled against his chest as he nestled close, his head on her breast.

Thinking about all of this now, Alice stood in the middle of her workshop, where the morning light was growing brighter every minute. She thought about the other incident, so many years ago.

She waited for the pain that always accompanied her memories of the accident that had taken her family. The horrible, sickening slug of guilt.

Outside in the garden, the sky was warming to a soft, fresh blue. The neighbours' rusty brown hens came through the hedge and pecked at insects on her lawn. Rainbow lorikeets fed noisily in the bottlebrush.

Alice waited a little longer for the tightening of her stomach muscles, the queasy weight in her chest, but the expected guilt didn't arrive. Instead of the usual anguish, she felt unexpected peace, the same sense of peace she'd felt last night when she'd sat in the twilight with warm, solid little Charlie in her lap. Alive and safe.

Rescued.

Wow.

She wondered if her healing had finally begun.

37

By six-thirty, Ruthven Downs was ready. From every window of the homestead, lights glowed softly in the purple twilight. Trestle tables loaded with shining glasses stood waiting on the verandah and out on the lawn. Within the house, tall vases filled with ginger and hippeastrums were set in strategic spots, and groups of candles twinkled in pretty holders.

The furniture in the dining and lounge rooms had been rearranged to host long tables covered with white cloths and loaded with plates and silverware. A crystal bowl filled with Hugh's favourite yellow roses from Burralea had pride of place on the sideboard.

Out on the lawn, tubs filled with ice held drinks that Flora and Xavier would serve, but guests would also be encouraged to help themselves. Inside the kitchen, a bank of slow cookers, casserole dishes, saucepans and ovens was keeping meals at the required temperatures, and the room was filled with mouth-watering aromas.

In her bedroom, Jackie stood before the mirror, making one last inspection. Her long, sleeveless dress in aqua and deep blue silk was cool and comfortable. Dangling earrings in a matching shade and silver sandals completed her attire. She'd taken extra care with her make-up, giving her lashes a final flick of mascara, and choosing a coral pink lipstick that lit up her blue eyes and fair hair. As tonight's hostess, she'd wanted to look casually elegant, and she was happy with the result.

Heading down the hallway, she passed Flora's room. Her daughter was leaning in, close to the mirror, blotting an eyelash with a tissue. She was wearing a dress in a pretty rose pink, a shade that had always suited her dark hair and dark eyes. But it was a warm night, so Jackie couldn't think why Flora had added a crocheted jacket, a black one at that, with long sleeves.

Pausing in the doorway, Jackie wondered if this was a new trend among the young people in Melbourne. Flora had been wearing long sleeves ever since she'd arrived home, but it didn't really make sense. This was October in the tropics, after all. Everyone in the north was shedding layers, not adding them.

It wasn't as if Flora had overly plump arms or body image issues, so why would she cover herself up?

Jackie was still pondering this when Flora turned from the mirror.

'Hi, Mum.' She smiled, then pursed her lips into a low wolf whistle. 'Wow, you look fabulous.'

'Thanks, darling.' Jackie hesitated in the doorway. There was a host of last-minute things that she should be attending to, but she was suddenly concerned for her daughter. The thought that something was wrong still nagged at her, and they'd never really had a chance to finish the chat she'd planned. 'I like your dress,' she said. 'That colour has always looked good on you.'

'Thanks.'

'But do you really need the jacket, darling?' Jackie was watching closely as she asked this and she saw the flash of alarm in Flora's eyes. It was gone in a split second, but a responding spark of fear shot through Jackie.

'It's become a habit, I guess.' Flora shrugged. 'The weather in Melbourne's so changeable, I always take a jacket with me, or a cardi, or some kind of sweater.'

Jackie wasn't inclined to accept this reasoning, but she nodded. Right now, with Hugh's party about to begin, it was the very worst possible moment to upset the girl.

'Well, it's not likely to cool down tonight,' she suggested. 'The forecast says it will stay quite warm. Wouldn't you be more comfortable without the top?'

This time, Flora couldn't hide her distress, or perhaps she didn't try to. Her eyes glistened and her mouth trembled.

In a heartbeat, Jackie was beside her. 'Darling, what is it?' But even as she asked the question, she guessed.

She swallowed, gently touched her daughter's elbow. 'There's something more to this, isn't there?'

Lips tightly compressed, as if she was struggling to hold back tears, Flora nodded.

Jackie's heart trembled. 'Tell me the truth, sweetheart. Do you have bruises?'

More than anything she wanted Flora to rear back in shock, to tell her she was crazy for suggesting such a thing.

To her dismay, Flora's face crumpled, and she sank onto her bed and burst into tears.

Alarmed, and close to tears herself, Jackie quickly closed the bedroom door and hurried to sit on the bed beside her daughter.

'Oh, Flora,' she whispered, slipping her arm around the girl's shaking shoulders. 'Sweetheart, what happened? Is this Oliver's doing?'

'Yes!' Flora wailed and she sank into her mother's arms, sobbing.

Eventually, Flora managed to stem the flow of her tears, and Jackie handed her the box of tissues from the dressing table. They sat in silence for a bit while Flora mopped at the mascara tracks running down her cheeks, and Jackie dabbed at her own eyes.

'I'm so sorry, Mum.'

'You don't have to apologise. If anyone should, it's me,' Jackie told her. 'I should have spoken up earlier. I sensed something was wrong and I've been worried about you.'

'You've been so busy.'

'That's no excuse. I should never be too busy for my family.' Jackie gave her another hug. 'Do you want to talk about it?'

'I guess.' Flora's dark eyes, with their smudged rings of make-up, looked huge in her pale face, giving her a childlike pathos that gripped her mother's heart. 'Actually, no, Mum. We don't have time.'

'I can make time.'

'Not now. God, the party's due to start any minute. Anyway, there's not a lot to tell, really.'

'But Oliver has hurt you? Physically?'

'Not too badly. Not enough to go to a doctor or anything. But – yes.' Flora peeled back the jacket to reveal a nasty purple bruise on her upper arm and several smaller ones, possibly finger-marks, on her forearm.

Jackie pressed a hand to her lips. This was so hard to believe. She knew, of course, that domestic violence could come from anyone, not just those you might suspect. But the man was an opera singer, for heaven's sake. He was supposed to be refined and cultured.

After all the hard work Flora had put into her music, the years of practice, of giving up other things she loved, this ghastly situation was so unfair. Flora had done so well, as an unknown girl from the far north, to have landed such an amazing, highly competitive position with Orchestra Victoria. The whole district had been proud of her. There'd been front-page stories and photos in the local newspaper.

It was appalling to think that the career satisfaction Flora had strived and sacrificed for might be spoiled by a self-centred, egotisti-cal prick.

'He texts you all the time, doesn't he?' Jackie asked. 'He wants to keep track of you?'

'How did you know?'

'I heard a talk-back show on the radio about men like that. And I've noticed that you always seem so worried when you're checking your phone.'

Flora nodded, gave a sigh. 'It's a control thing. Oliver – has issues. He's ambitious and he's an artist, so he's also very emotional. He puts too much pressure on himself.'

'That's no excuse, especially not if he takes it out on you.'

'I know,' Flora said sadly.

'So, was it your decision that he shouldn't come home with you?' Jackie suggested.

'Yes. I was scared he'd get bossy or even angry with me and I didn't want you guys to see him like that.'

'But Oliver didn't take it well?'

'He was so angry. Like you wouldn't believe.'

Jackie couldn't bear this. Her poor baby. She took her daughter's hand. 'Darling, you can't stay in a relationship like that.'

'I – I know.'

It was relief to hear Flora admit this, but Jackie wondered how hard it would be in practice for the girl to distance herself from Oliver. Even in a major city like Melbourne, musicians moved in small circles.

'It's been good to get away,' Flora said. 'To come home to all of you. It's given me some perspective. Things are clearer now.'

There was a knock at the door. Then Hugh's voice. 'Flora, have you seen your mother? Our guests have started to arrive.'

Flora stiffened. 'Mum, you've got to go. I'll be okay.'

From outside the house came the sound of cars arriving down the drive, of doors slamming.

'Are you sure, love?'

Her daughter produced a reassuring smile. 'Yes, after I've given my face a good wash and redone my make-up.'

'We haven't finished with this. We have to talk again. Work something out.'

'Yeah, sure. Thanks.' Raising her voice, Flora called, 'Mum's in here, Dad. She's coming now.'

They hugged.

'Is my make-up okay?' Jackie asked, turning to the mirror to check.

Flora took a tissue and dabbed at the corner of Jackie's left eye. 'It is now. Just remember to smile and you'll look perfect.'

'Right.' Jackie stood, blinked twice, took a deep breath, then crossed the room and opened the door carefully.

Hugh was in the hallway, looking worried.

'Flora and I were just having a mother–daughter moment,' she told him.

'Is everything all right?'

'Yes.' Jackie had promised herself there would be no more secrets, but this was hardly a moment for total honesty. She would fill Hugh in later. Now she smiled at her husband. He was wearing a new pale lemon shirt with crisp cream chinos, his favourite crocodile leather belt and well-polished RM Williams boots. 'You look scrumptious.'

He chuckled. 'So do you.' He took her hand, kissed her cheek. 'Come and greet our guests.'

Together, holding hands, they went down the hallway to the open front door.

———

When Alice arrived at Ruthven Downs, quite a few cars were already parked in rows on the lawn and people were gathered in groups along the verandahs, their happy voices rippling into the night. Somewhere among those groups Seth would be mingling.

Alice's pulse quickened. Tonight, she and Seth were supposed to be carrying on as if they were still a couple.

The idea had seemed so simple when she'd first hatched it, and her motives had been well-intentioned. She'd wanted to save Jackie any more stress. Now she felt distinctly uncomfortable about playing this role and deceiving the Drummonds. They'd all been so sympathetic and kind to her last night, almost treating her like a family member, when in truth, she was a total outsider.

Alice had always been an outsider. It was the role she'd deliberately chosen.

Even last night, when the Drummonds had been so welcoming and inclusive, she'd made a quick exit. She'd taken Charlie back to the cottage and read him three more storybooks before he'd finally settled to sleep. When Seth got back quite late, full of apologies, he'd told her that the meeting went well, but he'd given no details, which was to be expected – it wasn't any of her business – and she'd left quite soon after that.

She still had no idea whether the family's tensions had been resolved, or whether Seth was still tense or worried about the future. But, hey, she was simply a fill-in, playing the part of his girlfriend for one more night. After this evening, she would never pull up at the Ruthven Downs homestead again.

The problem was – and to Alice, it was starting to feel like a painfully major problem – she'd spent far too much time today thinking about Seth, dwelling on the precious moment of closeness last night when he'd been so understanding and sweet to her. With that fleeting act of kindness he'd made her *forget*, momentarily, that they had no future. And somehow, some-*crazy*-how, despite her best efforts to resist, she knew she'd foolishly fallen in love with him.

By the end of this party, she'd be a mess, with her heart in shreds, but it was too late to back out. Her goose was cooked. She had no choice but to straighten her shoulders and get on with it.

Collecting the small gift she'd brought for Seth's father, Alice climbed out of her ute and crossed the lawn. It was a warm summer's night and she was wearing a dress of soft white cotton, with shoestring straps and a border of flowers and leaves along the knee-length hemline. She'd scooped her hair up into a loose knot and her accessories were simple – gold hoop earrings and strappy, high-heeled green sandals.

As she reached the front steps, Jackie Drummond broke away from a group and hurried to greet her. 'Alice, there you are. How lovely you look.' Seth's mother kissed her warmly.

Seth's father was standing a few feet away, looking very relaxed and happy as he chatted with Brad and Kate Woods. If he was in any way upset about the meeting's outcome, he was hiding it well.

He turned and waved to her. 'Alice, good to see you again. Welcome.' He too came forward and kissed her cheek.

'Happy birthday, Mr Drummond.'

'Oh, please, you must call me Hugh.'

Alice offered him the gift and he responded with a reproachful smile. 'There weren't supposed to be presents, but thanks very much.'

'It's only a little thing from my shop.'

'Well, that's very kind of you, Alice. I'll look forward to opening it.' Setting the gift on a table, he gestured to an ice bucket where the neck of an opened champagne bottle stuck out invitingly. 'You'll have a glass of champers?'

'Thanks. That would be lovely.'

Hugh poured her a fizzing glassful. 'Here's to your good health.'

'And to yours. Cheers.' They touched glasses and she took a sip. The wine was icy and tickled her nose, and it tasted of Christmas and parties and fun. Both Seth's parents were beaming at her as if she'd pleased them hugely.

She wondered how their son would react.

Jackie introduced her to a group of their guests. There was an architect from Cairns and his elegant wife, another smiling couple who lived on the neighbouring property, a pale, serious doctor from Mareeba. Seth's aunt was also in the group, looking rather splendid in a purple and gold sari, with her long hair plaited and wound around her head like a crown.

'Alice is so clever,' Jackie told them. 'She restores old furniture and she re-silvered our sideboard mirror so it's as good as new. She has a lovely little shop in Burralea.'

The others responded with enthusiasm, asking questions. How did she learn her trade? Was she settling happily into Burralea?

It was all very pleasant, but after a bit, Jackie touched her on the elbow and leaned in to speak discreetly. 'I think you'll find Seth around the corner. The young people seem to have gravitated down there.' She nodded towards a side verandah.

'Right, thanks.' Of course she was expected to join Seth.

Jackie winked at her as she left.

Alice felt ridiculously nervous as she wove past the groups scattered along the verandah. As soon as she rounded the corner, she saw Seth. Dressed in a pale blue shirt, with long sleeves rolled to the elbows and his trademark jeans, he was leaning against the railing, beer in hand. His cousin Xavier was there too and his sister Flora, and other young people Alice hadn't met.

Two pretty blonde girls, who seemed to be identical twins, were gazing adoringly at Seth, totally awestruck.

Alice tried to ignore the pang this caused. Of course Seth would be hugely attractive to other women. Even if they knew nothing of his deeper qualities, Seth Drummond was a prize catch. Distractingly attractive, with that untidy dark hair and those stunning blue eyes, he was fun to be with, and he stood to inherit this place, or at least a worthwhile share of it. *And* he came with a cute little boy to fuss over.

Seth Drummond was probably one of the most sought-after bachelors in the district.

And I let him go.

Alice felt pretty damn wretched as she continued towards the group. Then Seth, who'd been laughing at someone's joke, turned and saw her. He went completely still. He didn't take his eyes from her.

Their little group fell quiet. Everyone else turned to see what had caught his attention.

Alice's heart thudded in her chest and for a dreadful moment she feared her knees would give way. Then Seth flashed her a grin, set his beer on a nearby table, and came towards her. 'I was beginning to worry that you might have changed your mind,' he said.

'I've been talking to your parents and their friends.'

'Right. Great.' He took her free hand and held her away from him, letting his gaze run appreciatively over her.

'You look beautiful. I mean, you always look beautiful, but tonight . . .' His throat worked and his eyes were a little too shiny.

'How's Charlie?' she asked him quickly.

Seth gave a slightly bewildered smile as if her question had caught him out. 'He's fine,' he said. 'Absolutely. What about you? You're not still worrying about him, are you?'

'No.' She was pleased she could say this honestly.

He leaned in to kiss her. On the mouth. A lovely, lingering greeting in front of all these people.

Help.

'Seth,' she whispered shakily. 'You don't need to overdo it.'

He frowned. 'Overdo what?'

'I know we agreed about putting on a good show in front of your family. About still being a couple. But don't you think this feels – dishonest?'

His eyes held hers and he still looked puzzled.

She swallowed. 'We've broken up, right?'

For a brief moment she thought she read dismay in his expression, but then he smiled so convincingly she knew she must have imagined it.

'Sure,' he said. 'Let's keep this honest.'

But he took her hand in his and kept a firm hold as he introduced her to the others.

———

Flora was in the kitchen refilling water jugs when Kate Woods found her.

'Flora, there you are. I was hoping to catch you. I haven't had a proper chance to hear all your news.'

Flora smiled carefully. In recent years, Kate had become a favourite among her parents' friends, and Flora almost looked on her as an aunt. But she couldn't help feeling tense about being cornered like this. Kate was a lawyer, after all, and she worked mostly on divorce and family issues.

Flora knew she was probably being paranoid, but she wondered if her mum had spoken to Kate about Oliver.

Was this some kind of well-meant intervention?

'How's your family?' she asked Kate, as enthusiastically as she could.

'Oh, they're great, thanks. Always doing something incredibly exciting. Adam's in Antarctica, would you believe? What about you, Flora? Are you enjoying Melbourne? You know we're all so proud of you, and we're desperate for news.'

'Melbourne's great,' Flora said. 'And I'm loving the orchestra.'

'That's wonderful. It must be so good to be working with people who are just like you, all mad about classical music and extraordinarily talented.'

Flora laughed as she pushed the lever on the freezer door and collected ice to add to the jugs. 'I must admit, it's cool to work with people who don't think I'm a nerd.'

Kate nodded. 'But you must be disappointed you couldn't bring your boyfriend home. We were all looking forward to meeting him.'

'Yes.' This time Flora couldn't manage to laugh or even to smile. The very mention of Oliver caused an uncomfortable tightening in her chest. 'It – it was a pity.' She began to slice a lime.

'How clever of you to snag a tenor,' Kate continued. 'Your very own Pavarotti.'

'Except that he's not Italian or fat or famous.'

'But loaded with charm nonetheless, I should imagine.'

'Oh, yes, he's a lot of fun.' It was true. Meeting Oliver had been such a thrill. Tall and dashing, he'd swept Flora off her feet with a charm offensive more flattering than anything she'd ever experienced.

'Flora,' Kate said gently.

The jugs were ready to be taken back to the tables, and Flora was keen to finish the conversation.

'Is everything okay?' Kate asked.

Hearing the concern underlying this question, Flora winced. 'Has Mum been speaking to you?'

Kate's smile was a tad guilty, but her eyes were warm with sympathy as she nodded. 'Sorry if I've come across as devious. Jackie's worried, of course. She's your mother.'

'But I told her I'm dealing with it. I'm not going to stay with him.'

'Well, that's certainly very good news.' Settling back against a kitchen cupboard, Kate folded her arms over her chest. 'I know you're not asking for my advice, Flora, but I'm going to give it to you anyway.' Her expression was deadly serious now. 'It's really, really important that you get out of this relationship as fast as you can.'

Flora nodded, but when she pictured herself actually walking out on Oliver, a shiver ran through her, a shiver of fear. She knew he was going to be angry. *Really* angry. He'd gone ballistic when she'd told him her excuse for keeping him from this party. She'd claimed there were limits on the numbers – not daring to tell him the truth, that she'd changed her mind and didn't want him to meet her parents.

If she was leaving him, there wouldn't be any point in trying to talk to him, he wouldn't listen. He wouldn't give her a chance. She would have to leave when he wasn't home. Sneak off to a friend's house and beg a bed, and hope that Oliver didn't come after her.

'It might not be easy,' Kate said, watching her. 'But the longer you stay, the harder it will be to leave. You know I'm a divorce lawyer. I've worked with a lot of women in unhappy relationships, but the women who actually file for divorce are rarely victims of violence. Too often, *those* poor women just don't get out.'

'Really?'

Kate gave a solemn shake of her head. 'They're miserable and they're hurt, but they stay. They're trapped. Trapped by the stories they tell themselves – that they're important to their man, that they can help him to face his demons. They tell themselves the guy will change. Or that he'll be nicer to them if they change their *own* behaviour.'

'Okay.' Flora held up a trembling hand to stop Kate. She was fighting tears. She couldn't bear this. It was all too painfully familiar. Too scarily close to her own thought processes.

Shit. How have I let this happen?

At least she'd turned her phone off tonight and left it in the bedroom. She hadn't wanted to let Oliver spoil this night, but she knew there'd be a gazillion messages on there from him when she got back. Tomorrow she would ring him and tell him how low she thought he was, trying to bully her from afar.

'I'm planning to leave him as soon as I get back,' she said tightly.

'Excellent.' Kate slipped an arm around her shoulders. 'I know it won't be easy, Flora. You'll still see Oliver at work, I imagine.'

'Sometimes.' She bit her lip to hold back tears.

'And you don't have family close by to back you up.'

'No, but I've made some good friends.'

'Great. And at least Christmas isn't all that far away. Does the orchestra take a break?'

'Yes, about a month.'

'So you'll be able to come home.'

'Perhaps . . .' Flora said, thinking of the big decision her family had made last night. When she saw Kate's surprise, she felt compelled to offer at least a partial explanation. 'Everything's up in the air at the moment. Mum and Dad will – um – no doubt tell you all about it very soon.'

'Oh?' Kate was obviously trying to cover her surprise and curiosity. 'Well,' she said quickly, 'if you can't come here, there's always our cottage in Burralea. You'd be welcome to stay there.'

Flora knew the cottage. It was a little timber place, painted pale pink, with white lattice and window boxes, and a picket fence. It was on the edge of the rainforest, cuteness personified, and she'd always loved it. Bonus, it was just down the road from Kate and Brad's office. For that matter, it was also close to Seth's girlfriend Alice's shop. Flora had really liked what she'd seen of Alice so far.

'But don't you rent the cottage out, especially at Christmas?'

'Not always. We often keep it free for family and friends, and I'm almost certain it's still free through December and New Year. We'd love you to make use of it.'

'Oh, Kate, that's so kind of you.' Flora could almost feel her tense stomach muscles letting go. No matter what happened family-wise, she could still come home to the far north for the Christmas break. For a whole month, she would be three thousand kilometres away from Melbourne, away from Oliver, safe in Burralea, in that sweet little cottage.

She would be able to regroup, and if she decided that she needed to look for a job with another orchestra in Australia, or even overseas, she could practise in the cottage to her heart's content.

'Thank you,' she said, giving Kate a warm hug. 'I'll let you know soon if I need the place. It would be perfect.'

———

The concept of honesty was clearly open to interpretation, Alice decided. Despite her brave attempt to set things straight with Seth, he kept to their original plan. All evening, he made sure she was at his side, proudly introducing her to the guests, always attentive, cheerful. *Tactile*.

The problem was, even the most casual touch from Seth was a major distraction for Alice, which made things rather difficult as they chatted to people. It wasn't easy to keep up her end of an intelligent conversation when every cell in her body was aware of the man at her side.

The party was lovely of course, a huge success. The eclectic background music set a happy mood and Alice met all sorts of interesting, friendly folk. The wine flowed, the food was amazing, and the speeches and tributes to Hugh Drummond were sincere and touching.

A neighbour, a balding, red-faced grazier, who kept hitching his trousers over his pot belly, became quite emotional when he told everyone how Hugh had saved his daughter from drowning when she was five. Brad Woods, the solicitor, talked about Hugh's university days in Brisbane when he was the star of the rugby team.

'Although I have to tell you,' Brad added, with a huge grin, 'I reckon Hugh's biggest achievement at Queensland Uni was when he lip-synced "Eagle Rock" at the Union College ball. You should have seen him back then, with his long, dark, seventies hair and his linen jacket, wiggling his hips and flapping his arms like Daddy Cool. The girls went crazy.'

Of course, this was greeted by roars of laughter and cheers and calls for a repeat performance.

'I always knew you were a cool dad,' yelled Flora, and that brought more laughter.

Other people spoke. Not surprisingly, Hugh Drummond had been a leader in the cattle industry, fighting for Beef Roads and cattle exports and helping on the committee of the Mareeba Rodeo. But beyond these predictable interests of a cattleman, he'd also been a great supporter of the Regional Art Gallery and a willing helper at the Multicultural Festival.

A rather brash, bearded young councillor even spoke about Hugh's term on the shire council.

'The best committee chairman we ever had,' he said. 'Should have been mayor.'

Then it was Hugh's turn to respond. Graciously, he thanked the speakers, thanked the guests for coming and thanked his family, especially Jackie. As he did this, he turned to Jackie, giving her a look of heart-stopping fondness as he held out his arms to her. The cheers were even louder as they hugged and kissed.

It was absolutely perfect, Alice thought, and she found herself swiping at tears. She didn't dare to catch Seth's eye.

Hugh kept his arm around his wife's shoulders as he continued with his speech. 'Good friends, while you're all here, Jackie and I have something rather significant to tell you.'

A hush fell over the crowd. All eyes were riveted on Hugh and Jackie. Alice shot a glance at Seth, saw the way his jaw tightened, and felt suddenly nervous.

Hugh said, 'We've decided – actually, the whole family has

decided – that the time has come to sell Ruthven Downs.'

A collective gasp broke from the crowd. Dropped jaws and stunned faces, even cries of 'Oh, no.'

Watching everyone's reaction, Alice felt sick. She was sure this decision was directly related to the documents she'd found behind the mirror. She looked towards Jackie, but there were no visible signs of strain as she stood there, smiling, beside her husband. Was she putting on a brave face?

Alice turned to Seth, but his gaze was fixed on his father, his expression hard to read. She glanced towards Flora and her aunt and cousin. None of them looked especially upset.

Hugh waited till the shock-waves subsided before he continued. He smiled at the crowd. 'So, as you can see, this party is more than a birthday for an old codger. It's also a kind of farewell, the end of an era, and the start of new beginnings for the Drummonds.'

Another ripple of reaction travelled through the guests. Hugh held up his hand. 'I know this is a surprise, but as I said, this is a family decision and we're all comfortable with it. It's nothing dramatic like a bust-up or a bank foreclosure.'

'But you're not leaving the district, are you?' someone called.

Hugh's smile was patient. 'I know there'll be lots of questions and you're all good friends, so you deserve answers, but let's leave that for later. Right now, I have some candles to blow out and a cake to cut.'

'And more bottles to open,' called Brad.

38

The joyous cheers for Hugh faded and Alice turned to Seth. 'Well, your dad certainly managed to surprise everyone.'

Seth cracked a wry smile. 'The surprise wasn't really planned. Just the way things worked out. Good timing, though.'

'I guess the whole district will know by tomorrow.'

'Yeah, we won't have to worry about spreading the word.'

Already, the crowd had begun to disperse. People helped themselves to fresh drinks, several women began clearing away plates, others were talking rather animatedly in groups.

Jackie and Deborah began to cut the cake into slices, while the Woods and the Kinsellas cornered Hugh, no doubt plying him with questions.

Alice waited till she and Seth were alone before she gave in to her burning curiosity. 'So, how do you feel about your family's decision to sell?'

'It had to happen,' he responded enigmatically. 'It was a unanimous decision.'

'But do you mind? You love it here, don't you?'

Seth turned to the railing and leaned forward, resting his

forearms on the timber ledge. 'There've been hassles and unfairness over the whole inheritance set-up,' he said. 'It was time to set things straight. We're going to form a family trust and everyone will have shares. It all has to be worked out very carefully and fairly, of course, but everyone's in agreement.'

'Well, that's good, I guess.' Alice studied his profile as he looked out into the garden. He looked and sounded calm enough, but she knew he'd lived here all his life and he must have expected to live here forever. 'Are you truly happy, Seth?' she asked cautiously.

'Yes, I am, actually.' He turned to her and smiled. 'You're as bad as everyone else. They've all been worried about me, especially Dad. He knows how much I love working with cattle, but I've been saying for ages now that I'd love to breed stud cattle, and this place has never really been suitable for cell grazing and stud breeding. The rainfall's not all that reliable.'

'Right. So you'll look around for a place of your own?'

'Yeah, I'm looking forward to a new challenge, to be honest. Starting my own venture.'

'That's great.' Alice tried to sound enthusiastic, but she couldn't quite pull it off. She was too painfully aware that she wouldn't be a part of Seth's exciting future. He would be on his own farm with Charlie – and she wouldn't be in that picture.

'Is something wrong?' he asked her suddenly.

She hadn't realised he was still watching her. 'No, of course not.' She managed to smile. 'I'm fine.' But she hoped Seth didn't expect her to elaborate on why she was so fine. Truth was, she felt miserable. Now that the major party event was over, things would start winding down. Her role at this ball was coming to an end. When the clock struck twelve, she would have to scurry away before her ute turned into a pumpkin.

'You're probably tired,' Seth said. 'You've had to drag yourself over here two nights in a row.'

'No, honestly, I'm okay, but I should help with the cleaning up.'

'No way, Alice. I'm sure there are plenty of –'

Alice didn't wait till he'd finished. She needed a little distance, some head space. Soon she would be saying goodbye to Seth and the Drummonds, and Ruthven Downs, and she needed to do be able to do this with dry eyes and a convincing smile.

When she reached the kitchen, however, she found a team of women busily working at the sink, wielding tea-towels, wiping down bench tops, stacking the dishwasher, all of them chattering non-stop as they worked.

'Jackie says she and Hugh want to do a whole lot more travel.'

'I heard they're talking of moving to Burralea.'

'But what about Seth? What will he do now?'

The chatter stopped as Alice appeared. 'Can I help?' she asked, feeling just a little foolish.

A woman in bright red spectacles shooed her good-naturedly. 'Thank you, dear, that's very kind, but we've had so many offers from the CWA girls, we can't possibly squeeze in another body. Off you go and enjoy yourself.' Her significant smile conveyed what she hadn't said – *enjoy yourself with Seth*.

Sure enough, when Alice returned to the verandah, Seth was waiting for her and, unfairly, he managed to look hotter than ever.

He was grinning at her too. 'Told you they wouldn't need you.'

She shrugged.

'Why don't we find somewhere quiet to sit for a bit?'

Under other circumstances, Alice would have relished a chance to slip away with Seth, but now nervous knots tightened in her stomach. Was this *it*? The goodbye chat?

'Why not?' she said as lightly as she could.

They took the small flight of steps leading from the verandah to a side garden. The night was warm, but Alice shivered as they crossed the lawn under a clear sky filled with stars, past a bed of lilies and a trellis covered in sweet-smelling jasmine to a seat in a secluded corner.

The long seat was made of wooden slats with curly wrought-iron arms and legs. They sat apart.

No more touching.

The time for painful honesty had arrived.

She was aware of the cooling night air on her bare arms and neck, and she was super-aware of the gorgeous man, some distance away, with his arms hooked over the back of the seat, his long legs sprawled. He reminded her of an athlete, exhausted after finishing a marathon.

She looked up at the sky to the silver half-moon and the astonishing dazzle of stars, and before Seth could start talking about the end of their relationship, she launched into a different topic. 'I'm so relieved that Charlie's had no lingering after-effects.'

'Yeah,' Seth agreed. 'You should have seen him running around today. It was hard to believe he'd had a close shave.'

'That's great. And the sitter hasn't had to call you tonight, so that's even better. You'll probably be able to start using sitters more often.'

'Mmm.' Seth frowned.

Alice looked back to the house, low and sprawling and rather splendid with its silver roof winking in the moonlight and the golden glow of house lights spilling over the lawn. She thought again about the Drummond family leaving all this – not just the house, but the hundreds of acres of bush and grasslands and dams and hills.

She still felt sad about it, but perhaps Seth was right. It was time for a change, for all of them.

'You must be so proud of your father,' she said.

'Yeah, he's a good bloke.'

Seth said this quietly – such a simple statement – but the note of sincerity in his voice conveyed a deep wealth of emotion.

You're a good father too, Seth. One day Charlie will speak glowingly about you.

Alice could so easily picture Seth in the future, running his cattle stud, a loving family man with a wife – possibly a local girl like one of those pretty blonde twins – and another child or two. He would be a pillar of his community. A salt-of-the-earth type. *A good bloke.*

'Alice.' Seth's deep voice broke into her miserable thoughts. 'Why don't we cut to the chase?'

She stiffened. 'What chase?'

Goodbye?

Seth turned to her, and in the moonlight, his eyes were a clear steel blue. 'We shouldn't be talking about my dad or Charlie or the damn babysitter. We need to talk about us.'

Us. Her heart began to pound. There was no *us*. 'But there's nothing to discuss.' She spoke tightly, sitting straight, hands gripping the edge of the seat. 'Once this party's over we say goodbye. You'll explain to your parents.'

'Is that what you want?'

'I – I –' His question totally threw her.

'You don't want to see me again?' Seth challenged.

Alice swallowed, fighting tears. 'It's not really a matter of what I want, is it? We broke it off, Seth. You were fed up with me and that was fair enough. The whole business with children. My hang-ups.'

A painful lump had ballooned in Alice's throat.

Seth's gaze was fixed on her. 'The thing is, I'm not sure I'm ready to say goodbye. I know you have issues, but I reckon we could still try to make a go of this.'

'This?' she squeaked, hardly daring to guess, to understand.

He'd moved closer, and now he dropped a kiss on her bare shoulder. 'This,' he murmured.

The warm imprint of his lips on her skin sent thrills streaking all the way to her toes, to her fingertips.

'I'm crazy about you, Alice.'

Zap. She tried to speak but no words came out.

She couldn't even see Seth. Her eyes were blurred with tears, but she felt his warm, strong hands as he cupped her face, sensed him lean into her, felt his lips brushing hers, lightly, gently, gliding seductively.

It was a kiss of sublime tenderness, making her feel as if she'd never been kissed before. A kiss filled with magic, touched by stars.

Closing her eyes, Alice pressed close, loving the familiar scent of Seth, the longed-for taste of him, the amazing intimacy of his lips on hers – soft and warm – unpicking her stitch by stitch with slow devastation. Teasing, teasing.

Oh, the sweetness of it. A soft groan broke from her. She couldn't help it. She wanted this man so badly she couldn't hold back. Weeks, days and nights of wanting blended into this single moment. Winding her arms around his neck, she pressed closer.

Instantly, Seth's arms tightened around her and his kiss became hungry, fierce. Gloriously possessive.

It was some time before they released each other, and they did so slowly, reluctantly, not speaking, as if they were both too shaken by the force of their feelings to find anything as trivial as words.

A gentle breeze blew over them. The sound of happy, innocent voices drifted from the house. In the trees by the creek an owl hooted.

Seth threaded his fingers through Alice's. 'So,' he said. 'I think we've answered my question.'

'I guess.' She hoped she didn't sound too over-the-top happy.

'I reckon both Charlie and I are crazy about you, Alice.'

She laughed.

'I suppose Charlie might still be a problem for you, but perhaps –'

'Actually –' Alice took a deep breath. 'I think I might be getting over that particular hurdle.'

Seth stared at her, his expression a mix of delight and caution. 'So last night's drama didn't totally freak you out?'

'I think it might have helped. I was absolutely terrified at the time, of course. But the amazing thing is, I coped.'

Seth gave her hand an encouraging squeeze. 'You did. You were wonderful. You did exactly what you had to do.'

'I didn't know I had it in me. I was always so sure I'd be a mess, hopeless with kids, dropping my bundle at the first hint of a problem.'

Some day soon, she would tell him the whole sad story that she'd shared with Tammy, but already it was losing it's pernicious grip.

He kissed her forehead. 'You were fabulous.'

'And for me that's a kind of miracle.'

'And I'll always be incredibly grateful. I'll probably be like our neighbours, the Hargreaves, telling everyone about it at your sixty-fifth birthday party.'

Alice laughed and felt herself blushing at the very thought of still knowing Seth when she was sixty-five.

'The really good thing is,' she said more seriously, 'I've felt really different today. I don't suppose I'm cured exactly, but I've been thinking about it all day and it doesn't make me panic any more. I can even picture caring for Charlie, or some other little kid, without feeling the horrible, crippling terror I've always felt. I think I'm starting to realise I can be like everyone else. There might be another crisis one day, but really, all anyone can do is try to be sensible and do their best. And – and most times that's enough.'

'Alice, that's right. Good on you. That's bloody fantastic.'

'I know. It's such a relief.'

They stayed there for ages, talking, kissing, talking some more in the moonlight.

Seth looked relieved and relaxed, almost boyish as he told Alice about his plans. He would probably look for a smaller property, somewhere more suitable for breeding. Closer to Burralea, perhaps.

Alice liked the sound of that. She was practically floating with excitement.

'It's good country over there and great pasture,' Seth said. 'Last year, a fellow near Burralea got the highest price ever paid in Australia for one of his bulls.'

'And you want to beat his record?'

'I can always try.'

He told her that Hugh and Jackie were thinking of moving closer to Burralea, too. They were going to look for a place down near the lake.

Alice loved the happy picture this conjured. This afternoon she'd felt so low and miserable, expecting to never see the Drummonds again. Now, within a few short hours, it seemed that she'd be seeing more of Seth's family than ever.

After all the years of missing her parents and Daisy, she longed to be part of a proper extended family. And now, she and Seth were even talking of taking Charlie to England to visit Joanna. And somewhere within the lovely countryside around Burralea, there'd be a farm, Seth and Charlie's farm, a stud farm, no less. A farmhouse on a sloping green hill, and Charlie's grandparents in their own house near the lake.

It all seemed too good to be true. She might have become teary if Flora hadn't suddenly burst around the corner of the jasmine trellis.

'Oh, there you both are.'

'Have we been missed?' asked Seth.

'Well, yes, you've been gone for ages. I suppose you've been snogging, but people are leaving and Mum thinks you should be there to say goodbye.'

'Then we'd better get cracking.'

39

It was after midnight, the guests were gone, and the Drummonds, plus Alice, were in the lounge room, winding down. Seth and Xavier had dismantled the trestle tables and taken them onto the verandah before dragging the lounge furniture back into a semblance of their normal positions.

Now Jackie and Hugh sagged with relief into the nearest chairs and Alice and Deborah handed round mugs of tea.

'Thank you, Alice,' said Jackie as she propped her aching feet onto a footstool. 'This is heavenly, exactly what I needed. And how clever of you two to find your way around the kitchen. It must be such a mess.'

'It's not too bad at all,' Alice told her. 'Your CWA friends did a wonderful job and we've stacked the dishwasher with a second load.'

'Oh, aren't they angels!'

Jackie sipped her tea and it was just the way she liked it, steaming hot and sweet. 'I must say, I think tonight went well.'

'It was a good party,' Hugh agreed. 'Hell, it wasn't just good, it was a bloody great party.' Over the rim of his mug, he sent Jackie a smiling wink. 'Thanks, love.'

'And to think you fought me tooth and nail to call it off,' she teased.

'Did I?' He gave a smiling shrug. 'Ah, well, wives always know best.'

'It's turned out to be a perfect celebration for all of us,' said Flora who was sitting on the floor near Xavier. Jackie had noticed that the two cousins had spent quite a chunk of this evening with their heads together, talking about music. She hadn't realised they had so much in common.

Seth, who was looking exceptionally happy, chimed in. 'The last big bash for the Drummonds of Ruthven Downs.'

'That's very true.' For a moment Hugh looked sombre and Jackie was terribly afraid that they would all become sentimental and tearful, she more than anyone else.

But before that could happen, Hugh said, 'You know what's missing tonight?' And he was looking directly at Flora.

'Oh, no.' Flora's smile was incredulous and she rolled her eyes. 'You're not going to ask me now, Dad.'

'Of course I am,' said Hugh. 'It's my birthday and you always play it for me.'

'Yes,' cried Jackie. 'We have to have "Danny Boy".' Flora had played this little piece for her father every year since she was eight, when she'd first learned the tune. Back then she had played it scratchily, with a few ear-splitting wrong notes, but with enormous pride, and it had become a tradition, one Hugh adored.

'Come on, Floss,' added Seth.

His sister needed no real urging. She was already on her feet, and was soon back from her room with her violin case.

Goodness, Jackie thought as she watched Flora remove the instrument and pluck the strings lightly, checking the tuning. *I'm going to become sentimental and teary after all.*

She drew a deep breath, fighting the impulse to cry as she

remembered what both Flora and Kate Woods had whispered to her during the night – that a decision had been made about Flora's future and it definitely included leaving Oliver. This was such good news.

It was a night for laughter, not tears. Their family's eyes were on the future, even though it was filled with uncertainties.

Now, Flora tightened her bow, lifted the violin and tucked it beneath her chin. The room was hushed, everyone watching her. Even Alice looked entranced as she sat close to Seth, her hand linked in his. There was an extra-happy glow about that couple tonight, Jackie had noted with secret glee.

Lifting the bow, Flora drew it tentatively over the strings, testing the tuning one more time and making a slight adjustment to the tension of a string. Then another small change, until she was satisfied. She flashed Hugh a fond smile. 'Happy Birthday, Dad.' And she played 'Danny Boy'.

The first beautiful notes of the haunting, familiar tune lifted fine hairs on Jackie's arms. Tears pricked her eyes and her throat ached, but she forced herself to smile.

The music swelled and soared. These days, Flora could add expert flourishes and trills, and each note was sweetly pitched, clear and perfect, filling the room, lifting to the high ceilings. Jackie looked at the others. Seth was grinning from ear to ear and Xavier looked rapt. But Hugh, her darling Hugh, was struggling just as she was to smile. Alice, with a tight hold on Seth's hand, also looked as if she was about to cry. Even Deb's eyes were shining with fondness and pride.

Behind them on the far wall of the dining room, as a backdrop to the scene, stood the tall sideboard, with its softly gleaming timber and shiny new mirror, and the family photographs in their silver frames. Generations of Drummonds.

Jackie thought of Stella, who'd also loved this place and had worked so hard to be a good wife and mother despite her secret heartache. Poor Stella had probably been terribly worried when she hid those documents behind the mirror, but thinking about it now, Jackie thought she'd been wise to put a freeze on a very difficult situation and to leave it for future generations to sort out.

We should try to keep that sideboard, Jackie thought. *It holds too many memories.*

The prospect of movable memories was a comforting one.

'Danny Boy' came to an end. The last notes lingered and a hush fell over the audience, until they broke into a burst of cheering and applause. Some wiped their eyes.

'That was marvellous, darling,' said Hugh. 'Thank you. You play it more beautifully every year.'

'It was awesome,' said Xavier.

Flora accepted the compliments graciously, and as she moved to put the violin away, Hugh said, '"Danny Boy" was my mother's favourite song, too.'

Flora nodded. 'I remember when I first learned to play it, Gran was even more excited than you were, Dad.'

'Yes,' said Seth. 'When Gran lived in that little place in Atherton, that friend of hers, the guy next door, used to sing it for Gran sometimes.'

Jackie stared at Seth in surprise. 'Her neighbour used to sing "Danny Boy"?'

'Yes, do you remember, Floss? When we used to stay overnight?'

Flora pretended to pout. 'You were always Gran's favourite.'

'You stayed there, too,' said Seth. 'But we had to take it in turns, because she only had that one tiny spare room with the single bed. Anyway, the point I'm getting to is that sometimes, when I stayed there, the fellow who lived next door to Gran used to come in and join us for a game of cards or Dominoes or whatever.'

'Or Snakes and Ladders,' chimed in Flora. 'Yes, I remember him.

He was a lovely old chap.'

'But do you remember that he also used to sing "Danny Boy" for Gran, because it was her favourite?'

Flora frowned. 'I'm not sure.'

'I remember it distinctly. Maybe he only ever sang it once or twice. He wasn't all that good a singer, to be honest, but Gran still loved it and he was a nice old fellow. An Englishman called . . .' Seth was searching his memory.

'Tom?' supplied Flora.

'Yes, Tom, that's right.' Seth frowned, staring into the distance, then shrugged. 'Can't remember his surname.'

'No, neither can I,' said Flora.

Not Kearney? Jackie almost cried, but just in time, she held her tongue. No, of course, it couldn't have been Tom Kearney. She was getting carried away, trying to slot together an ancient jigsaw when too many pieces were missing.

Even so, she found herself thinking about the nice old fellow who'd lived next to Stella. Seth and Flora were right. He was English. He had only a little hair and a longish face with deep creases running from the corners of his eyes to the sides of his mouth, and his lively eyes squinted when he smiled.

He'd come to Stella's funeral, too, and he'd been ever so sad.

Jackie turned to Hugh, and saw her own puzzlement mirrored in his face. Hugh nodded in silent acknowledgement and she realised he was wondering the same thing, but he was probably as doubtful as she was.

It couldn't be him.

Neither of them voiced their thoughts. It was late and this bizarre coincidence wasn't something to be shared with the others now. None of the younger generation had read Stella's diary.

'It's been a huge day,' Jackie said. 'I vote we all go to bed.'

'Yes,' agreed Hugh. 'You young people can keep partying if you must, but keep it quiet – make that *very* quiet – out on the verandah.'

'I need to rescue my poor babysitter,' Seth said, getting to his feet. 'She'll be desperate to get home.'

Everyone else rose too and there was a chorus of goodnights as people trailed away – Deborah to her room, Flora and Xavier to the verandah, Alice and Seth off to the cottage.

As Jackie followed Hugh into their bedroom her head was swimming. *Tom.*

No, of course it couldn't be him.

A lamp beside the bed cast just enough light to see by. In the semi-darkness she slipped off her sandals, unhooked her earrings and dropped them onto the glass tray on her dressing table. She looked again to her husband.

Before she could speak, Hugh said, 'Thanks so much for tonight. It was perfect.'

'I'm glad you had a good time.'

They moved towards each other, arms already reaching, slipping into a companionable hug as they had so many, many times. Jackie tucked her head against Hugh's shoulder.

'The party was just right,' he said. 'So much more than a birthday. It felt like a celebration of all the years we've lived here, and maybe a kind of staging point before the next chapter.'

'I'm glad,' Jackie said. 'And I know what you mean. I don't feel so bad about the thought of leaving here now, do you?'

'Not at all. I think I'm looking forward to it.' He kissed her forehead. 'As long as you'll be there too.'

She smiled up at him and when their lips met, their kiss felt familiar and dear, yet full of promise.

'I love you.'

'I love you too, Jackie girl.'

The words, so often shared, meant as much tonight as they ever had. Jackie's mind flashed to the rest of her family. To Seth and the difficult year he'd just weathered. To Flora and the brave decision she'd made. To Stella and Tom and their long years of separation and probable loneliness. 'We've had such a happy life, Hugh. We've been so lucky.'

'I know, I know.'

She went into their adjoining bathroom to remove her make-up and clean her teeth. She was applying moisturiser when Hugh appeared, wearing his striped pyjama bottoms.

'This Tom fellow who lived next to your mother,' she said as Hugh reached for his toothbrush. 'It must be a coincidence, surely?'

Hugh frowned. 'I suppose so. I don't know what to make of it, to be honest.'

'I wonder if he's still alive.'

Their gazes met in the mirror and Jackie knew Hugh was as desperately curious as she was.

He smiled. 'We could always try to find out.'

40

I've always wondered if this day would come, and now it has. Stella's son and his wife have visited me, and I liked them very much. They've found a diary of Stella's. Apparently it has been hidden for years, but everything's out in the open at last and I'm glad. I was never ashamed of my love for Stella and our story deserves to be told. They asked me to add a final entry, which I'm happy to do.

Looking back now, it's hard to believe that I almost didn't call on Stella. I had no idea what to expect after all that time . . .

When a strange vehicle pulled up at the front steps, Stella was home alone, busily packing in preparation for leaving Ruthven Downs.

Her first reaction was annoyance. She'd been making such good progress, sorting her clothes into piles – those to throw away, those for charity shops and those she would keep to take with her. She didn't want to have to stop now to make cups of tea and polite conversation.

She wanted this packing to be finished. After that, she planned to clean the house from top to bottom, to have everything perfect

and ready for Hugh and his new bride when they returned from
their honeymoon.

Outside, the car door closed and Stella heard firm footsteps on
the gravel. She went to the dining room and peeked through the curtains. And froze.

No.

It couldn't be.

She clutched at the back of a dining chair for support. Surely she
must be seeing things? She blinked and looked again through the
fine net curtain, and this time, even though she hadn't seen him in
more than twenty-five years, there was no mistaking the tall figure
mounting the front steps.

Her heart began to pound so loudly she barely heard his knock
at the front door, and her legs were so weak, she could scarcely make
it down the hallway.

When she opened the door, he didn't look any different. Not
really. More suntanned than ever, and greyer, of course. She thought
his receding hairline made him look even more intelligent.

'Hello, Stella.'

'Tom.'

Keeping a death grip on the door handle, she wished she wasn't
wearing her oldest house dress, wished she'd shampooed her hair,
wished she was one of those women who wore make-up around the
house.

'I finally got your letter,' Tom said. 'It was forwarded to my new
post in New Guinea. I've been working up in the highlands, so it
took a while to reach me.'

Stella nodded, still too surprised to speak sensibly. Over the
many, many years since their parting in Cairns, their letters had been
infrequent. Mostly, they'd been polite, a little stilted, dealing with
superficial news, but the contact with Tom had still been intensely
important to her.

Four years ago, she'd written to tell Tom about Magnus's stroke, and she'd found his letters incredibly comforting during the difficult long years that followed, nursing her bedridden and helpless husband.

Just six months ago, she'd sent the news that Magnus had died, and more recently she'd told Tom about Hugh's wedding and her own plans to leave Ruthven Downs.

Tom said, 'Port Moresby's only a quick flight away from Cairns, so I thought –' He hesitated and lifted his hand in a gesture of uncertainty. His smile had a nervous tilt, and the shimmer in his eyes caused a hitch in her breathing.

'It's good to see you, Tom.' She took a step back, opening the door wider.

'Is this – a convenient time to call?'

'Yes, of course. Come in.'

'Thank you.'

'Would – would you like a cup of tea?'

Tom smiled at her then. The skin crinkled around his grey eyes and she felt the same rush of tingling excitement that she'd felt on that very first night in Singapore.

'Yes, please,' he said politely. 'I'd love a cup of tea.'

She led him down the hallway and her heart picked up pace as she passed the doorway to the dining room and saw the sideboard where she'd hidden her diary pages and Magnus's letter. Her husband had discovered her history with Tom, but her children knew nothing, and she wanted to keep it that way.

'Would you like to wait here?' she asked, indicating the lounge room. 'Or would you prefer to come through to the kitchen?'

Tom nodded towards the room at the end of the hallway. 'The kitchen. Let's not stand on ceremony.'

While Stella boiled water and set cups and saucers on the counter, Tom stood at the kitchen door looking out over the paddocks.

'This is a beautiful property.'

'Yes, it's looking at its best. We've had a good wet season, so there's plenty of pasture.'

He turned from the view. 'And your son has taken over the cattle business?'

'Yes, Hugh's been looking after the cattle ever since Magnus had the stroke.' Not bothering to hide her motherly pride, she added, 'He's a very organised and businesslike grazier. This year, he made sure he'd mustered and sold off the stock before the wedding, so I haven't had to worry about the cattle while he's been away.'

Tom nodded his approval. 'And your daughter? Deb?'

Stella smiled, remembering the time in Cairns when Deb was a baby and Tom had sung her to sleep with 'Danny Boy'. 'Deb's not the slightest bit interested in cattle. She's off in Central Australia somewhere, camping with a group of artists and painting desert landscapes.'

She warmed the teapot, added tea leaves and boiling water and changed the subject. 'What about you, Tom? What have you been doing?'

They sat at the old kitchen table, drinking the tea and eating buttered slices of date loaf, and he told her stories about the places he'd worked, in South America, in India and now in New Guinea.

'You've always been an adventurer,' she said. 'Even before the war, you were in Malaya.'

'I've tried going back to England, but it just doesn't feel like home any more. It's so cold and grey and – and predictable. I've come to love the tropics.' Tom smiled. 'The heat, the strong colours, the chaos.'

And the women? The question jumped into Stella's head. She knew there must have been other women in Tom's life. He was too handsome and virile to have lived like a monk. But did she want to hear about his love life?

'You never married,' she said.

Tom didn't answer. He simply sat looking at her with a bemused, frowning smile, as if he couldn't quite believe that this fact needed to be stated. Stella felt her cheeks grow hot.

'So you're not going to stay here?' Clearly he was as adept as she was at changing the subject.

She shook her head. 'I want Jackie, that's Hugh's wife, to have free rein. I'd hate her to feel as if her mother-in-law was breathing down her neck.'

'That's thoughtful.' Tom picked up his teaspoon and seemed to study it carefully, even though it was a very plain little thing. He turned the spoon over, as if to check its hallmark.

Stella was remembering a time, long ago, when he'd held her hand as carefully as that, studying her fingers, kissing her knuckles one by one.

'Have you finalised your plans?' he asked quietly.

She had sudden difficulty breathing. Why was Tom here? Was he hoping she might go away with him?

How could she go now? She couldn't. Not without sharing awkward explanations with Hugh and Deb, with the risk of exposing details that Hugh, in particular, should never learn.

'I've bought a cottage in Atherton,' she said. 'It's about an hour from here, on the Tablelands. It's where I plan to live.'

The disappointment in Tom's eyes almost broke her heart. Again.

She did her best to explain. She told him about the most terrifying night of her life, when Magnus had hurled insults and accusations about their adulterous relationship. She told him about Magnus's letter to his lawyer, his misguided belief that Hugh wasn't his son, his plans to disinherit Hugh.

'I'm assuming this request wasn't honoured?'

Stella shook her head. 'It was only a few days later that Magnus had the stroke,' she said. 'He never mentioned the letter again. He was drinking heavily and rather confused and unwell right up until the stroke.'

'So you left things as they were?'

'I had to. I couldn't just hand the letter over. Magnus's judgement was so misguided. It was all so unfair. I couldn't let him cut Hugh off like that. But I couldn't bring myself to destroy the letter. That was a step too far.'

Tom frowned. 'What did you do?'

'I – I hid it.'

'And now, it's no longer an issue,' Tom said quietly.

This, unfortunately, was only partly true. 'I still feel dreadfully guilty about what I did. I don't want my children to know.'

Tom sat back, watching her through narrowed eyes, and she could see his mind working. 'You devoted yourself to your husband while he was ill.'

'It was the least I could do.'

'Stella, you can't live a life of self-sacrifice forever. Now it's time to consider your own needs.'

She had to ask. 'Why did you come here, Tom? What were you planning?'

'I came here with an open mind.' He gave her a rueful smile. 'And a hopeful heart.'

Stella dropped her gaze quickly, before he could see the tears stinging her eyes.

A hopeful heart.

She couldn't bear to think she might destroy that hope. But for so long, for almost thirty years, she'd kept the two worlds, the two halves of her life, so very carefully apart. It was far too late now to let them recklessly collide.

She had no guilt about her relationship with Tom, but she was terrified that if she told her children about him now, the whole truth about the will might somehow unravel. She couldn't let that happen.

'Look,' Tom said gently, as if he'd sensed her distress. 'I know it was a little unfair of me to land on your doorstep out of the blue. I wasn't planning to sweep you off your feet, or demand that you rush away with me.' He smiled shyly. 'But you must know you're very special to me, Stella.'

Reaching across the table, she touched her fingers to the back of his hand. 'It's wonderful to see you again, Tom.' Her throat tightened, but she forced herself to speak calmly. 'And I don't want to lose you again.'

'That's good to know.' He turned her hand over and lifted it to his lips, pressed a kiss to her inner wrist.

Stella shivered. 'You'll stay for dinner, won't you?'

Tom stayed for dinner, and he stayed the night. Miraculously, and to Stella's amazed delight, the years of their separation melted away. Although they were in their fifties now, they were the same in every way that counted, and making love was as natural and necessary to them as breathing.

Afterwards, as they lay together, their heartbeats gradually slowing, Tom let out a happy sigh. 'I tried to tell myself that this was just a wartime thing. That out of all that darkness and evil and brutality you were something good, but I shouldn't try to make it last a lifetime.'

'But it *has* lasted, hasn't it?'

'It has.' With a suntanned hand, he traced a line across her pale belly. 'So what are we going to do?'

If only she could throw herself wildly into his arms and tell him she'd go anywhere, anyhow, any time. But she couldn't risk opening a window on her secret.

Besides, she'd already made her plans. Until today, she'd been excited about her new place in Atherton. For the first time in her life, independence beckoned. She would make new friends, join a painting group or a gardening club, and still remain within easy reach of her family.

'We've been waiting for thirty years,' she told him gently. 'Let's not try to solve everything tonight. We'll work something out.'

The next day she took Tom to see her new house, travelling with him in his hire car, which felt like a very brave step.

'The garden's rather overgrown,' she admitted as they pushed the slightly rusty front gate open. 'But I'll enjoy knocking it into shape.'

The house was small, a low-set white weatherboard cottage with deep, timber-framed casement windows. They opened these wide to let in fresh air, and Tom dutifully admired the renovated kitchen, the generous, north-facing sunroom that looked out into the garden, the functional bathroom and two bedrooms.

There was no furniture so they picnicked on the back steps, eating the chicken and asparagus sandwiches that Stella had made and drinking mugs of coffee from a thermos.

'I guess I can always visit you here,' Tom said.

Stella almost hugged him with relief. 'I hope you do. I'd love to see you as often as you could make it down here, Tom.'

'At least New Guinea's just a step up the road, so to speak.'

'And maybe we can finally get to know each other properly.'

This brought a smiling frown from him. 'That's a funny thing to say after all these years.'

'I know, but it's true, if you think about it. We've only ever had desperately short snatches of time together and we've lived such separate lives for so long. I have no idea about so many things about you.'

'What do you want to know?'

Stella shrugged. 'Anything. Your favourite colour?'

'Orange,' he said quickly.

She stared at him. 'Really?'

'I like all the bright tropical colours.'

'Well, okay, maybe I could have guessed that if I'd really tried, but there is a host of other things I don't know. What kind of music you like, or your taste in books. Your favourite food. All we really have in common is how we feel about each other.'

Tom smiled at her again, watching her from beneath lowered lids, as he leaned back against the door frame. 'I look forward to getting to know you, Stella Drummond.'

'And I'm rather keen to know all about you.'

They laughed. She felt happy, truly happy, for the first time in ages. She and Tom were coming to a new understanding, and she was beginning to feel confident that they could make this work.

As they finished their picnic, she talked about her plans for the backyard.

'As you can see there are quite a few fruit trees that need pruning. I seem to have a mandarin and a lime, and I think that's a lemon tree hanging over the fence from the neighbour's place. I'm hoping the new owner won't want to cut it down.'

Tom raised an eyebrow. 'Has someone just bought the place next door?'

'Well, no. It hasn't actually been sold yet. The fellow who owns both these houses tried to persuade me to buy them together, a sort of job lot, but I'm not very interested in an investment and I don't really have the spare funds.'

Tom was on his feet now, trying to peer through the shrubbery to the neighbouring house. 'Have you looked at the house?'

'Yes, it's quite nice, a bit bigger than this place, actually, and I could have done with the extra bedroom. But I fell in love with this house's lovely sunroom.'

He turned back to her, his eyes bright in his tanned face. For a long moment he stared at her. 'You know what I'm thinking, don't you?'

Stunned, Stella stared back at him. 'You're not thinking of buying it?'

'Why not?'

She couldn't answer him, couldn't think. Her head was spinning.

'Wouldn't you want me as your neighbour?' he said.

'Well, yes, of course I would. I'd love it, but –'

'It makes sense, Stella.' Tom was grinning like an excited child. 'We're used to living apart. I'm not ready to retire, so I could keep working for the time being and have a base here. Next door.'

'Yes.'

'You could preserve your independence.'

And keep my secrets safe. His excitement was catching. She could feel it bubbling through her, as intoxicating as champagne. 'And we'd only have a fence between us.'

'Instead of oceans.'

Stella laughed. 'It could work, couldn't it?'

'It could work brilliantly.'

Now she was also scrambling to her feet. 'The agency's only a few streets away. We could go and get the key.'

'I don't need to look the house over, not if it comes with your recommendation.'

'But you may as well, Tom, while you're here. You never know, it might have white ants or something.'

Tom looked up to the sky and gave a disbelieving shake of his head. 'Are you always this practical?'

'Well, yes, I used to be a nurse, remember?'

His gaze met hers. He grinned. 'I certainly do remember.'

'And you're an engineer, so you should be practical too.'

'Okay, okay. I'll check the house out.'

'Now?'

'No, not now. Enough with the practicalities.' Tom beckoned. 'What you need, my dear girl, is more romance in your life. Come here.'

Stella was laughing as she floated into his arms.

ACKNOWLEDGEMENTS

Writers are often asked where they get their ideas from and often we don't really know. The ideas seem to filter in via the subconscious, the 'girls in the basement'. For this book, however, I do have a few specific sources of inspiration that I'd like to mention.

To begin with, I share Alice's love of old furniture. Even before I was married, I bought an English oak dressing table, which still has pride of place in our bedroom, and from early in our marriage, my husband and I collected old bits and pieces, including a silky oak sideboard. My husband, Elliot, developed an interest in restoring the sideboard and this involved getting the mirror re-silvered. And yes, he discovered papers behind the mirror – nothing as mysterious as an old will, but the front page of a newspaper from 1915. We were fascinated, of course, and we included a newspaper from the current day when we put the mirror back in place, and the idea of a deeper mystery hidden behind a mirror has teased my imagination ever since.

In terms of research, I'm deeply indebted to Noel Barber's wonderful book, *Sinister Twilight*, about the fall of Singapore in 1942. I should add that while writing the historical strand of this story, I chose to place Stella on the *Empire Star*, the one ship that made it safely back to Australia, despite bombing attacks and serious damage. However, I was very aware that I'd skirted details of the terrible fate that awaited many of the Australian nurses who left Singapore on the *Wah Sui* and the *Vyner Brooke*, and I would like to acknowledge here the inspiring courage of these women.

I'm indebted to the wonderful team at Penguin Australia who always work so hard to make sure that my books come to you in the best possible shape. These include deeply insightful Ali Watts, Clementine Edwards, Nikki Lusk, Fay Helfenbaum, Emma Dowden and Alexandra Hampton.

The Grazier's Wife is a story about generations and I'd also like to thank the four generations of my family who provide inspiration in so many ways. They range from my mum, Beryl, who is ninety this year, down to my beautiful grandchildren, Tom, Lucy, Lilly, Sophie, Milla and Jasper.

Finally, most importantly, my love and thanks go to Elliot, who not only restored the sideboard, but has also read every word along the way and has given me so much support, insight and unfailing encouragement.

Read on for a sneak peek of

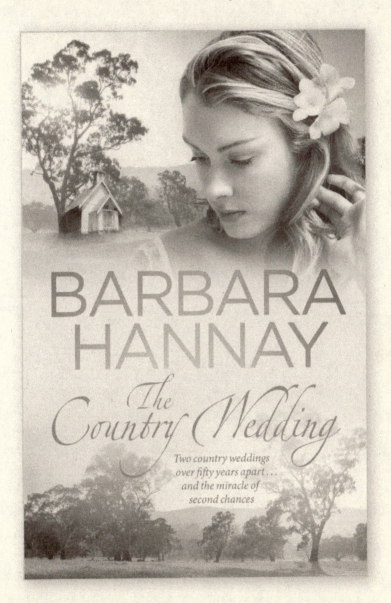

BARBARA
HANNAY

The
Country Wedding

Two country weddings
over fifty years apart . . .
and the miracle of
second chances

CHAPTER ONE

Burralea, 1958

The day was a stinker. The sun overhead was blazing and sweat trickled beneath the bridegroom's collar. Unfortunately, the weather wasn't the only cause of his discomfort as he waited outside the quaint white church perched on a rise above Burralea.

'You look like you could do with a smoke, Joe.' His best man, Cliff, shook out a packet of Camels.

Joe hesitated, remembering the aunts he would have to kiss once this ceremony was over. Then he thought about his bride, who was carrying his child, and who was about to head down the aisle in a fancy white wedding dress specially transported over a thousand miles from a Brisbane department store.

Stuff it. He needed a smoke. 'Thanks,' he said, taking a slim cigarette and then ducking his head to meet the flame held between Cliff's cupped hands.

'They reckon every bridegroom gets nervous,' Cliff suggested.

'Yeah. Course.'

'I s'pose the trick is to keep your thoughts fixed on the honeymoon.'

Joe dragged a little harder on his cigarette. Grey clouds hunkered on the horizon, but they offered no relief from the burning sun.

'You'll have a bonzer time on Hayman Island,' Cliff suggested. He'd been Joe's mainstay during the past few weeks, ever since the drunken debacle at Joe's twenty-first birthday party, the night that had started this wedding train rolling. The poor fellow was still doing his best. 'I hear it's really flash.'

Joe nodded, but he wasn't about to confess that the bride's father had coughed up the money for the luxury Barrier Reef resort. Ted Walker wanted the very best for his daughter, of course, and as owner of Burralea's one and only pub, a grand two-storey affair with a splendid fireplace and a magnificent silky oak staircase, Ted could easily afford it. He was footing the bill for the wedding reception, too. It was going to be held in the pub's enormous dining room.

Joe didn't have that kind of money. He ran a cattle property with his dad not far out of town. Kooringal was a modest place compared with the huge stations out west, but Joe and his dad turned out good quality beef, and they kept their heads above water.

He knew the Walkers weren't happy about their daughter marrying 'down', but when Gloria had told them she was pregnant, they'd had little choice. They'd demanded a wedding, and put on brave faces.

Joe knew how that felt. He needed a brave face now as the church's wheezy organ started up and Reverend Gibson popped his head around the vestry door. The minister beckoned to Joe and Cliff.

'Time, gentlemen.'

This was it.

A cold jolt of panic spiked through Joe. His legs felt hollow as he ground the cigarette into the dirt with his heel.

He didn't want to do this. He had no choice.

Cliff patted his coat pockets. 'Still got the ring,' he said with an encouraging grin.

Joe couldn't manage an answering smile. 'Good man,' he said.

Shoulders squared, Joe followed Reverend Gibson into the little church, packed with family and friends all dressed in their wedding finery. He saw his parents in the front pew, his mum looking dewy-eyed and his dad stern but proud. They were both disappointed that Joe's older sister, Margaret, hadn't come up from Melbourne for the big day, but Joe understood why she'd stayed away. Besides, he had bigger things to worry about today.

Now, his collar was choking him, but a whispering excitement buzzed through the congregation, and there was a stirring at the back of the church. No time to ease the knot at his throat. Already, too soon, the organist was striking the chilling chords that announced the arrival of the bride. Joe stiffened like a prisoner facing a firing squad.

He told himself that once the ceremony was over he'd be okay. He'd just get on with the rest of his life as best he could. He wouldn't be the first man to wed out of necessity, and he and Gloria would manage. Romance was supposed to be overrated anyway, although Joe, drowning in the very deepest of regrets, knew this wasn't true.

Uneasily, he turned and saw Ted Walker and a figure in frothy white making their way down the aisle towards him. A rustle of satin whispered at his side, announcing Gloria, looking pretty and surprisingly innocent, behind a misty veil. The music stopped.

Reverend Gibson's voice boomed. 'Dearly beloved, we are gathered here today in the sight of God . . .'

Joe took a deep breath and the time-honoured ceremony flowed seamlessly towards its inevitable end.

Afterwards, they posed on the front steps of the church for photographs. There were photos of the bridal party, photos with parents, with the aunts and uncles, with friends.

More clouds had gathered by this point, now darkening the sky and casting a gloom over the afternoon. Joe was blinking from all the camera flashes when he saw the lone figure in the distance.

From the church's position at the top of the rise he had a clear view down the street. About halfway, a woman was standing beneath a leopard tree, watching them.

His heart stilled.

She was wonderfully slender and wearing a green dress, a dress he remembered too well, with a scalloped neckline that sat neatly against her perfect pale skin, and a narrow belt that circled her slim waist. Despite the gathering clouds, her hair glowed like honey.

Hattie.

For bleak, gut-churning moments Joe stared at her. Helpless. Distraught. She was more than a hundred yards away, and he couldn't read the expression on her face, but he felt her desolation land like a blow, an axe to his heart.

He had tried to apologise to her for this heartbreaking mess, but no apology could undo his stupid, careless, unforgivable mistake.

'Hey, Joe, you're not smiling,' his Aunt Gertrude called rather bossily.

Joe swallowed, tried desperately to dredge up a smile as another flash went off and another cloud, dark as a bruise, rolled over the church's roof. A gust of wind came with it and all the wedding guests looked up, their faces a picture of dismay as they realised they were about to be drenched.

The rain arrived in a sudden, nasty scud that sent everyone scattering. Gloria's father stepped forward with a huge black umbrella held protectively over his daughter.

Down the street, the girl in green climbed into a small white VW and drove away.

***

Hattie tried to let herself into the cottage quietly, but she hadn't managed yet to oil the front door hinges and so they squeaked.

'Is that you, dear?' her mother called weakly from the bedroom.

Hattie stopped just outside the bedroom doorway, needing to compose herself before she went in. Closing her eyes, she took a deep breath and then let it out slowly, willing her rioting emotions to calm.

The unthinkable had happened. Joe was married and somehow she would have to find a way to keep going.

When she stepped through the doorway, her mother looked gaunt and sallow against the white pillow. In recent weeks, even her hair had faded, and now it was the colour of withered cornstalks. She was lying just as Hattie had left her, and the level of water in the glass on the bedside table was exactly the same.

'Have you been asleep?' Hattie asked her.

'I'm not sure. I think I might have dropped off.'

The rain was blowing in through a window. The white painted sill glistened with water and streaks of dampness showed on the floral curtains. Hattie crossed the room and closed the window. She would have to fetch a towel to dry the sill.

'Were you caught in the rain?' her mother asked, eyeing similar dark streaks on Hattie's dress.

'Only a few spots, really,' she said. 'I jumped in the car as soon as it started.'

'You went to watch the wedding.' It wasn't a question, but a matter-of-fact statement.

Hattie flinched. 'How did you know?'

'About Joe Matthews's wedding? Jenny Greeves told me yesterday.'

'Oh.'

Their neighbour had obligingly agreed to sit with Hattie's mother on Friday afternoons, while Hattie drove to Atherton to attend to the weekly business of banking, grocery shopping and getting her mother's prescriptions filled.

'You should have stayed well away from that church today,' her mother said now. 'You should have more pride, Hattie.'

'I kept my distance. No one saw me.' This was a lie, of course. She knew Joe had seen her.

Despite the distance between them, she had known the very instant that his careful smile left his face. She'd sensed his distress in the sudden way he'd become ramrod-still as he'd stared down the street at her.

It was no compensation for the unbearable pain he'd caused her.

'Darling, I know you're hurting, but I'm sure Joe can't have been right for you. What's happened is for the best. It has to be.'

Hattie wanted to challenge her mother, to demand how she could possibly know this. How could losing the one you loved ever be for the best? But she couldn't ask such a thing. Her mother was dying.

With a very thin, too-pale hand, Rose Bellamy patted the space beside her on the edge of the bed. 'Hattie, come here, please, darling. Sit here. There's something I need to tell you.'

Suddenly nervous, Hattie stayed where she was. 'What is it? Do you feel worse? Should I call the doctor?'

'No, no, I don't want the doctor.'

'I'll heat some more of that chicken soup.'

'Not now.' Her mother looked even more distressed than usual. 'There's something I need to explain. It's very important, and I don't want to leave it too late.'

A horrible chill crept through Hattie. 'What's this about?' she asked fearfully, as she edged towards the bed and took her mother's frail hand in hers.

'It's about you.' Rose squeezed her hand ever so gently. 'Firstly, I want you to promise that you'll go to England now. When this —'

She gave a small nod to indicate her failing body, the bed, the sick room. 'When this is over, you must go.'

Rose had written to Hattie's grandmother in England when she'd first learned how ill she was. The reply had been sympathetic and, in her grandmother's polite, remote, English way, she'd invited Hattie to come and stay with her. Indefinitely.

'I know you've been resisting, because you were so set on Joe,' her mother said, 'but there's no point in staying here now, is there?'

'I can still get a job.'

'Hattie!' The thin voice was surprisingly sharp. 'I'm not asking you, I'm *telling* you to go to England. I need to know that you'll do this. I'm sure there must still be enough money in the account.'

The last thing Hattie wanted was to distress her mother by arguing, but she didn't want to leave Burralea. This quiet country town was their home. She could scarcely remember anything else. And yet, she knew she would be miserable trying to stay here without her mother or Joe. Besides, how could she refuse her mother at this point?

'Yes, all right,' she said. 'I promise.'

'Thank you.' Rose looked more exhausted than ever and closed her eyes.

'I'll leave you to rest for a bit,' Hattie said.

The faded blue eyes flashed open again. 'Don't go yet. There's something else I need to tell you.'

'But you're tired. Leave it till later.'

This brought a bitter, dismissive little laugh. 'I'm always tired and this is important. It's something I should have told you long before this – about what happened when you were born. I need to explain about – about your father.'

Her father?

Hattie's mind had been preoccupied with Joe and her mother's illness, and she was totally thrown by this sudden mention of a father she'd never known. Her mind flashed to the photograph album they'd brought with them when they'd fled to Australia from China.

Hattie had been almost five when they left, so she had only shadowy memories of Shanghai, but the photos had helped to keep these memories alive. There were pictures of her grandparents' spacious, pleasant house in the French Concession, set back from a tree-lined boulevard behind tall wrought-iron gates.

Another snap showed Hattie aged four with her amah, Ah Lan. Hattie was wearing a party dress with a satin sash and a full skirt, with frilly socks and black patent leather shoes. Ah Lan was dressed simply in plain dark cotton and her hair was pulled back tightly from her round, smooth face to reveal her gentle smile. From beneath her skirt, her tiny, misshapen, bound feet peeked.

There were also photos of Rose, her mother, looking young and pretty, and of Hattie's glamorous Aunt Lily with her bright honey-gold hair cut into a bob and lacquered into waves like corrugated iron. Her Uncle Rudi with his dark, dark eyes and flashing smile. Her very proper and rather distant grandparents.

Then Hattie's mild-eyed father with his pleasantly handsome face and smart seaman's kit.

'My father's dead.' Her mother was well aware of this sad fact, of course, but Hattie felt impelled to repeat it now. 'He died when I was a baby.'

Rose had told her this story many times over the years, speaking of Hattie's father with a fond smile, as if her memories of him were comforting. Her story had never changed and Hattie found it terribly important to repeat it now. 'My father was Stephen Bellamy. He was English, a merchant seaman based in Shanghai, and his ship was bombed by the Japanese. He was terribly heroic, saving the lives of lots of passengers, but he was injured too, and he died.'

Over the years, Hattie had come to cherish a mental image of her father as a handsome and heroic seaman, a veritable knight in shining armour who had nobly sacrificed his life for others.

'I'm sorry, Hattie,' her mother said softly. 'I really am so terribly sorry.' Her pale lips trembled. 'I'm afraid the correct story is rather more complicated than that, and it's time you knew the truth.'

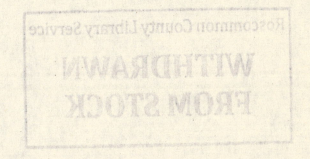